Find the River

*Merry Christmas and
have a great 2004!*

G. N. Str...

G. Nicholas Strohm

National Library of Canada Cataloguing in Publication

Strohm, G. Nicholas (Gregory Nicholas), 1962-
        Find the river / G. Nicholas Strohm.
ISBN 1-55395-094-1
I. Title
PS3619.T76F55 2002   813´.6   C2002-905874-0

Dedication

To Jessica, Kyle, Connor, my family and friends, thanks for
your support
Special thanks to Carolyn for all the time and ideas and to
Brenda for being patient with me. And Nancy, Christine, Jonny,
Beamer and of course to Mom.

KICKAPOO - 'he stands about' or 'he moves about, standing now here, now there'

Part 1
Chapter 1

May 22, 1873, Southwest Texas

The sun had barely risen over the mountains surrounding Eagle Pass as U.S. Colonel Ronald McKenzie's Fourth Cavalry finished setting up camp. The soldiers were bone weary and badly in need of rest after a successful pre-dawn raid on a sleeping Apache village . Sitting hunched over a small wooden table in his command tent, the Colonel unfolded the papers containing his orders. With his dirty blue battle coat slung over his shoulders to ward off the early morning chill, he rose and walked to the entrance of the tent. Sentries had been posted on either side of the tent flap. McKenzie turned to the young soldier to his left,

"Private, tell Lieutenant Smiley that I want to see him in my headquarters immediately."

The sentry tossed his muzzle-loaded rifle butt-end first to the ground with his left hand and saluted smartly with his right.

"Yes, Sir," he replied.

The Colonel returned to his small wooden stool and resumed his examination of the wrinkled papers. He paused and rubbed the stubble on his cheeks after stifling a yawn with his open hand. The long night had been exhausting and a little sleep would be well deserved. McKenzie looked up as Lt. Smiley entered the tent. The younger officer's dark blue uniform was stained with dirt and blood from the ambush, his face pale and drawn under his thick black beard.

"Is there somethin' you wanted, Colonel?"

McKenzie glanced back to his papers. "Do you remember our briefing before leaving Fort Clark?" He asked.

The Lieutenant's dark eyes betrayed anger as he answered in a tight voice, "Yes, sir, I do."

The field leaders voice dripped acid. "Oh, really, please refresh my memory, Lieutenant. What are our orders?"

Lieutenant Smiley thought for a moment before reciting, "After leaving Fort Clark, the Fourth Cavalry will travel south to the Mexican border. Any Indian villages encountered along the way are to be destroyed and the inhabitants taken prisoners."

McKenzie rose and strode to the tent flap, whipping the canvas aside.

"Prisoners?" He barked, his face taking on an unhealthy crimson hue. "Do you see any prisoners in this camp? I sure as hell don't!"

The young Lieutenant shifted his gaze to his dusty boots before agreeing, "No, sir, I don't see any prisoners, either, sir."

The Colonel leaned into the face of his junior officer and spoke in a tight, measured tone. "Listen to me, Lieutenant, we are supposed to bring back hostages for a reason. If we kill every Indian that we see, we will never get these people onto reservations where they belong. They will scatter into the mountains and hide until we're gone. You know as well as I do that those villagers were not responsible for the escalation of murders and scalping of whites. That was the work of a few marauders, and we will deal with them before we reach the border. Right now I need prisoners, not corpses."

Lieutenant Smiley nodded his head and said. "If you don't mind me sayin', sir, these people are savages. They are not going to go to the reservations without a fight. We suffered only one casualty last night, but if we give the Indians a chance we'll start losin' our men. That doesn't seem right to me, not for the sake of these animals."

Colonel McKenzie sat down at his table. After a brief silence he spoke quietly.

"Make sure the men are in their bunks. We'll break camp in 6 hours. The next village is Kickapoo, I believe, and it's less than a day's ride. I need the troops rested and ready to go." He paused. "And Lieutenant, no one is to fire his weapon until I give the command. Do you understand me?"

"Yes, sir, I do."

"Because anyone who does will be court-martial when we reach Fort Gibson, and you had better believe that includes you. Dismissed, Lieutenant."

A slight breeze blew in through the open tent flap as the junior officer made his exit. The scent of warming canvas filled the air. McKenzie sat on his cot and slowly pulled off his gritty boots. He slid wearily under the coarse woolen blanket and closed his eyes. As he waited for sleep to come, he thought about what Lieutenant Smiley had said about their low battle causalities. He did not entirely disagree that the Indian raiders that preyed on white settlers were savages. His men had seen the carnage the marauders had left behind. The Fourth Cavalry had come upon burned-out white settlements in their travels. The men and boys had been tortured, then scalped and mutilated. The women were gone, sold or traded by the Indian raiders once they had crossed the border into Mexico. He couldn't blame his troops for not feeling guilty about killing any Indians they saw. They were not killers of women and children under ordinary circumstances. Most of his men, like the Colonel himself, were veterans of the Civil War. Many of them had taken part in horrible battles and were haunted by those memories. They had joined the regular Army at the war's end because jobs were scarce, and they were accustomed to military life. Mostly northerners, the soldiers found the Texas environment harsh and the natives hostile. As many atrocities as they had witnessed in the war between the states, nothing compared to the carnage left behind by the Indian savages. Right or wrong, by killing innocents the soldiers were seeking justice for the murdered whites along with a large dose of revenge.

Lieutenant Smiley followed McKenzie's command by going from tent to tent, informing the troops that they would be breaking camp and moving out in six hours time. He told them of the Colonel's plan to attack the Kickapoo Village in another pre-dawn raid. Smiley left no doubt that hostages were to be taken this time, which brought grumbling from the men in response. When the Lieutenant had returned to his own tent, one of the soldiers spoke.

"I don't care what any officer says. I ain't gonna' sit back and let one of those red-skins shoot me and take my scalp. I'll shoot that son-a-bitch right between the eyes."

It was less than 24 hours before disaster would strike the Kickapoo Village at Eagle Pass.

Chapter 2

May 22, 1873

Hupa lay dreaming beside the smoldering campfire. The cool night air was filled with the sounds of mountain animals as the waning firelight flickered across the Indian's rugged face. The dream images were familiar, almost like old friends. Hupa had experienced this dream many times. As he slept he relived a time in the life of his Kickapoo ancestor, Seeing Eye.

Seeing Eye had lived long before, a time when the Kickapoo tribe had hunted in the woodlands up north, a time long before the white man had driven the Kickapoo south. In those days long past, hunting and trading with the Iroquois had been the tribe's chief concern.

Hupa knew the beginning, the middle and the end of his dream, but each time it played in his head was like the first. *He was running through the forest, the dense undergrowth slowing him down. His hunt had been cut short when a wolf pack had picked up the scent of the dead rabbits that hung from his belt. Seeing Eye's destination was Lake Kahooga up ahead that he had fished many times. The water would provide safety from the hungry predators. The menacing growls of the wolves were growing closer. The Indian pulled his knife from its sheath and cut the thin leather band that held his catch around his waist.*

The dead rabbits dropped to the ground as Seeing Eye continued to run. Now only the leather medicine bundles suspended from his belt and the sack on his back containing his bow and arrows bounced as he neared the lake. Within a few seconds of dropping the rabbits, Seeing Eye heard the snarling of the wolves fighting over their free meal. His tanned deerskin leggings protected the lower half of his body from the dense brush and downed tree limbs, but his exposed upper torso was welted and bleeding from many deep scratches.

Seeing Eye's fear gave way to elation as the lake came into view through the thinning trees. When his foot hit the dirt ledge that banked Lake Kahooga, he pushed himself with all of his strength, catapulting his body into the cool water. He sank slowly through the shallows to the murky lake bed. The water grew colder as he swam just above the rocks into deeper water. If the wolves had followed him, they would surely have lost his scent by now.

The Indian's long black hair wafted through the water as he used up the oxygen in his lungs. He rose slowly to the surface and barely creating a ripple, raised his head into the open air and turned to face the bank. Seeing Eye was able to stand on the tips of his bare toes, his eyes just above the waterline. The wolf pack would not be likely to venture this far into the water for a meal. They were excellent hunters on the land, but hesitated to swim in deep water. Scanning the trees and bushes on the shore, he knew instinctively that the creatures lurked, unseen, waiting for their prey to become vulnerable.

The dream shifted suddenly. Hupa was now tensely observing as the scene unfolded. He watched silently as Seeing Eye swam slowly toward the bank. *Seeing Eye pulled his bow from its leather quiver as he neared the shore. When the water was waist deep, he stopped. Without taking his eyes from the forest, he reached back to the quiver that held his arrows. His fingers skillfully examined the arrowhead at the end of each wooden shaft.*

Hupa knew what Seeing Eye was searching for and wished that he could help guide his ancestor's fingers.

Seeing Eye's hand passed over arrowheads carved from bone and flint until he found the arrow that he was looking for. He removed the arrow from the quiver slowly, almost reverently, and loaded the feathered shaft onto the sinew bowstring. The arrowhead had been blessed years before by Seeing Eye's grandfather, a powerful Kickapoo medicine man. Seeing Eye gazed at the arrowhead for a moment, remembering how honored he had been as a young boy to receive such strong magic.

As he always did at this point in his dream, Hupa/Seeing Eye stared at the sharpened stone as if transfixed. The arrowhead appeared to glow from within. If he gazed at it just long enough, the golden veins embedded in the polished flint seemed to writhe like tiny snakes captured in the smooth stone. Hupa's father had told him that the arrowhead had penetrated the hides of many deer, bear and buffalo over the years. The aim of the hunter who possessed it was always true.

Seeing Eye stretched the bowstring to its limit as he once again began moving toward the shore. As he stepped onto the bank, the only sound that he heard was the song of the birds in the trees high above him. The young Kickapoo warrior began slowly backing away from the place where he thought the wolf pack would be. A sharp snap from behind warned him, too late, seconds before the fangs of a huge gray wolf sank into his upper right arm. The animal pulled Seeing Eye into the forest with such force that he nearly lost his grip on the loaded bow.

Hupa was once again linked with his dream ancestor. Fear gripped him as Seeing Eye struggled with the fierce predator. His sleeping body twisted as he battled for his life.

The wolf threw Seeing Eye to the ground and held him down with its muscular frame. The animal would wait for its prey to weaken, presenting an opening for a quick, decisive strike to the throat.

The fallen medicine man took hold of the arrow shaft with his free left hand. He wanted to be ready when the strong jaws released his mangled right arm. By rapidly flipping his body, he was able to plunge the arrow into the muscular gray chest. As the flint pierced the animal's heart, both man and beast bellowed out a primal scream that echoed through the forest. The stunned wolf retreated a few steps, then fell shuddering to the ground. Blood poured from its wound, saturating the gray fur and forming a scarlet pool on the ground, dying instantly.

Drawing on a reserve of strength, Seeing Eye pulled the arrow from the wolf's heart. He cleaned the blood from the shaft with leaves and replaced the arrow in his quiver. He then pulled his knife from its sheath and made deft incisions on either side of the slain wolf's jaw. The power of the wolf lay in its jaw. Seeing Eye would build a fire to sear the flesh and fur away from the bone. He would then grind the jaw into powder and add it to the other contents of his medicine bundles to possess the great strength of the wolf.

The spirit of the dead wolf seemed to posses Hupa. Seeing Eye had fashioned the animal's dripping pelt into a crude headdress that he wore as he danced around a ceremonial fire. The gray fur cascaded down the Shaman's naked back as he danced and rejoiced in his victory, singing ancient songs to the Great Spirit.

Hupa's dream had always followed the same course, but now the dream changed abruptly into one that was completely unfamiliar. *Hupa was now alone, standing next to the remains of the fire that Seeing Eye had danced around. He bent to touch the ashes, surprised to find them cold. The fire had burnt out long ago. "The spirit of the wolf still hunts by this lake." The unexpected voice brought Hupa to his feet. His uncle, Kenekuk, stood before him. Hupa had been a young boy when the great Kickapoo leader had died, but they had spoken many times in dreams. Hupa still wore the floppy brown hat with the white eagle feather in the brim that his uncle had given him. As the two Medicine Men embraced with strong arms, Hupa realized how much he had missed the wisdom of the older Shaman.*

Finally, his uncle spoke again.

"The Great Spirit has sent me to you with a message. Do you remember long ago when I was still on this earth, I gave you a medicine bundle?" Hupa remembered very clearly.

"I told you that night, under a blanket of stars, that someday you would pass the bundle on to the next holy man of your village. It is now time to pass along the healing power of the Great Spirit." Hupa stood speechless. He knew the importance of what Kenekuk was saying.

Kenekuk continued. "The white army comes to the village at Eagle Pass in the early morning while it is still dark. You must abandon your hunt in the mountains now and return to your home quickly. There is little time left."

Not for the first time that night, Hupa felt real fear.

"Why do they come, Kenekuk?" He asked. "What more do they want from our people? We have given them all of the land to the north. We had to begin again in the desert. You know that the reservations will be death to the Kickapoo."

Kenekuk did know this. After fleeing Wisconsin years before, the Kickapoo tribe had split up into smaller factions. Some, like Kenekuk, had grown weary of being evicted from location after location by the white settlers. All they wanted was the freedom to hunt their native country, but their will had eventually broken. Kenekuk had given in and moved his small tribe to a reservation in Kansas. Within weeks of arriving at the reservation, they had seen much of the land that the U.S. Government had promised them sold to whites. Game was scarce on what little land remained for the Kickapoo. They were forced to rely on the white government for food. They soon found that their needs were largely ignored. With little food and shelter, the Indians began to succumb to illness. In 1853, three years after his arrival on the reservation, Kenekuk also sickened and died. His name was still revered by his people.

Kenekuk now placed a weathered hand on Hupa's shoulder.

"The white man is afraid of change. If he does not understand a thing, then that thing is evil and must be destroyed. It will take many, many moons before he learns to accept and benefit from what he does not know. Wake now and go to your village. All of your people cannot be saved from the white army. You must choose a handful of your best braves to stay behind in the village to do battle. Send the rest of your tribe to the mountains east of the village. Tell them to stay in the mountains for four days. On the fifth day they must cross the great river into Mexico where they will find safety."

Hupa looked deep into his uncle's eyes.

"What will become of the men who stay behind?" He asked.

Kenekuk replied sadly. "You and your warriors will join the spirit world. It is the only way that the others can survive. Do not be afraid, my loved one. I will be waiting to take you there when the time is right. There are many Kickapoo who await your arrival. You will soon understand the true beauty of the world and the sun and the stars overhead. Give the medicine bundle to your son so that he may help the Kickapoo who are left in the world of the living. You know that throughout your life your ancestors have guarded you, and now it is your time to enter the spirit world to watch over your own family. You must hurry now. Ride hard to Eagle Pass. Our people must hear your warning."

Kenekuk took a few steps backward. Hupa was startled to see that his Uncle's body was growing translucent. The old Medicine Man was slowly disappearing into a misty blue cloud, and he was soon gone altogether.

Hupa awoke by the smoldering remains of the fire he had started hours before. He lifted his head from his pillow of pine needles and slowly breathed in the cool night mountain air. Shaking off sleep, he threw aside his wool blanket and rose to his feet. He placed the brown suede hat with the proud eagle feather reverently on his head. Hupa hurried to his horse and untied the leather reins from the tree he had secured him to at the beginning of this long night. As he mounted the horse, he swatted its backside with the flat of his hand. Horse and rider sped into the darkness of the desert mountains. Hupa needed to reach his village before the white man's army arrived.

Chapter 3

The ride back to the village seemed to take an eternity. Hupa's horse was lathered from the hours at a full gallop as they finally rode into the sleeping village. The Shaman woke his tribe and gathered them around a smoldering fire pit in the middle of the village to deliver Kenekuk's instructions. They quickly scattered to their tipis and with fear in their hearts, they packed their meager belongings.

The sky was still dark as the families mounted their horses, ready to flee to the mountains. The handful of unlucky braves who were to stay behind said tearful good-byes to their loved ones. Hupa gently placed his two-year old son, Matachias, in his wife's waiting arms as she sat astride her black pony.

Tears flowed down her smooth cheeks as she bent to kiss her husband.

Hupa's voice was husky as he told her. " I will someday find you and Matachias. I promise I will search the desert and the mountains until our spirits are together again. Then our family will be one."

He untied the medicine bundle that he had prepared for his only son. Two others remained lashed to his belt. He looped the leather drawstring around Matachias' neck and gently tucked the deerskin bag under the boy's vest.

"The Great Spirit is with you now and forever, Matichias." Hupa told his son.

He turned to his wife. " The medicine bundle is to be given to him when he is old enough to respect it. You must make sure that no one else sees its contents, only our son. Tell him to travel into the desert alone and take each item out and hold them one by one. He will then understand their powers. When you reach the mountains today, tell the people of the village that Matachias is the chosen one. The spirit of Kenekuk assures you safety. Remember, hide out for four nights in the mountains and on the fifth day cross the great river into Mexico."

The small village was soon deserted. The small band of men who remained silently watched as their families disappeared into the early morning darkness. The young men knew that they would never see them again. Hupa interrupted their grief with terse instructions to gather their weapons and return to the center of the empty village. With little time left, the young men moved swiftly to prepare for battle.

Hupa entered his tipi and reached for the deerskin satchel that held his own bows and arrows. He took the weapons out into the moonlight and sat on the ground. After taking three of the arrows from the satchel he untied the carved bone arrowheads and removed them from their shafts. He opened one of the medicine bundles that still hung from his belt. He untied the bundle and carefully and reverently poured its contents out onto the hard ground. Three sacred flint arrowheads fell to the earth along with peyote flowers that Hupa's grandfather had dried years earlier. The desert Peyote only flowers every few years and was prized by the Kickapoo medicine men for it has many mystical powers. The flowers were dried and eaten before communicating with the spirit world.

One by one, Hupa kissed the arrowheads and placed them on the ground next to the three wooden shafts. He carefully tied each arrow tightly and returned them to the leather satchel.

Weapons in hand, the young braves took up positions in the woods surrounding the village. They would wait patiently for the white army to attack. The counter ambush would commence on Hupa's order. The white man's rifles were far deadlier than the

Kickapoo arrows, but with the element of surprise on their side, there was a slim chance of successfully defending the village. They talked softly as they waited high above the village. Their fear began to subside as Hupa told them of the conversation he had had with the spirit of Kenekuk. He spoke to the young braves of their forefathers who awaited them in the spirit world.

Just as dawn began to break in the eastern sky, the Fourth U.S. Cavalry crept silently into the abandoned village. The Kickapoo watched from the trees as the white soldiers shot into the empty wigwam with their powerful rifles. The acrid smell of gunpowder filled the air, and flashes of light exploded throughout the village. When the gunfire finally ceased and the rifle barrels were empty Hupa sounded the order to attack with a piercing cry. Arrows rained down on the white soldiers, piercing their bodies with the force nearly equal to that of their own rifle slugs.

The second wave of cavalry entered the village, this one on horseback, and found their comrades searching for cover.

"Those bastards are in the trees! Shoot into the trees!" One of the injured soldiers shouted. The men fired their rifles at random into the still dark woods hoping for a strike.

The Kickapoo returned their fire with amazing speed, inflicting a great deal of injury to an army that outnumbered them so heavily.

Hupa loaded the first of his sacred arrows into his bow. He pulled the sinew bowstring taut and took aim. The missile found its mark in the side of a soldier's neck. The man grabbed for the arrow as he fell from his horse. Hupa placed his second flint-tipped arrow into the bow string and once again took aim. This strike was deadlier than the first with a fatal hit to the chest of another white soldier. When his third and final flint arrow was ready to be fired, Hupa was overcome with a profound sadness. As he stared into the darkness, he realized that he had never taken another man's life.

He still held the bow string taut as the rifle slug burned into his stomach. The blow instantly crushed the air from his lungs, knocking him backwards. He released the arrow, sending it wildly into the trees. Unable to move, Hupa lay on his back listening to the fading sounds of battle. His vision began to cloud, and the woods around him gradually disappeared in a swirling haze. As suddenly as the pain in his stomach had begun, it was gone. The sounds of gunfire had been replaced with the sounds of laughter as he rose slowly to his feet.

"Welcome, Hupa! We are nearly ready to depart for the spirit world."

Kenekuk opened his arms to Hupa as he came closer. Still dazed, Hupa looked at his belly, searching for the bullet wound.

"Your injury is gone." Kenekuk said gently.

"There are no injuries or illness here."

Hupa looked around and saw some of his men who had stayed behind to face the white army. Their spirits seemed to beam with joy.

"We will wait for our other Kickapoo brothers." Kenekuk told him, "The battle will soon be over for them, too."

He rested a large hand on Hupa's shoulder.

"Before we enter the spirit world you must first go and greet the spirit of your son. He will be waiting for us."

"What happened to my son?" Hupa asked with alarm. " You said that my people would be delivered safely to Mexico."

Kenekuk's smile broadened as he answered. "He was delivered safely, Hupa. He has served his people as Shaman for many years. He is now an old man waiting for you to come and take him with us."

Hupa already missed his wife and son and was pleased to hear that he would be reunited with them soon.

"Come," said Kenekuk. "The Great Spirit awaits our arrival."

The veins in the flint arrowhead gleamed dully in the rays of the morning sun. It lay in a small clearing near the river and would rest there for many years to come.

Part 2
Chapter 4

Saturday, October 20, 1966 Devine, Texas

The fall of '66 had been unseasonably hot in south Texas, with the temperatures hovering near the 100 degree mark. This kind of heat could bring even the heartiest Texans to their knees. The weekend had brought some relief in the form of a cool breeze from the north. Laurie Logue decided that this would be a good day to finish unpacking the last of the boxes stored in their garage.

Laurie had moved to Devine from Clarion, Pennsylvania with her husband, Ryan, their son, Christopher, and his younger brother, Jonathan. Ryan had accepted a position as a laboratory supervisor with Horizon Powder Paints, a company located in nearby San Antonio. The new job offered not only a raise in salary, but less overtime than his job in Pennsylvania. Ryan would welcome more time to spend with his wife and growing sons. Having timed the move south in September to coincide with the start of the school year, the Logues had naively thought that they would avoid the summer heat, but they had not counted on the bright Texas sun. After a month in Devine, the family missed the lush pine forests and the green mountains of the Alleghenies. Ryan and Laurie had decided to hang onto the ten acres of land that they owned in Cooks Forest. Maybe in the most intense heat of the summer, they could hook their pop-up camper to the station wagon and escape to the woods up north.

Laurie stood in the open doorway of the garage, savoring the cool air that ruffled through her sandy blonde hair. She was anxious to finish unpacking and finally get her new home in order. She still did not feel entirely at home in the new ranch house that was so different from their old colonial back in Clarion. Laurie gazed out at the ten-year-old housing development and wondered how long it would take her to get used to the stucco ranches that were all the color of the sands of the desert to the west.

"Oh, well," she said out loud to no one. "At least Ryan likes his new job, and the boys are doing well at their new schools. Time to stop gathering wool and get to work, girl."

"Chris, Jon, I need some help in the garage," she called. She wasn't sure if anyone was within earshot.

"Hello, is anyone home?" She called, louder this time.

She heard movement in the house, and Chris came into the garage from the kitchen. At fourteen, Chris was nearly six feet tall with the slender build of an athlete. His dark brown hair and olive skin came from Ryan's side of the family, but his crooked smile reminded Laurie of her father.

"Is someone yelling?" He asked. Laurie was already up on a stepladder peering up into a square hole in the garage ceiling.

"I want to store some of this stuff in the crawlspace," she replied.

"I know you're busy, Chris, but if you hand me those boxes I promise I won't ask for another favor all day."

Chris began handing her the cartons as she bent from the top of the ladder, "Nah, I don't mind at all," he drawled, "Us Texans don't mind helpin' out purdy young heifers like you, ma'am."

"You'd better work on that accent, pardner, or you'll be in trouble around here," Laurie responded with a laugh.

"Where is your brother? He hasn't done a thing since we got here. His room is a mess, and he's still living out of boxes."

Chris handed her another carton and said, "He has a new friend two houses down. I think his name is Bill, or maybe Ben. He's in Jon's class at school."

"How about you, Chris, have you made any friends yet?" Laurie asked, climbing down from the wooden ladder.

"Well, yeah, there is one guy I met in science class. His name is Brian. He's not from around here, either."

Laurie surveyed the boxes that still cluttered the garage. She had hoped to fit all of them in the crawl space, but the small attic was already crowded. She sighed and ran her hand through her tousled hair.

"Chris, honey, you're going to have to get up there and stack those boxes for me. I need as much space as possible." Laurie instructed her son.

"Go on up and I'll hand the rest of these boxes up to you."

Chris pulled himself up into the crawlspace and began stacking the boxes that were already there.

Laurie was up on the ladder with another box that Chris took from her. "Do you know where Brian lives?" Laurie asked her son.

"Yeah, he told me how to get to his house. I think it's only a couple of blocks away." Chris replied. They were almost finished stacking the boxes, and the consolidation had left more space than Laurie had hoped for.

"When we're done, why don't you see if you can find Brian's house," she suggested. "It will give you something better to do than sit in your room listening to those awful records."

"What, you don't like my music? It's rock and roll, baby!"

Chris did enjoy listening to his albums. His parents had bought him a stereo for Christmas, and it sounded a lot better than his old record player. His favorite bands were the Beatles, the Rolling Stones, and the Kinks, all of the English bands. He would listen to the Yellow Submarine album over and over until Ryan lost patience and yelled for him to turn it down. In Clarion he had mowed lawns to get money to add to his album collection, but there wasn't much greenery in Devine, so Chris would have to come up with a new way to earn spending money. He wanted to buy a set of ear-phones, so he could play his music as loud as he wanted.

Chris came down from the attic and folded the stepladder, re-placing it at the side of the garage. "I think I'll go scout out the area on my bike. What time will dad be home from work?"

His mom considered for a moment before answering. "It's 2:30 now. We'll probably have dinner around 5:30. Try to be home by then."

Chris grinned. "No problem, mom. Have you ever known me to be late for a meal?"

Laurie shook her head as she watched her older son ride away. She was proud of both of her sons. They were good boys who were rapidly turning into men. The only thing that worried her about Chris was the fact that his hair resembled a mop. He was a good-looking kid, but she thought that he looked awful with that hair hanging in his eyes.

Oh well, as long as he keeps clean and doesn't get into trouble in school I guess he can do as he pleases.

"I'll give you five bucks if you get a haircut!" She called after him, unable to resist after all.

"No way!" He called back over his shoulder, "It takes too long to grow out."

Chapter 5

Sweat began to trickle down his face as Chris rode down his new street. He wiped it from his forehead with his tee shirt. Brian had told him to turn left at Winchester, continue on to Newton Falls road, then to hang a right on Iverson. Brian's house was on the corner. As Chris turned on Newton Falls Road, he could see the yellow house that his new friend had described. He parked his bike in the driveway. The garage door was open, and he could see someone inside. Brian stood hunkered over a bike that had been propped upside down on the dirt floor. He was attempting to replace the chain on the rear rim. He looked up as Chris entered the garage and smiled. Brian was shorter than Chris with the stocky build of a linebacker. He had a shock of curly blond hair and clear hazel eyes.

He greeted Chris warmly, "Hey, man, how's it goin'?"

"Okay, What happened? Did your chain pop off?"

"No, the inner tube had a hole in it so I patched it. I'm almost finished, do you want to give me a hand?"

Chris walked over to the bike.

"What do you want me to do?" He asked.

"Turn the pedals while I feed the chain onto the teeth back here."

Chris began turning the pedals slowly as Brian fed the chain onto the back rim. When he was finished, Brian flipped the bike over and dropped the kick stand.

"Thanks, man. You want to go in the house and have a soda?" He asked. "I'm thirstier than hell."

"Sure. Is it always this hot in October?"

"To tell the truth, I really don't know." Brian replied, wiping the grease from his hands with a shop rag. "My mom and I moved here from Chicago about six months ago. So far it's been like living in an oven."

Brian led Chris into a small kitchen. Chris looked around the room. The sink was filled with dishes, and the table was covered with old newspapers and empty cereal boxes. Brian saw the look on his friend's face and apologized.

"Sorry about the mess. I'm supposed to clean it up before my mom comes home at six. She's a nurse. She works at a nursing home."

Brian opened the refrigerator and took a quick inventory. "Hmm, looks like the Coke is all gone. How about a root beer?"

"Fine with me."

Brian pulled a can opener from a drawer and opened the two bottles. He handed one to Chris. "Hey, do you want to watch 'Lost In Space'? It should be on channel 3."

"Sure, I love that show."

Chris followed Brian into the living room and sat down on the blue sofa across from the television. Brian turned on the black and white set and stood in front of it waiting for the picture tube to warm up. Horizontal lines appeared and began rolling up and down the screen as the picture came into focus.

"Are you sure we're not watching 'The Outer Limits'?" Chris joked.

"I know " Brian said, "This thing takes forever to warm up, but it's better than nothing."

He fiddled with the buttons on the back of the set.

"Tell me when it stops rolling." Brian asked as the rolling increased.

"You went too far. Now it's going the other way."

Brian slowly turned the knob in the opposite direction.

"Stop right there... perfect."

Brian sat on the other end of the sofa. The boys had not missed anything; the opening credits were still rolling across the screen. They watched the show in silence, sipping their soft drinks. When the show was over, Brian asked Chris, "What do you want to do now?"

Chris thought for a moment. "I don't know. I have to be home by 5:30 for dinner." He reminded Brian.

"Do you want to come over to my house tomorrow and listen to records?"

"Nah, I can't," Brian replied.

"I'm going on a picnic with my mom and her new boyfriend, or whatever the hell he is. We're going to a park a couple of hours from here, mom wants to leave really early in the morning. I hate getting up early on the weekends."

The idea of getting out of town for a day sounded good to Chris.

"You don't seem to like your mom's boyfriend much. What's wrong with him?" Chris asked.

"I guess Matt's not such a bad guy," Brian admitted, "he sure is better than that jerk, Roger, she was with in Chicago. He's the reason we came down here. He was a mean drunk, and he used to beat her up all the time. I must have called the cops on him at least twenty times."

Brian sat staring at the television. After an uncomfortable silence, he got up and started spinning the channel button on the old console television. He finally decided that there was nothing on that appealed to him and turned the set off and returned to the sofa.

"So how about you, Chris, why did your family move to this Hellhole?"

Chris was a little embarrassed by Brian's story. He felt lucky that his parents got along so well even if they were kind of boring.

"My dad got a better job down here." Chris answered as he stood up. "Where's your garbage can?"

"Don't worry about it," Brian replied. "I better clean up this mess before my mom gets home from work, or she'll have a fit. Hey, why don't you ask your folks if you can come along tomorrow? I'm sure my mom and Matt won't mind. It'll give them some time alone."

Chris had been hoping that Brian would invite him.

"Sounds cool to me, I'll ask them when I get home, and I'll give you a call later and let you know. I'm sure they won't care."

Brian was beginning to feel better about the picnic now. Matt had told him that there were ruins of an old Indian village not far from the park. There were fossils and artifacts to be found if you were willing to hunt a little. He walked Chris through the kitchen and out to the garage where Chris had left his bike.

"Talk to ya' later," he called and waved as his new buddy pedaled away.

Brian was in his room when the phone rang at 8:00 that evening. His mother, Carolyn, called to her son: "Brian, pho-one!"

The voice on the other end of the line said, "hey, it's Chris. My parents told me that I can go tomorrow after the usual interrogation, of course. What time are we leaving?"

"I'm not sure. Let me ask my mom."

Carolyn was putting the dinner dishes away. She was exhausted after ten hours of work. Today's shift at the nursing home had been an extra day for her. She hated to leave Brian home alone, but she really needed the overtime. Brian's father had disappeared soon after his birth, and supporting herself and her son had not been easy on a Licensed Practical Nurse's salary. She told Brian that Matt would be picking them up at around 6:00 a.m.

"Tell him to bring his bike, so you two can go riding."

Carolyn hadn't asked Matt if Chris could come along, but she was sure that he wouldn't mind. He was the nicest man that she had ever been involved with. He delivered oxygen to the nursing home and had asked her out the day they met. She had put him off for a month because he was five years younger than she was, and the age difference worried her. He had been persistent, though, and had romanced her until she gave in. She hadn't regretted her change of heart for a moment of the two months that they had been dating. He was a gentle man, he and Brian got along right from the start. Unlike Carolyn, Matt was close to his own family. She had begun to think that maybe she and her son might have a place in that family.

Carolyn was sitting at the kitchen table with her feet propped up on a chair, savoring a glass of wine and a cigarette when Brian came in to raid the fridge for the last root beer.

"Thanks for letting Chris tag along tomorrow, Mom," he said.

"No problem, sweetie," she replied. "I'm glad you've found a friend. You haven't been very happy here, have you, kiddo?"

Brian hesitated before answering, "no, not really. Maybe having someone to hang around with help. Still hate the weather, though." Carolyn smiled and leaned over to run a hand through her son's hair. "Hang in there, buddy. I think things are going to be better for us here. Anyway, you know I love you, right?"

"Yeah, ma, me too."

After talking to Brian, Chris went to the garage to check the air in his bike tires. When he returned to the house, his parents were watching television.

"Chris, don't you want to watch 'Star Trek'? It just started." his father asked.

"No, I think I'll get to bed early. I have to be at Brian's by a quarter to six.

"Are you sure these people are O.K.? Ryan asked his son. "I mean, what does their house look like? Maybe I should take you there in the morning so I can meet his mother."

Chris sighed. His dad was beginning to irritate him. "Their house looks fine, dad. Don't worry about it. I think I'm old enough to take care of myself."

Laurie looked up sharply from the television. "Don't get smart with your father. We're entitled to know where you're going and who you're going with."

Chris let out a slow breath before responding. "Sorry, you're right. Brian really is O.K.." His mother smiled.

"Fine, partner. Go on to bed. If we don't see you in the morning, have a good time. Try to get home early, Monday is a school day, you know."

Chris escaped into his bedroom before his parents thought of anything more to say. He was looking forward to the next day's outing. It would be the first cool thing that he had done since moving to Devine. He set his alarm clock, turned out the light and crawled into bed. He was just dropping off to sleep when the bedroom door burst open with a bang. Chris sat straight up in bed, heart pounding.

Jonathan leaped onto the bed, landing on Chris hard enough to make him see stars. "You're going on a picnic tomorrow, take me with you," the little boy pleaded.

"NO, now get out of here, ass wipe," was his older brother's response.

"Aw, come on, Chris, please," Jonathan was beginning to whine. "I'll give you anything you want, just name it."

"I want you out of here" Chris said, shoving his little brother off of the bed.

"MOOOOM, tell butt face to get out of my room." Chris yelled.

Laurie's response was mechanical, "Jon get out of your brother's room, Chris, don't call your brother ' butt-face.'

"You're an asshole, you know that?" Jon sneered at Chris as he slammed the door.

"Yeah, goodnight yourself," Chris said quietly as he lay his head back on his pillow. Tomorrow was going to be a great day, he just knew it.

Chapter 6

The town was still asleep as Chris rode along the quiet streets to Brian's house early Sunday morning. As he approached the yellow ranch house, he saw two cars in the driveway, a Corvair parked near the garage and a big yellow Bonneville bringing up the rear. The Pontaic's trunk was open. Chris figured that the two bikes would fit in there easily enough. The kitchen door opened as Chris walked into the garage, and a handsome man emerged carrying a cooler.

"Hey, you must be Chris." He said in a deep Texas drawl, "I'm Matt, pleased to meet you." Matt was tall and rangy with dark curly hair. Chris thought that he looked a little like Mickey Dolenz from the Monkees.

"Nice to meet you too, " Chris replied, "Do you need a hand with that cooler?"

"Naw, go on inside. Brian's in the kitchen. Hey, why don't you wheel the bikes over to the car so I can pack 'em up right now, then go inside and see if Carolyn needs any help."

After moving the bikes, Chris went into the kitchen. Brian's mother was putting glasses into a picnic basket. She looked up and smiled at him,

"Hi, Chris, I'm Brian's mother, Carolyn."

The young man offered his outstretched hand. "Pleased to meet you, Mrs. Boscorelli."

Carolyn laughed. "That makes me sound too old, how about calling me Carolyn?"

"Okay, Carolyn, thanks for letting me come along."

Brian came around the corner into the kitchen, letting out a loud belch. "What's up, Chris, my man?"

"Is that absolutely necessary?" Carolyn snapped.

"Sorry, Mom, I didn't know that it would be that loud." Chris and Brian looked at each other and stifled their laughter.

Carolyn reached under the sink and rummaged around among the cleaning products and paper towels. Finally finding what she was searching for, she triumphantly held up a bottle of red wine. She added the bottle to the contents of the picnic basket.

Brian whistled under his breath. "Now I know why you want Chris and me to go off bike riding. You have plans for after lunch, huh?"

Carolyn blushed and waved him away.

"Never you mind, nosy. You boys go on out to the car now." She smiled as she thought about sharing the wine with Matt. Making love for the first time would be especially sweet on a blanket in the woods. She and Matt would have to make sure that the boys took a good long ride on their bikes. Matt's voice brought her back to reality.

"Is there anything else that needs to go in the car, honey?" he asked.

"Just this, Matt," she answered, handing him the loaded picnic basket. Matt pretended to have trouble carrying the basket.

"C'mon, pretty woman, daylight's wastin'. The boys are chomping at the bit to get going."

"Hmm," Carolyn thought, "keep sweet talking me and you may get lucky yet."

On the ride to the river Matt regaled the boys with stories of fishing trips that he had taken as a boy. After a few hours drive, the scenery began to change from brown to green. Chris was delighted to see that they were approaching a real forest. Not as green as Cook's Forest, but the closest he had seen since coming to Texas.

He asked Matt if the river up ahead was the Rio Grande. Matt laughed and explained that this was just a small tributary.

"The Rio Grande is a few miles south of here. This is a puddle by comparison. The water is low this time of year, but it can flood in the spring if there's a lot of rain. The Indians called this the Eagle River 'cause it runs through Eagle Pass, and they called the Rio Grande the Great River. The Bonneville turned off the main highway onto a narrow dirt road leading into the trees. The car threw up a cloud of dust and rocked from side to side as Matt navigated the rutted path. He explained that this road led to a spot where he and his father had fished many times when he was a boy.

"I brought fishing poles for everyone." Matt told them. "There are small mouth and rock bass in the river. If you don't want to fish, I'll show you the path leading to the ruins of the old Indian village that I told you about, Brian."

Brian spoke up quickly. "Yeah, that's where we want to go. Chris, remember I told you about that? We can look for arrowheads and stuff."

"Sounds cool," Chris responded.

Matt warned the boys not to expect too much. "You might find some pieces of broken pots or something, but I don't suppose there's too much left after all these years."

The road narrowed and became even more pitted as they neared the river. Brian and Chris laughed as they bounced around in their seats. Branches scratched the sides of the car, and Matt began to swear in a soft drawl, causing the boys to laugh louder. Carolyn shot them one of her patented mother looks, but she couldn't help smiling. The road had become a path when Matt finally stopped the car. The river was visible through the trees, winding in an improbable blue ribbon through the canyon known as Eagle Pass. The boys were out of the car before the Bonneville had come to a full stop.

"Wow, this place is totally cool!" Brian yelled. "Come on, let's check out the river."

He and Chris slid down a five foot embankment leading to the water.

"Hey ,you guys, help us unpack the car!" Carolyn called after them.

Matt opened the trunk. "Don't worry about it, honey. There's not that much," he said, pulling the bikes from the trunk.

"Hey Matt, we can see fish everywhere! The river is full of them. I hope they're biting," Brian called.

"I hope so, too," Matt yelled back. "They're probably scaring them all away." Matt smiled at Carolyn.

"Well, tell them to stop. I don't want them to fall in the river, either." Carolyn scowled as she tried to see what the boys were up to. Matt was trying to untangle the fishing lines without much success.

"Aw, let them horse around a little. It'll help them work up an appetite. Anyway, by the time I get these lines straightened up, the fish will be back."

Chris and Brian climbed up the bank and ran to the clearing. They flopped down, panting, on the blanket that Carolyn was in the process of spreading out on an even patch of ground.

"Hey, Mom, is it okay with you if we go check out the Indian village before lunch?" Brian asked, still slightly out of breath. "We can go fishing after we eat."

"It's all right with me; Is that okay with you, Matt?" Matt was still trying to untangle the fishing lines, but the harder he worked the more the clear line knotted.

"Holy smokes," he muttered under his breath. "Yeah, sounds good to me. I should have these lines straightened out by then. I'll tell you how to get there. Just follow the river until you see a big tree leaning out over the riverbank. You can't miss it. Cross the river there, it's pretty shallow, and go along the path right behind it. Take the path for about half a mile until you come to a clearing. The village used to be in the clearing. The path was used by the Indians when they went to the river. My dad took me there when I was a kid, and I found all kinds of stuff."

"Cool, what kind of stuff?" Chris asked.

Matt thought about it for a moment. "Let's see, I found some pieces of broken pottery, one time I found a bone arrowhead that I sold for ten bucks."

"Wow, ten bucks! I hope we find something that cool. I could use the cash." Brian exclaimed with a grin.

Chris and Brian were getting on their bikes when Matt cautioned them;

"Don't ride your bikes until you get across the river and up on the path. The rocks are sharp and you might cut your tires. Just walk your bikes for now."

The boys climbed off of their bikes and began walking up the rocky river bank.

"Keep an eye out, you'll see the tree pretty soon," Matt called after them. Carolyn asked if Brian had his watch and when he replied that he did, she told them to be back by noon.

"Yes, Mommy," Brian responded in a whining falsetto. "We'll be back in time for lunch," Chris laughed at his new buddy while Carolyn shook her head at her smart aleck son. The two amateur archeologists started off on their search for riches.

As Carolyn passed by Matt on his way on his way back to the car, she planted a quick kiss on his cheek and kept walking.

"Hey, lady, next time stay a little longer. "

"Maybe I will, cowboy," she said, sashaying away in her best Mae West imitation. Matt sat down on the blanket with a plop, the hopelessly knotted fishing lines still in his hand.

"This is going to take all day, " he sighed. Carolyn looked at the mess appraisingly.

"Why don't you just cut them and start over?" She suggested.

Matt had to agree. "Looks like you're going to get your first lesson on how to tie a fishing line," he told her, pulling a Swiss Army knife from his back pocket.

Carolyn shook her head with a laugh. "I think I'll pass. You can do the honors. Hey, does that thing have a corkscrew?"

"Sure does." Matt held the knife up proudly. "It has every-thing. I could build a house with this baby." Carolyn opened the picnic basket and pulled out the bottle of wine. "How about opening this for now? We'll build the house after lunch."

Matt's raised his eyebrows in mock surprise. He took the bottle from her and began to turn the corkscrew. "It's a little early for wine, isn't it?" he asked.

"Maybe, but the boys are gone for a few hours and this is a special occasion," she replied, leaning back on her elbows on the soft blanket.

"Why, ma'am, if I didn't know better, I would think you were trying to seduce me."

Matt had the bottle open and carefully poured the wine until the glasses were half full. He handed one of the glasses to Carolyn, and she held it out to Matt.

"Let's make a toast," she suggested.

Matt considered for a moment and then touched his glass to hers.

"Here's to new beginnings and special occasions."

Carolyn drained her glass in three quick gulps and held it out to Matt to be refilled. He thought about asking her to slow down a bit, but on second thought he decided that it might turn out to be an interesting day after all. He refilled the glasses, this time almost to the top.

Chapter 7

Chris and Brian crossed the river at the leaning tree and then climbed on their bikes and began peddling down the path to the site of the old Indian village. The path was overgrown and rutted, much like the road that they had traveled to reach the river. The going was slow, and the boys were careful to maneuver their bikes around the fallen tree limbs and brush that blocked their way. The movement stirred up swarms of deer flies that lived in the tall grass surrounding the path, and soon the boys were flapping their arms wildly to drive them off.

"Man, these flies are biting the crap out of me," Brian called behind him to Chris, who was bringing up the rear.

"Me too," Chris yelled back.

"Let's just speed through here as quick as we can. It can't be much farther."

"I'm all for that, " Chris agreed. "Maybe if we ride fast enough the flies won't be able to keep up."

They stood up on the pedals and pumped furiously. Chris could see Brian run his hands over his head. He realized that if the flies were on Brian's head, they were probably on his, too. He couldn't feel them because his hair was longer. He combed his fingers through his thick brown hair from front to back.

"Sure enough," he said, shuddering. With an effort, he ran his fingers through his hair until he couldn't feel the bugs anymore.

"Are you talking to me?" Brian hollered over his shoulder.
"No, let's just get the hell out of here!"

The path finally widened enough so that they could ride side by side. The sweat running down their necks onto the bug bites stung and the boys were running out of breath. Their legs were beginning to ache, and they stopped for a moment to rest. The swarm of deer flies had thinned to a stubborn few, and Chris swatted at them halfheartedly. Brian was looking around, trying to get his bearings.

"Hey, look, I can see the clearing! Let's go."

Once again they began pedaling as hard as they could. Once in the clearing, the boys could see that it had been used for partying. Empty beer cans and broken bottles littered the ground near the remains of a campfire. Chris and Brian were disappointed. They had hoped to find a wilderness, not a garbage dump.

"Why don't we clean up some of this crap?" Chris suggested. They had dropped the kick-stands of their bikes at the edge of the clearing and were walking around inspecting the debris. "We'll never find anything in this mess."

Brian wasn't too impressed with his friend's idea.

"I didn't come here to clean, man. I can do that at home anytime," he answered. "Why don't we look around at the edge of the clearing, over by the trees. There's not so much stuff over there," he said pointing toward the rocky hills about one hundred and fifty yards to the east.

They entered the woods, being careful to avoid the thorns on some of the bushes in the dense underbrush.

"How are we supposed to do this?" Brian wondered out loud. "Should we start digging or just look around on the ground?" They wandered through the trees, heads bent to the ground, picking up anything that didn't seem to be a natural part of the landscape.

"I don't see anything but a bunch of crap," Chris complained after about fifteen minutes. "It's getting hotter all the time, too."

"Oh my God, look at this!' Brian shouted.

Chris ran to where Brian stood staring at the ground.

"It's a rubber!" Brain explained. "It looks like it was just used."
Chris observed as they bent over to take a closer look.

"Gross."

He poked at the condom with a stick, finally working it into
the opening at the base. He slowly lifted the stick off the ground,
bringing it close to his friend's face. As Brian moved his head back
to avoid the condom, Chris flipped the stick toward him. Brian let
out a loud squawk and fell backward, landing squarely in a pricker
bush. Chris stifled a laugh and helped him up.

"I'm sorry, man. I was just kidding around." he apologized to
Brian. "Are you okay?"

"Yeah," Brian answered sheepishly. "I thought you were going to hit me in the mouth with that thing. You're lucky I didn't
puke. I have a weak stomach. One time I sniffed a carton of sour
milk and puked all over the kitchen floor." They broke into laughter simultaneously at the thought of Brian blowing chunks in the
woods.

"We'd better get back to work," Brian said after their fit had
subsided. "I'm going to start over toward those hills."

Chris looked around at the trees. "I guess I'll check out the
woods and work my way around the clearing. Don't call me if you
find another rubber." he advised, bending his head once again to
search the ground.

Brian was walking away, scanning this way and that. Chris
didn't think he was likely to find anything going that fast.

Dead leaves covered most of the soil. Chris picked up a stick
and began pushing the debris aside, bending even closer to the
ground. Beads of perspiration formed on his forehead and dripped
down his face as he moved the stick slowly from side to side. He
pushed aside rocks and leaves, trying to distinguish them from
anything that might be of value. Finally, he saw something foreign
in among the rocks. He squatted down to get a closer look. It was a
small shard of pottery, burnt red in color and about the size of a
matchbook. Chris examined it closely, turning it over in his hand.
There were no markings on the clay, but it was something, and

something was sure better than nothing. *Maybe where there's one, there's another.* He didn't see any point in telling Brian about one tiny piece of broken pottery. It might not even be old. Chris got down on his hands and knees and began combing through the rocks with his fingers. He soon spotted another shard of burnt red clay wedged in between some larger stones. He pulled the rocks apart and carefully extracted a curved piece of pottery shaped like a shell. The color was the same as the first shard, but with the addition of a black line that zigzagged across the outer surface. Chris's hand shook with excitement. He thought that this might be a real Kickapoo artifact. He called to Brian to come and help him search for more pieces, but Brian didn't answer. Chris stood up and began to look around for him.

Out of the corner of his eye, he saw movement in the woods, about fifty feet farther into the trees. He stood up to call again for Brian. His voice failed him, coming out in a rasping croak. The figure that stood before him was not his friend, but a tall Indian man. Although he appeared to be real enough, Chris felt the hair on the back of his neck stand up as he staggered backward, nearly losing his footing on the crisp dry leaves. The Indian man seemed to be young; his black hair was long and poker straight. He was dressed in leggings made of animal hide and wore a dark suede hat with an eagle feather in the beaded band. He was bare chested, his skin burnt nearly the color of his hat by years in the Texas sun. Standing as still as the trees, his face betrayed no emotion as he stared relentlessly at the shaking teenager. Chris tried to speak, to ask the stranger what he wanted, but his voice was now gone completely.

After what seemed like hours, Chris began to regain the use of his shaking limbs. His feet came back to life first, wheeling around and carrying him toward the clearing in an awkward sprint. A few yards from the edge of the trees, Chris risked a quick turn of his head to see if the man was in pursuit. The forest was deserted. He could detect no movement of the trees or brush, no sign of a retreating man at all.

Looking down at his clenched fists, Chris was mildly surprised to discover that he was still holding onto the broken pottery. Brian's voice sounded behind him, across the clearing,

"Hey, Chris, Where are you?"

Chris could manage only a hoarse whisper at first.

"In here, in the woods!"

He started walking in the direction of Brian's voice, slowly at first, then gaining speed in spite of the need to glance back over his shoulder every few seconds. The boys met up in the clearing.

"What's wrong with you, Chris boy? I heard you scream like a girl."

Chris stole one last glance over his shoulder and then held the pot shards out to his friend. "Well, I have bad news and good news," he answered sheepishly, " the good news is that I found these, and the bad news is that I saw an Indian in the woods, and I'm afraid he's pissed off. Are you sure we're not on somebody's property or something? I don't want to get shot over a few pieces of a broken pot."

Brian was grinning ear to ear as he examined the clay shards. "No, I think this is all state park land. I don't think Matt would send us up here if the land belonged to someone. These are totally boss. Do you think they're really old?" Chris shrugged.

Brian looked up at his buddy. "Hey man, you okay? You're a little green around the gills. Did that Indian guy say anything to you?" Chris shrugged again.

"No, he didn't say a word."

Brian gave him a little punch on the arm. "Well, c'mon then let's go back in the woods and see if we can find something else."

Chris didn't want to sound like a chickenshit, but he wasn't too keen on another trek into the woods either. "I don't know man, that guy was pretty spooky. I wouldn't want to meet up with him again. He might still be hanging around in there."

Brian snorted derisively. "I don't know whether to call you Chrissy or Sissy," he mocked, "What the hell do you think he's going to do, throw a tomahawk at us or something?"

Feeling a little ridiculous, Chris replied. " Okay, okay, let's go. If he throws a tomahawk, though, I hope he hits you."

Chris led the way back to the place where he had found the pottery, casting an occasional furtive glance into the trees as they went. He was able to find his way back easily by following the path that he had made through the brush on his hasty retreat to the clearing a few moments earlier. When they had reached the spot, Chris stopped and pointed down at the rocks.

"This is where I found the small piece and the larger one was over there." He hesitated before continuing. " The Indian guy was standing over there."

Brian looked in the direction that Chris was pointing. "Well, it looks like he's gone now. Maybe he was Sitting Bull, and he had to get back to the Little Big Horn," he laughed. Chris felt a little wounded by his friend's sarcasm

"I don't care if you believe me or not. I know what I saw."

Brian laughed again and delivered another little punch to his friend's deltoid.

"Hey, I'm just kidding. Don't get your panties in a bunch. C'mon, let's look for some more stuff," he suggested, dropping to his hands and knees on the forest floor. Rummaging through the leaves and rocks, he wished that he had brought a flashlight.

Chris was still staring at the spot where the Indian had stood. He could feel the hair at the back of his neck starting to creep upward again. He wondered if the man had been real. He looked real, but Chris couldn't understand why he had been so spooked.

The man hadn't said a word, and he hadn't really seemed angry or even mildly upset. There had just been something creepy about the way he was there one second without making a sound and then poof, gone without so much as the rustle of a dead leaf or the snap of a twig. The spirit of adventure was beginning to steal over the teenager again as his fear slowly evaporated. Now he wondered why the man had been watching him so intently, why he hadn't uttered a single word. Curiosity finally winning over caution, Chris made his way to where the Indian had been. There was no sign of anyone having stood there in a very long time, no broken twigs and no crushed leaves. Another chill passed over Chris, this one stronger than the first.

"Goose walking on my grave," he thought, then shuddered.

He jumped a foot in the air when Brian yelled. "Chris, I found some more pieces! Come over here and help me, will you?"

Chris took one last glance around to make sure he didn't miss anything. His eyes grew wide as he spotted a metallic glint among the rocks at his feet. He bent down to get a closer look. His heart skipped a beat when he realized that he was looking at an arrowhead nestled between two smooth stones. He picked it up carefully, then dropped it abruptly, his flesh crawling.

"The damn thing feels like it's alive!" He thought, looking around him wildly.

When his heart had stopped pounding, Chris reached toward the arrowhead, his hand twitching slightly. He touched it timidly, the way one would touch an iron to check if it was hot. The carved stone felt cool to his fingertips this time, just like what it was: stone.

"I must be losing my freaking mind," Chris thought. He examined the arrowhead closely. It looked like flint with tiny veins of gold and silver running through it. For a fraction of a second, Chris thought that he saw the veins move. He ran his left hand over his eyes and looked again. Nothing, no movement at all. Chris resisted the urge to giggle hysterically. *I hardly had anything to eat today, just one lousy piece of toast at the crack of dawn. It must be almost noon by now. I'm just hungry and thirsty, that's all. This is just a piece of stone, that's all, and a pretty cool one at that.* It was beginning to dawn on him that he might have found something of real value, and the heebie jeebies began to subside.

He turned and ran to where Brian was still crawling around peering under rocks and brush. Chris was now excited about his find, his revulsion at his first touch of the arrowhead forgotten.

"Brian, look, I found an arrowhead. I really found an arrowhead!"

Brian took the arrowhead from Chris with an expression of awe on his dirt-streaked face. "Wow, this is great! Where did you find it?"

Chris led him to the spot in the woods where the Indian had stood. "Right here, in these rocks." He said, pointing to the rocks where the arrowhead had rested for the better part of a century.

Brian handed the arrowhead back to Chris, along with more shards of pottery that he had turned up, then knelt and began carefully turning the rocks over one by one, hoping to uncover more hidden relics. Chris put the arrowhead into the pocket of his jeans and examined the pot shards that Brian had found.

"Hey, it looks like we have enough pieces to glue this together into a bowl." Chris said as he placed the shards on a tree stump and knelt to help Brian search.

Brian was growing tired and hungry. He was happy with his find and doubted that they would find anything more of interest.

"Do you think that the Indian was trying to show you where the arrowhead was?" Brian asked, wiping the sweat out of his eyes with his shirt sleeve.

That had not occurred to Chris, and he shivered a little in spite of the heat. He shrugged his shoulders and replied.

"I guess it's possible, maybe," although he knew with overwhelming certainty that it was so.

The forest was starting to look ominous to Chris, and he suddenly wished that he was back at the river with a fishing pole in his hand. He could almost feel the presence of the mysterious Indian man close by. He tried to appear nonchalant as he stood and dusted himself off.

"Man, it's getting late. I don't know about you, but I'm getting hungry. What time is it, anyway?"

Brian pulled his watch from his pocket. "Holy shit, it's eleven 11:45! We'd better get going." Chris reached the clearing with a strong sense of relief. Brian had gathered up the broken pieces of pottery on the way back to their bikes.

"I'll tell you what," Brian said, "I'll carry these pieces back if I can keep them. That arrowhead blows these hunks of clay out of the water, anyway. I'll glue them back together and see what we've got."

Chris had intended to give the pot shards to Brian, but he couldn't resist messing with his friend's mind a little.

"What are you talking about? I found the first few pieces, so I should get first dibs." He looked down at the ground as he walked, so his eyes wouldn't give him away.

Brian's face fell. " Are you serious? Do you really want to keep them all?"

Chris laughed at his friend's wounded expression. "Of course not. I'll let you keep them if you let me help put them back together. Deal?"

Brian grinned sheepishly, realizing that he had been had. "Deal. Here, help me with these things. I'll pull my tee shirt up and carry them like this," he said, folding the front of his shirt up to form a pouch.

Chris placed the pieces of pottery gingerly into the pocket. The boys started back to the river, Chris shooting out in front of Brian, taking advantage of Brian's fragile burden. This time he wouldn't be bringing up the rear when they rode through the deer flies.

Chapter 8

Matt and Carolyn were duly impressed with the Indian artifacts.

"Wow, look at that arrowhead. It's a lot better than the one that I found!" Matt enthused. "This one looks like it was carved from flint. I think you boys have something special here. Did you find it in the clearing where the Indian village used to be?"

Brian was a little disappointed that his mom and her boyfriend didn't seem overly impressed with the shards of pottery that he had found, but getting to tell the story of the arrowhead would make up for it a little.

"No, we really didn't search the clearing too much. It was full of trash, beer cans and broken glass everywhere. We split up and scouted the woods separately." Chris wondered if Brian was going to tell the part about the condom, but figured that it was probably too embarrassing to talk about in front of Carolyn. He thought that since his find seemed to be more valuable than Brian's, it would be nice to give Brian credit for finding the pot shards, so he left his part out as he took up the story.

"While Brian was digging up the pot shards, I saw an Indian man in another part of the woods. Are you sure we weren't on someone's property, Matt? He didn't look too happy to see us."

Matt's eyes widened at the mention of the Indian man.

"No, I'm sure that the area is all part of the State Park. What did the man look like?" Matt listened intently to the boy's answer.

"He was about thirty or so, with dark skin and long black hair. He was wearing suede leggings and no shirt. Oh, yeah he had on a brown hat with a white feather sticking up, and he had a couple of leather bundles hanging on a thong around his waist."

Matt let out a whistling breath before asking. "Did he say anything to you?"

"No, " Chris replied, "he just stood there and stared at me."

Matt's voice was excited as he told Chris that the man in the woods was undoubtedly the ghost of an Indian Medicine man who had died in a massacre in the Kickapoo village in the 1870's.

"Wow, Cool!" Brian yelled.

Chris had grown pale and wasn't sure that seeing a ghost was all that cool.

Carolyn had returned to the blanket and was in the process of setting up lunch, pulling hot dogs and hamburger meat wrapped in waxed paper from the picnic basket. Brian's shout caught her attention.

"What's this about a ghost? Are you joking, Matt?"

"No, I'm serious," he insisted. "There's a legend around these parts that the U.S. Cavalry massacred the villagers during the Indian wars in the 1870's, but before they could attack, the tribal Medicine Man sent the women and children to the mountains west of the village. The men stayed to do battle with the cavalry and to keep them from following the rest of the tribe. All of the Indian men left behind were supposedly killed in the ambush. Anyway, when the Medicine Man sent his wife and son to the mountains, he told his wife that he would walk the earth until the time came to be reunited with them. According to the legend, his spirit still walks in the woods around the village waiting for them."

The boys were silent for a moment, digesting Matt's story. Brian regained his voice first.

"Holy crap, Chris, you saw a ghost!"

Chris was skeptical; he thought Matt was putting them on, trying to put a scare into them. He still didn't like the idea that he had been face to face with a long dead Indian.

"He sure didn't look like a ghost, " he protested, "there must be some Indians still living around here. Maybe the man I saw was searching for artifacts just like we were."

Carolyn agreed with him. " Matt, why don't you give your imagination a rest," she chided gently. "And start the charcoal. I don't know about you guys, but I'm starving."

Matt replied that he was starving, too, but as he piled the briquettes into the portable Hibachi and poured on the lighter fluid he defended his story.

"I'm not making this up. My dad told me the story when I was little, and later when I was a Boy Scout we used to camp here. The Scoutmaster swore that the story was true. We never did see the ghost, though," he admitted, sounding a little disappointed.

Chris and Brian washed the pieces of pottery in the river while Carolyn and Matt finished preparing lunch. After they ate, the adults settled down on the blanket for a catnap while the boys spent the afternoon fishing and talking about the existence of ghosts.

On the ride home Brian asked his mother if Chris could stay for dinner. They wanted to work on putting the pieces of pottery back together.

"I don't care. Chris, do you think your parents will mind?"

"They're not expecting me home 'till about nine. We should be back in Devine by seven or so. I'll call them when we get back to your house if that's alright with you."

Carolyn sighed. "Fine, now I'd appreciate a little peace and quiet, guys. It's been a long day."

Chris and Brian used airplane glue to put the old bowl back together. They were short a few small pieces, but Brian was very proud of it, anyway. He would keep it on his dresser for years to come, showing it off to anyone who visited.

Chapter 9

Laurie and Ryan were impressed with the arrowhead that their son had found, and Jon was positively green with envy. Chris didn't tell them the story of the ghostly Indian. He didn't think that they would believe him, he didn't know if he really believed it himself. The memory of the morning had taken on an aura of unreality this late in the day.

After a brief description of the other events of the day, Chris excused himself and went to his room, shutting the door behind him. He didn't want to be disturbed, especially by his bratty little brother.

Chris kept most of his collectibles in the bottom drawer of his dresser, he rummaged around until he found what he was looking for. He sat on the bed and studied the shark tooth necklace that his parents had bought for him during a vacation in Hilton Head several years earlier. A thin brass wire looped around the tooth and then looped again on either side of the root. It looked to Chris as though the craftsman had twisted the wire into a sort of hangman's knot tied to a leather thong. Chris couldn't quite figure out how the necklace was made, but he guessed if he took it apart that he could see how to put it back together again.

He slowly untwisted the brass wire from the shark tooth, paying close attention to how the wire was looped so that he could string the arrowhead properly.

"God, I hope I don't break this," he whispered as he began to straighten the bends in the thin wire.

The arrowhead was only slightly bigger than the tooth, so Chris was able to closely approximate the original construction of the necklace. Once he had the pendant completed, he attached it to the leather thong and yanked on it to test its strength. The thong seemed pretty secure. He tied the thong around his neck and modeled it in front of his dresser mirror, striking a pose like the pictures of Charles Atlas on the back of his comic books.

Exhausted from the day at the park, Chris decided to shower in the morning. He crawled into bed and thought about the Indian in the woods. Although he hadn't admitted it to the others, Chris was fairly sure that the man he had seen was the ghost of the Kickapoo Shaman. He didn't know why he didn't want to share this with his friends and family. *Maybe*, he thought. *This experience was just for me and not meant to be shared. I was the one destined to find the arrowhead, otherwise why had the Medicine man not shown anyone else the way in all these years?*

Destiny or not, the arrowhead was special; Chris felt it in his bones. He fell asleep remembering how the veins in the flint had seemed to move. He dreamed that night, a dream that would become more than familiar in the years to come. As he grew older, Chris would have dreams about the things all teenagers dream of: sex and love, school and friends and family, nightmares of flying and falling and being naked in study hall. The dream he had on that Sunday night, the one that would come to him so many times in the future, was one of a kind. *He was running through a forest, a pack of wolves close on his heels. The largest wolf in the pack caught him by the arm and dragged him deeper into the woods. He struggled with all of his strength and finally managed to stab the wolf with an arrow that bore an arrowhead carved from flint that was veined with gold and silver. The dream ended as he donned the wolf's bloody hide and danced around a fire, singing ancient songs of glory.*

Chris awoke with his heart pounding, pumped full of adrenaline.

Strangely, he wasn't scared. He was exhilarated, as though he had won a marathon, not like a boy who had just had a nightmare.

Part 3
Chapter 10

Saturday, May 31 1969

The buzzing of the alarm interrupted the dream that Chris had come to think of as *the wolf dance*. When something disturbed him before the end of the dream, he would start the day with a feeling of having unfinished business.

Chris had to go to work this morning. He took a long shower to help shake off the cobwebs and dressed in his cotton painter's pants and a tee shirt, tying his shoulder length hair in a ponytail. The long shower having eaten up anytime he had for breakfast; he made do with grabbing a piece of toast to eat in the truck on the way to new office building he would be painting today.

It was straight up 8:00 as he pulled up behind an old step van that had M&M PAINTING AND RENOVATING stenciled on the side. The company owners, Mike and Mark, were already inside the building unloading equipment. The two affable young men had started the company two years earlier. They had bought out the contracts of a painting contractor who was retiring and had managed to build a successful business. Mike had hired Chris to work part-time at the beginning of April, he and Mark had been very pleased with his work.

He had learned the job quickly and was now trusted to work without supervision. In two months' time Chris had salted away

$350.00 in a savings account and had another $200.00 stashed in his bottom dresser drawer. He planned to enroll at the University of Texas in the fall, and his father had told him that he could use whatever money he earned that summer for spending money at school. With his first paycheck, Chris had bought a ten year old Ford pickup for $100.00 and hoped to take it to with him to college. The truck had lost most of its shine, but the body was in good shape otherwise, and what was more important it ran great.

As his father had said. "The damn thing handles like a tank, and there's no stopping it."

The sanders had finished the drywall in the first floor offices on Friday. Mike told Chris to start dusting the drywall with a push broom so that the walls could be primed that afternoon. By mid morning the air in the office was thick with white dust, Chris had to clear his throat with each breath. He decided to take a break to get a little dust-free air and headed down the hall to find his bosses. Walking down the corridor, he looked into each room as he passed. The drywall was finished on this floor, but the carpenters had not hung the doors yet.

"Mark, Mike, where are you guys?"

"I'm in here, Chris."

Chris followed the sound of Mark's voice and finally found him painting in a back office.

"Holy snowflake, Batman," Mark laughed when he saw Chris, a specter covered with white powder, "aren't you and that drywall dust getting along today?"

Chris shook his head, sending a white cloud billowing out around him. "I have to get out of here for a second, or I'm going to die," came the choked reply.

Mark understood his young employee's discomfort, he'd been there many times himself.

"Why don't you go outside and take a break. While you're out there you can get a clean dust mask out of the van." Chris was trying to clear the dust out of the corners of his eyes with a clean rag.

"Yeah, I think I will. I'll be back in a few minutes."

Leaning on the truck, Chris pulled off his tee shirt and shook off the dust. At 18, he stood over six feet tall and his body was lean and athletic. He had been on the track team for a few years, but had lost interest in his senior year. Girls, study and work took up most of his time now. He looked in the side mirror of the van and wiped the dust from his face. Pulling the rubber band from his ponytail, he ran his fingers through his thick brown hair and shook his head vigorously, stirring up another small cloud of white dust. He pulled the arrowhead necklace over his head and blew the dust off of the stone as well as he could, then polished the flint with the inside of his tee shirt. He didn't like to get the arrowhead dirty, but he didn't like to take it off either. He had worn it around his neck since the day he had found it. He believed that the Indian had meant him to find it for a reason and he didn't want to tempt fate.

Opening the back doors of the van, Chris took a few new dust masks from one of the shelves and returned to the building. As he entered the foyer, he heard Mike calling to him from one of the side hallways. Chris found him dusting the walls in one of the front offices.

"Here, "Chris said, tossing one of the dust masks to his boss.

"Thanks, "Mike said, discarding his old mask. "Didn't you tell me that you had a friend who might want to do some work for us?"

Chris nodded. "Yeah, my buddy, Brian, said he could use a little cash."

"Well, we're getting behind on this job, and we could use another set of hands. Why don't you take an early lunch and see if you can find him. He could work the rest of the afternoon and I'd pay him cash money."

Chris looked at his watch. It was just after 11. He didn't like to take lunch too early, it made the afternoon drag. Mike saw that Chris wasn't too thrilled with the idea.

"Why don't you go home for lunch. You can call Brian from there. Take an extra half hour and I'll pay you for your travel time."

The extra half hour and the paid travel time clinched the deal.

"Okay", Chris grinned. "I'll see if I can find him. He doesn't spend much time at home these days. He's been hanging around with a new crowd lately." There was an edge to his voice that Mike had never heard from the likeable young man.

"Judging from the look on your face, I take it you don't think much of Brian's new crowd."

Chris sighed. "No, they think they're a bunch of bad-ass's and they have Brian buffaloed into thinking that he's a bad-ass, too. He's really a pretty good guy, just a little screwed up."

"Well, see if you can get in touch with him. Maybe if we keep him busy, he'll stay out of trouble." Mike said.

"Yes, sir, boss man." Chris replied with his crooked grin as he turned and headed for his truck.

Pulling up to his house Chris saw that the garage door was open and his father's car was gone. He parked on the street so that he wouldn't have to move his truck if Ryan came home before he went back to work. Jon was on the couch watching television as Chris came through the front door.

"Where's mom and dad?" he asked his younger brother.

Without looking up Jon replied, "I don't know. I guess they went shopping or something." Chris walked into the kitchen in search of food.

Early lunch sounded pretty good to him now. He took a package of sliced ham and a half gallon of milk out of the refrigerator and placed them on the counter. He opened the bread box and found the bag almost empty, just the two bread heels left. He hoped that his parents had gone grocery shopping. He washed his ham and bread heel sandwich down with two glasses of milk and scouted around the kitchen for some cookies.

Jon called to him from the living room.

"Pam called right after you left this morning."

He had been dating Pam Case for a few months. She was a strawberry blond with the most beautiful green eyes Chris had ever seen. He had been a little jealous of Brian when he had begun seeing Pam in their junior year, then uncomfortable about asking her out after she broke up with his best friend, but Brian knew that Chris had the major hots for Pam and had assured him that he couldn't possibly care less who Pam dated. Brian had treated her like dirt, so Chris believed him when he said that he didn't care if Chris caught her on the rebound.

Chris thought that it was a little weird that she had called when she knew that he was working.

"Did she say what she wanted?" He asked Jon.

"Yeah, she said that she wanted your body, stud." Jon replied.

"Why don't you shut up before I kick the crap out of you, you little asshole." Chris wasn't in the mood for any of his little brother's smart mouth.

Polishing off a package of Twinkies that he had found in one of the cupboards, he gulped down a third glass of milk, then called Brian's house. Carolyn answered on the first ring.

"Hi, Carolyn, this is Chris. Is Brian around?"

"No, honey. He didn't come home last night, and I'm really worried about him. Did you talk to him at all last night?"

Chris was torn between making something up to cover for his friend and lying to a woman who had always treated him like one of the family. In the end, he chose honesty as he usually did. "No, I haven't talked to him. I was just calling to see if he wanted to work with me this afternoon painting some new offices. I thought he might want to make a little money. I'm sure he's okay, Carolyn."

She sighed. "I wish I was sure of that. Chris, what do you know about the kids that Brian's been hanging around with? He hardly talks to us at all anymore."

She and Matt had married two years earlier, and Brian had been delighted. Matt treated him like a son, Brian had been thrilled to finally have a dad. For the first few years of marriage, Carolyn was relieved that Brian seemed to be thriving in his new family. He had a few minor scrapes in school, smoking in the john, cutting class now and then, but nothing major. She didn't think that Brian's grades would be good enough to get him into college, but maybe he would find a trade school that interested him. Lately, though, his grades had begun to slide as he spent less time with Chris and more time with boys that she knew nothing about but suspected were no good.

Chris had always believed in Brian and had helped him with his school work. Carolyn felt that Chris had always been a good influence on her sometimes rebellious son, and she was very grateful. Now she was hoping that Chris could help her to head Brian back in the right direction.

Chris hesitated before answering Carolyn's question. He thought that Brian's new friends were the scum of the earth, but he knew that Carolyn and Matt would come down hard on Brian if they found that out, he didn't feel right ratting out his friend. He also figured that Brian would see what losers Tommy and Jeff were and would lose interest in hanging around with them sooner or later. Carolyn seemed oblivious to the fact that the war in Vietnam was open for business, that the draft was a fact of life for 18 years old boys who were preparing to graduate from high school, especially those who hadn't been accepted into college. Brian hadn't even applied to any schools and didn't seem to have a plan for after graduation. When Chris brought the subject of the draft up, Brian would just laugh and tell him that he would have no trouble convincing the Army shrinks that he was insane. Chris suspected that Brian would not have to act too hard.

"Chris? Are you still there?" Carolyn's voice brought Chris back to reality.

"Brian is probably with Tom, Tommy Mannington and Jeff Linden. They go to our school, at least Jeff still does. Tommy may have dropped out. I haven't seen him around lately." His reply seemed safe enough, but Carolyn wasn't through with him yet.

"What are they like, these boys? What do you know about them?"

Chris sighed. He wasn't going to get off the hook easily. "I don't really know them all that well, Carolyn."

That much was the truth. Chris wouldn't be caught dead hanging around with punks like Tommy and Jeff. He had heard rumors, though. Jeff was still officially enrolled in high school, but probably wouldn't last until graduation. He and Tommy were into drugs, too, if the rumors were true. Chris didn't mind smoking a little weed now and then, but Jeff and Tommy were into harder drugs than pot. They weren't adversative to a little stealing to support their partying either, but Chris wasn't about to share this with Carolyn. In fact, he was liking this conversation less and less.

"Listen, Carolyn, if I hear anything else I'll give you a call, but right now I have to get back to work." Carolyn sounded as though she was on the verge of tears, which made Chris feel as guilty as hell. He wished that he could help her, but Brian was a big boy. Chris could only do so much.

"Thanks anyway, Chris. You know that you're the best friend that Brian has, don't you?" Carolyn asked, her voice breaking.

"I know. He's the best friend I have, too. Good-bye, Carolyn."

As she replaced the phone in it's cradle, the tears that had bubbled just below the surface all morning finally rose to the top. Carolyn began to sob and ran to the bathroom for a tissue. She sat on the edge of the tub and cried until her head hurt.

After his disturbing phone conversation with Carolyn, Chris returned to his job site. He walked down the corridor of the office building, calling out as he went.

"Hello, is anybody home?" There was no reply. In the room where he had last seen Mark, Chris found an open gallon of paint with a note lying on the lid. "Mike and I went to lunch. The walls are dusted, so you can start rolling them. We'll be back soon. P.S. The primer is in the open can right below this note."

Chris went to work priming the walls, pleased that his bosses trusted him to work alone. As he painted, he thought about his friend, Brian. Chris couldn't help feeling guilty about dating Pam no matter what Brian said. When the three of them were together, Chris could sense that Brian and Pam still cared for each other, but Pam swore that she would never go back to Brian. He had hurt her deeply.

In spite of his reassurances to Carolyn, Chris also worried about Brian hanging around with a couple of losers like Tommy and Jeff. If he hadn't gotten this weekend job, maybe Chris could have kept Brian busy.

"If Brian gets shipped off to Vietnam, maybe I'm partly to blame," he thought then tried to shake the thought away.

He had tried more than once to get Brian to come work with him, but Brian just wanted to play. *He's a big boy, whatever shit he gets into is his own damn fault.* Chris decided, but the nagging worry stayed with him for the rest of the afternoon.

Chapter 11

Hours of working in the hot, dusty offices had drained every spare ounce of fluid from Chris's tired body. Standing in the shower, he held his breath as the warm water washed over him, replenishing the lost fluids. The dust, sweat and paint embedded in his hair made it seem as brittle as spun glass. He shampooed gently several times until his hair finally felt clean. Turning off the shower, Chris dried off standing in the tub. His father had a pet peeve about getting the bathroom carpet wet. Ryan worried about water damage to the floor underneath, so his sons humored him by being extra careful to keep the carpet dry.

Wrapping a towel around his waist, Chris returned to his bedroom. He pulled the thong with his prized arrowhead around his neck and brushed his wet hair, gazing at himself in the dresser mirror. His hair was still badly tangled, so the process was slow torture. When he had finished, he felt as though he had pulled half of his hair out by the roots. Gingerly tying what was left into a ponytail, he vowed to wear a do-rag the next time he worked. Appraising his image in the mirror, he wondered what he would look like in short hair. He had started wearing his hair long six years earlier when he discovered the Beatles. He had always liked the way he looked with long hair, and it had been his one minor rebellion against his parents' middle class values. Since he had begun to work, the need for hair maintenance had increased dramatically. Now Chris wondered if it might be more trouble than it was worth.

He no longer felt any real need to rebel. His parents treated him pretty much like the responsible adult that he was maturing into. *Man, I'd look like a total greaser if I cut my hair short. Pam would totally freak,* Chris chuckled to himself as he turned his head, trying to imagine what it would look like .

He dropped his towel on the floor and opened his underwear drawer, or at least he tried to. His mother had stuffed his clean underwear and rolled socks in the drawer so tightly that Chris had to squeeze his hand into the opening and push on the piles of socks to clear the opening, pulling on the drawer handle with his free hand.

"Why does she have to make this so damn hard?" he muttered to himself as he worked at the drawer. Then it occurred to him that his mom picked his dirty clothes from the floor, washed them and replaced them without complaint. Chris decided that it wouldn't be in his best interest to confront his mother on this particular issue. She might very well tell him that if he wanted his socks and underwear laundered a certain way, he could just do it himself. He knew that his days of being pampered were limited. His mom wouldn't be in the college dorm to pick up after him. "Or in the barracks if I get drafted," Chris thought out loud.

Getting accepted into college had lessened the chances that he would be drafted right out of high school, but the possibility still existed. Like most parents of teenage boys, Chris knew that they would dread the thought that their son would be sent off to war.

Ryan had served in Korea and was proud of it, but in this war the issues were muddier. World War II was ancient history, and the mood of the country had changed. In the 50's, Americans were still infused with a 'My country right or wrong' spirit of fervent patriotism, but times had changed. The Vietnam War had its share supporters, but as the war dragged on, more and more loyal Americans questioned the wisdom of losing so many young men in a war that didn't appear to be winnable.

Ryan and Laurie were torn between supporting their government and wanting their son to be home and safe. When Chris had been accepted into the University of Texas, they had breathed a sigh of relief. By the time Jonathan turned eighteen, the war would surely be a thing of the past.

Chris dressed in a pair of cut-off jeans and a black tee shirt with a picture of Jim Morrison and the Doors silk-screened on the front. Switching his stereo on, he tuned to the new FM station that played an entire album side without commercials. Until recently, he had always listened to AM because most stations on the FM band had carried nothing but religious shows or boring talk shows. Carefully tuning out the static, Chris listened for a familiar song. His efforts were rewarded with the voice of Keith Moon singing the part of *Wicked Uncle Ernie* from the rock opera, *Tommy*.

"Cool, the Who," I hope they play the whole thing, he thought, reaching under the bed for his leather sandals.

As soon as Chris had sat down on the bed to pull on his sandals, Keith Moon was interrupted by the ringing of the phone. Looking at the clock on his dresser, Chris realized that it was already 6:30. *She's early tonight*, heading for the hall phone. Pam usually called at 7:00 on the Saturdays that Chris worked. He planned on taking her to see *Midnight Cowboy*. He had been told that there were some good sex scenes in the movie. Maybe they would put Pam in the mood, he just might get lucky later. He felt a little guilty at how sexist that sounded, but what the Hell, they were both eighteen, and he hadn't pushed her to go past second base. It was high time they consummated their relationship. Chris really did care about Pam although he didn't know if he was in love with her. He hoped that their relationship would last for the whole summer, but he didn't know what would happen in the fall. Pam would be going to college in Colorado, and he would be in Texas. Chris didn't have much faith that he and Pam could survive the distance. He wouldn't try to keep her from dating other guys in college. If they were meant to be together they would find out after they both graduated from college.

No reason we shouldn't go all the way now, though, as long as we're careful.

Pam's voice didn't have its usual upbeat lilt, in fact she sounded like she was on the verge of tears.

"Hi, Chris, it's me. I've got some bad news."

Chris tried to lighten the mood. "Oh, no, don't tell me that they didn't have the blouse that you wanted at the mall," he joked. Pam didn't respond.

"Okay, honey, I'm sorry. How about if I pick you up right now, you can tell me your news on the way to the movie?" H e asked.

"Chris, I don't think we'll be going to the movies tonight," she answered, her voice tight. "Brian has been arrested. He's in jail in San Antonio."

Chris felt as if he had been punched in the stomach. "Arrested?" he asked, his voice a raw croak.

"For what?" He was stunned by her reply.

"He was picked up last night, running from the police in a stolen car."

Chris had known that Brian would get into trouble sooner or later, but nothing as serious as Grand Theft Auto.

"What the hell was he doing in a stolen car?" he asked, though he had a sneaking suspicion that Tommy and Jeff were involved somehow.

"He was with some other guys who got away. Chris, his mother doesn't know yet, or I'm sure she would have bailed him out by now. Brian knew that you were working today, so he called me. He wants you to tell Carolyn."

"Why me? Why doesn't he just call her himself; he's the one who messed up, not me. I knew that hanging around with those scumbag's would catch up with him."

Chris never felt so pissed off at Brian. "Did he tell you why the hell I should tell his mom?"

"No," Pam sighed. "The police told him that since he will be 18 next month he could be tried as an adult. I think he's just scared to tell his folks. Carolyn loves you, you know that. Maybe Brian thinks that she'll take it better coming from you. Chris, what are we going to do? Just turn our backs on him?"

Chris was beginning to get mad again. "I've never turned my back on him. He's the one who wanted to drink and party, not me. I tried to get him a job, he just ignored me. I'm not the one who told him to hang around with those asshole's!" Chris realized that he was yelling now. When he stopped to take a breath, there was silence on the other end of the phone line.

"Pam, you still there?" He asked, feeling guilty for taking his anger out on her.

"What's wrong with you, Chris?" Pam shot back. "Whoever said that it was your fault that Brian is in trouble? I never said that. I just want to know if you're going to help him or not."

"I'm sorry, Pam. I'm just upset is all. I'll go talk to Carolyn and Matt. Boy, that's going to be a real barrel of fun," Chris laughed bitterly.

"This is going to cost them a bundle. Brian told me that they've been saving to buy a house. If they hire a lawyer for him that will probably take care of their savings. I hope Brian is happy."

"I doubt if he's very happy right now," Pam replied. "I know he'll appreciate you going to talk to his folks though. I appreciate it, too. I'm sorry about our date tonight; I'll make it up to you, Chris."

"I'll hold you to that, honey." Chris liked the sound of promise in Pam's voice.

"Call me when you get home," she added.

"Okay, 'bye."

Keith Moon was still singing *Fiddlin' about, fiddlin' about* as Chris hung up the phone and returned to his room. Collapsing on the bed, Chris felt the knot in his stomach tightening. He took a few deep breaths to try to loosen up. He was still in shock at the thought of his best friend in jail, maybe on the way to prison. This was Brian's first offence, but cops and judges in Texas didn't think much of long haired hippie types. Chris had received his share of disrespect from adults due to his long hair even though he was a straight "A" student and kept himself scrupulously clean. He had heard the phrase "long haired hippie freak" whispered as he walked by. Brian hadn't been keeping himself too clean lately, so Chris was sure the San Antonio police didn't feel too kindly toward him. *"Oh, well"*, he thought, *"better go and get this over with."*

He dreaded the thought of delivering such bad news to Brian's family, but at least Carolyn and Matt would be relieved to hear that Brian was still alive. Chris was sure that they were thinking the worst by now. They hadn't heard from their son in at least 24 hours.

Laurie was in the kitchen cleaning up the supper dishes as Chris headed out the back door. He told her that he was going over to Brian's house and would be back early.

"Have a good time, sweetie," she said, kissing his cheek as he leaned over to grab a slice of cold roast beef from the platter.

"Yeah, mom, I will," Chris replied ruefully.

"A real blast," he thought as he pulled his pickup away from the curb.

Turning onto Newton Falls road from Winchester, Chris could see both Carolyn's and Matt's cars in the driveway. The front door was open, he could hear the television as he tapped lightly on the screen door.

"Hey, it's Chris. Mind if I come in?" He called softly. Carolyn opened the screen door, her face tight with worry.

"Chris, come in. Have you heard from Brian? Has something happened to him?" she asked. Her eyes were red from crying, she looked as though she hadn't slept much lately. Matt sat in a high backed chair with his feet up on an ottoman. He looked tired, too.

"How ya' doing, Matt?" Chris asked, holding out his hand for Matt to shake. Carolyn sat down on the ottoman by her husband's feet.

"We haven't heard a word from Brian since last night," Matt explained to Chris. "We're worried sick. Have you talked to him?"

Sighing deeply, Chris answered. "No, but Pam has," Chris stared at his leather sandals as though seeing them for the first time. "He's, ummm, he's in Crystal Springs jail."

There was a moment of stunned silence as Carolyn and Matt absorbed the news. Carolyn's eyes puddled with tears for the hundredth time since Friday, Matt slumped in his easy chair, his handsome face dark and weary.

"Is he okay?" Matt asked quietly. "He's not hurt or anything?" He didn't seem surprised at his stepson's predicament. He barely heard Chris's mumbled reply; "I think he's okay, probably scared, though."

Matt watched his wife's face as she tried to regain her composure. "*Poor Carolyn*," he thought sadly, "*she doesn't deserve this*."

Matt realized that neither one of them had asked why Brian had been arrested. Somehow, it didn't really matter too much. They had tried so hard to keep Brian on the right path, to keep him out of trouble. Now he had crossed a line, and no matter how this turned out things would never be the same between them.

Carolyn rose to her feet as Matt kicked the ottoman out of the way and got up to turn off the television. He sat back down on the edge of his chair and with a deep sigh, finally asked the question.

"All right, Chris, what the hell is going on?"

Chris told them what Pam had told him that he was arrested running from the police in a stolen car.

"Running from the police?" Carolyn asked, incredulous. "Was he alone?"

"I'm not sure," Chris replied. "But I don't think he was alone. He was the only one who got caught though."

Matt considered this for a moment. "It would help if he wasn't driving. If he was driving he'll probably be charged with reckless operation as well as grand theft and resisting arrest. Either way, he really screwed up this time."

Carolyn had heard enough. "Matt, you'd better call your lawyer friend. We need to get Brian out of that place and we're going to need help." Matt got up and headed for their bedroom.

"I don't know if we'll be able to get him out until Monday, but we'll try. I'll call Curtis from the phone in the bedroom."

Carolyn smiled at Chris through her tears. "Thank you for coming to tell us, Chris. It was sweet of you to take the time out of your Saturday night."

"I wish I had known he was doing this kind of stuff. I would have tried harder to get him away from Tommy and Jeff," he replied. "I'm sorry that I couldn't help him more."

Carolyn leaned over and took Chris's hand. "Chris," she said softly, "it's not your fault. He's been messing up for a while now. I always thought of you as a positive influence on him, but you can only do so much. I know that these boys are not your friends, and now I know why. Brian has been getting failing grades in school all year, the only reason that he is still there at all is because I've been begging Mr. Lindsay not to expel him for truancy. This time I'll be dealing with the police instead of the high school principal. And this is a lot worse than not getting a diploma."

Despite her best efforts to be strong, Carolyn started to cry again. Chris tried to think of something to say to make her feel better, but he couldn't see any bright spots in her son's situation. "I really thought we had a chance when we came to Texas," Carolyn continued. "He was happier when we first came here than he had ever been. I should have left Chicago a lot sooner than I did. Goddamn it, why didn't I just pack up and leave? If it's anybody's fault, it's mine," she sobbed, getting up and heading toward the bathroom for a fresh supply of tissue.

Chris waited for her to sit back down on the sofa before replying. "Don't blame yourself. Brian told me more than once how proud he is of you for having the guts to pick up and move to another state. He knows that you did it for his sake. He's an adult now, he's to blame for his own troubles."

Carolyn's smile was a little more convincing this time. "Thanks, Chris."

Matt returned to the living room with a paper in his hand. "I called my friend, Curtis. He doesn't handle criminal law, but he referred me to an attorney who does. Curtis said that we won't be able to get Brian bailed out until Monday after he is arraigned, and the judge sets bail. At least that will give us time to talk to a bail bondsman. I'll go call the other lawyer and see if he can come to court on Monday. I'll also ask if we can go and see Brian tonight or tomorrow. Honey, can you find me a cigarette?" he asked, patting his wife on the shoulder.

Carolyn stood and kissed Matt's cheek. "Sure, I'll be a minute." Chris thought that this would be a good time to escape. He felt uncomfortable witnessing the grief of his friend's parents and was relieved that things had gone as well as they had.

"Well, I'd better get going." he said. "Have Brian call me when he gets home, will you?"

"Sure, honey," Carolyn replied, sounding a little like her old self. She gave Chris a quick hug. "Thanks again." Chris hugged her back.

"You're welcome. Hang in there."

Chapter 12

Talking with Carolyn and Matt had pretty much worn Chris out. He decided to call Pam to tell her how Brian's folks had taken the news. It was after 9 o'clock by the time he finally flopped down on the living room sofa. Ryan and Laurie were sitting in their reclining chairs watching television.

"You guys are really lazin'," he observed. "You're in the same spot you were in when I left. Is TV that good tonight?"

"Not really," his father replied, "we're just lazin' like you said. What are you doing home this early on a Saturday night? Did you and Pam have a fight?"

Chris shrugged his shoulders. "No. I'm just tired from painting all day and decided to get to bed early."

Laurie looked up from a needlepoint pillow that she had been working on. "I have to get up at 6:00 tomorrow to help prepare the pancake breakfast at the church. Do you want me to get you up for work?" she asked.

Chris thought about it for a moment. "No, I don't think I'm going to work tomorrow. I need a day off to catch up on some stuff that I've been neglecting. I'd appreciate it if you'd call Mike for me before you leave for church. The number's on the pad by the phone in the kitchen. I could stand to sleep in for a change."

Laurie smiled at her son before returning to her needlepoint. "Sure, honey. You've been working too hard lately anyway. You don't have much longer to be a kid, so enjoy it while you can," she said, rather wistfully.

Chris went into the bathroom and fished his toothbrush from the dispenser. He heard his mother's voice coming from the living room.

"Since you're not working tomorrow, why don't you come to church?"

Chris hastily stuck the brush in his mouth without toothpaste and answered around it, "mrumph," hoping that the mumbled response would satisfy her. He turned on the water and shut the door. He brushed his teeth again with toothpaste this time.

Laurie didn't really expect her son to go to church with her, but she still asked once in a while. The boys had attended Cove Methodist Church in Pennsylvania regularly and had participated in church activities. They had enjoyed the Youth Fellowship classes and had both gone to Boy Scout meetings in the church basement. Laurie and Ryan had joined the Grace Methodist Church in Devine, but the boys had not shown much interest in church since moving to Texas. After much discussion, Ryan and Laurie had decided not to force religion on the boys for fear that they would become resentful and stay away from church to rebel. They were disappointed, though that this family activity had pretty much gone by the wayside. Jon still went to church once in a while, but less and less lately.

On Sunday morning Laurie mercifully let Chris sleep, he didn't stir until almost noon. After a quick shower and shave he took Pam out for lunch. Over burgers, he told her the details of his conversation with Matt and Carolyn.

"All in all, it sounds like they took it pretty well," she said when Chris had finished. "What did your parents say when you told them?"

"I haven't told them yet," he answered, "it was rough enough telling Carolyn and Matt. I guess I'd better tell them tonight, though."

After lunch Chris took Pam to see *Midnight Cowboy,* but the movie didn't put either one of them in the mood for love as Chris had hoped. He thought it might be best to give Pam some space to sort out her feelings for Brian. She still seemed to care about him a great deal, Chris suspected that it was more than just friendship for old time's sake. He wondered if his relationship would weather this particular storm or fade out before the summer ended.

Chapter 13

Tuesday, June 2, 1969

Brian opened his eyes and stared at the ceiling for a moment before realizing, much to his relief, that it was his own bedroom ceiling and not the cracked and water-stained ceiling of the Crystal Springs Jail. The mattress he had slept on the last three nights had smelled of urine and other things that he did not wish to consider. When he finally got home on Monday afternoon after Carolyn and Matt had bailed him out, Brian had stripped off his filthy clothes and showered the minute he walked in the door. When he felt that at least the first layer of jail scum had washed off, he stuffed his face with Carolyn's cooking and then showered again before going to bed. In the light of morning he tried to make sense of the mess he was in.

Brian couldn't believe that those idiots Jeff and Tommy had bailed out on him when the cops finally caught up with them. Come to think of it, he couldn't believe that they had stolen a car. When they came to pick him up for a night of partying on Friday, Jeff had told them that he had borrowed the Chevy Impala that he was driving.

"What a fool I was to buy that!" Brian thought, punching his pillow in his frustration and anger at himself for being so stupid. *Who would lend anything to that ass, never mind a car!* The police hadn't believed his story for a minute even though he was in the

backseat of the Chevy when they caught up to the car. Tommy Mannington had been driving down some back country roads when the chase had begun. Brian had yelled at Tommy to pull over, but Tommy had ignored him. When he had realized that the police cruiser was gaining on them, and they had no hope of escape, Tommy had yanked the steering wheel to the right and skidded the car to a stop, kicking up a cloud of dust. *Just like in the movies.* In the blink of an eye, Tommy and Jeff had leaped out of the car and had bolted for the trees nearby, leaving Brian to twist in the wind. He was struggling with the front seat lever as the police cruiser slid to a stop behind him and before he realized it he had a .38 caliber revolver being pointed at him by a very serious state trooper. The look in the young trooper's eyes told Brian that he had better do what he was told. He was hustled off to the back seat of a patrol car, handcuffs clanking, feeling like an animal in the zoo.

Brian had suffered silently through the long weekend, too ashamed to call his folks. He had almost cried with relief when Carolyn and Matt had come to see him on Monday morning before his arraignment. He wondered how much it had cost them to hire a lawyer. A lot, he supposed. The arraignment had not amounted to much, just a judge charging him with grand theft auto and resisting arrest. The judge had then set his bail at two thousand dollars. Matt had then paid a bail bondsman, and Brian was released to go home with his family. The lawyer had told Carolyn and Matt that he would talk to the prosecutor, and as this was Brian's first offence he might be able to cut a deal. The ride home had been quiet. Matt and Carolyn had asked him if he was all right, when he assured them that he was the 3 of them had lapsed into silence. Brian had told his side of the story over dinner, they had said that they believed him, but he wasn't so sure they were really convinced. He wasn't sure he blamed them for doubting him, he had not been much of a son lately. Now all he could do was hope for the best. With that thought, Brian drifted off to asleep again.

Waking again after noon, Brian got up and checked out his reflection in the bathroom mirror. He had let his hair grow long, like many other boys his age, but instead of growing straight to his shoulders, it had grown upward into a brown fuzzy 'fro. Kids at school teased him about his hair, asking how high it would grow if he left it alone. The 'fro did fit well with his thick neck and square jaw, making him look intimidating. Now, however, he laughed at his image in the mirror. Going to sleep with his hair wet had caused it to become sculpted into a point on the top of his head resembling the head of a hatchet.

"*If my friends could see me now,*" he thought, reaching for a brush.

Brian was polishing off the last of three bologna sandwiches that afternoon when Chris stopped by on his way home from school.

"Hey, jailbird," he said, punching Brian lightly on the biceps. "Sounds like you had quite a weekend."

"Yeah," Brian answered, a bitter edge to his voice. "Jeff and Tommy screwed me good. They left me hanging while they ran for their pathetic lives."

Chris took the bottle of Coke that Brian held out to him and took a swig. "Seriously, man, what happened?" he asked. "What were you doing in a stolen car? Didn't you think that you might get caught or even killed?"

The arrowhead that Chris wore around his neck shone in the afternoon light coming in through the kitchen window.

Brian stared at the necklace and sighed. "I sure could have used some of that good luck you have hanging around your neck on Friday night." He looked utterly defeated.

"Come on, man," Chris said gently. "What really happened?"

"Tommy and Jeff pulled up to my house in a car that Tommy said his aunt had let him have for the weekend since she was going to be out of town. They didn't tell me that the car had been stolen by Tommy's older brother for parts until they were well into their second six-pack of beer. Then Jeff was spotted by the police when he threw his empty can out of the passenger window, now I am so screwed," Brian told Chris. "The cops interrogated me all damn night, trying to get me to tell them who I was with, but I never did tell," he said proudly.

"Why the hell didn't you just tell them?" Chris asked, incredulous. "Why would you want to protect those two asshole's?"

Brian's answer sounded bitter. "In the first place, Tommy and Jeff would beat the crap out of me the minute they got bailed out if the cops even believed me. In the second place, when people found out that I ratted out my buddies, how many friends would I have left?"

Chris answered softly. "You'd have me."

"Yeah," Brian replied, his voice cracking, "I know."

"So what are you going to do now?" Chris asked after a moment of awkward silence.

"My folks got me a lawyer, thank God. He says he's going to try to cut me a deal. I guess I'll just lay low and try to stay out of trouble 'til we see what happens."

Anger, fear and shame were boiling just below Brian's calm surface. Chris, not aware how close his friend was to losing control, decided to push the accomplice issue a little further.

"Tommy and Jeff are losers, Brian. Don't mess up your whole life to protect them. In my mind, you have two choices: either you hold your tongue and serve prison time, or tell the cops what they want to hear, and maybe get probation. Who cares what people think? Are the kids at school going to help you? People don't care unless it's their ass on the line."

Brian jumped from his chair, knocking it over. Angry tears had begun to well in his eyes. With a sudden unexpected burst of violence, he kicked the fallen chair across the room.

"You know what, you're right," he screamed, "nobody gives a shit about me. I really don't care, either! I'll just go to jail and become someone's girlfriend, or better yet, get gang-raped in the shower by all the damn inmates. I'll be the new bitch on the cellblock, and no one will give a good goddamn!"

Tears were streaming down Brian's face now; his hands were bunched into angry fists. Chris was silenced momentarily by his friend's outburst. He tried to think of something to say to calm Brian down and came up with the exact wrong thing to say.

"That's why you have to tell the police about Tommy and Jeff. It might just keep you out of prison."

Brian's face went beet red and he delivered another swift kick to the fallen chair.

"I AIN'T NO RAT", he screeched, his voice husky with tears. "Man, you're just as big an asshole as the rest of them! You act like you give a shit, but you're going to leave me behind, just like everyone else in my life. First my father left, then my mother dragged me to this hell-hole, then she married Matt, and it's like, she didn't need me around anymore."

Chris interrupted, defending Carolyn. "Hey man, what are you talking about? Your mom has a right to a life too, you know. She and Matt have always been there for you."

Brian leaned close to Chris, his face contorted with rage. "Now how would you know that? Do you live here? I haven't seen you in six friggin' weeks, and now you're going to tell me that my life has been just peachy. This time next year you'll be finishing your first year of college, where will I be? Will you have time for a loser like me?"

Chris knew that Brian was probably right, but his self-pity was beginning to get old. If Brian hadn't seen him in six weeks, it was his own damn fault. Chris had tried to call, but Brian was never home anymore. Chris got up and skirted around his still angry friend, heading for the side door.

"Listen, man, I have to get going. I have some errands to run."

He didn't think it was prudent to tell Brian that he and Pam had a dinner date.

"We'll talk later when you're in a better mood."

Brian slammed the kitchen door behind his retreating friend. "Thanks for coming over to cheer me up," he shot after him.

Chapter 14

Brian's appointment with his new lawyer, Dennis Z. Steiner, was scheduled for 2:00 p.m. on Tuesday afternoon. Carolyn had taken the afternoon off and had rushed home from the nursing home to get her son to the attorney's office on time, but finding a parking space in downtown San Antonio had proved to be almost impossible. She glanced at her watch as Brian held the door to the office building open for her.

"1:55, not bad timing," she told her son.

They were greeted by a young blonde receptionist in Steiner's plush outer office. She sat behind an oak desk that held four telephones and several stacks of black file folders. The nameplate on her desk read: Megan Granfords. She looked up at Carolyn and Brian and smiled.

"May I help you?" she asked in a soft, pleasing drawl.

"Yes," Carolyn answered nervously. "I'm Carolyn Wheeler and this is my son, Brian. We have an appointment with Mr. Steiner at two."

The receptionist, Megan, ran a finger down the list of names on her scheduling book and circled their names with her pen.

"Have a seat," she said. "Mr. Steiner will be with you shortly. There's a coffee machine in our kitchen. It's the first door on the right. Help yourself."

Brian stole another glance at the receptionist as he turned toward the waiting area. Megan wore wire rimmed glasses and had her honey-blonde hair pulled up into a demure french twist. She was a little younger than his mother was, and there was something sexy about her. She reminded him of a librarian that he used to fantasize about in tenth grade study hall. With a rush of shame he realized that she probably knew why they were there. He could feel the blood rushing to his face as he turned away. Carolyn answered as she looked quizzically at her son, wondering why he had such a strange expression on his face.

"No, thank you. We're fine."

They took seats in leather wing chairs and leafed through the magazines on the glass and brass end tables. Brian chose a copy of *Life* magazine and sat flipping through the pages. He was too nervous to read the articles, so he just stared at the pictures, not really seeing them. Carolyn sat cradled in the soft leather, trying not to think about anything. The family had spoken very little since Brian had come home. Carolyn and Matt knew that any conversation about the events of the previous weekend would surely escalate into fireworks, and they were still too raw with shock to deal with the situation rationally. Brian had stayed in his room, catching up on lost sleep while his parents went about their daily business in stunned silence. There was no point in talking about Brian's future until they talked to the attorney and found out a little more about what the future was likely to bring.

After what seemed like an eternity, Dennis Steiner appeared in the hallway leading past the kitchen.

"Hi, Mrs. Wheeler," he said holding a hand out to be shaken. "How are you all today? Better, I hope."

Carolyn took his outstretched hand as she rose from her chair. "I'm much better today, thanks."

"And how about you, Brian?" The attorney asked genially. "Feeling better after a few nights sleep in your own bed?"

"Yes, sir," Brian answered politely. "Thank you for getting me out of there. I don't think I could have made it another night. That place stunk."

Steiner laughed. "Yeah, it sure does stink," he agreed. "Please, come on back to my office," he pointed down the hallway. "It's the last door on the left." He waited until both Carolyn and Brian had passed in front of him and followed them down the hall.

Once they reached his office, Steiner asked Carolyn and Brian to sit in the two chairs across from his massive mahogany desk. Brian watched the lawyer as he walked around the desk and sat in the black leather swivel chair. Brian had been so tired and nervous on Monday morning when they had met just before court; he hadn't paid much attention to the attorney's appearance. Dennis Steiner looked ten years younger than his forty-six years. Only the gray at his temples betrayed his true age. He was dressed in a black suit, and matching Italian leather shoes. His dark hair was freshly cut, and his manicured fingernails gleamed in the soft light of a green glass desk lamp. His smile was well rehearsed.

He chose a beige file folder from his cluttered desktop and quickly skimmed through the papers within.

"I want to thank you again for helping us on such short notice," Carolyn said.

"You're quite welcome," Dennis replied, looking up from the papers. "I had a chance to talk to Curt Ambrose this morning. He told me that he and your husband have been friends for quite a long time. Curtis is a good man, I've known him for a few years myself."

"Curtis told Matt that you are the best criminal lawyer that he knows. I can't tell you how relieved we are that you are willing to help us, Mr. Steiner," Carolyn said, her voice cracking with emotion.

"Please, call me Dennis," he said returning his gaze to the papers in the folder. "Well, let's see what we have here."

Dennis sat back in his chair and ran a hand across his face, suddenly looking tired. "Well, son, I'm sorry to say that I don't have much good news. I talked to the prosecutor this morning, and I'm afraid that he's prepared to throw the book at you as they say in the movies. The charges include aggravated auto theft, which is a first degree felony, resisting arrest, possession of criminal tools..." Brian interrupted. "What criminal tools? We didn't have any tools that I know of."

"A screwdriver and a pair of pliers were found under the front seat. Because the car was involved in a crime, fleeing the police, that is, these can be considered criminal tools. This would constitute another felony. There are also assorted misdemeanor charges involved; reckless operation of a motor vehicle, littering, and a few others that will probably be thrown out of court. Son, you could be in serious trouble here if you don't play your cards right. If I'm going to represent you, you're going to have to be completely honest with me. Are you prepared to do that?"

Brian looked down at his hands. They were trembling, and he tried, without success, to still them.

"Brian," Carolyn said sharply," answer him."

Dennis tried again. "Brian, I can help you, but how this ends up is up to you, do you understand?"

Brian continued to study his shaking hands. He felt like crying more than he ever had in his life, but he wasn't about to cave in.

"Yes," he answered softly.

"Good," Dennis replied. "Now I can tell you the good news. The police and prosecutor don't really care all that much about nailing you to the wall. They really want to get their hands on Tommy Mannington and Jeff Linden, and they're willing to use you to get to them."

Brian looked up, speechless. He slowly became aware that he was working his open mouth like a fish stranded on the dock.

"How do you know about them?" he was finally able to ask.

Dennis laughed. "Son, the police aren't stupid. They knew that you weren't alone in that car. All they had to do was ask around to find out who you've been palling around with lately. The police know that Mannington and Linden have been involved in a number of felonies, auto theft, drug dealing, breaking and entering to name a few. They also know that you were pretty much just along for the ride. Unfortunately, they don't have enough evidence to put them away. Without your cooperation, that is."

Carolyn, sensing that things were beginning to go their way at last, choked out a sob of relief.

Brian's tongue felt thick, and his throat was dry. He had a hard time choking out his next question. "What do they want me to do?"

Dennis wove his fingers together on the leather desk pad. "If you testify against Mannington and Linden, the prosecutor is willing to drop the charges against you, with one other condition."

"What condition?" Brian asked warily.

Carolyn interrupted, her voice rising to a shriek. "Who cares what condition? You will tell the police anything they want to know!"

Brian's face reddened. "You don't understand if I rat out these guys, my life won't be worth a nickel! I'd have to move to Brazil!"

Dennis stood up and came around the front of the desk. "Listen, you two, fighting isn't going to help. Brian, your mother is right. If you don't testify against your so called friends, you're looking at some serious jail time. You seem to forget that you wouldn't be in the mess you're in without Mannington and Linden. These guys are real criminals, not just petty thieves. They're the real thing. Carolyn, Brian is right about being in danger if he testifies. That brings me to the other condition that I was starting to tell you about."

Brian and Carolyn sat back in their chairs, their anger temporarily abated.

Dennis continued. "The police aren't going to be able to protect you from Mannington and Linden if you testify against them. The prosecutor has made it a condition of the plea bargain that you join the military ..."

Carolyn sat forward in her chair. "The military?" She asked. "You mean like the army? Do you mean to tell me that Brian has a choice of going to prison, being killed by punks, or going to Vietnam? Maybe we should think about Brazil." She started to cry softly.

Dennis offered her a tissue and turned to Brian. Brian's face had gone white, and he seemed to have sunken into the soft upholstery.

"I know this is a tough decision for you, son, but you have to think about your future. Even if you got a short prison sentence, and I'm not sure that you would, you would still have a criminal record. If you take the deal that the prosecutor offered, you would have to make a deposition informing on your buddies Tommy and Jeff, but then you'd be pretty much off the hook." He directed his next remark to Carolyn as much as to Brian.

"Even if none of this had ever happened, you would have been a likely candidate for the draft, you know. Joining the army will get you out of town after you testify, which isn't such a bad idea under the circumstances."

Brian absorbed this information in silence. He was aware that Carolyn was talking about him being killed in a foreign country.

"I'll tell them what they want to know," he blurted out suddenly.

Carolyn turned to look at him, her face a mask of tears. Brian reached over and patted her hand. He felt sorry for her and guilty as hell for putting her through this.

"Mom, listen, I don't want to have a criminal record for the rest of my life. Anytime I apply for a job I'll have to admit that I'm a convicted felon, and who is going to hire me once they know that? I really screwed up, and this is the best way to handle it. I'd probably get drafted anyway just like he said."

Carolyn shook her head. She knew in her heart that he was right, but she still was not ready to accept his decision.

"He's right, Carolyn," Dennis said gently. "This is the best option that Brian has. He'll only have to serve one year overseas. An honorable discharge will get him a lot farther in life than a criminal record. The D.A. will help to expedite Brian's enlistment after he gives a deposition, of course. I'll arrange a meeting for tomorrow afternoon. Will you two be able to make it?"

Carolyn had been sitting with her eyes shut, and her head resting against the back of her chair. She opened her eyes slowly as though waking from a nap.

"My boss won't be too happy," she sighed, "but we'll be here."

Dennis stood, signaling that the meeting was at an end. "All right, I'll set up the appointment with the prosecutor. I'll have Megan call you later on and let you know what time to be here tomorrow."

Carolyn and Brian both had a lot to think about on the ride home. Brian alternated between feeling relief that he wouldn't be going to prison and being afraid that he wouldn't make it to enlistment if Jeff and Tommy found out that he was ratting them out. Curiously, he wasn't afraid of joining the Army. He had thought about doing it on his own anyway.

Carolyn had her own demons to wrestle with as she drove. She and her son had never been apart, and now that he was in trouble the only way out was to send him to fight in Southeast Asia. As she drove she prayed that God would intervene and somehow right this terrible situation. Only a miracle could get her son out of this jam.

Chapter 15

That evening Chris stopped by to see Brian. He was anxious to find out how the meeting with Brian's attorney had gone, and he also hoped to mend a few fences. He and Brian had rarely fought in all the years of their friendship, and Chris was sorry that they were fighting now when Brian needed a friend the most. Brian was in his bedroom, sprawled across an old easy chair that was covered with a bed sheet. He didn't mention the argument, and Chris decided that maybe it was for the best. Brian began filling Chris in on what Steiner had advised.

"Well, what do you think?" he asked when he had finished his synopsis of the afternoon.

"You have to join the army? You know damn well that you'll be shipped overseas," Chris sighed, "I guess it's better than the alternative, though."

"Yeah," Brian agreed, "raped in prison or killed in Vietnam. What a choice."

Chris considered his words carefully. Brian didn't seem to be pissed off at him anymore, but he didn't want to say anything that might start him off again.

"I hate to see Jeff and Tommy get away scot free while you're getting shot at by the Viet Cong," he said cautiously.

"Don't worry about that," Brian replied. "I have to meet with the prosecutor tomorrow to give a deposition. I'll be telling them everything I know about the whole fucking fiasco. Just call me the singin' canary," he snorted.

Chris walked over to the window and gazed out into the backyard. The sun was setting over the wooden stockade fence that separated the yard from the neighbors.

"There is nothing wrong with ratting on those two losers. Man, they left you hanging. Personally, I'm glad to see them get what they deserve."

Brian rested his head on the back of the chair and closed his eyes. For the hundredth time in the last week he looked utterly defeated.

"I'm not really worried about what happens to them," he told Chris. "Tommy's brother is involved in this, and a lot of other crap, too. There's gonna be a lot of people out to get me. What's the difference if I get killed in Vietnam or Texas?"

Chris felt a wave of sympathy for his friend. Brian was the first person to treat Chris decently when he had come to Texas, and now he was the best friend that Chris had, in spite of the way he had acted in the last few months.

"Do you have a choice of which branch of the service you go into?" he asked.

"Not much of a choice. I couldn't handle the Navy with my weak stomach, and I would need a diploma to get into the Air Force, so that just leaves the Army or the Marines. I don't think I'm really Marine material."

Chris didn't think that joining the Army was the worst thing that Brian could do. His life had been going nowhere lately, and his feelings about the war were mixed at worst. He sat down on Brian's bed and cleared his throat. He didn't know how Brian would react to a pep talk, but he felt compelled to give it a try.

"You know, before I came over here I was watching the evening news. They were interviewing a soldier over in 'Nam. He said that he was over there because his grandfather had fought in World War I, and his father had fought in World War II. He was proud that they had helped to win those wars. They were fighting to protect our freedom, and he said that it was his duty to do the same, no matter how he felt about the war personally. Maybe he has a point, Brian," he concluded.

Brian grinned at Chris and applauded. "Man, you should be a lawyer," he laughed. " You have taken me from being a car thief to being John Wayne. Now can you get me through the next year without being killed? Or better yet, seeing as how you're so gung ho, why don't you join up with me? We'll fight the V.C. together. I heard that the whore's are cheap, and the weed is the best you'll ever smoke."

Brian wasn't seriously trying to interest Chris in joining up. His sales talk was mostly for his own benefit. Despite the alternative, Brian was beginning to grow a little nervous about the prospect of going to war halfway across the world.

Chris flopped down on Brian's bed. "Well," he laughed, " if I did join I probably wouldn't live to see boot camp. My parents would kill me. My dad is dead set on me going to college." "Oh, I see," Brian responded with a touch of sarcasm. "You feel strongly about stopping communist aggression as long as you aren't the one doing the fighting. Is that what you're saying?"

Brian had scored a point, but he secretly hoped that by some miracle he wouldn't be doing any fighting, either. Chris was wounded by his friend's attitude. Brian had brought this on himself, but reminding him of that now would most likely start another argument, and Chris wasn't in the mood.

"How long before you have to enlist?" Chris asked, trying to steer the conversation in a safer direction.

Brian sighed. " As soon as word gets out that I'm testifying against Tommy and Jeff there will be people looking for me, and I'd rather not be around. I guess I'd better join up as soon as possible."

Chris got up to go. "Just stay in the house," he suggested. "I doubt that even those guys will break in to get at you. They're in a world of shit as it is."

Brian thought about that for a moment.

"Yeah," he replied, the ghost of a smile forming on his lips for the first time in a week.

"They're really going to be pissed when the cops come to get them. Man, can you picture Tommy's smug face in the back of a cop car?"

They both started to laugh at the mental picture of Tommy and Jeff being led to jail in handcuffs. "Ain't so bad now, are you, tough guys?" Brian chortled, wiping tears from his eyes.

Chris was relieved to see that his friend was getting his sense of humor back. It was good to see him laugh again.

"Listen," he said, giving Brian a shot on the biceps, "I gotta head home and get something to eat. All I've eaten today is a banana, and I'm starving. Why don't you give me a call when you get home from the lawyer's office tomorrow? I'd like to know how it goes." Brian nodded as he opened the door.

"Chris," he said, hesitating for a second. "Thanks, man, thanks for everything." He held out his hand, and Chris grabbed it.

"I'll always be there for you, Brian. You'll see." He didn't know how true those words were.

Chapter 16

Laurie Logue was starting dinner when Chris came home from school the next day. He headed straight for the refrigerator as always.

"Hi, Chris, how was school today?" He shrugged as he surveyed the contents of the fridge.

"Okay, I guess. It's pretty boring now that finals are over. It doesn't seem like it's worth going now. Is there anything to eat in here, Mom?"

Laurie leaned over her son's shoulder and pointed out a tin foil packet on the second shelf. "That's some leftover pork chops. You could heat them up under the broiler. It won't take a minute," she said, turning back to the sink.

She retrieved a clean plate from the dish drainer and dried it with a towel that was decorated with orange mushrooms. She turned to hand Chris the plate just in time to see him polishing off the last of the cold pork chops.

"Geez, Chris, you could have used a plate and silverware. We do live in the 20th century, you know." She tossed the towel to him.

Chris grinned. "No need Mom," he said, wiping the grease from his hands. "Now you don't have another dish to wash."

Laurie retrieved the towel from him and took off her apron, hanging them both on a hook beside the sink.

"What time do you have to be at work?" she asked.

"I'm not going to work today. I'm going to take a little nap actually. I feel kind of lazy today," he replied, getting up from the table. He hoped he could escape to his room to wait for Brian's call.

"You haven't been working much lately. Are you feeling all right?" Laurie sounded just like a mom and sometimes wished that she didn't.

"Yeah, mom," Chris said gently, sensing his mother's mood. "I'm just burned out from working too much and finals and all. I just feel like taking a break."

Laurie patted Chris's hand. "You'll have the rest of your life to work. A little break will do you good. Do you want me to wake you for dinner?"

Chris headed for his room. "Yeah, Mom. Wake me up if Brian or Pam calls, okay?"

As he lay on his bed waiting for sleep, Chris wondered when he would work up the nerve to tell his parents about Brian's problems with the law. He had tried to tell them a dozen times, but he never felt like answering all the questions they were sure to bombard him with. He wondered why he felt so defensive about this. For the hundredth time in the past week, he told himself that he wasn't responsible for his friend's troubles.

"Then why the hell do I feel so damn guilty?" he asked out loud.

Chris was standing on a branch in the fork of a tall tree. Crickets chirped their night songs in the steamy darkness that surrounded him. He looked down at his body, and as his eyes adjusted to the dark. He was surprised to see that he was dressed in olive drab Army fatigues and heavy black boots. Somehow he knew that there was an enemy hiding in the black forest below him. A voice startled him, and he squinted into the darkness. "Kenekuk will come soon to take us to the spirit world." Chris turned toward the sound of the voice and saw the shadow of a man standing on another branch of the same tree. Chris had managed only to blurt out "What?" when the shot rang out. Something hit him hard in the stomach, the force of the blow knocking him from his perch. He fell backward toward the ground.

"CHRIS!" His mother's voice startled Chris from the dream. "Wake up, Brian's on the phone!"

His brain fogged with sleep, his nervous system still jangled with the rush of falling from the tree. Chris ran his hand over his eyes and struggled to lift his head from the pillow as he called out in a hoarse croak. "Alright, I'll be right there."

The brain fog lifted slowly as he staggered to the phone in his parent's bedroom.

Brian sounded chipper, almost like his old self. "Hey, Chris, what's going on?"

Chris stifled a yawn as he replied. "You tell me. How did it go today?"

Brian's voice lowered slightly. "Well, it's official. I'm the rat man of Devine. They were actually pretty nice to me, though. No dark rooms with bright lights shining in my eyes or rubber hoses."

Chris laughed at the mental picture of a fat southern prosecutor shining a gooseneck lamp in his friend's eyes and growling. "Tell us everything you know, boy." He had half imagined that Brian's session with the prosecutor would go something like that, though.

"When are they going to arrest Tommy and Jeff?" he asked.

Brian told him that the police had found fingerprints on the car that belonged to Brian's former buddies and were putting a case together as quickly as possible.

"They want to put them away as soon as they can. Man, it's going to be wild. I need to get out of Dodge pronto."

Brian's lawyer had brought enlistment papers to the deposition and had Brian and his mother sign them on the spot.

"I'll be officially enlisted in the U.S. Army as soon as I take the papers to the recruiter's office in the morning. That's where you come in, my friend. I need a ride to the recruiter's office, and Mom has to work. I don't think she could handle it, anyway. Can you help me out?" Brian asked. Chris agreed without a second's hesitation. He didn't care if he was a little late for school. The last week was bullshit, anyway. He was also curious about what the recruiter would have to say.

"Man, I can't wait to see the look on your face tomorrow," he told Brian with a laugh. "Holy cow, this is going to flip everybody out."

Chapter 17

At promptly 8:00 a.m. the following morning, Chris pulled his Ford pick-up into the parking lot in front of the recruiter's office. The spaces in front of the office were filled, so he turned into a spot in front of the Dairy Isle. He and Brian looked at the oversize photos of ice cream cones, sundaes dripping hot fudge, frosty milk shakes and red, white and blue Bomb Pops.

"Man, I could go for one of those monster milk shakes right now," Chris said, gazing longingly at the poster. "Oh, well. Are you ready? Your future awaits."

The side wall of the recruiter's office was lined with folding metal chairs. The window seat of the storefront was cluttered with pamphlets. There were four green metal desks in the rear of the office. Brian thought that the office seemed kind of disorganized for a military office, but he had a bad case of dry mouth going, so he decided to keep his opinion to himself. A handsome, dark haired man somewhere in his thirties sat at one of the desks talking on the phone. The office was empty otherwise. Chris didn't know too much about the Army, but he knew that the three stripes on the recruiter's sleeve meant that he was a Sergeant. After hanging the phone up, the Sergeant raised his index finger and beckoned to the boys.

"How you doin', fellas? How can I help you?"

Brian stepped forward and handed his papers to the recruiter.

"My name is Brian Boscorelli. I was told to bring these enlistment papers to you."

The recruiter took the papers from Brian's trembling hand and leafed through them casually, making sure each paper was signed and dated.

"Mr. Steiner called yesterday," he said, standing and offering Brian his hand. "I'm Sergeant Gary Nichols, and I'll be processing your papers. We need you to be here Tuesday morning for a physical. You will then take a bus from downtown San Antonio to Fort Hood, then to basic training. We can take you to the bus station from here, or you can have your family take you. You might want to spend as much time with them as you can. You will have a leave after basic training though."

The Sergeant's smile was friendly enough, and neither boy noticed that it didn't reach his dark eyes.

"Welcome to the Army, soldier."

"So I'll be leaving Tuesday, huh?" Brian sighed and continued without thinking. "Less than a week 'til I lose everything."

Sergeant Nichols looked at Brian sharply then turned and pulled a sheaf of papers from a gray filing cabinet. Returning to his desk, he finally spoke.

"I wouldn't say that joining the Army made me lose anything, Brian. In fact, I'd say that it was the best thing that ever happened to me. I joined when I was the same age that you are now." This was the standard first line of Sergeant Gary Nichol's sales pitch. He always used it when he wanted to sell the army to a young man who came into his office or when he visited Career Days at local high schools. He knew that Brian's enlistment was in the bag, but if he could get the other boy to sign up, he would have a nice commission in next month's paycheck. He hoped that by convincing Brian that joining the Army had been a good choice, he might be able to sell the other boy as well.

"You're joining at the right time, you know," the sergeant continued, "everyone knows that the conflict in Vietnam is coming to an end soon. Who knows, by the time you finish boot camp there might not be any reason to ship you overseas, except maybe to Germany or Italy."

Chris and Brian looked at each other. They hadn't thought of that. Brian nodded his head in agreement. Maybe this wouldn't be so bad after all. Sergeant Nichols sensed that he was gaining on them. "It's possible that you'll stay stateside, of course. The National Guard needs our help right now to control college protests and rioting. Usually we lay back and wait until the worst is over and then move in to keep the peace. That's considered active duty. Once you've completed a year and a half, your active duty is over." The recruiter paused for a moment to let this sink in.

Now was the time to reel in the kid with the ponytail.

"You know, Brian, once your two year hitch is up, you'll be eligible for a lot of government benefits, such as college tuition and low interest housing loans."

Chris interrupted his spiel. "You mean that he gets all that for only two years?"

"That's right. The government understands that you are serving your country, and in return they want to offer you an opportunity to go to college, buy a house or do whatever you want to do with the rest of your life. The time you spend in the service will help you to focus on the future and help you to move in whatever direction you choose. You'll get training in the Army that will help you to decide what you want do for a living. When I joined the Army, I had no idea what I wanted to do with my life. Now, ten years later, I'm making more money than I would be in civilian life. I'll be able to retire from the military when I'm forty and can move on to a whole new career if I choose, with a good pension from the government. Right now I take it a year at a time because I have the freedom to do what I wish, and I can't think of a better way to make a living than this."

Both boys were nodding now. A good salesman knows when his pitch is working, and Sergeant Nichols was a good salesman. He felt the familiar rush of adrenaline coursing through his veins and took a deep breath before he moved in carefully for the kill. He smiled at Chris and held out his right hand.

"Sorry, son, I didn't get your name."

Chris shook the hand that was offered to him. "My name is Chris, Chris Logue."

"I'm pleased to meet you, Chris," the sergeant replied warmly. "What are your plans after graduation?"

"I'm thinking of enrolling at the University of Texas, but I haven't decided yet." Chris was a little surprised by his own response to the recruiter's question. Until this moment he hadn't had any doubt that he would be going off to college in the fall as his parents expected.

Brian spoke up. "What do you mean, you haven't decided? I thought everything was settled."

Chris paused and cleared his throat before saying the words that Sergeant Nichols wanted to hear.

"If I were to join right now, would I be able to leave with Brian and serve with him the whole two years?"

Brian interrupted as the sergeant started to answer. "Chris, don't be crazy. You can't go with me. I'll be fine, you'll see. You should go to college like you planned to."

Chris shook his head. "Listen, man, my dad doesn't have the money to send me to college. He's just doing it because he thinks that he has to. It will be a real financial drain on the family. Besides, I've just spent the last thirteen years in school, and I still don't know what I want to do when I graduate. Like Sergeant Nichols said, I can use the time in the service to figure out what kind of career I really want."

The recruiter sat back down at his desk to let the boys discuss this on their own. It looked like a done deal. He thought with satisfaction. Brian, however, was not through trying to talk his friend out of what could be the mistake of a lifetime.

"Come on, man, you've got to be kidding. How am I going to live with myself if you get killed in Vietnam? What will I say to your parents. I'm a screw-up so now your son is dead?"

Chris grinned and gave Brian a quick punch to the deltoid. "Hey, I told you I wouldn't let you down, remember? You're stuck with me for another two years, buddy." He turned to the sergeant. "Will you be able to keep us together if I sign up today?" he asked. The recruiter shrugged. "I don't see a problem with that at all. There's a few questions I need to ask you and some paperwork to fill out. It won't take long at all."

He grinned widely, looking like a shark that has just had a good feed. Chris and Brian didn't notice. Had either boy been thinking clearly, they might have realized that the sergeant hadn't really promised that they would be able to stay together. After Boot Camp, in fact, all bets would be off.

Chris was nearly drunk with the excitement of making his first truly adult decision. A small voice in the back of his head was telling him to slow down and think about what he was doing, but he wasn't in the mood to listen.

"Go ahead and shoot," he said to Sergeant Nichols with a laugh, "That is what they say in the Army. Let's get the paperwork done."

Chapter 18

The Dairy Isle had opened by the time Chris and Brian left the Army Recruiter's office. Chris noticed the *open* sign as he headed for his truck and changed course immediately.

"C'mon, Bri, let's go get one of those Monster Shakes. I have a feeling that we won't be having milkshakes for a long time, so we might as well live it up." Brian nodded in agreement as he followed Chris.

They sat on the tailgate of the Ford and drank their shakes in silence. As the morning air began to heat up, Chris thought that he might just be dreaming that he would wake up any time now and realize that he was late for school. He couldn't believe that he was old enough to join the Army. A loud belch from Brian brought him back to earth with a startled laugh.

"Do you remember the first time I met your mom and Matt?" he asked. "You let out a bodacious belch, and your mom got pissed. You haven't changed a bit."

Brian agreed. "Yeah, but I've given my mom a lot more to be pissed about than my bad manners," he observed sadly. Chris didn't want his friend to start beating himself up again. Brian had taken a positive step to get his life on the right track, and it was time for him to move forward.

"You know, we have a few more days of freedom," he pointed out, "why don't we take advantage of it and do something different? I don't want to hang around here all weekend."

Brian thought for a moment. Getting away from Devine sounded like a good idea, but he had reservations.

"Won't our folks want us to spend all of our free time with them before we go to basic training?"

The monster shake became a cold lump in Chris's stomach when he thought about telling his parents that he had joined the Army. He had managed to push that thought aside in the excitement of making a major life decision. Suddenly he felt like a scared kid. He shook the feeling off and continued.

"I'll probably be better off if I get out of Dodge for a few days after I tell my folks that I joined the Army. It'll give them time to let the news sink in. Let's do something really outrageous. Let's go to Mexico tomorrow. We can come back Saturday and still have time to spend with the families."

Brian looked at his friend as though he had never seen him before. This kind of spontaneity was rare for careful Chris.

"Man, you're really pulling out all the stops today," he said with a laugh. "When are you going to tell Pam? On the way to the bus station?"

Chris felt his heart sink with a thud. "What a heel I am," he thought. He hadn't even given her a minute's consideration. For a time he had thought that he loved Pam, so how could he make such a major move without even discussing it with her?

"Oh, man," he sighed, "what a selfish bastard I am. We were going to spend the summer together. This is a hell of a way to break up."

Brian tried to think of something to say to bring back the spirit of adventure that his friend had shown just moments before.

"Pam is a reasonable person," he offered. "She'll understand. Besides, how can she be mad at you for serving your country? If you guys have a future together, she'll wait for you. You weren't going to the same college anyway. Maybe she'll think it's romantic to have a soldier for a boyfriend."

Chris snorted. "Yeah, maybe she'll bake me some cookies to eat on the way to 'Nam."

All of his life his parents had taken care of Chris, made decisions for him, seen to it that he was never hurt.

He realized now how much that meant to him. He suddenly knew that being a man was not just about having the freedom to do whatever he wanted to do. A big part of being a man was the fact that the choices he made had an impact on the people who cared about him. Chris was overwhelmed by the awesome responsibility of being an adult.

Brian sensed that his friend was thinking deep thoughts. He was glad that he was never troubled much by his conscience. He didn't wanted to hurt anyone, mind you, but worrying too much about other people put a damper on his party spirit. Chris was becoming entirely too serious. It was time to bring him back to here and now.

"So, tell me about this trip to Mexico," he prodded, "when do you want to go?"

Chris had almost forgotten about the weekend. He would have to talk to Pam this afternoon and break the big news to his parents tonight.

"How about tomorrow morning? We can go down Route 57. Piedras Negras is just over the Rio Grande a few miles south of Eagle Pass Park. Maybe we can stop and fish on the way back for old times sake," he added.

They threw their empty shake cups into the wire trash can that stood on the sidewalk outside of the Dairy Isle. Chris slapped Brian on the back and started the truck.

"C'mon, we've got a lot to do today and only a few days of freedom left. I don't want to waste my time here."

Chris was waiting in the school parking lot at noon when Pam came out for lunch. She readily accepted his suggestion that she skip school for the afternoon and have lunch with him in the park. Over carry-out burgers he broke the news of his enlistment to her. Pam took the news better than he had expected. Running her fingers through her auburn hair, she lay back on the blanket that they had spread on the grass.

When she finally spoke, her words were measured carefully. "I always knew that Brian would split us up somehow. I just didn't know how it would happen." Chris began to protest, but Pam held a slender hand up to shush him. "Oh, I know that he may not have done it on purpose, but he did it all the same."

She started to cry softly, and Chris held her to his chest and stroked her hair until she stopped. He still wasn't sure how he could leave a great girl like Pam, but he couldn't argue that Brian had always stood silently between them. He suspected that she was crying as much for losing Brian as she was for him.

They spent the rest of the afternoon on the blanket in the park, talking over old times and about what the future held for them. By the time he pulled up to her driveway at 6:00 p.m. and kissed her goodbye, they had decided to wait and see how they felt about each other when his Army hitch was up.

Chris felt a mixture of relief and sadness as he pulled away from the curb. Heading for home, he knew that telling Pam had only been a dress rehearsal for telling his folks. The worst was yet to come.

Chapter 19

Laurie and Ryan were sitting on the sofa watching the 6:00 News, the way they had done every night that Chris could remember. He stood in the kitchen doorway and watched them for a moment. He wondered if the knot in his throat was fear or love. *Maybe both,* he thought with a sigh. Squaring his shoulders, he walked into the living room and sat down in a soft side chair.

"Hi, Chris, where have you been?" Laurie asked without waiting for an answer, "your boss, Mark, called looking for you a half hour ago."

"I spent the afternoon with Pam."

Ryan turned away from the TV set reluctantly. "Are you quitting your job? I don't care if you do, but you owe your bosses more consideration than too just not show up."

Chris cleared his throat. "Mom, Dad I have something to tell you."

Laurie felt a cold finger run down her spine at the tone of her son's voice. Whatever he wanted to tell them, she knew instantly that it wasn't good. In the few seconds before he continued, her mother's mind ticked off a laundry list of possible disasters that might have befallen her oldest child: flunked out of school, girlfriend pregnant, car accident, drug problem...

Her list was cut short when he blurted out. "Brian and I joined the Army today."

Laurie couldn't believe that she had heard him right. *That wasn't even on the list,* she thought. She looked at her husband. His face betrayed no emotion as he calmly folded his newspaper. Chris was surprised at his parent's lack of a reaction. He thought that maybe they hadn't heard him and was about to repeat himself when Ryan spoke, his voice low and even.

"What the hell are you talking about?" He asked. You are kidding us, right?"

Chris shook his head. "No, Dad," he replied, "I'm not kidding. I've been thinking about this for a while, and it's what I really want to do. I went to the Recruiting office this morning and signed up."

Laurie spoke up, sounding like a mommy who was scolding her little boy for bringing a stray puppy home. As the words spilled out, she knew that she sounded ridiculous, but she couldn't stop.

"You know, Christopher, your father and I aren't going to let you go off and fight a war, so you just better go back and tell that recruiter that he can scratch Chris Logue's name off his list."

Ryan tried to keep his own tone from betraying the rage and frustration that were building steadily. He couldn't believe that Chris was stupid enough to throw away his future, never mind his life away on a war that could never be won.

"Chris," he said, "I know that you haven't decided on a major yet, but once you start college you'll figure out what you want to do soon enough. You know that I've always wanted you to become a chemist, but I want you to do what makes you happy. We can figure out a way to get you out of this and then you can go to college in the fall the way we had always planned."

Chris knew that he was fighting an uphill battle; convincing his parents that he wasn't throwing his life away would be nearly impossible, but he was determined to give it his best shot. He was grateful to them for everything they had done for him, and he truly wanted them to be okay with this.

"Mom, Dad, this is my choice to make. I'm not a little kid anymore. I want to be able to take care of myself and not spend all of your money to go to school. This way I can pay my own tuition and get government help to buy a house when the time comes. I can't take this back. I signed the papers this morning, and I'll be leaving for boot camp on Tuesday."

Laurie's voice quivered as she spoke. "Tuesday morning. That's not even a week from now. Chris, please stop clowning around. This isn't funny any more."

Chris stood and approached his mother as she started to cry, intending to give her a comforting hug. Before he reached her, Ryan leaped from his chair with a sudden burst of fury and slammed his son to the floor, knocking the wind out of him. Amazed, Chris thought that this must be how a quarterback felt when he got hit by a linebacker.

Chris had expected Ryan to explode anytime. His father was usually a pretty even tempered guy, but he was capable of ranting and raving on occasion. What Chris hadn't expected was physical violence. He had never seen his father hit anyone ever. Stunned, he lay limp and unresisting as his father shook his finger inches from his face and screamed.

"YOU ARE NOT GOING ANYWHERE. DO YOU HEAR ME? NOW GET THE HELL UP AND GO FIND THAT RECRUIT-ER'S PHONE NUMBER!"

Laurie was pulling on Ryan's shirt and crying. "Stop it, Ryan, you'll hurt him."

Ryan paid no attention to her. He grabbed his son's shirt collar and pulled him to his feet and headed for the kitchen, sweeping his wife away effortlessly with his free hand. Reaching the kitchen, Ryan shoved Chris toward the wall phone, releasing the grip on his shirt. Chris stumbled and then righted himself. Turning abruptly, he ran through the door into the hallway and into his bedroom, slamming the door behind him.

Knowing that his father would be after him in a heartbeat, he pulled open the bottom drawer of his dresser and grabbed the $200 that was hidden beneath it, stuffing the money into the pocket of his jeans. Not knowing what his father might be capable of in his present state, Chris was determined to get the hell out before round Two started.

The door burst open, and Ryan stormed in as Chris was pulling his gym bag from the closet shelf.

"WHERE THE HELL DO YOU THINK YOU'RE GOING?" Ryan screamed.

Chris began shoving clothes into the gym bag and replied calmly, "You know, when you thought that I was going to college, you were ready to stand behind me all the way because I was doing what you wanted me to do." His voice began to rise, "Why can't you stand behind me when I do something that I think is right? I'll tell you why because you think that my life is all about the kind of son you want. You won't even take a second to think about how I feel, and what I want." He finished jamming clothes into the bag and zipped it shut.

Ryan's anger had not abated. His fists opened and closed, opened and closed until his knuckles turned white.

"Oh, really, Chris?" He shouted, "Why don't you tell your mother and me how you feel about being shot and killed in some stinking jungle? We'd really be interested to hear how you feel about that!"

Chris had enough. He started to push his way past his father, but Ryan grabbed his shirt collar before he could escape.

"I'll be damned if you're leaving this house, soldier boy, so you'd better just turn around and get back in here!"

As Ryan yelled, he gave his son a shake for emphasis. Chris twisted away from his father's grip, tearing his shirt in the process.

"You aren't going to do jack shit to me because I'm 18 years old, and there's not a thing you can do about it! You are going to have to find a way to live with that!"

Chris was screaming now. As he pushed open the screen door, banging it into the far wall, he caught a glimpse of his mother's face. She was sobbing now, but Chris was still too angry to feel guilty for causing her pain. There would be plenty of time for that later.

Ryan chased Chris to the lawn and stood watching as Chris peeled the truck away from the curb, but he was silent now. Chris was relieved that his father hadn't brought the argument out into the yard for the neighbors to hear.

Chris drove around Devine for the next 3 hours, wishing he had some place to stay. He was reluctant to spend his money on a hotel so he finally headed home. When he pulled up to the house the lights were off, much to his relief. He was mildly surprised that Ryan and Laurie hadn't waited up for him, maybe they had been worn out by the evening's rumble. He crept into the house as quietly as he could and climbed into bed. He couldn't remember ever being so tired. Maybe the battle with his folks would help to prepare him for the rigors of boot camp. He was drifting off when his bedroom door opened.

"Chris, may I come in?" His father asked softly, "I'd like to talk."

"If that's what you want, dad," Chris replied. "I'm a little too tired for another wrestling match, though."

Ryan sat in the chair next to the bed. "Don't worry. I'm worn out, myself. Chris, I'm sorry. I got carried away. You really threw me for a loop. I know you've heard this before, but you'll understand how I feel when you have kids of your own. I just always thought that you wanted to go to college. You never gave us even a hint that you wanted something different. If you had, your mother and I would have tried to understand. Hell, we're trying as hard as we can to understand this. I just want to be sure that you know what you're getting into. We've never talked too much about politics, and now I wish we had. I happen to think that this is a useless war. If I thought that the United States had a good reason to be in Vietnam, I might feel differently about you joining the service. You were right before when you said that you are a man now and you have a right to your own opinion, but I hope that you're doing this for the right reasons. Convince me, son."

Chris sat up in bed and leaned back against the headboard. He finally told his father about Brian's problems with the law, and why his friend had to join the Army. Chris explained that when he was trying to put a good spin on the situation to make Brian feel better. He had realized that signing up was the best thing for him too. He wiped a hand over his tired eyes.

"Dad, I just couldn't let him go by himself," he finished.

"Chris, you are not Brian's keeper. If that's the reason that you're doing this, then you're making a big mistake," Ryan said.

"That was the reason at first, but now I really do think that it's the right move for me for a lot of reasons. It's time for me to grow up and take care of myself, and I'll be a better person for it. You'll see," Chris answered. "Dad, I promise, and I mean promise that I'll be home safe and sound in a year. The rest of my service will be stateside and even that will be over by the time you know it. I can graduate from college by the time I'm 24."

Ryan got up and leaned over the bed, enveloping his son in a bear hug. When he finally spoke, his voice was hoarse.

"Chris, I love you, and I'll be there for you whatever you do. Your mother and I just want you to come home in one piece."

Chris figured that this was as good a time as any to tell his father about the trip to Mexico. Ryan sighed as he headed for the door.

"Oh well what's two more days anyway?" He asked not expecting an answer. "I'll explain it to your mother," he sighed, "she'll come around eventually. I guess. Good night, son." He turned to look at his little boy one more time ."I love you, son."

Chris smiled and slid back under the covers. "Good night, Dad. I love you too."

As he drifted off to sleep for the second time that night, Chris was aware of the cold smooth stone of the arrowhead against his chest. He had not been able to tell anyone about the feeling he had that the Kickapoo ghost had a part in all of this. No one would believe him, anyway.

Chapter 20

Brian shifted in the seat of the Ford pickup. "According to the map if we just passed LaPryor we should be at the border in about an hour."

He was using the cover of a matchbook to scale the miles between Devine and the Rio Grande river on the road map in his lap. "Man," he exclaimed. "It's only about 120 miles from Devine to Mexico. Why haven't we ever gone there before?"

Chris shrugged. "Beats' me. Every time I knew someone who was going, I either didn't like them, or I had other plans."

Brian folded the map as best he could and slid it into the glove compartment.

"Yeah, that's true," he agreed. "I guess I've had a couple of chances to go, myself. Anyway, this is going to be fun. I hope it's as wild as I've heard."

They had been driving for over an hour, and they had kept the conversation light. Brian stared out the passenger window at the desert, his mind wandering. They had not been able to pick up anything on the radio except static after they got out of the range of the San Antonio stations. As he drove, Chris drummed his fingers on the steering wheel and hummed the song *Light my fire* by the Doors. It was last song that they had heard before the static took over and Chris had it stuck in his head now. He was glad that he liked it at least.

After a time, Brian sighed deeply, startling Chris.

"You know, maybe when we cross the border we should just keep going south. How long do you think we could live in Mexico on $200.00?"

Chris laughed. "I don't know, not long I guess. The thought had crossed my mind too though. We'd probably have to live in a tent and eat cats and dogs. I'm sure that we'd adjust."

Brian wrinkled his nose in disgust. "C'mon, that's friggin' gross. I think I'd live in the mountains and hunt wild animals before I'd eat a dog or a cat."

Chris began singing softly, repeating the words that had been going around in his head for the last half hour: *"C'mon,baby,light my fire,C'mon baby,light my fire,Try to set the night on fire."*

Brian moaned, "Man, I wish we could listen to the radio."

Chris gave him a mock-withering look. "What's a matter? You don't think I sound like Morrison?"

Brian shook his head, grinning. "Just don't quit your day job. Oh, wait, I forgot. You don't have a day job anymore. You're in the Army now."

"Oh, wait, I forgot, so am I. Shit." They both had a laugh at that one.

Chris turned and looked at his friend. "But seriously, folks, I think that we should stop and get something to eat before we cross the border," he suggested. "It might be a good idea to get a big meal in our bellies, so we don't get sick on Mexican food. I don't feel like spending our whole vacation sitting on the john."

Brian was all for it. He was getting hungry, anyway.

The blue truck rolled down the dusty highway. Waves of heat rose from the blacktop, and the surrounding desert seemed to bake in the early afternoon sun. As they neared Eagle Pass Park, trees began to sprout from the desert, breaking the monotony of the beige rocks and scrub. The intermittent shade came as a relief, cooling off the truck bed and giving Chris's eyes a rest. Thirty minutes later they came to a crossroads. Chris pulled over to the side of the highway, so they could get their bearings. As Brian studied the road signs, Chris checked out the dozen or so nondescript businesses that were scattered at the side of the road. They included a rather neglected looking motel, a gas station with a body shop at the rear, a lumberyard, and, glories be, a set of golden arches.

Brian spoke up, "This is where 277and Route 57meet. See, the sign points to the right. That will take us right to the border. Just make sure you stay on route 57, and we'll be fine."

Chris thought that sounded good. "Let's hammer some Big Macs first," he suggested as he pulled into the parking lot of the McDonalds.

They made short work of their burgers, fries and shakes and headed back toward the road. "You might want to crotch that bag of weed," Chris suggested. "I doubt that we'll get checked out on the way into Mexico, but it's better to be safe than sorry. I'd hate to get caught trying to smuggle weed across the border. We don't want to end up in jail for the weekend."

Brian pulled the plastic bag from his pocket and stuffed it down the front of his jeans.

"They'll have to look under my balls to find it now," he said, twisting in the seat to adjust his underwear.

"You ready?" Chris asked.

"Let's do it." He turned the Ford back onto the highway, heading south.

"I'm really looking forward to seeing the Rio Grande. I've heard that you can do some really wild rafting on it. Judging by the size of the mountains and the river width on the map, I'll bet it gets cooking pretty fast." Chris adjusted the rear view mirror as he spoke.

Brian pointed to a road sign and let out a loud whoop. "Here we go!"

Both heads followed the sign as they passed.

"United States/Mexico customs 1 mile." Brian adjusted the small bag of marijuana nestled in his crotch. "Man, I'm a little freaked-out with this weed in my pants. What if they frisk us?" He asked nervously.

"They won't check us now," Chris answered. "They want us to spend our American dollars in their country. We'll have to be careful on the way back though. That's when the border guards will be looking for contraband. We'll have to smoke it all up before we come back," he said with a grin.

"No problem, man." Brian laughed and let out another whoop. "YeeeHaaaa, " he screamed, his head hanging out the window.

Chris slowed the truck as they approached the border check point. There were a half dozen cars in each line with newcomers jockeying for shortest line. Chris darted into the far left lane, which was a good move. The car at the customs booth was pulling ahead, and there were only four cars left in line. They didn't have long to wait. The green Pontiac ahead of them drove through after only a few moments, and Chris pulled ahead. The customs officer was American. He had close cropped blond hair and stood square shouldered and erect.

"How are you fellas doing today?" he asked, his voice clipped and neutral.

"We're fine thanks," Chris replied, rolling his window down.

"Why are you boys traveling to Mexico?"

Chris tried his best to sound casual. "We're just going down for a couple of days as tourists."

The customs agent asked if they planned to stay for more than 30 days. Chris replied that they would be coming back to the states on Saturday. The agent left the booth and walked slowly around the Ford, pausing to look in the truck bed. He noted the two gym bags and looked up at Chris's reflection in the side mirror.

"What's in the bags?" he asked.

"Just the clothes we brought for the trip."

"I'd like to inspect the contents," the agent said, locking eyes with the young man reflected in the mirror as if to gauge his response.

Chris shrugged and told him to go ahead . He felt a little nervous and a little guilty about the weed in his friend's pants, but he was able to hold the steady gaze of the customs agent. The agent gave the contents of the gym bags a cursory search, and then walked around the truck and stopped at Brian's half open window.

"Hi, how are you today?" he asked.

Brian replied that he, too, was fine, thanks. The agent asked if Brian had any I.D. Brian wordlessly fished his driver's license out of his wallet and handed it over. The officer glanced at it and handed it back. Both boys followed him with their eyes as he walked around the front of the pickup. They breathed a sigh of relief in unison as he turned and headed toward the booth.

"You boys have a good time now and be careful down there." He waved them off with a smile.

Chris called after him, "Do you know of a decent motel in Piedras Negras?"

The guard thought for a moment before replying. "I'm no travel agent, but you might try the Hacienda. It probably has the friendliest cockroaches." He pointed to the bridge. "Just stay on Route 57. It's on the right side of the highway right on the edge of town. You can't miss it."

Chris thanked him and headed the truck toward the Route 57lane.

Brian felt like he had been holding his breath for an eternity. He breathed out now in a long whooshing gasp.

"Man, why did you talk so long?" He asked when he was finally able to speak. "This weed feels like a boulder in my crotch. I was starting to freak out."

Chris shrugged a response.

"If he had wanted to pull us over, he would have done it right at the get-go. Besides, now we have an idea where we can bed down. I'm betting that there are a lot of nasty places down here and I'd rather not sleep in somebody else's business if you know what I mean."

Brian agreed reluctantly. Now that they were back on the road he was beginning to relax a little.

The Rio Grand was visible now. Chris slowed the truck so that he could get a look at the river. It was even wider than he had imagined. He whistled softly under his breath.

"Man, just think of the people who crossed the river before the bridges were built. I can imagine the settlers getting to the edge and saying 'Okay, this is too wide to cross. Let's just make this part of Texas, too.' I wouldn't try to cross without a bridge, either. It looks like death to me."

Brian nodded in agreement. "No one would ever find your body if you drowned in there. You'd float right out to the ocean."

They passed a sign printed in Spanish and English:

PIEDRAS NEGRAS 3 MILES

Brian grew contemplative as he gazed out of the window at the surrounding countryside. "Isn't it weird that I've never been out of the U.S. before' and now I'll be leaving twice in two months."

At the far end of the bridge there was a sign welcoming them to Mexico. The scenery on the Mexican side of the river was in stark contrast to that of the United States side. Many of the buildings were so dilapidated it was surprising to see them standing. Broken glass, doors hanging on hinges, and overgrow lawns were the norm in the area.

"There sure is a lot of garbage around here," Brian noted. "I can't wait to see what the Hacienda looks like. I wonder if there'll be any cheap nasty whores in the lobby. Jerry Martin told me that when he was down here he got a blow job from a hooker who had no teeth and only charged 3 bucks."

Chris wrinkled his nose in disgust. "Even Jerry Martin should be able to get a senorita with teeth."

Brian explained that the prostitutes had their teeth pulled so that they could give better head. Chris was no prude, but the thought of being gummed by a toothless hooker appalled him.

"Listen, Pal, you can have your fantasies. I'll take a pass on this one."

A mile beyond the customs booth they entered the town of Piedras Negras. Most of the buildings on the outskirts of town were drab one-story houses and businesses. The natives were dressed in colorless clothing, matching the facades of the buildings that surrounded them.

Brian pointed to a sign announcing the Hacienda Motel. The
motel was built on two levels, the main portion facing the dusty
street with a smaller wing jutting out on either side. The blue paint
was peeling and sun bleached. The parking lot was nearly empty
but there was a light on in the office and a red neon *VACANCY* sign
buzzed over the door. Chris parked in front of the office door.

"I guess it looks okay," he said dubiously.

Brian observed that all of the rooms had balconies.

"We can see beautiful Route 57 from the veranda any time we
want to," he said, drawing out the word "verahandah." He fidgeted
in the truck seat. "Why don't you go in and get the room?" he
suggested. "I don't want to go in there with this weed stuffed in my
crotch. I'll take it out when we get to the room."

"Yeah, whatever," Chris replied, getting out of the Ford. He
felt a stab of irritation at his friend. They hadn't really discussed
how the trip would be financed, but he noticed that Brian didn't
jump to offer any money for the room. *I guess I should have as-
sumed that I'd be paying for everything* he sighed to himself. *Brian's
great at getting out of everything* as it happened, Brian also as-
sumed that Chris would be bankrolling most of the trip. After all,
Chris was the one with the job, and Brian had provided the dope,
which he considered a significant contribution to the festivities.

After a few moments Chris climbed back into the driver's seat,
handing Brian a key that was hanging from a chunk of wood.

"Room 113, my man, and we both have our own bed," he said,
pulling the truck around to the back of the right-hand wing. "Oh,
yeah," he added, "I gave up the veranda for the second bed. So
much for the scenic view of Route 57."

The faded curtains were closed, and the atmosphere in the room
was stifling. Chris turned on the room light and checked the ther-
mostat by the door, finding the hoped for air-conditioning setting.
He turned the control to 'cool' and pushed the 'on' button. A blast
of hot air blew from the vents and gradually turned cold. Brian
held his hand above the vent.

"Feels like it's working, but it's gonna take awhile. Man, it's like a sauna in here."

Chris threw his gym bag down on the nearest bed and went into the tiny bathroom, switching on the light. The room was shabby, but appeared to be clean enough and even had a paper strip across the toilet seat to show that it had been sanitized. Chris kind of doubted that, but he removed the strip anyway. He had been driving with a full bladder since McDonald's, and he didn't care how clean the john was at this point. He returned to the room to find Brian fishing the bag of pot from his jeans.

"Why don't we check out the area and let the room cool down for awhile," he suggested. "I'd like to take a shower, but in this heat I'd start sweating again as soon as I finished."

Chris sat down on the bed and tested the mattress with a few bounces.

"You know, this place isn't half bad. The bathroom is pretty clean, and the towels look fresh." He walked over to the window and opened the curtains, looking out over the small town. "I always thought of Mexico a third world country, you know, poor people who haven't had a bath in a year and with flies all over them. This isn't that bad. It isn't Hawaii, but there is a tradition and a heritage that you can see and feel."

Brian was sitting on the far bed opening his gym bag and searching around for his cigarette papers.

"You mean it's ancient," he laughed. "Let's fire one up, and then we'll take a walk toward the center of town. It can't be that far, and I'm sure there'll be plenty of places to drink along the way."

Chris saw that beads of sweat were popping out on Brian's forehead and his normally ruddy complexion was taking on an alarming hot pink hue.

"C'mon," Chris said. "Let's forget the joint and just go. You look like you just ran a marathon."

Brian tucked the bag and the papers back into the bag.

"You're right," he agreed. "I can't breathe in here."

A breeze wafted in through the door as Chris opened it. The air was warm and dry and smelled of the desert, but it was refreshing as it kissed their skin. The boys felt like foreigners as they walked down the street. The people went about their business without paying them any attention, but they still felt out of place.

"This is weird," said Brian in an anxious stage whisper. "What if someone tries to rob us? Where do you have your money?"

Chris answered that most of it was wrapped around his ankle inside his sock.

"I have 20 bucks in my pocket. If we're attacked, I'll just throw that at them and run." He really didn't think that they had too much to worry about. The town looked pretty peaceful. A multicolored neon sign caught his attention.

"Well, what do you think? Should we give it a try?" Chris asked as they stood looking at the small tavern.

The building stood alone, set back slightly from the street. There was nothing on the sign except the flashing neon bottle with the word *BEER* in the middle. Brian noted that much of the advertising that they had seen so far was in English. The tourist trade must be a major source of income around here. The sign visible in the front window of the nondescript building. Curtains that looked as though they have been there since the Korean War draped limply on either side of the neon bottle. The building itself was cracked and weathered from the desert wind and sun. Brian was dubious about entering the seedy looking tavern. "I don't know. It looks spooky, like something out of a ghost town in an old western movie. What if a loco bandit wants to shoot us?"

Chris couldn't help grinning. Brian sounded more like a little boy than a soon-to-be soldier.

"What if, what if. Is that all you can say? What if we just stand around all day wondering what a cold beer would taste like? Come on, let's do it."

They crossed the street and were about to open the door when Chris stopped short.

"Drink out of the bottle, man, just to be on the safe side," he cautioned.

Now it was Brian's turn to grin. "So much for recklessness," he thought as he pulled the door open.

The boys were momentarily enveloped by the darkness inside the tavern. As their eyes adjusted to the dim light, they saw a bar that ran the length of the room. The bar stools were covered with cracked and faded red leather that had been patched with duct tape. They were empty except for a lone Mexican man who nursed a beer at the farthest stool . A middle aged Mexican couple sat at one of the high tables that lined the walls. No one paid any attention to the young grinning touristas. Brian and Chris sat at the bar and waited for a bartender to appear. Brian took a long look around the nearly deserted tavern and leaned toward Chris.

"Wow," he laughed. "This place is really hoppin'. Which chick do you want dibs on?"

Chris was a little annoyed by the sarcasm.

"Hey, man, it's cool enough in here, and I for one don't mind starting out with a nice, quiet beer."

Chris looked at the door at the end of the bar wondering where the bartender was. The old man glanced up at the same time, and their eyes met briefly. They exchanged nods, and the old man returned his gaze to his half empty bottle of beer. As Chris scanned the bottles of liquor lining the shelves behind the bar, the door to the back room opened, and a woman emerged. At first glance, Chris judged her to be about forty, slightly plump with bleached blond hair. She stopped in front of them and flashed a smile full of even white teeth, and Chris decided that she was younger than he had thought, and not bad looking to boot.

"Hi, guys, what'll you have?" She asked in English with a slight southern drawl.

Chris was relieved that there was no language barrier to overcome.

"Boy, am I glad that you speak English." he said. "I don't even know how to order a beer in Spanish."

"Cervesa, por favor," she replied. "My name is Ann, and we'll do anything to please our customers. Well, almost anything," she finished with a pleasing laugh.

Chris decided that she really was pretty after all. "It's nice to make your acquaintance, Ann." Chris was being as smooth as he knew how. "I'm Chris, and this is my friend Brian. We'd like a beer, bottle or can, whichever is colder. Two cervesas, por favor, I mean." He corrected himself with a crooked grin.

Ann smiled and nodded in Brian's general direction and then looked back at Chris. His patented crooked grin had obviously worked it's magic.

"Well, honey, the coolers are working fine today, so you can have your beer however you want it." The innuendo in her voice was clearly lost on Brian, who replied quickly.

"I'll have a bottle, then, the biggest you've got." Chris ordered the same and laid a 20 on the bar.

As Ann bent to open the beer cooler, Chris winked at Brian with a little nod in her direction. Brian shrugged and nodded, signaling that she met with his approval, too. The barmaid returned with the amber bottles, two mugs and a basket of popcorn. Brian and Chris both ignored the mugs that she placed in front of them and drank directly from the sweating bottles. Ann laughed and told them that the popcorn was safe as it came out of a bag. Chris thanked her and they dug in, washing the salty popcorn down with great swigs of the cold beer.

Between gulps of beer, Brian asked if there was a cigarette machine in the bar.

"Sure," Ann replied, pointing toward the rear of the building. "It's right through that doorway. There's a jukebox and a pool table back there, too. All of the machines take quarters. The pool table is a quarter, cigarettes are a buck, and the jukebox plays three for a quarter. I don't think there are many songs that you'd like, but I talked the owner into putting in a few American Rock'n Roll tunes for my sake."

Chris gathered up the change that Ann had placed on the bar in front of him. He held out four dollar bills.

"Can you give me 3 dollars in quarters? The other dollar is for you."

Ann flashed another smile as she took the money.

"Thanks, Chris. That's sweet of you. I'll turn the light on over the pool table."

She flicked a switch under the bar and a fluorescent flickered on, casting an eerie glow in the small room. Brian got a pack of Marlboros and checked out the jukebox selections as Chris slid a quarter into the coin slot on the side of the pool table and racked up the pool balls. Ann came into the back room with a handful of quarters.

"There are only a few good cue sticks in the bunch," she said, nodding in the direction of a lopsided rack hanging on the wall.

Her hand felt like cool velvet as it lingered on his provocatively. He looked into her eyes, and in the bright white light he could see that they were a soft aqua blue. She broke the spell with a toss of her blond hair.

"Don't drop any, now," she said softly.

"Huh?" asked Chris, momentarily bewildered. "Oh, the quarters. Hey, why don't you play some eight-ball with us? Or we could play cutthroat so we could all play at the same time. If you shoot pool, that is..." His voice trailed off, sounding lame in his ears.

"If I shoot pool? Buddy, I could put you two to shame," she replied confidently. "I can't right now, though. The after work crowd will be in shortly." She started back toward the bar and then slowed, glancing at him over her shoulder. "I get off work at seven. If you're still around, maybe we could play a few games then."

Chris thought that being around might be a very good idea, indeed.

Brian had played three of the four Rock'n Roll tunes on the ancient Wurlitzer and they chose two of the straightest cue sticks. He tossed one to Chris and suggested that they make a friendly wager to make the game more interesting.

"We could play for tequila shots," he said, chalking the end of his cue stick. "After five or six games, we'll see who is still standing."

Chris turned out to be the better player, and at the end of an hour Brian had consumed three shots along with his mug of beer.

"Do you want to play one more, or have you had enough?" Chris asked as he sank the last of Brian's striped balls. Brian's reply came out a little slurred.

"No. I think I've had enough for now. Let's go back to the motel and get cleaned up. Maybe even take a little nap," he added as he headed for the door, staggering slightly.

Chris returned the cue sticks to the rack and scooped up the empty glasses. He returned to the front room of the tavern and placed the glasses on the bar. The bar was crowded now, and Ann leaned over the wooden counter in order to be heard.

"Thanks for bringing these up," she said with a smile. "Maybe I should be tipping you. Hey, which one of you drank the shots?"

Chris pointed to Brian, who stood weaving by the front door. Ann's grin widened to a laugh, and she shook her head. Chris smiled back at her, and their eyes locked.

"We're going back to the motel to clean up," he told her. "We should be back in an hour or so, maybe we could shoot that game of pool?"

Ann's reply was light. "The last time I did anything after work, Kennedy was still president." When she saw Chris's deflated look, she realized that he had mistaken her flip response for rejection, which what was not at all what she had in mind. She reached out and lightly touched his hand.

"Don't hurry on my account," she said softly. "I'll be here."

Chris was smiling broadly as he steered Brian back in the direction of the Hacienda. Brian raised a hand to shield his eyes from the bright Mexican sun.

"Man, you don't actually want to go back to that mortuary, do you?" He asked as they crossed the street.

The street was much busier than it had been when they went into the bar. The faces in the crowd were now mixed, Caucasian faces among the Mexican. The touristas seemed to be mostly family groups at this hour, but Chris suspected that after dark young party goers would replace the families. He told Brian that the tavern might be a good jumping-off point for the evening, and that Ann would be able to steer them to some better night spots. He didn't add that he wouldn't mind getting to know Ann a little better since he was going to be in the Army in a week. He doubted that he would have much female companionship in basic training. The sudden memory of Pam brought on a pang of guilt.

Chris marveled at how quickly he had come to think of her in the past tense. He rationalized that he didn't want to tie her down while he was in the service then remembered that she hadn't exactly offered to wait for him anyway. *Oh, well*, he thought. His life had changed so much in the last couple of days. This trip was for fun, not serious introspection.

The cool air that escaped from the motel room door as Chris opened it was a welcome relief from the oppressive afternoon heat. Brian lost no time plopping down on his bed. Fatigue from the drive combined with the heat and tequila had finally caught up with him. His stomach threatened to reject the alcohol he had consumed.

"Oh, man," he moaned. "I don't feel so good. Is this room spinning, or is it me?"

Chris noted that his friend's normally pale skin had graduated to a deathly pallor.

"It's you," he replied. "You gonna be okay?" He asked.

Brian felt a little better now that he was lying down.

"Yeah, I'll twist up a joint and take a couple of tokes. That'll help."

Chris headed to the bathroom, undressing as he went. The arrowhead necklace swung back and forth lazily as he bent to pull of his jeans. He didn't think that smoking weed would improve Brian's condition, but he had realized a long time ago that giving his friend advice was a waste of time and breath.

"I guess you know best," was all he said.

The stream of water from the motel shower was stronger than Chris had expected. He felt revived after hosing off. When he turned off the water, Chris was startled to hear voices speaking in rapid fire Spanish coming from the bedroom. He realized with a rush of relief that the voices were coming from the ancient black and white television that sat perched on top of the dresser. Brian was sound asleep, curled up in the fetal position and snoring softly. An unlit joint lay in the ashtray on the night stand. Chris kicked the bed gently, then harder when he got no response.

"Hey, Brian, wake up!"

Brian didn't even stir. Chris grabbed his gym bag from the bed and turned the television off. He dressed in a clean T-shirt and jeans then fished the remaining cash from his dirty sock and stuffed it into his pocket. Walking back to Brian's bed, he raised his voice a notch as he pled with Brian to wake up.

"C'mon, don't pass out on me now. You'll feel better if you get up and take a shower. We've got a long night ahead of us." He shook his friend's shoulder and finally got a response, although not the one he had hoped for.

"Leave me alone, or I'm gonna be sick. In fact I feel like I could yak right now," Brian groaned.

His head flopped back down on the pillow, and he curled up tighter, drawing his knees up until they nearly touched his chest.

Chris stood over him shaking his head in disgust.

"I can't believe this. If you think I'm going to stay here and watch Mexican TV and baby-sit for you all night, you're crazy."

As he sat on his bed pulling on his sandals, Chris's aggravation at Brian receded into the distance. Unbidden, the thought of going overseas and killing strangers popped into his mind. He tried to imagine himself carrying out orders to take Vietnamese prisoners and burn villages to the ground, and he didn't think that he would ever be able to do such a thing. Atrocities committed by

American soldiers against the Vietnamese were well documented in the media, and Chris knew also that the Viet Cong were killing Americans at an alarming rate. Images of the faces of men he had known who had fought in Vietnam flashed through his mind. Some of the men were alive and well, some barely alive, permanently damaged in their bodies and minds. The faces that were most vivid were those of his acquaintances who had come home to Texas with American flags draped over their coffins. Chris tried to push the horrifying images away, but he felt as if he was caught in a nightmare from which he couldn't wake. He remembered Les Klink. Les had gone to Marine Corps boot camp about this time the year before. He was older than Chris, but they had mutual friends. Chris had last seen Les at a going away party for a half dozen Devine High grads who had joined the Army. Les had the same hopes and dreams as Chris did about serving his time and the going to college on the G.I. Bill. He had been so confident that his future was secure.

Brian and Chris had attended Les's funeral just before Christmas. He had been killed at the Laotian border. The Marine Corp. had told his family that Les had been killed by mortar shrapnel in a firefight. He had been awarded a Purple Heart for his bravery. Les had been buried with full military honors. The 21- Gun Salute honoring their son's death had seemed to bring comfort to Les' family.

Les had been dead less than a month when his brother Jimmy told Chris the real story of his death. A marine who had been in the same company as Les had told Jimmy that they were behind enemy lines trying to evacuate dead American soldiers when Les was killed. The squad didn't understand why their commanding officer had ordered them into enemy territory when he knew that the Viet cong were still heavily entrenched in that sector. Just as they reached the bodies of their fallen comrades, the enemy had opened fire from the tree lines. The Marines had been sent behind enemy lines to locate the Viet cong artillery positions so that a counter attack could be launched. The young marines had been pawns in the deadly chess game of war. Their commander had known that the Viet cong would be waiting to slaughter them. The order was given, and American shells rained down on the Vietcong and on the Marine rescue squad alike. Unbelievably, the Marine squad completed their mission and crossed back into their own territory, carrying the dead soldiers. An American mortar shell exploded in their midst. Les had been killed instantly. His buddy cried as he told Jimmy the story, and Jimmy had cried as he told Chris. Les's buddy had been spared simply because the dead soldier that he carried slung over his shoulder had taken the brunt of the hot shrapnel raining down around them like death-hail. He had shrapnel wounds in his arms and legs, wounds that kept him in a military hospital for two months of painful rehabilitation, but he felt lucky to be alive. Chris had never heard the term 'friendly fire' before; being killed by the men who were on your side didn't sound too friendly to him. As he played the story over in his head, he wondered why he had gotten himself into this situation.

Brian moaned loudly in his sleep, startling Chris out of his waking nightmare. He stood over his motionless friend and yelled one last time

"Hey, Brian! I'm leaving now!" Brian didn't move. Chris shook his head and tucked the joint that Brian had rolled into his pack of Marlboros. A bulldozer could knock down the motel and not wake Brian.

Chapter 21

The tavern was crowded now. Nearly every barstool and table was occupied. Chris found an empty stool at the bar between two middle-aged men and a young man about his age. Ann popped out of the back room carrying a tray of clean glasses. She scanned the bar to see who needed a refill, and her eyes lit up when she spotted Chris. She filled a mug at the beer tap and placed it on a napkin on the bar in front of him.

"You made it back, I'm surprised," she said with a smile.

"I said I would be," he replied. "I lost my other half. I should have never let him drink those shots. His brain thinks that he's a big drinker, but his stomach knows better."

Ann took the 5 dollar bill that Chris had set on the bar and returned with his change.

"Is he okay?" She asked, genuine concern clouding her features. "Tequila has a strange effect on some people. What if he starts throwing up or something?"

Chris dismissed her fears. "He'll be all right. He's sleeping like a baby. He's going to feel like hell in the morning though."

He drank his beer while Ann waited on a few new customers. She returned with a fresh beer and wiped the bar in front of him with a rag.

"I have some bad news," she said. "The girl who is supposed to relieve me isn't going to be in till ten o'clock. She's having car trouble or some bullshit. I was hoping that you and Brian, well just you now.....” her voice trailed off. “Well, anyway, if you want to, you can stick around until ten, and then we’ll shoot that game of pool.” She didn’t sound too hopeful.

Chris took the pack of cigarettes from his shirt and removed one, careful not to pull out the joint. He only smoked when he drank beer. Somehow the two tastes just went together. It was a quarter to 8, over two hours to wait until Ann’s relief arrived. Chris was beginning to feel stranded.

“Yeah,” he said finally. “I guess I could hang around for a while.”

He wondered what the hell else he could do. He sat, feeling miserable, and watched as Ann walked up and down the length of the bar, refilling beer mugs and pouring shots. From time to time, she would replenish a tray brought to her by a harried looking young Mexican waitress who was waiting on the tables and booths.

The conversation that buzzed around Chris was all in Spanish. He felt like an American island. It was impossible to break into a conversation when you didn’t understand a word that was being said. He didn’t think he could sit here until ten o’clock watching Ann as pretty as she might be. Going off on his own didn’t seem too appealing either. He had no clue where to go to find a decent and reasonably safe club.

Chris had just about decided to go back to the motel and see if maybe he could rouse Brian out of his stupor and maybe salvage the evening when he felt a nudge on his right shoulder. He turned to face the young Mexican man sitting to his right. He was surprised when the young man spoke to him in a soft Texas drawl.

“Excuse me, could I borrow one of your smokes? I’m too lazy to get up and buy a pack from the machine,” he grinned.

Chris sized the young man up. He seemed to be in his early twenties. He had a round face framed by jet black hair and at second glance, looked to be more Indian than Hispanic. Forgetting the joint, Chris pushed the cigarette pack toward the young stranger.

“Sure, help yourself. I hope you like Marlboros.”

The young man picked the pack up and shook out a cigarette, rolling the joint onto the bar as well. Stunned, Chris shot his arm out like a coiled rattlesnake striking and snatched the joint off of the bar and out of sight. The young man laughed easily as he lit his cigarette.

"Don't sweat it, man," he said, blowing out a puff of smoke. "Nobody in this place cares about a little weed."

Ann stopped in front of them as Chris slid the joint back into the pack of Marlboros.

"How you guys doing? Need another beer?"

Both mugs were more than half full, so both men shook their heads.

"Hey, I should introduce you two. Tory, this is Chris . . . I'm sorry I guess I didn't catch your last name."

Chris held out his hand. "Chris Logue," he said as the young man shook his hand firmly.

"My name is Salvatore Amairro Zingale," the young man replied. "But only my family calls me Salvatore. Everyone else calls me Tory."

Ann moved off to the other end of the bar to wait on some new arrivals. Chris started to speak but was interrupted by a loud growl coming from his own stomach. He and Tory laughed, and Chris told Tory that he had been about to ask if there was a decent place to eat nearby. Tory thought for a moment. When he had first come to Mexico about six months earlier, his aunt had cooked meals that would burn a hole in his stomach. He wondered what Chris would think of the hot peppers that authentic Mexican food usually contained. It might be kind of funny to see smoke coming out of his ears, but Chris seemed like a nice guy, and Tory didn't think that playing such a crummy trick on him would cement a new friendship. For some strange reason, Tory felt a kinship with the stranger sitting next to him at the bar. It was like he had known him for years, or at least like he should know him.

"There's a taco stand a few blocks from here," he said finally. "The tacos are pretty tasty and only about 10 cents each."

Chris had almost finished his beer. He swallowed the remainder and stood up. He leaned over and whispered in Tory's ear.

"I'm going to get some of those tacos. Do you want to burn that joint with me?"

Tory jumped off of the bar stool as though it had suddenly caught fire. He gulped the rest of his beer and wiped the foam from his lips with the back of his hand.

"I'm all yours, Gringo," he answered with a grin.

Chris waved to Ann. He fully intended to come back for that game of eight-ball and whatever came next and wanted to be sure she knew that. When he told her that he and Tory were just going out for a bite, her face fell. Not being experienced with older women, Chris didn't understand that the look on her face spoke of too many broken promises. She recovered her poise quickly though, and told him with a smile that she would be there when he got back. She knew that he wouldn't be coming back.

The two young men walked out of the bar and into the waning sunlight. More people were out and about more than before. Tory suggested that they go sit in his van to smoke the joint. The van was parked in the back lot, and he doubted that anyone would bother them there.

"So what brings you down this way?" he asked as they passed the joint back and forth. "Did you come to visit Ann?"

After holding the pungent smoke in his lungs for a minute longer, Chris released his breath with a small cough. He cleared his throat before answering.

"No, I came down with my buddy, Brian. He drank some tequila and a few beers this afternoon and an hour later he was gone. Now he's passed out at back at the motel."

Without being asked, Chris found himself telling Tory about Brian's trouble with the law and his own impulsive enlistment in the Army. The combined effects of the beer and marijuana had loosened his tongue considerably.

Chris felt an enormous sense of release as he confided his fear of having to kill or be killed in a far off country. Tory listened sympathetically, amazed that the young man he was sharing a joint with had been willing to risk his life to keep a friendship together. Tory wondered if Chris was the most generous person he had ever met, or if he was just plain shit out of his mind.

"Damn," he whistled under his breath when Chris had finished his story. "That's some heavy stuff, dude." Chris was inclined to agree. They sat in silence for a while. Tory stared out of the windshield at two men who had left the bar and were getting into an old pickup truck. The joint had gone out, but he could still smell the sweet aroma of the pot hanging in the stuffy air inside the van. Tory hadn't really talked openly about his own experience with the draft. To tell the truth, he had been ashamed of what he was, but somehow, the stranger sitting next to him seemed like the right person to open up to.

"I'm from El Paso," he said softly, startling Chris out of his marijuana haze.

"I came down here six or seven months ago to live with my aunt and uncle," Tory continued. "I guess I'm what you would call a draft dodger." He glanced at Chris to gauge his reaction, thinking that his companion would be disgusted, but Chris appeared to be unfazed by his confession.

"When were you supposed to go in?" Was all he said. "Right before Thanksgiving," Tory replied. "My parents arranged for me to move in with my mom's sister down here. I haven't seen my family or friends since. Sometimes I wonder if I did the right thing. I think about what my parents went through to become U.S. citizens so that they could raise their kids in America, and then when the time comes, I don't even want to give anything back."

He fell silent, drumming his fingers idly on the steering wheel. He had felt a catch just beginning to form in his throat, and there was nothing worse than a goddamn crying drunk. A chicken shit crying drunk, no less. Tory had told his family that he couldn't fight a war that he did not believe in, but he had kept his night-mares to himself. Every night he would watch the news, and the images of dead and wounded soldiers being carried on stretchers and the sight of helicopters spreading napalm scared him shitless. He would sleep fitfully and as often as not woke up screaming. Tory did not want to go to war because he did not want to die, it was as simple as that, and he was damned if he would share that with anyone.

The silence in the van had gone on long enough to become uncomfortable. Chris understood how Tory felt without being told. The truth was, he was scared shitless himself. He looked down at the half-smoked joint that was still between his fingers. Leaning toward Tory, he held out the roach. His head felt a little cloudy.

"Here," he said, his voice sounding far-off in his ears. "Why don't you keep the rest of this for later? I really don't smoke much, so a little goes a long way with me. If I smoke anymore, I'll fall asleep."

As Chris leaned over to hand over the roach, the arrowhead necklace caught Tory's eye. The hair on his arms stood up, giving Tory's skin a peculiar crawling sensation. His eyes widened in surprise, and he suddenly felt stone cold sober. In the dying sunlight that streamed in through the van windows, the little veins in the stone seemed to be moving, undulating slowly like a nest of snakes. The crawling sensation in his skin increased and Tory shuddered. He closed his eyes until the feeling passed, and when he opened them, the veins in the arrowhead were still. *Trick of the light*, he thought. *Or too much good weed.*

Trying to appear casual, he took the joint from Chris and tucked it in his shirt pocket.

"Thanks, man," was all he said.

Chris was staring at him quizzically, but Tory didn't tell him what he had seen. He knew now why he had felt a connection to Chris. He didn't know how Chris had come by the arrowhead, but Tory's gut told him that it was a Kickapoo relic, and an important one, at that. It didn't matter how Chris had come by the carved flint it was a part of his spirit now, and instinct told Tory that Chris had been meant to have it. He looked at Chris's open, apple-pie

American face and knew that Chris had no idea what the necklace really signified.

Maybe Tory could open up his new friend's mind a bit. Maybe that was why fate had brought them together in a seedy bar in northern Mexico. All thoughts of a war in a far-off place had vanished. This was way more important, and might bring Chris back from Vietnam alive.

"Let's go for a ride in the desert," Tory said as he started the van's engine. "The sunset is unbelievable out there, and I have someone I'd like you to meet."

Chris didn't object as Tory pulled the van out of the parking lot and headed south.

Chapter 22

Tory had been right about the desert sunset. The sky was streaked with brilliant reds and oranges on the horizon followed by the deepening blue shades of night. Chris had a ringside seat with the passenger window on the western side of the van. The sun was disappearing over the scrub hills, and the desert was coming alive as the animals of the night began to stir. Chris decided that being a little stoned didn't detract from the light show.

Chris was a little surprised, but not alarmed when Tory pulled over to the side of the freeway. In fact, Chris wasn't in the least bit nervous to be traveling in the middle of nowhere with a total stranger, in a foreign country, no less. He supposed that it was because all of the above would be his way of life in a few short weeks or months. At least no one was shooting at him here. He also had a nagging sensation that there was some tenuous connection between himself and Tory. He guessed that sometimes you just felt an instant rapport with some people, like you had known them all of your life, but this time the feeling was especially strong. Maybe being a little stoned didn't hurt there either. Tory turned the engine off, and without preamble asked Chris a startling question.

"Have you ever done any mescaline, Chris?"

Chris shook his head. He had heard of it and had known a few kids in school who had used it, but he had never done anything but smoke a little pot, and not much at that. He responded with a question of his own.

"It's like LSD or some thing, isn't it?"

Tory snorted in disgust. "No, man, that shit is man-made and poisons the mind and spirit. In my opinion, most people use it for worthless reasons. Mescaline comes from a cactus that grows wild in the desert. It's hallucinogenic, a little like LSD, I guess, but it's not a man-made chemical. The Indians around here have been using it in their tribal ceremonies for centuries. I have a little Kickapoo blood in my veins myself. That's one of the reasons that I brought you out here. There's an old Medicine Man just south of here who is a distant relative of mine. He must be a hundred years old. My grandfather told me that the shaman was an old man when my grandfather was a child. My grandfather knows a lot of Indians from the Kickapoo tribe, and he says that they still use mescaline. He's seen some weird shit happen at their rituals."

Chris barked out a laugh. "They're taking hallucinogens, man. I'd be surprised if he didn't see some strange shit."

Tory looked wounded. "I'm telling you, Chris, this stuff just opens up your mind."

He pulled a bag out of his jeans pocket. He extracted a small square of clear of plastic with some reddish brown powder sealed inside and handed it to Chris.

"I go out to the desert once in a while and get this stuff myself," Tory told him. "I process it and package it at home and sell a little of it to the touristas in Piedras Negras. I seal the powder between two pieces of tape. Just chew the tape between your front teeth. Don't worry, I make the doses small so you won't freak out."

Chris shook his head and laughed, but the laugh didn't have a pleasant ring to it.

"Man, you brought me all the way out here just so you could sell me this?" He handed the little piece of tape back.

Again Tory looked wounded.

"No, it's yours man," he said, pushing the mescaline away. "I just thought it would be cool to have your mind a little more open when you meet Matachias. He's the Medicine Man I was telling you about. He lives a few miles south of here." Chris's mouth went dry at the mention of the old shaman's name. His hand, which still held the little square of tape, had begun to shake, and he stared at it, dumbstruck. He knew that name. Chris didn't know how, but he did. *The dreams,* realizing with sudden clarity. *I've heard that name in my wolf dreams.*

With no more hesitation, Chris popped the mescaline in his mouth and chewed. The drug tasted bitter, or maybe it was the glue on the tape. When the plastic had turned to a sticky pulp, Chris swallowed.

"Tory, take me to meet the Medicine Man," he said, his voice betraying his excitement. Laughing, Tory almost spit out his own square of mescaline. "Dude, slow down," he chortled. "What's your hurry all of a sudden?"

Chris didn't know how much he wanted to confide to Tory. This shit was really weird. *What the fuck,* he thought. *Tory was the one telling me about the Indian ceremonies.* Chris pulled the arrowhead necklace from around his neck and handed it to his companion. Hesitantly at first, but encouraged by the look of interest on Tory's face, Chris told him about finding the arrowhead at Eagle Pass Park and about the recurrent dreams ever since. He was convinced that the two were connected and hoped that the Shaman could tell him something about the stone.

Tory handed the necklace to Chris in silence. He found the story fascinating and believed every word. Hadn't he seen the veins in the arrowhead squirm? Didn't the stone feel unnaturally warm in his hand, making his flesh crawl just a bit? He had been glad to get it out of his hand.

"Yeah, sure," he answered when the silence had gone on too long. "Maybe Matachias can tell you something about the arrowhead. It was a real lucky find."

The last part didn't sound too convincing, mostly because Tory didn't really mean it. If there was luck connected to the stone, Tory would have bet that it was bad. He drove south for a few miles. A small shabby village appeared up ahead as if it had sprung from the cactus and scrub pines. Tory stopped the van in front of a small shack that stood alone on the outskirts of the village. The shack sat back from the road surrounded by weeds and rocks. It had an air of abandonment that was mitigated only slightly by the feeble light that shone in one window.

Now that they were here neither Chris or Tory seemed to anxious to get out of the van. Tory finally broke the nervous silence. "I'm sure he's in there. He's been living there forever. My grandfather told me that the old man can't die until the spirit of his murdered father returns to him. When Matachias was a baby, his father sent him and his mother to Mexico to hide before their village was attacked. The story goes that Matachias's father vowed to search for his family until they were reunited, and that he still searches for them out in the desert."

Chris shivered in spite of the dry desert heat as a finger of fear tickled his spine. *He's just telling me a ghost story, a legend,* he thought, but his gut told him that the story was true.

They walked up the dirt path to the wooden porch. There was a sign on the front door written in Spanish.

"It says to go to the back door," Tory said, heading around to the side of the small dwelling. "I think he has a little shop set up back there."

Chris tried to get a closer look at the building as they maneuvered around rocks and weeds. The gray wood was old and weathered from exposure to the elements. It was obvious that it hadn't seen a paintbrush in a good many years. As they rounded the back of the house, they came to a screened porch with a wooden door hanging slightly askew. The upper hinge had pulled away from the frame, and the rusted screws still dangled in their holes.

Chapter 23

The old man sat on folded woven blankets that padded his rocking chair. A long awaited evening breeze wafted through the brittle screen as the old man's head nodded with the first stages of sleep. His hair, long ago turned gray, hung in a limp ponytail between his thin shoulders and the wooden rungs of the rocker. His tan Chino shirt was wet with perspiration, and the two smooth leather pouches that hung from his belt had fallen to his side and were wedged between his hip and the side of his chair. His ancient face was deeply wrinkled and as weathered as the wood on the sides of his shack. The knobbed knuckles of the hands that rested in his lap were swollen with arthritis. His head lolled to the side as his chest rose and fell with the steady breath of sleep.

His deep sleep had brought with it a dream that took the old man back to his childhood. The interior of the wigwam was hot and airless. His mother sat next to him on a brightly woven blanket. Her face was young and beautiful and content as this was still in the time before his father's death. The old man smiled as the dream brought peace to his weary spirit.

"It's time to wake up, Matachias. Your father is coming and he will need you. Strangers are about to arrive, and the ties to this life will soon be cut. We will all be together soon, and all that is splendor to the spirit will be yours."

The old man awakened slowly, reluctant to let go the feeling of peace and well-being he was experiencing in his dream.

As the cloud of sleep lifted, the old man saw the form of a tall man standing in the darkness. Matachias was not startled only curious as he had seen many spirits in his long life. The tall form moved toward him, and the old man was overjoyed to see that it was his father, Hupa. With a smile the vision held out his hand. The old man stood up and took the hand that had been offered. It felt warm and dry and familiar as though he had touched it just hours before, not the better part of a century. The two men embraced, and tears began to fall from Matachias's eyes.

"My father," he said, his voice choked with his tears. "You have finally come for me. I have waited so long for you to arrive. Now I am old and weak."

Hupa stood back, and his smile widened that of a proud father admiring the man that his son had become.

"Looking at you now, Matachias, I still see the young boy who rode off with his mother into the dark desert sky. I have watched you grow into manhood, and I have seen all the help that you have given to your Kickapoo brothers and sisters. You have much strength and good will to carry with you into the spirit world." He took a step back and laid a hand on the old man's shoulder. His expression was one of deepest compassion. "It is not yet your time to join us, my son," Hupa said sadly, "There is still someone left for you to heal, and by helping him you will be helping many others. Once the seeds of fate are sown, people may learn to throw the hatred from their hearts and allow the love to enter. Do not fear, my son, the spirits of your forefathers will be with you until I return to you."

The tears of joy in the old man's eyes were replaced with tears of bitter disappointment.

"I am ready to go with you now, my father," he said, his voice hoarse. "This world is still infected with hate and war. One man kills another because he prays to a different God or because the color of his skin is different, just as in the time when you lived. How can one tired old man change that?"

Now both of Hupa's hands were on his son's thin shoulders. His grip was firm and his brown eyes sharp and hypnotic.

"You must understand that your time on earth is for you to learn the ways of the Great Spirit. You have done that work all of your life by healing people. Those people carried that knowledge and medicine to others, creating a chain that you started. Your work is almost complete, but there is still work to be done, and you are the chosen one."

As Hupa spoke, Matachias could feel the grip on his shoulder begin to lighten. Now he could see a shadow of the back wall of the shack through his father's translucent body. When the spirit of the Shaman spoke again, his voice was thin and hollow. Matachias had to strain to hear his father's final words.

"There are many waiting in the spirit world to welcome you when it is your time. My love is with you, my son."

The image that had been translucent began to waver like heat waves in the desert then vanished altogether. The old man sat back down in his rocker with a soft thump. The visit had been bittersweet, but he rejoiced at the thought of returning to his family.

The voices outside the cabin were muffled at first, but they became clearer as they neared the screened porch at the rear of the shack. The old man rose again and listened closely. The voices were those of two men speaking in the white man's tongue. The words meant nothing to him as he had never learned to speak much of the language.

"I thought you wanted to go get some tacos," Tory was saying as he pulled open the ancient screen door. He was looking over his shoulder at Chris, and when he turned his face toward the shack, he found himself staring directly into the eyes of the old man. Tory stepped back with a startled grunt, and Chris, not expecting his guide to stop, ran into his back, pushing him toward the old man.

"Why the hell did you......" Chris asked irritably, his words trailing off as he saw the Indian. He felt a shock of recognition that felt like electric current in his veins. This man was a much older version of the man Chris had seen so long ago at Eagle Pass Park.

Both Chris and Tory jumped as the old man smiled and boomed "WELCOME," thereby exhausting most of the English that he knew. While Tory spoke to the old man in Spanish, Chris looked around the dimly lit room. Wooden crates were stacked against one wall. The wall directly behind the medicine man was lined with shelves from the dusty floor to the ceiling. The rickety wooden shelves were crammed with glass and clay bottles of all shapes and sizes. Some of the clear glass bottles were filled with murky liquid while others overflowed with what looked like dried herbs and roots. The mescaline had a firm hold on Chris now. In his fascination with the strange room, he had tuned out the conversation between Tory and the old man without even realizing it. Chris heard his name being called, startled and confused, Chris was surprised to see that the old man was surrounded by an undulating yellow aura.

"He wants to see the necklace, Chris," Tory repeated impatiently.

Mechanically, Chris pulled the arrowhead from under his shirt and wrestled the leather thong over his head. The old man gasped when he saw the stone, and the gnarled hand that reached for the necklace was shaking. He began to mumble in a weird singsong that made the hair on the back of Chris's neck stand up.

"What is he saying?" Chris whispered the question.

"Beats the hell out of me," Tory whispered back. "I don't know what language that is, but it sure ain't Spanish."

Chris hated the feeling that his flesh was going to crawl right off of his body. He didn't know how much of the unpleasant sensation came from the mescaline and how much was from the old man's chanting, but he thought he might lose control at any time. He felt like bolting out the door and returning to the city, forgetting about this whole experience. He started to plead with Tory to get him out of here, but was stopped short when Matachias turned to face him. The old man had taken on a look of humble submission and no longer seemed the least bit threatening. He began to speak to Tory again and in Spanish this time, never taking his dark eyes from Chris. Tory nodded at the old man and began to translate slowly.

"He says that the arrowhead belonged to his tribe for hundreds of years, and he needs to get it back before he goes to the spirit world." Tory hesitated for a moment before continuing with a nervous laugh. "Here is where it gets kind of spooky. He says that the spirit of his father was here just before we got here and told him that he had to stay to help you with what is ailing you. He says that you should know what that means."

Chris considered for a moment. His health was excellent, so that couldn't be it.

"Maybe he means that something is upsetting me," he answered finally. "I can't believe I joined the army so spur of the moment. I keep thinking I'm gonna get killed or have to kill someone else. That goes against my beliefs. I'm not even sure I believe in the war. If he can get me out of that, the arrowhead is all his."

Tory recognized the sarcasm in his new friend's tone, but repeated his reply to the old man verbatim. Matachias kept his steady gaze on Chris as he spoke again through Tory.

"He says that he can do anything that you desire because the Great Spirit has been with you since you found the arrowhead. He can channel the power of the arrowhead and give you anything you want." Tory shook his head, "man, this is getting too deep for me."

A wave of clarity washed over Chris and seemed to take the effects of the mescaline with it. He suddenly saw the humor in the situation and began to giggle. If he didn't control himself, he would soon be laughing hysterically. Maybe the mescaline wasn't entirely gone.

"Man, I don't want to be rude," he finally managed to say, choking off his laughter. "But this is fucking nuts. If you expect me to believe this mystic mumbo-jumbo crap then you are both, as they say, loco. Get my necklace back and let's get the hell out of here."

The old man looked at Tory quizzically, waiting for a translation and an explanation for the young gringo's unexpected reaction to his offer. Tory's voice took on a soothing tone as he tried to talk some sense into Chris.

"Take it easy, my friend. Matachias is not your enemy, he's trying to help you the only way he knows how. Maybe what he says is true, and besides, what have you got to lose?"

He didn't add that he had seen some amazing shit since he had come to Mexico. He also didn't add that he liked Chris and didn't particularly want to see him come home from 'Nam in a box. If the old man could prevent that, why not?

Chris took a deep breath as he thought it over. The old man was now staring at him expectantly, and he still gave Chris the heebie jeebies, but what the hell. No use being a poor sport about it. He let out his deep breath slowly as he replied. He tried to keep the sarcasm out of his voice and almost succeeded.

"Okay, Tory, I'll play along. Tell him that I don't want my friend, Brian, and me to go to Vietnam. Tell him that right now I want to go back four days before I joined the army. Better yet, how about if he transfers me to the future? Ten years, twenty, no wait, how about thirty years? Yeah." Chris was beginning to enjoy the game of make-believe. "Yeah, thirty years. The war will no doubt be long gone by then, and I'd like to see the end of the twentieth century. Can you imagine the New Years Eve parties in 1999? Sure beats the hell out of sleeping in a rice paddy in 'Nam." His voice was beginning to rise with his hysteria, and Tory and Matachias regarded the yelling gringo with growing alarm. Chris was amused to note that they now seemed to be more afraid than he was.

He sighed, and when he continued his voice was quiet and resigned as though the game was over, and he had already lost. "Just tell him to beam me out of here like on *Star Trek* to where my life can be normal again."

Tory hesitated before translating this odd request, thinking that Chris would stop him, but Chris was silent. He was thinking of Ann back at the bar and wished that he had never left. He had no idea how much time had gone by since he told her he would be back soon, but he doubted that she would still be there if he returned now.

The old man didn't bat an eyelash as he listened to Tory's translation. When Tory had finished, he turned to Chris and shrugged his bony shoulders ever so slightly and nodded as though the young man had requested nothing more complicated than a drink of water or directions to the nearest filling station. Moving stiffly as if in pain, Matachias pulled an old card table to the front of his rocking chair and sat down. He reached down to his waist and gently removed one of the worn leather bags from his belt. After placing the bag on the table, he carefully untied the thong and removed an ancient looking bone and laid it reverently on the cracked vinyl tabletop. The bone was the jaw of a great wolf, and Matachias aimed to summon the power of the wolf to help him fulfill the young gringo's wish. The moment that he had touched the arrowhead he had known that the wolf's power was captured in the stone. He would now set that awesome power free. He sat back in the rocker and closed his eyes, beginning to chant softly.

As Chris watched the old man, he felt the old familiar sensation of the flesh-crawling, this time accompanied by nausea. He noted that Tory was watching the old man's ceremony with rapt interest, but showed no sign of fear. *Figures,* Chris thought miserably. *"He's a lot more used to peyote than I am, and the old geezer isn't casting some cockamamie spell on me. I should have stayed with Brian in the motel."* Mexican TV sounded pretty good to him right now.

Matachias was leaning forward now, his lips moving faster as he mumbled the ancient chants. He began to rub the arrowhead and the jawbone together gently. After a few moments, he placed the jawbone on the table and rubbed the arrowhead with both thumbs as if polishing the smooth stone. Chris and Tory stared at the hypnotic rhythm of the old man's hands. They were both startled when the muttering ceased abruptly. They looked up at the weathered face. Matachias' eyes began to roll from side to side under his closed eyelids, and his head lolled weakly against the back of the rocker. With a raspy, shuddering sigh, the old man collapsed into the rocking chair as if he had been suddenly deflated. A thin line of spittle rolled slowly from the corner of his slightly parted lips. The silence in the shack was deafening. Tory jumped when Chris croaked. "Holy shit, is he dead?"

Tory leaned over Matachias in the dim light of the shack and looked for signs of life. He shook his head, and when he answered he sounded relieved.

"No, I can see his chest moving. I think he's in a trance or something." He backed away from the old man's chair. "Man, I ain't ever seen anything like this before. Maybe you're right Chris. Maybe we should just get out of here."

Chris thought that leaving sounded like a fine idea, but they couldn't just leave the old man like this. He looked like he was one step away from the grim reaper. He took a few steps closer to Matachias, thinking of trying to shake him awake, then stopped. He stared at the ancient piece of bone lying on the table. It was several inches long and yellowed with age, but the two teeth still embedded in the bone gleamed white. He reached out gingerly and picked up the bone, hesitating as though it still had the power to bite. As his hand closed around the jawbone, Chris was blinded by a sudden flash of blue light, and he was overcome by a feeling of euphoria. He suddenly felt weightless as if suspended in a wonderful dream. He looked down at his hands, but they had disappeared, along with the rest of his body. All that was visible was the swirling blue light that surrounded him.

Dark shadowy images appeared out of the fading blue light. Chris shook his head and closed his eyes, and when he opened them again the images were becoming more distinct. He was standing in a patch of trees. The bed of pine needles was soft beneath his feet, and the sweet aroma of pine was strong in the air around him. Turning to his left, Chris saw a lake. *Lake Kahooga.* On the opposite shore, two men sat, talking. A large gray dog lay sleeping between them. The men were Indians, and Chris felt a shock of recognition; one of the men was the old Kickapoo medicine man, now magically young and darkly handsome. He watched with amazement as the men talked and laughed together. There was something strangely familiar about the lake shore. He knew that he had been here before, but when? With in moments it came to him. This was the setting of the dreams that he had been having ever since he found the arrowhead. The bank of the lake where the two men sat was the battleground where he had fought the wolf so many times. The circle of ash that had once been a roaring fire brought back vivid images of dancing around the flames wearing the bleeding pelt of the defeated beast. The dog raised his head and turned toward Chris, and he saw that it was not a dog at all but a wolf, the one that he had killed so many times in his dreams. As he stared at the wolf, the image faded then vanished altogether. The two men had stopped talking and were staring straight at Chris, their bodies eerily motionless. Chris was caught off guard when he heard the unmistakable sound of a branch snapping in the woods behind him. He wheeled around in time to see the huge gray wolf lunging toward him. He screamed and threw his body backward to avoid the snarling animal.

Chapter 24

The wooden crates tumbled down around Chris as his body slammed into them. Shocked and alarmed, Tory ran to Chris and pulled him from the jumble of splintered wood and dried herbs that had spilled from the broken boxes. The pungent smell of the herbs permeated the stale air in the cabin and made Tory's head ache.

"Chris, are you all right? Can you hear me?"

Chris could hear Tory's voice, but it sounded hollow and far-off. As Tory's face gradually swam into focus Chris tried to stand, wincing and gingerly touching his forehead. The beginnings of a purple goose egg were already beginning to form where his head had hit the crates. He stumbled a little and then righted himself with Tory's help.

"Man, what happened to you? Did you freak out or something?"

Chris shook his head, bringing a new stab of pain to his forehead. His eyes came to rest on Matachias. The old medicine man was still unconscious, but he was beginning to stir now, mumbling and moaning. Chris still wasn't sure what the hell had happened here, but he was damn sure that he did not want to be in this scurvy old shack when the Indian woke up. He lurched forward, his legs still unsteady, toward the old man's rocker. Careful not to touch him, Chris snatched the arrowhead that was clutched in the old man's swollen fingers. Pulling the necklace over his head, he turned

and brushed past his astounded friend, heading for the screen door
at the back of the porch.

"Hey, man, where ya' goin'? "Tory called after him.

Without answering, Chris ran unsteadily out into the desert
night, the screen door slamming behind him with a resounding
whap. He started to follow, but was stopped by the sound of the old
man's voice.

"No need to go after him. He will gather his thoughts as he
waits for you."

The medicine man looked exhausted, but otherwise okay, much
to Tory's relief. Killing an old man would not be a perfect way to
end the evening even if he was older than dirt. Matachias was sitting up straight now, and some of the color that had drained from
his grizzled face was beginning to seep back.

"Don't you want me to get the arrowhead back?" Tory asked.
"He did promise to give it to you."

He was relieved again when Matachias smiled and shook his
head. Chris had looked more than slightly crazy when he had run
from the shack, and Tory had a sneaking suspicion that getting the
arrowhead back might not be all that easy.

"Do you want me to stay with you for awhile then? You don't
look so good."

Again, the old man shook his head slowly. "No need. Go to
your friend now. The ceremony is over, and his wish will be granted
when it is time. He still needs the arrowhead for a time, but he will
be back. He will be back."

Speaking seemed to have worn the old man out and he rested
his head on the back of the rocker. Tory took a tentative step toward him but the old man waved him away. "Go now, son," he said
and closed his eyes.

The medicine man had been right about Chris waiting. Tory
found him sitting in the passenger seat of the van. He grinned sheepishly in the dim dashlight and apologized to Tory for being such an
asshole. Tory laughed off the apology.

"Don't sweat it, man. You gringos just can't handle your peyote."

They rode back to town in silence. Chris was still too shaken by his hallucination to want to talk about it. The whole thing seemed to fucking real. He didn't really believe that the old geezer had put some kind of spell on him, but he couldn't shake the feeling that something truly powerful had happened back in the cabin. The old man had seemed so damn familiar, and the fact that he had genuinely seemed to recognize the arrowhead flat out gave Chris the willies. He was pretty sure that it didn't have anything to do with the dope either. At least not much. He wished to hell that he had been sober when he met Matachias, but nothing in the world could ever induce him to go see the old man again.

Chapter 25

It was nearly midnight by the time Tory pulled into the parking lot of the Hacienda Motel. Opening the van door, Chris turned to face Tory, his face deadly serious.

He held out his right hand for Tory to shake and said, "Good to meet you man." As he turned to get out of the van, he looked back over his shoulder and added, without so much as a smile, "And thanks for a lovely evening." After a beat, Tory cracked up and was still laughing as he pulled away from the curb.

Chris let himself into the motel room as quietly as he could so that he wouldn't wake Brian. He doubted that Brian was anywhere near ready to wake up, but Chris was still relieved to see his friend sleeping peacefully. No way did he want to recap the evening. It would definitely lose something in the translation. His heart was still hammering in his chest, and he was bathed in sweat in spite of the air conditioning. He crept into the bathroom and splashed cold water on his face before lying down on the empty twin bed still in his T-shirt and jeans. He lay on his back in the cool darkness, trying to erase the image of the snarling gray beast lunging at him from the trees. Each time he closed his eyes, the haunting faces of the Indian men sitting by the lake appeared, uninvited, followed by the unmistakable sound of branches snapping behind him. The inevitable snapping that announced the leaping wolf who would surely kill him one of these nights. The nightmare played over and over in his head like the last song you hear on the radio before going to bed. The dream had become so familiar over the years since he had found the arrowhead that it hardly scared him anymore, but this had been different. More reality than nightmare, and he was sure as shit that the old man had done this to him somehow. Chris had gone to the medicine man's cabin to find out something about the arrowhead, but this had not been what he had in mind. True, the old man had answered his question about the origin of the arrowhead, and had pretty much confirmed Chris's belief that there was something supernatural about the ancient stone, but Chris didn't feel the least bit satisfied with the answers that he had gotten.

What the hell had the old man meant when he said that the arrowhead would help him to grant Chris's greatest wish? Tripping out and hallucinating about being attacked by the wolf of his nightmares had definitely not been his greatest wish. The medicine man hadn't even bothered to ask Chris what his wish was, but on the ride back to town, Tory had assured him that his wish had been granted at least according to Matachias. What the hell had the old man done to him? Turning his experience in the cabin over and over in his mind, Chris came to the rational conclusion that the old man was nothing more than a con artist, like a gypsy fortune teller at a traveling carnival. He had taken advantage of Chris's drugged state to plant a suggestion in his head and Chris' imagination had done the rest, conjuring up his worst nightmare, literally.

Maybe Matachias and Tory had cooked the scheme up together, Tory feeding him drugs and then taking him to the old man's shack to be conned out of his vacation money. What an asshole he had been! He had been taken in like the stupid, unsuspecting tourista that he was. He was lucky that he hadn't passed out from the mescaline that he had bolted from the cabin when he had. He could have lost all of his money, or worse. There were a million places in the desert to bury a stupid tourist.

Chris knew with his rational mind that he had simply been the victim of a couple of seasoned con artists, but he wished that his gut was as easy to convince. He still couldn't close his eyes without conjuring up the terrifying image of the lunging wolf, Christ;

he could even feel the animal's hot, rank breath on his face and smell the sour, gamy odor of the wild beast and try as he might, Chris couldn't rationalize away the expression of genuine joy on the old man's face as he took the arrowhead from Chris with his shaky old man's hand. Sighing, Chris decided that there was still some mystery attached to the arrowhead like barnacles on a ship, and if he didn't put the whole thing out of his mind, all he would get for his mental effort was a long, sleepless night.

Chris was seized with a sudden panic that seemed to leap at him from the darkness like the wolf, followed by an overwhelming urge to leap out of bed, throw his stuff into his bag [or not], and drive as far away from Piedras Negras and Matachias as he could. Of course, he couldn't very well leave Brian here, and Brian didn't seem to be anywhere near waking up. As if in response to an unspoken question Brian rolled over, snorting and mumbling. He came to rest on his back and began to snore loudly.

Chris fought the urge to laugh. *Yeah, this sure is the perfect end to the perfect evening,* he thought with wry amusement. He envied his friend and couldn't help wishing that he had gotten pig drunk while they had shot pool and ended up like Brian, sleeping it off without a care in the world.

Chris didn't think that Brian would care if they left Mexico in the morning, but he wouldn't want to go back to Devine so soon. The longer Brian could make himself scarce, the healthier he would remain. Come to think of it, Chris didn't exactly relish the thought of going home to face his parent's grief and the guilt that it was sure to produce. He suddenly felt inspired. Maybe they ought to spend the rest of their little vacation kicking back and relaxing. There was good fishing at Eagle Pass Park, and it was on the way back to Devine. Chris still had enough money left to pick up the supplies that they needed to fish and camp for a couple of nights, and enough left over to buy food and beer. There must be some place between here and the park where they could pick up provisions. It would be kind of cool to spend their last days as free men at a place they had enjoyed so long ago. The irony of camping at the same park where the arrowhead had come into his life was lost on Chris for the moment.

Occupying his mind with listing the things they would need to buy for a fishing trip chased his demons away and finally, Chris slept, for a change he didn't dream.

Chapter 26

Chris was awake shortly after dawn and immediately hopped into a hot shower to clear the cobwebs. He had seen a coffee pot in the motel office, and after pulling on cut-offs and a T-shirt, he stepped out into the cool morning air to buy some liquid stimulant for himself and his sleeping friend. Returning to the room with two steaming paper cups, he leaned over Brian and cleared his throat loudly.

"Hey, party boy, it's time to rise and shine," he hollered into his friend's ear.

Brian moaned, then turned and opened his eyes, staring blearily up at Chris. Moaning again, he turned onto his back and covered his eyes.

"Holy crap, my head hurts," he whined. "I can't believe I got that fucked up so fast. What time is it?" He asked, rubbing his throbbing temples.

Chris was combing his hair in the dresser mirror.

"It's almost eight o'clock," he replied, pulling his hair into a ponytail. "There's a cup of coffee for you on the night stand, so drink up. We've got stuff to do today."

Brian sipped the hot, bitter coffee gratefully.

"What did you do all night while I was sleeping?" He asked between sips.

Plunking down on the empty bed to strap on his leather sandals, Chris debated how much to tell Brian about the night before.

He really didn't feel like getting into a long, involved story this early in the morning. In truth, he still didn't know how he felt about what had happened. In the end, he responded with a lie, trying to keep his voice casual.

"Oh, I just went back to the bar and had a couple of beers, then I came back and went to bed early."

Brian bought the lie, no reason that he shouldn't, really.

"Did you and the barmaid ever hook up?" He asked.

"No, she had to work late, and I didn't feel like hanging around all night." That part was true, anyway. Chris was growing anxious to leave, but he was careful not to let it show. He didn't want Brian to start asking questions.

"Listen, I was thinking that maybe we should get out of here. I was thinking that maybe we should go camping, you know, like at Eagle Pass Park. We could fish, you know, and swim. It would be fun." Chris realized that he was beginning to sound lame.

Brian was looking at him quizzically.

"I'm just not in the mood to drink anymore, and it looks like that's all there is to do around here. Besides, you look like you could use a break from the tequila, yourself," Chris added.

Brian lay back and closed his eyes while he considered the prospects. Camping didn't sound all that good, but he had a helluva hangover and wasn't really in the mood to party anymore. The thought of another shot of tequila made him gag. Going back to Devine wasn't an option either. He didn't feel like spending the next few days looking over his shoulder. Maybe a little fishing would do him good.

"Sounds good to me," he said, getting out of bed carefully so as not to jar his aching head. "As long as we don't go back home. That's the last place I want to be. You know Tommy and Jeff have to be wondering where I am," he added, laughing bitterly. He went into the bathroom and stood over the commode, swaying a little as he emptied his taut bladder.

Chris had warmed to the idea of a camping trip and was prattling on about what they would need to buy when Brian came back
into the room, pulling his grimy T-shirt over his battered 'fro.

"Tell you what," Brian interrupted, "Why don't you go round
up the supplies while I take a shower. I'm still wearing yesterday's
clothes and I could use a nice, long shower. If you could pick up
some aspirin when you're out, maybe I can get rid of this hangover. I sure could use something to eat, too."

Chris felt a stab of irritation. He had figured that they would
go shopping together on their way out of town. Once again he would
be doing the work, not to mention spending his money. He wondered if Brian was ever going to grow up and take some responsibility. *Oh, well,* he thought ruefully, *maybe the army will force him
to grow up.* Brian had hurried into the shower, so asking him to
contribute was out. Chris promised himself that he would ask him
to kick in a few bucks for the provisions later. Besides, he was
starving to death. He never had gotten his tacos last night. He decided that he owed it to himself to find a decent breakfast before he
went shopping. Brian could just eat whatever Chris could find to
take on their trip. It would serve him right.

Chapter 27

The motel clerk had given Chris directions to a café that served a pretty good breakfast. Chris felt better after he had filled his gnawing stomach, and didn't mind driving around town to look for someplace to buy some camping gear. Much to his surprise, he managed to find a large general store that carried reasonably cheap sleeping bags and pup tents. They even had some fishing gear. The store was located on the main drag of town and obviously catered to the tourist trade. They carried lunch meat and Wonder bread, so at least Chris and Brian wouldn't starve even if they didn't catch any fish.

It didn't take Chris as long as he had thought it would to stock up, so his mood had lightened up a little by the time he got back to the motel. He was pleasantly surprised to find Brian dressed and ready to go. Their bags were even packed. As they put their belongings into the bed of the truck, Chris tossed a loaf of bread and a pound of bologna to Brian.

"There ya' go, breakfast!" he exclaimed with a grin. Brian grinned too, and busied himself making sandwiches to devour on the trip north.

Getting through U.S. Customs was even easier on the way north than it had been going south, much to their surprise. The Customs agent waved them through after a few perfunctory questions. Brian decided that it was the fishing gear and the Wonder bread that made them look like all-American boys. His hangover had eased up after a few aspirins and sandwiches, and he was glad to get out of Mexico. He and Chris agreed on that though for entirely different reasons. After giving it a little thought, Brian was looking forward to spending some time at Eagle Pass Park. Maybe it would bring back some memories of a better time in his life, a time before he had fucked everything up. Hanging around a campfire with his good buddy, smoking some weed and drinking a few beers might be a good way to spend his last few days as a free man. He considered going into the Army to be pretty close to going to jail, only less dangerous. If he went to prison and anyone from Tommy or Jeff's gang ended up in the same cell block, his life wouldn't be worth shit. At least he stood a chance in Southeast Asia.

Chris wasn't thinking about camping or the army either. The farther he got from Matachias, the happier he was. Even in the light of day, he was having trouble getting the old man out of his head. He could still smell the aroma of the herbs emanating from the smashed crates, and the bruise on his forehead throbbed like a toothache. Oddly, Brian hadn't asked him how he had gotten the bruise. Chris guessed that like always Brian was busy thinking about his own troubles.

The faded blue pickup kicked up clouds of dust as the tires rolled over the dirt road leading into the park. As they approached the line of trees leading into the woods, Chris and Brian began to reminisce about sitting in the back seat of Matt's old Bonneville, heading into Eagle Pass Park for the first time. The park looked exactly the same as it had four years earlier, so Chris didn't think that he would have any trouble finding their old fishing spot.

"Hey, do you remember how excited we were finding that old Indian stuff?" Brian asked. Chris laughed uncomfortably.

"Remember it, hell," he replied. "I'm still wearing my relic around my neck."

I'm still having the freaking nightmare that it brought to me four years ago, Chris thought to himself. He had never been able to bring himself to tell anyone about the dreams that he had been having since he found the arrowhead. He had started to talk to

Brian about them a few times, but always stopped short. Brian would think he was nuts, or at least would ask why Chris didn't just throw the damn thing out if it gave him bad dreams, and Chris didn't have an answer. Not a good answer, anyway. In fact, he had thrown the damn thing out.

At least a dozen nights he had awakened, hot and sweating, after the dream, and his shaking fingers had pulled the necklace over his head, had felt the stone warm from his skin, warm and dry like the flesh of a reptile. On those nights Chris had hurled the cursed thing into the trash with a shudder of revulsion and had spent the remainder of those nights tossing and turning the bedroom light on. A dozen times he had thrown out the arrowhead, and a dozen times he had sheepishly fished it back out of the wastebasket the next day. It was only a piece of stone, carved to a point. It had felt warm from his skin that was all and it would be stupid to pitch it out. Surely, it was worth something.

Brian grabbed his arm, startling Chris out of his reverie.

"There!" Brian shouted. "There's the path to the river!"

Chris turned the truck onto the rutted tire tracks that ran parallel to the river. As they bounced along the tracks, brush scraping the sides of the pickup, Brian and Chris craned their necks to the left, trying to get a glimpse of the river through the trees.

"This is kinda cool coming back here," Brian said. " I've always wanted to come back here and check out the old Indian village for more stuff."

The last thing Chris wanted was more Indian stuff, but he doubted that Brian would do much searching after a few beers.

"Do you think this is still open to the public?" He asked.

Brian shrugged. "I don't see any *NO TRESPASSING* signs. Besides, we're only going to be here a couple of nights. As long as nobody comes back here, who's gonna know?"

They came to the clearing where Matt had parked the Bonneville, and Chris turned the wheel to the left, stopping the truck by the same stand of trees. By memory, they walked over to where the embankment dropped down to the rocky river bed where they had fished after eating a picnic lunch four years earlier. The river tumbled along the rocks, glittering in the morning sun. It looked deeper than Chris remembered.

"We could pitch the tent right here," he said, pointing to the ground between two tall pines. Brian nudged the toe of his boot into the thick bed of pine needles, turning up a bed of small sharp stones. "How do you think we're going to be able to sleep here with all these rocks and roots? We're going to have to find someplace better than this."

The ground was rocky and uneven everywhere they looked. Chris was getting discouraged when Brian made a suggestion that made him cringe.

"Why don't we go find the Indian village? There might be a good spot to set up camp in the clearing."

Chris shrugged. What had happened the night before was still with him, but he had to be rational about it. He wasn't a kid anymore; it was high time he stopped being spooked by a stupid piece of rock.

"Sure," he said finally. " Why don't we go check it out before we drag everything back there. It might be too overgrown to pitch the tent."

"Or too full of shit," Brian added.

Chris led the way as they started up the shoreline. Before long, they came to the old tree that hung out over the river. The tree was still performing its balancing act, looking as though it would fall into the river any minute now.

"Here's where we cross," Chris said, pointing to the tree.

They waded into the cool water, moving slowly to keep from losing their balance on the slippery rocks as the river swirled around ankles, then knees. Reaching the riverbank on the other side, they had some trouble finding the path to the village, and had to search for a while. The field that separated them from the village was overgrown with weeds and brush. The foliage grew thicker as Chris and Brian moved away from the river. Before long, any trace of the path that they had ridden their bikes on had vanished, replaced by weeds, grass and pricker bushes. It was slow going, and they had to stop from time to time to make sure they were heading in the right direction.

To make matters worse, patches of dark clouds were moving in overhead, blotting out the bright sunshine. The clouds brought an occasional cool breeze that ruffled the tall grass and relieved the simmering afternoon heat. Stopping to get his bearings, Chris looked at the darkening sky with dismay. He turned to Brian, who was a few yards behind doing battle with a pricker bush.

"Hey, man, look at those clouds. I hope to hell it doesn't rain."

Brian stopped chopping at the weeds with his hands long enough to check out the sky. The black clouds were closing in quickly now. The cool breezes were becoming sharp gusts of wind.

"Man, where did this come from?" Brian asked. " It was sunny a few minutes ago."

"I don't know, maybe it'll pass," Chris replied doubtfully as he continued to work his way through the undergrowth.

The weeds and grass began to thin out now as they neared the spot where the clearing had been. Brush that had been chest high was now waist high, then knee level. What was left of the clearing where the Kickapoo village had been looked familiar, yet changed. It was not as littered with beer cans and broken glass as it had been four years earlier. Most of the trash was covered now by dirt and weeds. Mother Nature was slowly reclaiming her land and covering up the mess that man had left behind, sweeping it under a lush green carpet.

"Doesn't look like anybody's been back here for awhile," Chris observed. "I can't even see any traces of campfires."

As they scouted around for a good spot to set up camp, kicking up a can or broken bottle once in a while, the rain began to fall. At first just a few warm fat drops spattered on their skin then a few more. Brian looked up and was alarmed by the angry black clouds that were now directly overhead. Thunder rumbled in the distance.

"Maybe we should head back to the truck," he suggested, still looking up. "I gotta feelin'...."

He was cut off mid-sentence by a clap of thunder that sounded perilously close. Before Chris could respond, the sky opened, unleashing a torrential downpour that caught them off guard and drenched them both in a few seconds.

"Should we try to get back to the truck?" Brian yelled.

Chris looked around frantically for anything that would offer some shelter. Lightning was streaking the sky now, and he knew that being under the tall trees was as dangerous as hell.

"I say we run over to the base of the mountains," Chris screamed, fighting to be heard over the wind and rain. "There's gotta be some protection there!"

They began to run toward the hills. The wet grass was as slippery as an ice rink, and they struggled to stay on their feet for the fifty-yard dash to the rocks. Brian caught his toe on a protruding root and tumbled face first into the wet brush. Chris caught him by the back of his tee-shirt and half-dragged him the rest of the way to the hillside. The sheer face of the nearest hill shielded them from the downpour, and they stayed close to the jagged rocks until they came to a break in the hillside. Chris almost sobbed with relief at the sight of an indentation in the rock, a patch of bare earth that was sheltered by an overhanging ledge. They collapsed, panting and dripping, to the ground under the ledge. Clumps of mud and weeds clung to their skin and clothes.

Brian finally caught his breath and sat up, leaning back against the cool stone. Groaning, he hung his head between his knees.

"I feel like I'm going to puke," he said weakly.

Instinctively, Chris rolled away from his friend. "Would you mind barfing over there?" he asked testily, pointing out to the field, "we may be here for a while, and I don't feel like sitting here with a pile of puke."

Brian didn't answer, only nodded and groaned again, resting his head on his knees.

After a few minutes Chris stood and walked shakily to the edge of the rock shelter. The wind had settled down a little, but it was still pouring steadily, and thunder rumbled close by. The patch of sky that was visible through the tree limbs remained dark and angry. He wondered if there was any chance that it would let up soon enough for the ground to dry up before nightfall. He had lost track of time, but reckoned that is was early afternoon. He didn't like camping enough to sleep in the rain. *You'll be doing plenty of that in 'Nam*, an evil voice in his head reminded him. Chris sighed heavily and wondered how he had gotten into this.

Here he was, trying to enjoy his last few days of freedom, and he couldn't even return to the comfort of his own bed without endangering Brian. Chris loved Brian like a brother, but he sure could be a giant pain in the ass.

He turned to look at Brian, huddled, muddy and miserable against the rock wall. His normally pale complexion had taken on a sick greenish cast. Chris felt a wave of pity for his friend even knowing that Brian was usually the cause of his own troubles, including his current hangover. He hadn't had the cushy life that Chris had as a kid with a stay-home mom and a loving, supportive father. Chris wondered what his own childhood would have been like without his dad if Laurie had had to go to work and struggle to keep a roof over his and Jonathan's head. Carolyn had done the best she could, but Chris knew that she hadn't been able to watch over Brian as carefully as she would have liked. If the tables had been turned, Chris wondered if he would have ended up flirting with disaster the way that Brian always seemed to. *Well ,shit,* he thought ruefully. *What difference did it make anyway? We're both in the same boat now, heading off to the army in a few days.* Chris couldn't remember ever feeling so depressed. *What next? Maybe the fucking rock ledge would get hit by lightening and crush them both.*

He walked over and plunked down next to Brian.

"Man, you look awful. Didn't the aspirin help at all?"

Brian lifted his head, and Chris had to stifle a laugh. Brian's normally fluffy 'fro hung in sopping ringlets, sending muddy rivulets down his sallow cheeks.

"I gotta lie down, or I'm gonna pass out," he moaned. "I think I'll be okay if I rest for awhile..."

Chris patted his shoulder gently, "sounds like a good idea. The rain doesn't look like it is letting up anytime soon. Maybe if we take a nap, it'll be dry when we wake up."

Chris didn't really believe that, but who knew? These fierce summer storms could pass as quickly as they started.

Brian curled up on his side in the soft dirt using his bent arm as a pillow. He seemed oblivious to the muddy mess that his tee shirt and jeans had become. Chris looked down at his own clothes and realized that he didn't look much better. He doubted that he would be able to sleep, but he suddenly felt like closing his eyes for a bit. The adrenaline rush from the dash for shelter was wearing off, replaced by an aching weariness. The few hours of fitful sleep from the previous night were catching up to him. He took of his wet tee shirt and rolled it into a clammy pillow.

A gust of wind blew into the shelter, raising gooseflesh on his bare chest. Lying on his side, hugging himself for warmth, Chris just knew that he wouldn't be able to sleep. The soft rhythm of the rain became a lullaby, and he soon drifted off into a sound, dreamless sleep.

While they slept, the rain continued to fall steadily in cold gray sheets punctuated by flashes of lightning that split the sky. The water running from the mountains filled the dry creekbeds that ran to the swelling river. The clear river water was washed away and replaced by coffee colored rapids that were swift and strong.

After two hours Chris opened his eyes and sat up stiffly. He reached over and gave his still sleeping friend a shove.

"Hey, Brian, wake up."

Brian mumbled and rolled over. Chris stood and looked down at his clothes in dismay. The mud on his jeans had dried into a mess of caked dirt. He tried without success to brush some of it off but soon gave up and pulled his damp, filthy tee shirt over his head with a sigh of resignation. Retying his ponytail didn't go much better. He decided that it didn't much matter since they would soon be soaking wet again. The rain had let up, but not enough to hope for a dry night. Chris didn't have any idea how long he had slept. He felt as though he had just closed his eyes.

"Come, on Brian, wake up." This time Chris shoved a little harder, and Brian awoke, staring blearily up at Chris through bloodshot eyes.

"Wha'?" Was all he could manage to say in response.

"We gotta get outa here," Chris said with as much patience as he could muster. " I don't think the rain is going to stop. Let's head back to the truck and dry off. Maybe we could eat some sandwiches while we decide what to do next."

He was all for going home, and the hell with Tommy and Jeff. Maybe he could talk Brian into staying at his house until they left for basic training. He would be reasonably safe there. Or at least they could find a park that had cabins to rent. He wasn't about to sleep out in the rain.

Grunting, Brian managed to sit up. Leaning against the rock wall, he ran his fingers through his damp hair. He still looked pale, but his skin had lost its greenish hue.

"How long have I been asleep?" He asked groggily.

Chris shrugged. "I don't know. A few hours, I guess." He was watching the rain continue to fall steadily. "I'd say this camping trip is a wash."

Brian was up now, but not without a lot of effort. He felt like he had been hit by a bus, his muscles aching from the run through the woods and his arms scratched and bruised from his losing battle with the pricker bushes. He took a deep breath to clear his head.

"Well, I guess we might as well get going. It ain't gonna get any easier, and I could use something to eat. A beer wouldn't taste too bad either."

Chapter 28

Chris and Brian left the shelter of the rock ledge and started toward the field that led to the river. The trees offered a little protection from the rain, but they were pretty well soaked before they reached the clearing. The field had become a muddy swamp, and they waded in reluctantly. The ankle deep mud sucked at their shoes, threatening to leave them in their socks at anytime. Their clothes were drenched and heavy with water, making the going even harder. As they neared the edge of the clearing, Chris was alarmed by the sound of rushing water up ahead. He couldn't see the river yet, but it sure sounded a lot higher than it had a few hours earlier.

"I think we may be in some deep shit, Brian," he called back over his shoulder.

"No shit, Sherlock," he grunted in response, concentrating on keeping his shoes on as he sloshed through the muddy water.

Their relief at heading back into the sheltering trees was short-lived. The river was visible now, the muddy brown water cresting the banks as it rushed by. The leaning tree wasn't leaning anymore, now it appeared to float as the water washed over the lower branches.

Chris felt his heart sink. He leaned against a nearby tree, slid down the rough bark, landing on his ass with a wet thump. "Fuck," was all he could think of to say. Brian had caught up and sat heavily next to Chris.

"Fuckin' A," he agreed solemnly, "How deep do you think it is?"

Chris wasn't worried about the depth of the river. He and Brian were both good swimmers, thanks to summers spent at the public pool in Devine. It was the current that scared him. He had never been swimming in anything more turbulent than chlorinated pool water, and he didn't think that Brian had either . The rocky riverbed had been slippery on the way over when the water only reached their knees. God only knew how they would keep their footing with the water sweeping by at waist height, or was it chest high by now?

"I have absolutely no idea, man," he finally answered.

They sat quietly for a few minutes, catching their breath from the trip to the riverbank.

"Is there any other way to get across to the truck?" Brian asked finally.

Chris shook his head. "I don't think so, at least not close by. Maybe if we found some walking sticks, they would help us to keep our balance in the river."

From the way the water was swirling by, Brian doubted that anything would keep them on their feet, but he didn't want to stay on the riverbank getting soaked for the rest of his life. As they looked around for some long sticks, Brian caught sight of the truck on the other side of the river. He was stunned to see that the tires were halfway submerged in water. That was the final straw as far as he was concerned. He was about to get stranded out here in the middle of nowhere while he watched their only transportation float away.

"C'mon," he said, gesturing toward the river. "It's now or never. If we get stuck out here all night, we'll freeze to death. No one even knows we're out here. If we get to the truck, we could still make it out of here."

What Brian said did make some sense, but the thought of wading into the raging water still scared the shit out of Chris.

"I don't know," he answered. "The current looks pretty strong to me, it could suck us under in a second. I say we wait until it stops raining. We could go back to the rock shelter to wait it out."

Brian was heading for the river, and he stopped at the edge and turned to face his friend. He swept his arm toward the water.

"Are you kidding me?" he snorted. "This will take days to drain out. If we wait any longer, you might as well kiss your truck good-bye, then where the hell will we be?"

Chris looked skyward for any sign of relief and wasn't a bit surprised that he didn't see even the smallest break in the clouds. Brian was right. Chris agreed reluctantly. It really was now or never.

"Okay man, but we have to have a plan here, not just go jumping in."

Brian began to laugh. "Man, I always said you can't take a dump without having a plan."

Chris knew that Brian was right, but he felt wounded anyway. The one time in his life that he had really acted spontaneously, he had ended up going off half-cocked and joined the Army, so maybe spontaneity wasn't all it was cracked up to be. He decided to let the insult pass though. No point in arguing now.

"Let's head up the river a bit," he said. "If we get swept downstream then maybe we can grab onto the leaning tree and pull ourselves to shore. We need to stick together,"

He cautioned. "We can help support each other."

In truth, Brian had always been a little in awe of his friend's natural leadership and had often wished that a little of it might rub off on him, but it never had. Like always, Chris was thinking straight in the pinch while Brian was ready to just jump in literally. He knew that if they were to make it across the river, it would probably be because Chris had a plan and would remain cool enough to carry it out.

Chapter 29

They waded up river with Brian in the lead, staying close to the bank. He stopped a few hundred feet from the leaning tree and turned to Chris.

"Well, this looks like as good a place as any to start across. Chris looked farther up river and didn't see anyplace that looked better.

"Okay, man," he agreed reluctantly.

When he continued, his expression was serious, "No kidding, Brian, if we're struggling too much we have to turn around and go back and wait it out. The truck's not worth drowning for. Are you sure you're up for this?"

Brian nodded, watching the foamy brown water roar past. His stomach was churning as violently as the river, but he ignored it. He was ready to go back to Devine, and fuck whoever and whatever was waiting for him there. He just wanted to go home.

He started inching his way down the bank and into the water. He was soon ass deep, water swirling around him as he held his arms straight out from his sides, trying to keep his balance. Chris watched him uneasily. His danger radar had been going off steadily, and now it was screaming. He was in thigh deep now, and ahead of him Brian was struggling desperately to stay on his feet in the slippery silt. Glancing up river mechanically like a child looking both ways before crossing the street, he saw a large tree limb tumbling toward them, bobbing up and down in the swift current. Brian was staring straight ahead at the opposite shore as if in a trance, oblivious to the branch that was bearing down on him.

"Watch out!" Chris screamed at his friend.

He realized with a feeling of sick dismay that the limb was only the tip of the iceberg. The branch had bounced off of a protruding rock revealing, just for an instant, that a large part of the tree trunk was still attached and riding under the surface of the water.

Brian looked up at the sound of Chris's voice, and his eyes widened in shock. He flailed his arms to fend off the branch but was totally unaware of the submerged trunk. It caught his ankle like a grappling hook and swept him off his feet with stunning speed. His scream was cut off as he was pulled under the surface. Chris plunged into the roiling water, fighting his way upstream toward his helpless friend. Brian's head emerged from the water a few seconds before Chris reached him. He was coughing and gasping for air, pistoning his arms wildly in a desperate attempt to stay afloat. The current was pulling the tree to the middle of the river and Brian along with it. Chris was swimming as hard as he could, trying to follow Brian, but he wasn't able to make much headway against the rushing water. He was being swept down river faster than he could swim to the middle of the raging river.

They were both being swept along now, Brian caught in the upper branches of the fallen limb, Chris fighting to swim against the current. Driven now by panic, Chris lunged under the water and was able to grasp Brian's trapped foot, still tangled in the tree limb. They rushed along in tandem, Chris trying frantically to wrench his friend's ankle free. With the last of his strength, he twisted Brian's foot, and it finally pulled loose. Weakened from his efforts, Chris drifted for a moment, realizing that he was being pulled deeper into the water by a strong undertow. Unable to hold his breath anymore, he sucked in a mouthful of brackish water. He pumped his aching arms madly to get back to the surface. He was fighting for his own life now.

The burning pain in his arms forgotten, Chris swam frantically and finally broke free of the undertow. His head rose above the swirling water, and he sputtered and gasped to take air into lungs that felt ready to explode. He tried to tread water, but his arms had turned to limp straws, and all he could manage was a weak dog paddle. Brian was about twenty feet ahead of Chris, bobbing up and down, arms flailing helplessly as he was carried along by the rushing water. With a little oxygen in his lungs, his head beginning to clear a little, Chris saw that his friend was heading straight toward the leaning tree. The tree was level with the river now, and if Chris couldn't stop him Brian would crash into the trunk headfirst.

Chris knew that he would never reach Brian in time and tried to scream, but his voice had been reduced to a rasping croak, rusty from the dirty river water that he had inhaled.

"Brian, turn around or you're gonna hit your head!"

Brian could hear his friend's voice above the roaring water, but the water in his ears made everything sound muffled, and he couldn't make out the words.

"Help me, Chris, I'm losing my strength," he cried weakly.

"Brian, turn around NOW!" Chris yelled, louder this time, but it was too late.

Brian turned in time to see the tree for a split second before his forehead hit the bark with a sickening thud. Chris shrieked and forced his screaming muscles to move again, kicking madly toward the tree, and his friend floating face down in the water, bouncing against the tree trunk as the water turned dark red around him.

Chris slid his arms under Brian's armpits and flipped him over. Blood bubbled from the jagged gash on his pale forehead, and for a moment Chris was sure that his friend was dead. He choked back a sob and felt Brian's limp form begin to slide away from him. His arms were numb from shock, and Chris had to force his hands to tighten their grip. Brian moaned softly as the cold fingers dug into his arm, and Chris sobbed with relief. He was losing his one-handed grasp on the slimy tree bark and the force of the roiling water threatened to pull them back out to the middle of the river.

Kicking against the current, Chris began to inch his way toward the riverbank, digging his fingernails into the tree bark and dragging the limp body of his unconscious friend with one arm looped around his neck. After what seemed like an eternity, his hand felt not solid tree trunk, but a gnarled root. He crooked his right elbow through the root and hung on tight, resting his head on his shoulder. He didn't think that he would be able to hold on for very long, and the riverbank seemed miles away. Chris knew that he didn't have the strength left to pull them both to shore, but he couldn't just let go of Brian and watch him drift away. If they were both going to die out here, that was the way it would have to be.

Growing numb from the cold, Chris closed his eyes. He couldn't feel his right arm any more and wondered how long it would be before the arm went limp and allowed the current to sweep them back to the deep water. The warmth of a hand on his elbow startled him and Chris realized that he had been losing battle to stay conscious. He looked up and found himself staring into the face of the Indian that he had seen in the woods on the day he found the arrowhead. *Shit, I'm hallucinating,* Chris thought, but the hand that held his elbow felt warm and real against his skin. The man smiled down at Chris and began to pull him to the riverbank. Chris managed to keep his hold on Brian until only a few inches of water lapped at their bodies. Chris let go of Brian and rolled over onto his back. He fought to keep his eyes open against the exhaustion that crept over him. He lay still as the Indian man knelt beside him. The man reached out and drew a circle on Chris's chest with the index and middle fingers of his right hand.

"You saved our lives, thank you," Chris said weakly.

The man smiled and nodded to acknowledge the thanks but said nothing. Standing, he pointed to Brian's motionless body still lying half in and half out of the water.

Chris rolled over stiffly and crawled to his friend. Blood oozed from the wound on Brian's forehead, tinting the muddy water red. Chris dragged him farther up the bank and put his ear to Brian's cold chest. The heartbeat was faint, but he was still alive. Chris cradled Brian's head in his arms and struggled not to cry with relief. He turned to thank the Indian again, but the man was nowhere to be seen. Somehow, Chris was not surprised. With shaking muscles, he managed to stagger to the truck, half dragging, half carrying Brian. He welcomed the occasional moan that his friend emitted, relieved that Brian was still alive. Chris loaded his friend's dead weight into the passenger seat as gently as he could, padding Brian's head against the back of the seat with what was left of his shirt.

Before climbing into the driver's seat, Chris turned to gaze out to the river one last time. He wished that their guardian angel hadn't disappeared so soon, he had something that he wanted to tell him. Maybe the Indian could still hear him.

"Thank you for saving our lives," he whispered into the rain. "I don't know what this all means, but I know that I've been chosen for some reason. I promise that someday I'll come back and return the arrowhead to your son. I'm sorry that I didn't give it to him last night. Please watch over my friend until I can get him some help." The arrowhead that connected him to his guardian angel felt cold against his chest.

Chapter 30

The next six hours were a blur for Chris. Brian was still unconscious when Chris got him to a medical center in Carrizo Springs. They administered emergency treatment and quickly transferred him by ambulance to Southwest General Hospital in San Antonio. Chris had called Carolyn and Matt from Carrizo Springs, and they met him in the Intensive Care unit waiting room at Southwest General. Carolyn was near hysteria and clung to Chris while the neurologist spoke to them about Brian's condition. Dr. Zubik felt that Brian's prognosis was reasonably good. He explained that Brian's coma was due to swelling of his brain from his impact with the tree trunk. They were administering IV steroids to reduce the swelling and narcotics to reduce the chance of bleeding. He felt confident that Brian would regain consciousness in a few days. Dr. Zubik did caution, however, that there might be some residual brain damage from the trauma that they wouldn't know for sure until Brian woke up and could be tested.

Carolyn seemed comforted by the doctor's explanation and asked Chris to come with her to Brian's bedside. She didn't seem to be rattled by the sight of her son hooked up to the heart monitor, with tubes protruding from every orifice, but her tight grip on his hand told Chris that she was scared that she could be losing her son.

The next few days found Chris at Brian's side when the ICU staff would allow, and sitting in the waiting room trying to read the outdated magazines when not allowed to see Brian. When Carolyn arrived at the hospital after her shift at the nursing home, Chris would go home and spend the evening watching television with his parents. Or rather, staring at the TV screen. As he lay awake in bed at night, Chris could never remember what shows he had seen. The nights were the hardest for Chris. Sleep eluded him as the image of his friend lying helpless in the ICU swam before him. If only he hadn't suggested that fucking trip, Brian would be going off to basic training with him on Tuesday instead of being in a coma. Chris had tried to be loyal to his best friend, had even joined the Army to stay with him, and now he would be going off to war by himself.

That thought invariably made him feel guilty for thinking about himself at a time like this and fueled his misery. He was able to remain stoic in front of his parents, and Pam and Brian's folks but at night, alone in the dark, all he could see was Brian's face. The gash on his pale forehead seemed to glow in the darkness like a hellish nightlight.

On Monday, the ninth of June, Chris took Pam to the hospital to see Brian. Brian had not regained consciousness in a few days as predicted, but his doctor's were still hopeful that he would recover. They were not as reassuring as they had been about how much of Brian's injured brain would be intact when he awoke.

Chris watched as Pam touched Brian's face with heartbreaking tenderness. He tried to remember if she had ever looked at him with that much love and decided that she had not. The question of their future together was answered in that moment. For a time, Pam and Chris sat at Brian's bedside and reminisced quietly about their friend, remembering the good times with Brian. Chris wondered if Brian could hear them and understand what they were saying and tried as he always did to not talk as if Brian was dead. A few hours had passed when Brian's nurse told them that Carolyn was waiting to see her son and reminded them that Brian was only allowed two visitors at a time.

Pam offered to go talk to Carolyn for a moment so that Chris could have some time alone with Brian. Chris would be going off to boot camp in the morning, and she knew that he needed to say goodbye in private. She kissed the tip of Brian's nose and started to cry as she left the cubicle.

Chris sat on the bed next to Brian and leaned in close. Not caring a damn any more if someone saw him in a less than masculine position, he took Brian's cold flaccid hand in his own.

"I hate to think that I might never see you again, but friend, that just might be the case," he whispered. Hot tears tracked down his cheeks and fell to the white sheets below. "I'm really scared, Brian," Chris moaned. "We were supposed to do this together. Now look at us. You could be this way for the rest of your life, and I might never make it home."

He rested his head on Brian's chest, and to hell with what anyone would think if they saw him. He was crying uncontrollably now and fought to regain his composure. After the tears had subsided, Chris sat up and wiped his face with the back of his hand. He pulled the arrowhead necklace from around his neck and gently placed it around Brian's.

"You keep this for me, buddy," he said softly. "You need someone to watch over you, and I won't be here to do it. The Indian man didn't pull us from the river just to let you die in the hospital and me in Vietnam. I'll be back soon, and things will be good again, you'll see."

Chris heard footsteps approaching and turned to see Carolyn entering the cubicle.

"Hey, Chris, how ya' doin'?" she asked with forced brightness.

"I'm okay," he answered with a wan smile.

Carolyn could see that he had been crying, but said nothing. She reached down and touched the arrowhead that rested on her son's chest.

"For good luck," Chris explained.

"So tomorrow's the big day, huh?" She asked sadly.

"Yeah," Chris answered. "I have to be at the bus station by four a.m. The bus leaves for Fort Hood at five a.m. sharp. You know, I'm not even sure how long it takes to get there." Though he was talking calmly about leaving in the morning, it still didn't seem quite real.

Carolyn leaned over the bed and enfolded Chris in a hug.

"Honey, I'm so sorry that Brian got you into this. If it hadn't been for him . . . " Her voice trailed off as she started to cry. Chris patted her back tenderly.

"It's okay, Carolyn. I made the choice to do this myself. It's not Brian's fault. You have enough to worry about now without worrying about me."

She stood and smiled crookedly at her son's best friend. "I can't stand the thought of losing both of you," she whispered hoarsely, the tears threatening to start again.

Chris stood and hugged her.

"I'll be okay, " he said firmly, meaning it this time. "Pam's waiting for me. I'd better go now."

Carolyn turned and looked at Brian. "I'll make sure that the necklace stays with him, Chris. That was very sweet of you to give it to him. I know how much it means to you."

Chris smiled and nodded. He took one last look at Brian and saluted, turned and walked out of the cubicle.

"You'd better write!" Carolyn called after him.

Chris took Pam back to her house after they left the hospital. Her mother had gone to play Bingo, so they had the house to themselves. They made love in her bed, but Chris knew that Pam's heart wasn't with him. She cried and held him tightly afterwards, but he wondered if the tears were for him or for Brian. Probably both, he decided.

They sat on the porch late into the evening, sipping cokes and mostly making small talk. They made plans to stay in touch while Chris was in boot camp and to see each other when Chris came home on leave. They didn't talk about Brian, but he was with them as surely as if he were sitting in the wicker chair across from the swing. In the small silences that punctuated their conversation, both of their thoughts drifted to him, lying in the hospital bed that would be his home for God knew how long.

Chris was almost relieved when Pam's mom returned. It gave him an excuse to leave. He knew that his parents already resented the time that he was spending away from home during his last few days in Devine. They understood his staying at the hospital with Brian, but he felt guilty anyway.

The Logue family spent the rest of the evening watching television. Ryan seemed quiet and distracted, and Laurie looked like she would start crying at the drop of a hat. Only Jonathan was his old self, talking excitedly about the adventures that his big brother was going to be part of in the army. When Laurie finally shoed him off to bed at nine-thirty, Chris breathed a sigh of relief. He loved his little brother, but the prattling was wearing on his nerves. At 10:30 Ryan stood and switched off the television set.

"We have to get you to the bus station early son," he said as if anyone needed to be reminded. "We'd all better get some sleep."

Laurie's tears finally came, and Chris hugged her affectionately.

"I'll be home in six weeks, mom," he assured her. "And I'll finally have that haircut that you've been bitching about for so long."

Laurie scolded him for swearing, but she was smiling through her tears.

Chris was in bed by 11:00 p.m., but sleep never came. When the alarm buzzed at 3:30, he was still wide awake, wondering what the next few years would bring.

Part 4
Chapter 31

August 28, 1999

"Make goddamn sure you clean that sink out when you're done!"

Jack King could hear his grandmother's screech all the way from the living room. Her voice made him jump, and he almost cut himself. He resisted the urge to yell at her to shut the fuck up. He still had half of his head to shave and didn't want to lose his concentration. Jack hadn't been shaving his head all that long and he was just now getting to the point where he didn't have to walk around for an hour with bits of toilet paper stuck to his skull after every session with the razor. He carefully pulled the razor across his lathered scalp and surveyed the results in the bathroom mirror, pleased to see that there were no nicks this time.

The thought of the old woman sitting in her bathrobe in her scabrous blue recliner, a coffee mug of sour mash whiskey on the stained table beside her, irritated the shit out of Jack. He looked at the stubble in the sink and chuckled to himself as he walked to his bedroom. Jack would ignore his grandmother's demand the way he always did. He enjoyed jerking on the old bat's chain.

His grandmother's voice hit Jack's ears like fingernails on a chalkboard as he reached his bedroom doorway.

"Did you clean that sink out? I'm telling you right now that you'd better start doing something around this house, or I'll throw you out on your ass! Do you hear me?"

Jack stopped in the doorway and leaned around the corner to face her. She looked like a cartoon Halloween witch to him with her tangle of gray hair and the dark circles under her eyes. She had always been a drinker, but having Jack come to live with her two years earlier had shoved her over the edge into full-blown alcoholism. When he was fifteen, his mother had given and packed him off to El Paso and a reluctant grandmother.

In fact, his mother had given up on Jack long before his fifteenth birthday. She had considered him nothing but a burden after his father ran off when Jack was four. The kid was in the way of her bar-hopping and partying. She just wanted to find a new man to take care of them. Jack's no-good father certainly wasn't going to support his brat.

Jack hadn't been an easy teenager to live with. He was sullen and angry most of the time, doing badly in school when he bothered to show up at all. His grandmother had never figured out how to cope with her own kids, and she didn't have a clue how to help her troubled grandson. She loved him, but she didn't understand his anger, and she was a little afraid of him, so she took the easy way out and simply retreated into the bottle, and let Jack go his own way.

"It's almost seven o'clock," Jack sneered at her with contempt. "Why haven't you passed out yet you old bitch?"

She lit a cigarette with shaking fingers and blew the smoke out in response.

"You'd think you would show me a little respect. You're living in my house and eating up my pension check, you know. You're just like your worthless mother, always using people and never giving anything back."

Jack laughed bitterly and waved his hand expansively around the shabby living room.

"Yeah, some great mansion you have here, grandma. It's not even a house, it's a fucking trailer, and a crappy one, to boot!"

He turned and went into his bedroom. Just before slamming the door, he turned and shot back over his shoulder, "I don't have time to argue with you, I've got stuff to do. And leave my mother out of it."

There was no mistaking the menace in his voice as he spat out the last sentence. His grandmother took a deep drag on her cigarette and reached up to rub a tear out of her eye. She would never let that little bastard know that he made her cry.

"What did I ever do to deserve to be treated like this?" She whispered. Then she poured another shot of whiskey into her chipped glass.

Jack sat on his bed and tucked the legs of his olive green camouflage pants into his black boots with long slender fingers. Muttering to himself, he laced up his Doc Martin's and tied the laces with unnecessary vigor.

"Fuck you, you drunken old bitch, throwing my mother in my face just to piss me off. And fuck you too, mom, wherever the hell you are."

He didn't need his sorry-ass family anymore. His friends in the Old World Order were all the family he needed now, and he would die for any one of them. They ruled their own world, and now Jack was one of them. For the first time in his young life he felt that he belonged that he had a purpose. The Old World Order was going to rid the country of the vermin spics and niggers that diseased the streets of America with AIDS and drugs, and the Jews that would hold a dollar over a hardworking white man's head and laugh while he jumped for it. The white man was on his knees, and the Old World Order was the group that would lift him up and return him to his rightful place.

He had joined the organization three months earlier and had instantly felt a sense of power and control that had been missing his whole life. He was working his way up in the ranks and still had a long way to go, but he was treated with respect and acceptance by everyone in the group.

Jack stood and inspected his image in the cloudy mirror over the dresser. His bald head made his face appear thinner than it already was. He would have been almost handsome, but the shining scalp and angry eyes made his face look hard. A growth spurt in the last two years had transformed Jack from a pudgy adolescent into a lean six-footer. He turned to the left and then to the right, admiring the twin black swastikas tattooed on his upper arms.

Jack rummaged through the plastic garbage bags that held his clean clothes, searching for his favorite shirt. Finding the prized black tee shirt with the O.W.O logo on the front, and the message OUR TIME IS HERE emblazoned on the back, he pulled it from the bag and smoothed the wrinkles with his hand. He pulled the shirt over his head and tucked it into the waistband of his pants. He rolled the sleeves until the swastikas showed. Now Jack felt like he was in uniform.

He was heading to a warehouse party with his friends in the O.W.O. The popular thrash band, Mushroom Head, would be playing and they usually whipped the mosh pit into a frenzy. Jack leaned over and opened the top drawer of his night stand. A .22 caliber Baretta sat on top of a stack of papers. He considered tucking the gun into his pants pocket then decided against it. He planned on moshing that night, and the gun might go off. *Shooting my pecker off would sure wreck the evening*, he thought. Before turning out the light, Jack saluted the black and white poster of Adolph Hitler that hung over his bed. After closing the door of his room, Jack locked the deadbolt that he had installed and slipped the key into his pocket.

Jack's grandmother started in on him as soon as he reached the living room,

"Why do you keep your door locked? Is there something in there that I should know about?"

Her speech was more slurred than before, and Jack noted with disgust that the level of the whiskey in the bottle on the table had gone down considerably. "Just stay the fuck out of there if you know what's good for you. What's in my bedroom doesn't concern you." He didn't think that he had much to worry about. She would be passed out in no time. Her slack face grew anguished as she saw the swastikas on his arms. The tattoos were a recent addition, and until now Jack had been careful to keep his arms covered when he was at home. He left the trailer without a word.

Leaning against the signpost at the entrance to the Sunset Trailer Park, Jack sighed and lit a cigarette. His friends weren't due to pick him up for 15 minutes, but he couldn't stand to stay in the depressing atmosphere of the trailer anymore. He looked back down the row of trailers until his eyes came to rest on his grandmother's home.

Remembering the look on the old woman's face when she saw his tattoos, he felt a momentary pang of guilt. She had worked at menial jobs her whole life to take care of her kids, and she sure as hell didn't have much to show for it. His mom had thrown him out, and he would have had no place in the world to go if his grandmother hadn't taken him in. No one else would have cared if he lived or died. The words 'biting the hand that feeds you' popped into his mind, but he dismissed them. *The old bat probably thought that I would get a job and support her in her old age, and do all the work around that shit hole, too,* he thought contemptuously. He shook his head and took a last drag of his cigarette then threw the butt into the rutted trailer park driveway. *Maybe it's time to get a job and get out of this crappy trailer park and that old bat,* he sighed.

Chapter 32

"WOO-HOO Let's go, big guy!"

Todd's rebel yell startled Jack more that the screeching brakes of the mint 1976 blue Camaro that pulled up next to him. Judging from the crooked grin on Todd's face, he was well on his way to Drunkville. He waved a beer can at Jack in greeting with his left hand as he pushed the back of the passenger seat forward, so Jack could climb into the back. As Jack settled back into his seat, Lenny Rittman handed a cold can of beer over to him from the front seat. Jack and Lenny had met in Occupational Education class in high school during one of the few spells that Jack actually bothered to show up. The class was designed to allow troubled students to take classes in the morning and get additional credits and some on the job training at a part-time job in the afternoon. It was usually the last step before the problem students dropped out or were expelled. Jack and Lenny hit it off immediately and dropped out of school a few weeks later. Jack didn't bother to tell his grandmother that he had quit school. Lenny's parents were gone during the day, and the boys spent most days at Lenny's playing video games or just hanging out. That ended when they joined the Old World Order.

At 27 years old the Camaro's driver, Rich Shanack, was the oldest of the car's occupants. He and his twin brother, Ronald, were among the founding members of the O.W.O. The Shanack twins were high ranking members of the organization and had helped to recruit Lenny and Jack. Todd Harris sat in the Camaro's front passenger seat. He was a friend of Lenny's older brother and had introduced Lenny and Jack to the Shanack brothers. Rich and Ron had immediately pegged Jack and Lenny as potential candidates for the O.W.O. Both boys were on a fast track too nowhere. Neither one had any direction in life and were in the market for someone to blame for their failures. The Shanack brothers also recognized the anger that could, with a little training and hate rhetoric, be channeled into violence against the enemies of the order especially in Jack's case. The raw recruits had come to believe in the white supremacist propaganda that had been constantly fed to them by the hatemonger in the front seat.

The Camaro's four occupants bore an eerily striking resemblance to one another with their shaved heads, black O.W.O tee shirts and shiny Doc Martins. All four sported matching swastika tattoos. The Old World Order was made up of young men who were willing to become one for their cause and women who were willing to follow. Individuality was suppressed in favor of unity.

"So, what's going on, gentlemen?" Jack asked, popping the pull tab on his beer can.

Todd answered, casually glancing over at Rich and then back out the open passenger window. "We were thinking of cruising around in the mountains for a while. We figure the party won't be hoppin' 'til at 11:00 and we have plenty of supplies."

He held his beer can in the air. Todd was smiling as he turned to Jack, but there was something dark beneath the smile that made Jack uneasy.

They drove south on Route 20, and Jack caught an occasional glimpse of the Rio Grande out of his window. The conversations was lighthearted, banter about the latest action movie or their favorite wrestlers, punctuated by raucous laughter. Jack laughed the loudest when Rich and Todd began bragging about female conquests though he had the least experience with the opposite sex. The O.W.O. attitude towards women was strictly male chauvinist. Women had been created to take care of the needs of their men and to produce babies. Men ruled, and women followed the rules, period. Men had the right to enforce the rules as they saw fit.

Chapter 33

"Hey, Jack, are you still fucking that bitch from your trailer park?" Rich called over his shoulder as he negotiated the curves in the narrow mountain road.

Jack felt his face redden as he tried to maintain his composure. If his friends saw any sign of weakness in him, they would rag on him, unmercifully.

"Nah, I cut her loose a couple of weeks ago. She wasn't all that bad, but she has a kid, and I ain't ready to be anybody's daddy, so I left her in the dust."

He hoped that he sounded heartless enough to suit Rich. He sipped his beer, remembering the night that Stacey had told him that she didn't want to see him anymore. Jack and Stacy had started dating four months earlier, just after she moved into the trailer park. Her father had bought the trailer for Stacey and her two-year-old son, Kevin, after the breakup of her marriage. Stacy was twenty, divorced, and raising Kevin without support from her ex. She worked the morning shift at a nearby diner, leaving Kevin in the care of a sitter.

Stacey was a petite blonde with dimples that lit up her face when she smiled, which was often. Jack had been immediately attracted to her sense of humor and her upbeat, independent out-looks. She saw only the good in Jack, that is until he had proudly shown her the Nazi memorabilia and Old World Order posters that were on display in his room. She had recoiled and asked Jack if that was the way he really felt about the other people that he shared the planet with. Her reaction had surprised him. When he answered her by explaining the mission of the O.W.O., he had expected her to understand how important the organization would be to her son's future. Instead, Stacey had told him to stay away from her and Kevin and had walked out of his life just like dear old mother. Jack had relived his mistake every day for the past two weeks. He had waved to her several times as she passed by his grandmother's trailer on her way to or from work, but she had ignored him. He still hoped to convince her to see him again, but he wouldn't give up his membership in the O.W.O. for anyone, no matter how much his heart still ached for Stacey. He would just have to chalk it up as a sacrifice for his beliefs.

The foursome continued south on Route 20, drinking beer and joking as they passed McNary and then Esperanza. Rich headed the Camaro toward the mountains on Route 54, the Baylor and Delaware ranges to the east and the San Diablo to their west.

The afternoon sky was graying into dusk as they reached the twisting road that led into the mountains. The valleys already bore the shadows that warned of the night to come. Rich took it easy on the hairpin curves. M.P.s from the nearby Army base patrolled the mountain roads regularly and he didn't want to risk getting pulled over. Not tonight when they were on such an important mission.

The sun was a memory now, only a soft orange glow behind the mountain peaks. The heat of the afternoon was giving way to cool mountain breezes. The red bicycle reflectors caught Todd's eye as they rounded a curve. The bike path that ran parallel to the road held one last biker trying to beat the coming darkness. Todd nudged Rich and nodded toward the young Hispanic woman aboard the mountain bike. A blue spandex biking suit hugged her curves and a long black braid swayed from side to side as she pedaled. Rich drove past her without slowing, he didn't want to spook her.

"Hey, Jack, did you know that you have done absolutely nothing to earn the O.W.O symbol that you wear so proudly on your scrawny pigeon chest?" Rich asked the question without turning around.

The undertone of menace in the driver's voice sent a thrill of fear up Jack's spine. He couldn't tell if Rich was joking or not. He glanced over to Lenny and laughed nervously, but Lenny was staring out the window as if his life depended on seeing something in the distance.

"We think it's time you show how dedicated you are to the cause," Rich continued, pulling the Camaro off the road and setting the parking brake.

"See that spick chick on the bike?" Todd asked.

Jack nodded, though Todd was still staring straight ahead.

"We want you to take her out, and I don't mean on a date."

Everyone laughed at Todd's wit, everyone except Jack. His mouth had gone as dry as the washes that ran down the sides of the surrounding mountains. He turned and strained to see the bikes tail light disappearing behind them. When he righted himself in the seat the others were staring at him, their expressions blank in the soft glow of the dash lights. Jack knew that they were dead serious, and if he didn't do as he was told, he would be the one to be taken out.

"How am I supposed to do it? I don't have my gun with me and I don't want to get some shank's blood all over me."

Jack was trying his best to sound tough, but his voice had a whine to it that made him cringe inwardly. Todd leaned his face over the seat until Jack could feel his beery breath.

"We're dropping you off right now. You'll have to do it with your hands, man, you know, the primitive way, like a real man. She'll be here in a minute, you'll have to figure it out yourself."

Todd's grin was pure evil and made Jack feel like the victim.

"There's a lake up ahead," Todd continued. "We'll park there for a while and then come back and get you, and the spick chick had better be dead when we get back."

Todd opened the passenger door and got out of the car, motioning for Jack to follow. Jack nodded numbly and got out of the car on shaking legs, hoping that his friends couldn't see how scared he was. Rich started the Camaro and circled it back onto the road, without turning the headlights on.

"Remember, you'll be doing the world a service, killing off one of the breeders," he grinned as he drove away.

Jack felt a wave of nausea lurching up his esophagus and wished that he hadn't drunk all that beer on an empty stomach. *This isn't the way it's supposed to be*, he thought miserably. *We're supposed to work as a unit.* He had imagined himself marching with his comrades in the Old World Order, a well oiled, well armed machine, wreaking havoc on nigger peace marches or maybe bombing Indian casinos. It had never occurred to him that he would have to work alone in the dark. *This sucks*, he thought bitterly.

He heard the woman biker coming around the curve before he saw her. Trying not to panic, Jack looked around wildly for something to use as a weapon. Spotting a tree limb on the ground, he picked it up and hefted the branch over his shoulder like a Louisville slugger and hid behind a nearby tree at the side of the bike path. Jack's heart raced, and he wiped the sweat from his bald scalp then wiped his trembling hand on his pant leg as he peeked from behind the tree. He didn't want to miss his opportunity to knock his prey off of her bicycle as she approached.

Jack closed his eyes and leaned against the tree until the whistling of the bike spokes rang in his ears. Leaping out from behind the tree, Jack swung the tree branch with all of the strength that he could muster. To his surprise, the branch connected with the biker at chest level with a sickening thunk, tearing her grip from the handlebars and sending bike and rider crashing to the ground.

The woman laid on her back. He was panting, his lips curled in a crooked, hellish grin of triumph. It had been so fucking easy. Jack was high on adrenaline now, and the shock and terror in the woman's eyes were an aphrodisiacs to him. Blood ran from her nose, and the sight of the viscous red liquid excited him even more. Jack tossed the tree branch aside, he would stomp her to death with no weapons other than his boots.

"Please don't hurt me anymore, I'll give you anything you want," she whispered hoarsely. "My bike is worth $500.00 dollars, take it."

Jack cackled demonically and smashed his right Doc Martin against the right side of her face with all of the force that his thin leg would allow. Jack bent over and grabbed her by the arm and dragged her back into the tree line, eliciting a ragged moan from his victim. He didn't want to be interrupted now; this was too fucking good.

After he dumped her, writhing in pain, behind the trees, Jack ran back to the road to check for oncoming cars. The road was deserted. He returned to the trees and knelt over her inert form. In the dim twilight, he could see that the side of her face was already purple and swollen. She lay helpless. her open left eye had the unmistakable look of a terrified animal.

"You stupid fuckin' Mexican bitch," Jack sneered at her. "This is your own damn fault. Why did you have to come here tonight? You were in the wrong place at the wrong time."

He ran a finger across the blood that flowed from her mouth and nose, then rubbed his hands together. "They have to think I killed you with my bare hands," he explained patiently.

He looked more closely at her face. She looked older than he had thought at first. Except for the expensive spandex suit and bicycle, she looked like an average spick chick, all right, pretty though, except for the blood and bruises, he decided.

She began to mumble, and Jack brought his ear closer to her mouth, so he could make out what would very likely be her last words. Her words were not in English or Spanish either. He listened intently, trying to make out what she was saying, then realized that she was chanting in an Indian language.

"Hey, you're an Indian," he exclaimed. "You should have stayed on the reservation where you belong."

Jack looked up the mountain for a sign of headlights, but saw none. They would be back for him soon. He had to finish the squaw off, or they would finish him off for sure. He stood and looked down at the helpless woman at his feet. All it would take would be one sharp stomp of his boot on her slender neck, but Jack hesitated. The adrenaline rush had dissipated, leaving him weak and trembling. He didn't know if he had the stomach to take a human life one on one like this. Shooting someone from a distance or planting a bomb was one thing, but that brown eye staring up at him gave him the willies.

She spoke again, this time in English.

"You have to help me, I'll die if you leave me here. I don't want to die, please don't let me die, please," she pleaded, tears rolling down her cheeks and mixing with her clotting blood.

Jack raised his right foot then looked away and shut his eyes. *What if I don't kill her?* He thought. Would she be able to identify him? He doubted it. She was no doubt in shock, and there wasn't much light. If she did wind up dead, there would be an investigation, and he had no doubt that his companions would turn on him in a heartbeat to save their own skins. They could pin the murder on him all right. His mother's voice came to him, from a time long ago when she had tried to give a shit about him. "What kind of friends do you have, anyway? If they jumped off a bridge, would you jump, too?" He probably would have back in Brunswick. In his early teens, Jack had been such an outsider that he would have done just about anything to be accepted as a part of a group even the group of misfits that he had hung around with. Now he wasn't so sure anymore. Jack felt betrayed by his so-called friends in the O.W.O. They had made him feel like a kid who had been ambushed by adults and forced into this heinous crime he didn't want to do.

What the fuck is the point of killing a squaw out here in the middle of nowhere? Jack thought, looking down at the pathetic woman on the ground at his feet. He didn't give a damn about her, but he didn't have the stomach to finish her off either. *No one is going to connect her death with the Old World Order. This won't do a thing to advance the cause the white man*, Jack decided. He knelt down and pinned her to the ground by planting his right knee on her chest.

"You'd better do what I tell you or you're heading for the happy hunting ground, do you hear me?" Jack hissed at her, leaning close to her face.

She resisted the urge to spit in his eye and nodded, gasping, "Yes."

Jack let his knee up a little, "just lay here and don't move a fuckin' muscle. If my friends see that you're not dead, they'll shoot us both. Believe me, they mean business. You tell the newspapers that the Old World Order is going to change the country. This is just a wake up call. Can you remember that?"

She nodded again. Jack stood and walked to the edge of the road, she took a chance to suck in a ragged breath. Jack saw headlights coming down the mountain. The lights were a good distance away, but they were moving fast. He hoped to hell that the lights belonged to the Camaro. It had occurred to him that they might just leave him here to get caught with a corpse.

Jack turned to look at her. In the moonlight, she looked like a mannequin that had been twisted out of shape, then tossed at the side of the road. He felt no pity for her or remorse for injuring her so grievously. She was just a means to an end. Like he told her, she was in the wrong place at the wrong time that's all.

"This is it, lady," Jack said. " Just stay down 'til we're out a here, and you might survive."

She began to speak, and he was stunned by the strength and venom in her steady voice, "I call upon the Great Spirit to curse you. You are evil, and evil will always be with you. One day you will be hunted like the animal that you are and robbed of your soul by the horned panthers of the underworld. Take care what you wish for, devil, because you will get what you want and only the Great Spirit can save you."

Jack's shock turned to rage. After giving her a chance to live, the fucking squaw had the balls to lay a fucking curse on him! Jack leaped at her, his boot connecting solidly with her rib cage, sending an explosion of pain coursing through her chest. She choked back a scream and sobbed quietly.

"Now are you gonna shut the fuck up?" Jack screamed at her, his voice shaking with fury. "This is no fucking joke!"

He could hear the Camaro's engine now. He jumped over the guardrail and into the road, waving his arms at the approaching car.

Rich stopped the Camaro, and Jack ran to the open driver's side window. Rich leaned his head out of the window.

"Well, did you do the deed, sonny boy?" he asked, his voice dripping sarcasm.

"Yeah, it's done," Jack replied, struggling to sound casual. He walked around the front of the car and reached for the passenger door handle.

"Not so fast," Todd said, opening the door and starting to get out. "We'd better check to make sure she's good and dead not that you'd lie to us, right?"

Jack's stomach tightened. He had hoped that they would take his word for it. *She'd better be good at playing possum*, he thought desperately.

"I wouldn't lie to you, man," he answered. "I'm sure she's dead. I didn't check her pulse or anything, but she sure looks dead." Maybe if he back pedaled a little, they would go easy on him.

"Well, let's just have a little look-see," Todd sneered.

"These asshole's are going to kill me," Jack thought miserably.

Jack was meekly following Todd to the guardrail, trying to think of a way to save his skin when he spotted headlights coming slowly down the mountain toward them.

"Hey, man, someone's coming," he yelled, trying not to sound relieved.

Rich had seen the lights in his rear view mirror and called out to Todd and Jack, "C'mon, we gotta get out of here," as he started the Camaro's engine.

They piled into the car, and Rich had started to pull away when a noise in the woods behind them caused Jack's heart to leap. He looked over his shoulder and saw a small tree swaying among the otherwise still brush. Jack's mouth went dry, and he wheeled around to see if anyone else was watching. To his relief, Todd and Lenny were popping beer cans open and laughing, talking about what a great job Jack had done, and how cool the blood on his hands was. Rich was driving down the mountain, so Jack figured he didn't have anything to worry about, then he saw Rich's eyes in the rearview mirror.

The blue eyes were glaring straight at him and Jack knew that Rich had seen the tree move and had understood exactly what it meant.

"Yeah, Jack, way to go," Rich's tone of voice was as cold as his eyes, but only Jack heard. Lenny and Todd were too drunk to notice.

Jack took the beer that Todd handed to him and wondered what the hell was next. He was quiet on the way back to town. By the time Rich parked the car on Gunter Road, the beers that he had drunk along the way had eased his nerves a bit.

Chapter 34

Gunter Road was a few blocks away from the warehouse that served as headquarters for the Old World Order. Parking a safe distance away from the party protected their transportation in the event of a police raid, and since violence usually erupted at O.W.O. parties, police raids were common. The four men formed a human wall as they walked side by side toward the warehouse. They scanned the area around the entrance before entering. The vestibule was dark and silent, sending up a red warning flag. A guard was always stationed at the entrance to ward off gate crashers. The police, FBI, and local media were anxious to infiltrate the organization, so anyone who looked at all suspicious to the guard would be ejected unceremoniously.

The warehouse was a three level building that served as storage for several local companies. Every few months, the stock dwindled enough to make room for a large blow-out or a rally. A close friend of the Shanack twins, Ron and Rich, owned the building, so Ron had access to one of the five offices in the front of the warehouse.

Rich led the others through the dark hallways that led to the back of the building. A clock on one of the office walls read 11:17, so the party should have been in full swing, but there was no sound coming from the storage area where the bands usually played.

"Wonder what the fuck happened?" Todd asked quietly. "There were supposed to be two kegs of beer here tonight."

Rich shushed him as they entered the loading dock. Now they could hear the muffled sounds of music and voices. Rich relaxed a little and motioned for the others to follow him. As they rounded the corner into the main storage, they saw 40 or so party goers scattered into small groups, laughing and holding cans of beer. A boom box set up on a wooden crate blasted punk rock, but the sound couldn't fill up the cavernous space, and no one was dancing. The turnout for their parties was usually over 200, so something was definitely wrong.

"Man, I hope Doug Griffiths showed up," Lenny whispered to Jack, nudging him in the ribs with a bony elbow. "He's supposed to bring these two runaway bitches that he's been hanging around with. They'd do just about anything for a place to stay, know what I mean?"

Jack was still too nervous to care, so he just shrugged. The first group they came to consisted of Doug Griffiths and four girls. None of the girls looked to be over 16.

"What the fuck's goin' on, Doug?" Rich asked as they approached the group. "This is not what we were expecting."

The group stopped talking, and Doug turned to Rich. He was only a year older than Jack, and Lenny and his boyish John Denver good looks were deceptive. The blue eyes behind the wire rimmed glasses were as cold as the eyes of a shark. Doug was loyal to the cause and would do anything that was asked of him, including murder.

"Man, the guys that went for the beer got busted. I guess they were under age," he answered. "Ron decided to get rid of anyone under 18, except for the girls that is."

Rich laughed and shook his head. Before long, he and Todd left to mingle with the others. Jack looked around and saw that most of the faces were familiar. He didn't see anyone worth leaving the company of the young girls for. As usual, males outnumbered females at the party two to one. If Jack had any chance of scoring one of the girls, he'd have to make his move before the night got too old. After an hour, he and Lenny had managed to steer two of the girls away from the herd. The girls were listening to his stories intently and laughing in all the right places, so Jack was beginning to feel pretty confident about his chances. They seemed to be impressed with his exaggerated tales of living life on the edge.

Normally a quiet guy, Jack was working hard to keep up a steady patter. During the periodic lulls in the conversation, his mind flashed back to the Indian woman lying in the dirt, broken and bleeding. The mental picture brought a chill up his spine. What bothered him the most was not her pain, but the sound of her curse still ringing in his ears. He knew that the curse was bullshit, the ravings of a woman in shock, but he could picture the horned panthers that she ranted about. He imagined the sleek black beasts crouching invisible at his feet, waiting to pounce and seize his helpless spirit the second that he let his guard down. The last thing that he wanted to do was to go home alone to his passed-out grandmother and his empty bedroom.

The two teenage girls giggled as Jack, and Lenny competed for their attention. They tried to top each other with stories of their adventures in the Old World Order, mostly made up. Jack hadn't worked up the nerve to suggest that they leave the party, and he was running out of bullshit, so he was relieved when Lenny changed the subject.

"Hey, did either of you ladies ever check out the O.W.O. website?" he asked.

Both girls shook their heads, "we don't have computers," one of them explained.

"Oh, man, you've got to check out the Internet," Lenny exclaimed, "it's really cool. Ronny's got a chat room set up so you can talk to people all over the world. You should read some of the E-mail that comes in. It makes you realize how many people believe in our cause. There's a lot of other cool sites to check out. Hey, Jack, did Ronny show you that website where you can talk to Vietnam Vets? They tell some awesome war stories."

Jack was nodding in agreement at Lenny's enthusiasm about the Internet. He and Todd had found some porn sites that captured most of their interest, but he wasn't quite drunk enough to discuss sex.

"Yeah, I was over at Todd's house, and he pulled up the Vietnam Vet website on his dad's computer," he answered. "This one vet was tellin' about how they used to take gook prisoners and tie their right arm and leg to one helicopter and their left leg and arm to another, then they would bet on which chopper would be able to take of first and score the biggest half."

He and Lenny laughed hysterically at the story, but judging by the looks on the faces of their female companions, they didn't think it sounded funny. In fact, they both looked grossed out by the graphic visuals that they were getting. *Well, fuck em' if they can't take a joke*, Jack thought.

"Most of these stories are probably bullshit, anyway," Jack said, not bothering to add that the story he had just told was, in fact, total bullshit, since he had just made it up. The girls smiled tentatively, though, ready to go on with the party.

Jack couldn't resist one last brag. He took a swig of his beer and puffed out his chest.

"Sometimes I wish I had been around 30 years ago. I would have joined the Army in a freakin' "heartbeat," he assured the girls. "That would have been great, runnin' around the jungles, shooting gooks. I'd fuckin' cut their heads off with my bayonet and leave 'em hanging from the trees."

Lenny laughed and gave Jack an approving high-five. Neither he nor Jack noticed that they were losing their audience. The girls had signaled each other with glances that maybe it was time to see if the party had anyone better to offer. Jack, oblivious to their lack of interest in his violent imagination, continued on.

"Yeah, I think I was born in the wrong time. I would have fit right in over there. The thought of putting a bullet in one of them slanty-eyed little scum-bags thrills me to death. I mean, what the fuck good are those people? They're parasites that suck off of the rest of the planet."

The girls were slowly inching away from Jack and Lenny, but they didn't seem to notice. Jack was on a roll now, and Lenny was all rapt attention. Their raucous laughter had caught the attention of some of the other part goers, and a few people drifted over, wondering what was so funny.

Delighted to have a bigger audience, Jack became even more expansive.

"I'll tell ya' I wish I could go back to the jungles of Vietnam. I'd love to come face to face with some Viet cong. I'd pick that little fucker up and pile drive that prick into the ground."

His new audience laughed appreciatively, but Jack didn't hear them. He had been distracted by a low, growling noise that seemed to fill the air around him. He glanced around furtively, but he couldn't find the source of the noise. No one else seemed to hear anything odd. *Probably just the music*, he thought, dismissing the odd sound. Seconds later, he was startled by the unmistakable snarl of a wild animal. This time it was so close Jack could almost feel the hot breath of the creature on his back. Panicking, he spun around, not stopping to think how he looked, certain that a dog was preparing to attack him from behind, and a large dog at that. The snarl didn't sound like it came from a dog though, or even a wolf. It sounded for all the world like a Bengal tiger he had seen on a TV special about endangered species.

The memory sparked an image of the horned panthers that the Indian woman had ranted about. Jack tried to shake off the mental image. "She's full of SHIT!" He thought wildly. *I'm just spooked, that's all, and drunk*, he reminded himself.

"Damn, Jack, what's the matter with you?" Lenny asked, "You afraid the cockroaches gonna get you?"

Jack managed a weak laugh. He realized that he must have looked pretty stupid, hopping around like a flea on a griddle, but he was too shaken up to be embarrassed. He cleared his throat and tried to sound casual.

"Did you guys hear a dog or somethin' ?" He asked, knowing what the answer would be.

"I swear it sounded like it was right behind me you had to have heard it," he pleaded.

His friends shook their heads as Lenny hooted, "Hey, them cockroaches are barking now!" This brought a fresh gale of laughter from the group.

It dawned on Jack that his friends were playing a joke on him. It just wasn't possible that he was the only one who had heard the snarl. It was too fucking loud. *What a asshole I am*, he thought. *Them bastard's really got me.* Maybe if he played along they would tire of the game.

The thump to the back of his knees knocked Jack off balance, and he stumbled to keep from falling. His companions were momentarily startled, then burst out laughing. This was the best entertainment that they had all night. Jack wheeled around, hands clenched into fists, ready to punch the crap out of whoever had blind sided him. This wasn't funny anymore. There was nothing behind him, but the vast empty warehouse space that provided no place to hide. He could have dismissed the animal noises, but someone or something had whacked him across the legs.

"You'd better take it easy on the beer, man," Lenny sputtered through tears of laughter. "Or we'll have to take you home and have granny tuck you in."

Jack wanted desperately to gather up some of his lost dignity, but he didn't have a clue how he could explain away his bizarre behavior. Grace under pressure had never been Jack's long suit.

Maybe if he casually excused himself and went to the bathroom for a few minutes, his friends would get tired of talking about his strange antics and move on to another subject. Maybe whatever had gotten under his skin would just go the fuck away and leave him be. With a few minutes to himself, he would at least have time to make up some lame excuse.

Jack's casual getaway problem was solved when Todd walked up to him and announced that Ronny wanted to talk to him.

"He's over in the office by the dock. Go grab a beer, and I'll
meet you over there," Todd instructed, then turned and headed back
to the loading dock.

Jack shrugged and breathed a sigh of relief as he swaggered
toward the Styrofoam cooler that held the cans of cold beer. He
hoped that no one would notice his shaking knees. He glanced furtively over his shoulder a time or two before he reached the cooler,
making sure that nothing was sneaking up on him from behind.
Jack's hand trembled as he cracked open a cold beer, and he was
grateful for a minute alone to collect his wits. Ronny was a powerful man in the organization, and Jack had to better be on the ball, or
he could be in deep shit.

As he walked down the lighted hallway toward the shipping
office, Jack squared his shoulders and sucked in a deep breath to
clear his head. His stomach churned, and he wished that he had not
drunk so much beer.

"Hey, guys, what's goin' on?" Did you want me for something?"
He asked, trying not to sound nervous.

Ron Shanak was sitting on the desk with Todd and Rich hovering close by. Jack had no trouble telling the twins apart. Ron was
powerfully built, a good 30 pounds heavier than his twin was, and
with his dark goatee, he resembled a pro wrestler. He glanced at
Todd and Rich and then at the door. Without a word, they got up
and filed out into the hallway, leaving no doubt who was in charge
here. Ron hopped off the desk and walked over to the window then
turned to face Jack.

"Rich and Todd told me what you did tonight up in the mountains," he said mildly. "I must say I'm impressed. Too bad it wasn't
someone on my list, but I'll have to credit you nonetheless. Now
that you've proved that you're one of us, I have another little job
for you. I want you to go with Rich. The job shouldn't take too
long, so you can get back to your little sweeties in the warehouse."

Jack stood silently for a moment, absorbing the praise and
waiting for Ron to give him more details about the job, but Ron
had turned to face the window again. Jack had the feeling that he

had been dismissed, and it irritated him. He deserved to relax a little after what he'd accomplished, or at least to be told something about the mission he was being torn away from the party for.

He gathered up his courage and asked, "So, Ron, what's goin' on?"

Ron turned to look at him, surprised that Jack had the nerve to question his order. He thought about telling the little shit to just do as he was told, but if Jack has performed as well tonight as Todd and Rich had said, he was worth keeping around.

"I need you to go with Rich to bag a nigger drug dealer. A contact in spook town tells me that he carries a sizeable wad of cash, but I'm sure he carries a piece, too, so I need you to go with Rich to see that nobody gets hurt except the nigger and some of his tribe if they get in the way." Ron spoke as matter-of-factly, as if he was sending Jack to the store for milk.

Jack felt his gorge rise and was surprised by his own anger. He knew that he had to do as he was told if he was going to get anywhere in the Old World Order, but what Ron was ordering him to do was an insult. He hadn't joined a white supremacy organization just so he could rob nigger drug dealers like a common street junkie. Kicking the shit out of an Indian woman was bad enough.

"You gotta be kidding me," Jack blurted out.

Ron's eyebrows shot up, and his back stiffened.

"I did what you guys wanted me to do, now I'm getting pretty fucked up, and I know I can get one of them bitches into bed tonight," Jack continued.

Oblivious to the hard stare that Ron was leveling on him.

"Make someone else go with him. I've fucking had enough for one day."

Ron continued to stare at Jack without speaking, just shaking his head. Jack was beginning to regret talking back when Ron walked over to the desk and opened one of the drawers. Jack sucked in a breath, and his eyes widened. He was sure that Ron was going for a gun, but there was no way that he could escape, not with Todd and Rich standing right outside the door. When Ron stood and held his hand out to Jack, it contained only a crumpled can. Not a gun. Jack took the empty can and stared at it in puzzlement then looked at Ron. The can was the same brand that they had been drinking in the car on the ride into the mountains.

"What you're holding there is one of the five cans of beer that you drank after you became the killer-man of the mountains," Ron explained, his voice low. "I have four others that have your bloody fingerprints all over them. You should see the first two that you drank from. The cops wouldn't even have to dust those things, just hold them and compare them to your hand." Ron's grin was pure evil.

Jack stood, staring mutely at the crumpled metal, wondering how he could have been so fucking stupid. Of course, Ron didn't know that the squaw was still alive, or at least had been alive when Jack had left her. She could connect the attack to the O.W.O, and the beer cans would seal Jack's fate. He realized now that by flapping his gums to her about the Old World Order, Jack had risked the entire organization. That didn't seem to matter anymore. Now that this asshole was casually talking about blackmailing him, as if Jack was as disposable as the empty beer can in his hand.

"You can't do this to me, Ron," he pleaded. "I believed in the O.W.O. I believed that what you're trying to do is good for the country, but I'm not going to be your hit man. I've been a loyal member, so why are you turning on me?"

Ron raised his eyebrows at Jack's outburst, but remained unperturbed.

"I'm not turning on you. The organization has to protect itself," he explained slowly as if he was talking to a not-too-bright child. He pointed to the bloody can that Jack still held in his hand. "I don't want to have to use that, but you aren't leaving me any choice. You have to learn to follow orders without question."

Jack began to seethe with a black anger that seemed to come out of nowhere and might get him killed if he allowed it to boil over. He had dropped the can, and his hands were balled into fists that were so tight that his knuckles ached. He unclenched them with some effort and stole a glance out of the window that led out to the hallway. He couldn't see anyone out there standing guard, but that didn't mean that Rich and Todd weren't close by. There didn't seem to be any way out of this. If he did as Ron told him, he would be his stooge forever. If he didn't, he was sure that Ron would eliminate him with no more thought than swatting a fly. Holding his anger in check, Jack squared his thin shoulders. He wasn't going to be pushed around for the rest of his life.

"I'm calling your bluff, Ron, so you can go fuck yourself. If I cave in now, you'll just keep on using me. If the police come sniffing around me, I swear I'll kill you."

His heart pounding with a mixture of fear and anger, Jack turned around and was heading for the door when a bark of laughter from Ron stopped him in his tracks.

"You're gonna kill me, you little pissant?" Ron roared. "You think that I don't have friends everywhere? With what I've got on you, I guarantee that you'll end up in the state pen before you know what hit your sorry ass!"

Ron wasn't laughing anymore. He leaped at Jack with surprising speed, grabbing the back of his neck and spinning him around with a flick of his massive wrist.

"My friends in the pen will love you," he sneered in Jack's face, drawing out the word "love" obscenely. "You got such a cute little ass."

Jack stared into Ron's cold dark eyes, and something in his head suddenly snapped. Without being aware that he was even moving, Jack grabbed the metal gooseneck lamp from the desk beside him and smashed the heavy square base into Ron's left temple with stunning force. His eyes wide with amazement, Ron began to fall sideways, blood spurting from the ragged wound, showering Jack in the viscous red liquid for the second time that day. His fury unabated, Jack pounced on Ron before he hit the ground wrapping the lamp's electrical cord around Ron's neck and pulling it taut in one movement. Eyes popping, Ron tried to scrape the smaller man off of his back against the wall, looking absurdly like a bear scratching his back on a tree. Jack held on tenaciously, grunting as he pulled the cord tighter until it bit into the flesh of Ron's bull neck. After what seemed like an eternity, Ron's body went limp, and he crumpled to the floor. Jack got to his feet slowly, the strength draining from him like water from a bathtub. He stood panting over Ron's inert form, surveying the damage he had caused with astonished satisfaction. Blood was smeared over the big man's face, running into his bloodshot eyes and bubbling from his purple lips as he fought to take a breath of air. His doughy fingers tore at the cord that was still embedded deep in the flesh of his neck. Red foam spewed from his mouth in a sickening arc as Jack brought a booted foot down on Ron's stomach with all the force that he could muster.

"Just stay the fuck away from me," Jack advised his former leader in a rasping croak. "If you come near me again, I swear I'll kill you."

Ron could only manage a wheezing groan in response, but Jack didn't think that it would take him long to come around, and he didn't want to be anywhere near him when that happened. He turned and ran from the office on shaking legs.

To Jack's surprise, the hallway leading to the exit was mercifully deserted. Jack realized that no one had bothered to stay around to protect their leader. Who would have thought that the boss would need protection from his scrawny little underling? If anyone had suggested to Jack that he would be kicking Ron's ass that evening, he would have laughed his butt off. *I guess I showed those asshole's*, Jack thought triumphantly. Not being a total idiot, he also knew that his victory would be short-lived if anyone at the party discovered what he had done to Ron before he could make himself scarce.

Jack hurried to the fire exit and out to the parking lot. *Elvis has left the building*, he thought with gleeful relief as he closed the door quietly behind him. He breathed in huge gulps of the crisp night air as he crossed the parking lot, and he began to run as soon as he reached the street. He ran as far as he could, looking over his shoulder periodically. No one followed.

After running a few blocks, aching weariness forced Jack to slow to a trot then finally to an unsteady walk. He looked fearfully over his shoulder one last time. Behind him the street was dark and silent. Streetlights cast empty pools of light on the pavement. Jack couldn't believe that Ron hadn't come around enough by now to send someone after him, then the truth dawned on him with sickening force. His former friends had no need to follow him into the night. They knew where he lived. The Old World Order had all the time in the world to deal with him.

Home was not the safest place in the world that Jack could go right now, but he had nowhere else to go. He had no friends that weren't a part of the O.W.O., which meant that now he had no friends at all. Stacey would surely turn him away if he showed up on her doorstep in the middle of the night. After a lifetime of feeling alone, Jack had finally hit rock bottom. All he could think about now was his comfortable bed, five miles away in the Sunset Trailer Park. He would worry about his future if he had one in the morning.

As he trudged along, Jack caught a glimpse of his image in a storefront window and was horrified to see that he was covered in Ron Shanak's blood. *Oh, Christ*, he thought. *What if a cop comes along?* He hurried down a side street, peering down driveways until he spotted a garden hose coiled by the side of a garage. The house was dark. Jack crept silently to the side of the garage and turned the spigot on then pulled the hose along the driveway to the far side of the garage. He hosed himself off quickly, clenching his teeth and shivering as the icy stream of water stung his skin. When he felt cleansed enough, he dropped the hose and continued in the direction of his home and his bed.

He glanced over his shoulder from time to time sure that those assholes in the O.W.O. would come screeching up behind him any minute. He wouldn't stand a chance if they found him. When it finally dawned on him that they might not be coming after all, fear gradually gave way to anger. *They played me for a fuckin' gofer, the big bad Old World Order is nothin' but a bunch of muggers and thieves. They don't give a flying fart about improving the lot of the righteous working white man.* It never occurred to Jack that he had never worked a day in his life. *I'll show those asshole's,* he decided, *and that bitch squaw for putting a curse on me.*

He thought about the Indian Jamboree that was coming up in a few short weeks, and the rifle that leaned against the wall of his bedroom. *I'll take out a few of those squaws relatives. That'll make 'em sit up and take notice of ol' Jack King. I'll bet the TV reporters will be falling all over each other to get an interview with me then.* Comforted by the picture of his future glory, Jack continued toward his warm bed.

Chilled before his impromptu shower, Jack was numb to the bone by the time he reached the front gate of the Sunset Trailer Park. He stumbled into his grandmother's trailer and was not surprised to find her asleep in her ratty blue recliner, a weight-loss infomercial blaring from the portable television. His grandmother had her own bedroom, but she preferred to have the company of the television as she slept. The sound of human voices helped to alleviate the old woman's loneliness. At one time she had looked forward to having Jack around, but he had been surly from the start. He had never given the old woman a chance to get close to him and she hadn't been up to the challenge of earning his trust.

Jack turned the television set off, the overhead light. He unlocked the door to his bedroom and went inside, locking the deadbolt behind him. He stripped off his still-damp clothes and collapsed onto his bed gratefully. It took all of the strength that his trembling arms had left to pull the covers up over his exhausted body. As he fought off sleep, Jack tried to make sense of all that had happened that endless day, but his thoughts fluttered around in his head like demented butterflies.

He was still furious about being treated like dirt by those asshole's in the Old World Order. He would have to do something to show them that Jack King was no mere lackey. In the dim light that shone under the door, he could see the outline of the assault rifle that sat propped in the corner.

Jack remembered a poster he had seen in a local mom and pop store that advertised a jamboree for Indian children that would be held in nearby park the following weekend. He could do some damage to some fuckin' redskins with his trusty rifle. That would make those shit-heads in the O.W.O. sit up and take notice, all right. He tried to formulate a plan of action, but sleep had laid claim to his body the moment that his head had hit the pillow, and Jack finally gave up and surrendered to it. There would be time to think about it in the morning.

Two horned panthers of the Underworld sat by the side of Jack's bed as invisible and silent and as patient as death. They waited for the right time to take possession of his cursed soul.

Part 5
Chapter 35

August 28, 1969

Chris Logue had completed his Army basic training at Fort Hood and had been assigned to the First Air Cavalry Division. Chris had thought that he was in pretty good shape, but boot camp had proved to be physically and mentally exhausting. Before boot camp, Chris had been worried that he would never be able to take a human life, no matter what the circumstances, but two weeks of Advanced Individual Training had changed all that. Still nervous about going off to war, Chris also felt a growing sense that he would be able to do whatever it took to get home alive. The Army had not only given him a pistol and a rifle, but he had been imbued with a passion to kill the enemy.

Aboard a troop transport plane flying high above the blue waters of the China Sea, Chris sat with a pad of paper on his lap. The plane would be landing in Chu Lai soon, and he wanted to get one last letter off to his parents before joining his platoon in the jungle. Chris stared at the blank sheet of paper and tried to think of something to write. It had been hard to keep his letters upbeat during basic training, but for his mother's sake he had done his best. What he had on his mind now was not only the overwhelming fear of dying, but the nagging certainty that if he survived the war, he would be forever changed. Not exactly subject matter for a sunny letter to the folks. Chris sighed and started to write.

Dear Mom and Dad,

    In an hour we'll be landing in Vietnam. Even though the butterflies are
    fluttering in my stomach, I feel ready to serve my country. I want to thank you again for driving to Fort Hood for my graduation. It was really great to see you guys again (even Jon,ha ha). We'll know more about where we're going to end up once we land. I'll write as soon as I can to let you know how things are going. I don't want you to worry about me too much. I think I can take care of myself and believe me, I plan to be as cautious as I possibly can. Once again, I'll write to you every chance I get. Until then, I love you and miss you all very much.

Love, Chris

P.S. Tell Jon not to forget to start my truck every week. I want it to be in good running order when I get back! Thanks.

    Chris clipped the pen to the pad of stationary and returned it to his duffel bag. Out of sheer habit, he brought his hand up and reached back to touch his ponytail. He laughed when he remembered, for the umpteenth time that Uncle Sam had shorn him like a sheep two long months ago. The nervous habit of tugging on his hair was hard to break. His ponytail had been a part of him for such a long time.
    He sat with his head against the wall of the plane, lulled to a state of near-sleep by the vibration of the powerful engines. His mind wandered to Brian, still lying in his hospital bed. He was out of the Intensive Care Unit now, but he had a long way to go. The doctors called his condition a light coma now. They said that it might be a year or longer before they could determine the extent of

his brain damage. Carolyn would be moving him and the life support to their home as soon as possible because she and Matt couldn't keep up with the hospital bills. She would be quitting her job at the nursing home to stay home and care for her son. There was no way that she and Matt could afford to keep him in a nursing home or rehabilitation, center and Carolyn had confided to Chris that she would be Brian's best chance at someday resuming a normal life. Chris thought the she was probably right, but he wondered how they would manage on Matt's income as a truck driver. Carolyn's letters to Chris in boot camp seemed to be more optimistic than the situation called for, but he could understand why she would hang on to hope with all of her might. Brian was her only child.

Ryan had told Chris that Brian was wearing the arrowhead necklace every time that they visited him. Carolyn had said that she had instructed the nurses to keep it on him at all times as a good luck charm for the safe return of her son and his best friend wherever they were.

Thinking about Brian brought tears of guilt and pain to Chris's eyes, as always. He closed his eyes and was soon rocked to sleep by the gentle rolling of the airplane. He dreamed of Pam, walking on a tree lined street on campus, her books cradled in her slender arms. He had never envied anyone more in his life.

Chris did not wake up until the troop transport was preparing to land on Chu Lai. Dawn was breaking in the eastern sky as the plane banked during its final ascent. Chris felt a stab of homesickness as he watched the pink streaks in the sky turn to pale yellow washed with blue as the sun rose over the water. He imagined his mother starting breakfast as she hollered for Jon to hurry up and get out of bed. He knew that with the time change the sun wasn't really rising over Devine now, but that didn't matter. He wanted to be home more than he had ever wanted anything in his life.

After the plane had landed, the raw recruits were herded unceremoniously into lines to await their orders. The young soldiers sat on their duffel bags in the steamy heat of southeast Asia as they were called into the command tent one or two at a time to receive the number and location of the platoon that they would be joining in the field. The soldiers talked nervously among themselves, wondering where they would end up and what their lives would be like in the jungle. Chris heard the names of so many Vietnamese villages that he wasn't sure any more which ones were hostile and which were friendly. After a few hours of sitting in the stifling heat, Chris began looking around for the mess hall. Maybe he would have time for a real meal before his name was called. He couldn't remember when he had eaten last, and he would be living on c-rations and stagnant water soon enough. As he stood, Chris heard his name being called. Inside the tent, a young sergeant told him that he had been assigned to Platoon B with the 163th3 Infantry. The 163th3 was currently based in the A Shau Valley in the southeast corner of the Thua Thien Province near the Laotian border. The platoon needs replacements for the soldiers who were going home and for those who had been wounded. The A Shau Valley was an annex to the Ho Chi Minh trail. The North Vietnamese used the valley as a supply pipeline to the Viet cong in the south, and the fighting there was often fierce. The Army and Marines had been trying for the past two years to shut off the stream of enemy supplies with some success, but the Viet cong still had control of half of the mountains that surrounded the valley. Air strikes were common, and Chris was advised to stay close to his platoon at all times.

Chris would be leaving by helicopter at 1800 hours. At the city of Hue, he would join other troop reinforcements and then head west to the A Shua Valley. The sergeant finished by instructing Chris to stay in the compound and suggested that he get a 'hot and a cot' before departing for Hue. He pointed out the supply hut and the mess tent and gave Chris a clap on his shoulder as he wished him luck. A meal and a nap sounded good to Chris. He was starving by this time' and he was still exhausted from the long flight.

After a tasteless meal in the mess tent, Chris made his way to the supply hut. He was issued a folded cot and told to set it up in the holdover area at the back of a nearby barracks. The morning sun had warmed the plywood barracks, and Chris had to stop and wipe perspiration from his forehead as he walked down the aisle past the vacant bunks that lined the walls. He struggled to carry the wooden cot along with his backpack and duffel bag.

The holdover sleeping quarters were empty except for a few discarded cots that lay scattered on the wooden floor. Chris guessed that their former occupants were already somewhere 'in country.' He set up his own cot and took off his fatigue shirt and boots. Sitting on the narrow cot, he pulled his rolled army blanket from the straps of his backpack. Using the blanket as a pillow, he laid back on the cot, falling into a fitful sleep while listening to the sounds of the compound through the thin plywood walls.

The camp was alive with the roar of heavy equipment engines punctuated by the voices of men talking and laughing as they walked nearby and the muffled voices of men yelling in the distance.

Chris drifted in and out of a fitful sleep throughout the afternoon. From time to time an unusually loud noise would startle him awake, and he would look around groggily, trying to remember where in the hell he was. When he realized where he was, hell seemed to be the right word. The dry heat of west Texas had not prepared him for the stifling humidity of the jungle. Chris felt like he was trying to take a nap in a hot shower. The constant flow of sweat running down his neck finally became too vexing, and he sat up on the rickety cot and swiped at his face and neck with the hem of his tee shirt.

Sitting cross-legged on the cot, he opened the side pocket of his backpack and took out a silver-faced wristwatch with a broken leather strap. His father had given him the watch years earlier when he had gotten a new one for Christmas. Chris had been proud of the watch but had never worn it and had never bothered to get the strap replaced. When he was packing the few belongings that he would be taking overseas, he had tucked the watch into his pocket on impulse. It still kept good time, and Chris found it comforting to have something of his father's with him. He stared at the second hand as it swept rhythmically within the small circle. How depressing it was to see his life tick away. At 4:45 he sighed and gently returned the watch to the pocket of his backpack. Soon he would be joining his unit, but there was still time to write a short letter to Pam.

Chris opened the letter by telling her that he hoped that she was adjusting to college life and that he wished that he was there with her, which was certainly the God's honest truth. He updated her on his whereabouts, downplaying how close he was to the enemy. As he tried to decide if it was right to scare Pam by sharing his own fears with her, he was startled by a deep voice from the doorway.

"Are you Private Christopher Logue?" A tall man with a handlebar moustache barked. The brim of a green camouflage cap and mirrored sunglasses hid the rest of his angular face.

Chris shot up from the cot, dropping his pen and paper and trying to salute at the same time when he read the nameplate on the man's breast pocket.

"Captain Thomas Wallace," the man announced.

"Yes, sir," Chris replied sharply.

The captain walked over to the fallen paper and picked it up. He glanced at it, and Chris saw the ghost of a smile cross his thin lips. Wallace dropped the letter onto the green canvas cot and turned to face Chris. A little of the edge was missing from his voice now.

"Finish up your letter to your sweetie and get your things together, Logue. We'll be heading out soon. I'll see you at bird number 4287 in 15 minutes." As he turned and left the barracks.

Chris stuffed the pen and paper back into his duffel bag and rolled his blanket tight again. After strapping the blanket onto his backpack, Chris reluctantly slipped his shirt back on. His fingers trembled as he pushed the buttons through their holes and tucked the shirttails into the waistband of his pants. He loosened the strap that held the helmet to his backpack and pulled it free, then dropped the helmet onto the cot as he hoisted the backpack onto his right shoulder. His head began to sweat as soon as he donned the metal helmet. Carrying the duffel bag in his left hand and his M16 rifle in his right, he hurried to the helicopter pad.

He found Captain Wallace standing by the tail section of the UH-1 helicopter that had the numbers 4287stenciled on the side. Chris transferred his rifle to his left hand and saluted. The captain returned the salute and motioned to the chopper.

"Hop in, Private Logue. It's just you and I today, no copilot and no gunner. We're gonna need all the cargo space we can get once we load the ammo we're picking up in Hue."

Chris pulled himself into the Huey and inched toward the tail. He stowed his gear in an empty footlocker strapped to the side of the chopper, then climbed into the co-pilot seat. Captain Wallace climbed into the pilot's seat, and the mirrored sunglasses turned to Chris.

"There's a couple of things I gotta tell you before we take off. First, since we've got no gunner, I'll need you to man the 70 if we get into heavy fire," he said, pointing to the M70 machine gun that was mounted by the passenger side door. He laughed at the look of dismay on Chris's face as he regarded the machine gun.

"Don't worry, Logue, all you have to do is pull the trigger and sweep. I'll tell ya' which direction," the captain said, putting on his own headset. "We should be all right during our day flight, but after dark it might be a different story. After dark, I'd advise you to sit on your helmet instead of wearin' it on your head. If one of them fuckin' VC get a bullet into the belly of this bird you'll be glad you did. It might just keep you from gettin' your balls shot off."

Chris took the advice with alacrity, and by the time the captain had fired up the Huey's engine, he was trying his best to get his ass into the helmet.

Chris felt his stomach lurch as the powerful rotor blade lifted the helicopter into the air, but once they were airborne, he found the colorful landscape below fascinating. The noise from the chopper's engine and blades made normal conversation impossible even with the headsets, so Chris had an hour to take in the view. It didn't seem possible that the serene rice paddies surrounded by verdant green jungles were the settings for death and destruction.

After an hour in the air, the Huey began to descend toward a clearing in the jungle a quarter of a mile ahead. As they neared the clearing, Chris saw a man on the ground signaling the aircraft with arm gestures. Chris was grateful that the Huey's landing was surprisingly soft. His ass was balancing precariously on the helmet, and he couldn't handle a rough landing. As soon as they touched ground, Chris scrambled out of the chopper on the Captain's signal. The ground controller was running toward the Huey, and they met 50 yards away from the swirling props.

The controller pointed to the pilot and shouted, "Is that Captain Wallace?" Chris nodded in response.

The controller ran to the pilot's side of the Huey and opened the door. Chris watched as the two men shouted into each other's ears for a few moments, their clothes billowing in the wind from the propeller blades. The soldier ran back to where Chris stood.

"See that truck?" He yelled into Chris's ear.

Chris nodded as his eyes followed the young controller's hand pointing to a camouflage-painted supply vehicle sitting 50 yards away from the idling Huey.

"Private Baldwin will be helping you unload the first pallet of ammo into your bird," the soldier continued, "Just take the first pallet and double time it. Captain Wallace has casualties to lift out once you get to Hue. There was a pretty heavy exchange of fire this morning and we got some wounded."

Chris marveled at the 'exchange of fire' euphemism for a gun battle as he ran for the supply truck. He caught a glimpse of the nearby camp and decided that this was what he had expected Vietnam to look like. In the camp, surrounded by lush green jungle, some of the soldiers hurried around, performing various duties as others lounged in the hot sun, smoking cigarettes and playing cards. A line of Vietnamese natives walked single file along side of the dirt road that skirted the camp, a few of them leading oxen laden with food-filled baskets.

A soldier was already starting to unload the wooden pallets from the rear of the truck when Chris got there. He turned to face Chris and held out his hand with a wide grin.

"How ya' doin? I'm Phil Baldwin."

Chris shook his hand. "Chris Logue," he replied, "Good to meet you."

Baldwin was a good six inches taller than Chris and outweighed him by 50 pounds. His hand engulfed Chris's.

"Damn, Chris," he laughed. "You look as shiny as a new nickel. How long you been in country?" Phil resumed unloading the wooden ammo crates, and Chris pitched in.

"I've been here about 10 hours," Chris replied as he hefted one of the heavy crates.

They were going to have a hell of a time getting the ammo to the waiting Huey. Baldwin took hold of the rope handle on one end of the wooden crate and started for the chopper, dragging Chris along by the other handle. Chris stumbled as he hurried to keep up with the big man.

Baldwin talked as they walked, his voice rising to a shout as they neared the helicopter.

"Man, you gotta be shittin' me! Ten fuckin hours!

You're the cherriest of the cherries." He laughed companionably, but his face was serious as he continued. "Let me tell you, Chris, I was in communications when the call came in from our unit. They've been fighting all morning with north regulars in the valley. This isn't the first Air Vac they've needed today. One of the guys I know in B Platoon was killed. I gotta feelin' we're gonna be goin' in hot!"

Chris didn't need an interpreter to figure out what that meant.

After they had loaded the last of the ammo crates, Phil ran back to the truck to retrieve his backpack and rifle. Knowing that this might be his last chance for a while to get mail out, Chris pulled the letters to Pam and his folks out of his duffel bag and ran them over to the ground controller.

"Could you get these mailed to the states for me?" He asked, trying to catch his breath. The soldier took the letters from Chris' hand.

"Yeah, sure. Mail will be going out tomorrow."

Chris waved his thanks and hurried back to the Huey. Climbing back into the co-pilot's seat, he was relieved to see that Private Baldwin was positioned by the M70. He wasn't sure that he could handle the powerful weapon. Before takeoff, Captain Wallace yelled instructions to Chris through his headset.

"We're gonna be in the air for about 15 minutes, and we'll probably draw some fire. If Baldwin can keep that '70 going, it ought to keep them in their hole. Make sure you feed Baldwin what he needs." He cocked his thumb in the direction of an open ammunition crate behind Chris. "I hope to hell Baldwin doesn't jam up the '70 or we're in deep shit," the captain added as the Huey lifted off, stirring up a cloud of dust and leaves.

Chris looked over his shoulder at Private Baldwin, and the two young soldiers shrugged in unison. As scared as Chris was, he figured that now was as good a time as any to be initiated into the world of jungle combat. His special training was fresh in his mind and a part of him was ready to kick some ass.

Chris sat silently in the Huey's co-pilot seat, glancing over his shoulder at Private Baldwin from time to time. They were still 5 minutes away from the A Shau Valley when he began to experience an odd, floating sensation. He closed his eyes to quell the dizziness, but it grew steadily worse. When his stomach began to roll, Chris decided that he'd better tell Captain Wallace that he was sick. Opening his eyes, he was surprised to see that the interior of the helicopter was suffused with an eerie blue glow, which was darkening rapidly. The sound of Huey's turbo engine was fading, replaced by a soft, insistent buzz. Chris vaguely recalled having had this peculiar sensation before, then remembered that it had been when he had touched the ancient wolf's jawbone in the medicine man's shop back in Mexico. That night the blue cloud had

transported him to another time and place, and now it was engulf-
ing him again.

Chapter 36

August 28, 1999

Jack King's body glistened with sweat as he writhed in his bed, twisting the sheets into sodden knots. He was deep in the most terrifying nightmare of his life. *He was running, stark naked, through a dense forest. No, it wasn't a forest, it was a jungle. Jack's body ached from exhaustion, his lungs burned from the effort of sucking in hot, dank air. He had no idea where he was, but he had to keep going at all costs. He was being pursued relentlessly and the voices behind him were getting closer. The pain in his feet was excruciating but a fear drove him on. He knew that if whoever was behind him in the jungle caught up to him, he would die a horrible death.*

Chapter 37

Hupa sat with his legs folded and his arms to his sides. His son Matachias to his left and his Uncle Kenekuk to his right. A slight breeze slid across Lake Kahooga ruffling his long black hair and the eagle feather atop his suede hat. "The Great Spirit has heard the cries of our people that suffer from the hands of evil. It is now time to strip the one called 'Jack King' to his soul. He must see the evil that festers inside his heart and poisons his mind." Matachias and Kenekuk nodded in agreement. "The horned panthers wait by his bedside, they will take his soul and torture him forever! What if we are too late?" Matachias asked. "The horned panthers of the Underworld will take Jack King's soul, but first they will play with him like a panther plays with its injured catch before he devours it." Kenekuk answered.

Chapter 38

Jack fell to his knees on the floor of the jungle, choking and gasping. The strange voices were closing in, and he knew he didn't have the stamina to outrun them. It was time to hide. He wrenched handfuls of lush green foliage from the soft ground. Maybe he could hide in the thick brush and use the uprooted plants as camouflage. Jack lay motionless, trying to quiet his labored breathing as the dark figures drew closer. The pounding of his heart was so loud in his ears that he feared that they would be able to hear it.

Without moving his head, Jack watched as the dark silhouettes walked past. His eyes widened in fear, and he drew in a sharp, searing breath as he made out the unmistakable shapes of rifles in their hands. Now Jack heard his pursuers speaking clearly, but he couldn't understand a word. What the hell language were they speaking? Chinese? Japanese? *Oh, God*, he thought. This *isn't happening*. In his panic, Jack forgot that he needed to lie perfectly still. He began to groan and shake his head violently from side to side.

As Jack shot upright in his bed, his head was still shaking. He stared around the room wildly and slowly began to recognize the familiar surroundings of his own bedroom. He realized that his hands clutched not at palm fronds, but at damp bed sheets. Still panting, he lay his aching head back on his pillow and closed his eyes then opened them again as images of the nightmare flashed before him.

There was a rising uneasiness in his stomach that was hard to ignore. He tried, gulping in mouthfuls of night air. Maybe if he just lay still for a while it would pass. No such luck. Jack's stomach spasm painfully, threatening to rid itself of all the beer he had drunk that night. He threw the covers to the floor and stumbled toward the bathroom, cursing thickly as he fumbled with the deadbolt on the bedroom door. He reached the bathroom in time and collapsed on the cold tile, hanging his head scant inches above the water in the toilet bowl. Dizzy and weak, his stomach churning, Jack rested his head on the white porcelain.

Eyes half closed, Jack looked around the room, and it dawned on him slowly that something was very wrong. This wasn't the cramped bathroom in his grandmother's trailer. Somehow, he was in the bathroom of his mother's house in Brunswick, Ohio. *Oh, Christ*, he thought miserably *I'm still dreaming*.

Jack forced his body to sit up, bringing on another retching, painful stomach spasm. Sour bile rose in his throat, and he spit into the bowl.

"What the fuck am I doing in Brunswick?" he moaned. "This doesn't feel like a dream anymore."

Jack wished he could get the hell out of the bathroom, but the agonizing waves of nausea were coming faster now, keeping him glued to the toilet. After what seemed like hours, the muscles of his abdomen convulsed, sending the contents of his stomach north to his esophagus. As the mass reached his throat, Jack gagged, then he vomited explosively.

Resting his head against the side of the toilet, Jack's eyes flew open wide in shocked surprise as he felt a strange, fluttering movement in his mouth. When he saw what was pouring out of him, he leaped backwards, gagging in horror, and sprawled backwards into the bathtub, arms flailing helplessly. Jack ignored the pain as his head hit the edge of the bathtub. He was unaware of the trickle of blood from the gash on the back of his head. All he could see was the swarm of shiny brown insects that buzzed up and out of the toilet bowl, flying toward him. The buzzing of their iridescent wings grew louder as they approached, bringing on a fresh wave of nausea. Jack vomited again, spewing out another vile stream of insects. They made a soft clicking sound as they hit the side of the tub. Jack tried to scream, but his throat had constricted so that all he could manage was a thick *Uuuuh.* The small bathroom seemed to pulsate from the hum of the thousands of tiny wings. Like moths drawn to light, the winged demons flew at Jack, covering his face and body in their mission to return to the nest. They burrowed their heads into his ears and nose. With each gasping breath he took more of the disgusting creatures into his mouth. Jack swiped at them desperately trying to free himself of the intruders. The harder he struggled the more the swarm threatened to suffocate him.

Weak from lack of oxygen, Jack finally succumbed, dropping his arms to his sides as he lapsed into blessed unconsciousness. The last sound he was aware of was the drone of the insect wings, a drone that shifted subtly, metamorphosing into the sound of helicopter blades as the darkness closed in around him.

The steady "whup,whup, whup" of the chopper blades was the first sound Jack heard as he swam back to consciousness, but he didn't know what he was hearing. He grunted and spat and swiped wildly at his mouth. Shuddering as he brushed away the insects that were no longer there. It took a few fuzzy seconds for Jack to realize that he was able to breathe freely again, and he gratefully sucked delicious air into his lungs. Still, in a pool of darkness, his vision slowly began to clear. He looked around and was puzzled by what looked like the blurred outline of a soldier sitting behind a machine gun. *Oh, shit, not another fucking nightmare!*

Then the soldier spoke. "You okay, Logue?" Private Baldwin asked.

Jack realized that the question was being directed at him. As he opened his mouth to ask who Logue was, the first bullets slammed into the Huey's side.

The helicopter listed to one side as Captain Wallace tried to maneuver out of the line of fire. Jack slid toward the port side of

the chopper, scrambling to keep from hitting the crates that lined
the wall. As the helicopter righted itself, he sat up. In the dim light,
he looked down at his body. He was dressed in camouflage Army
fatigues. The boots on his feet weren't Doc Martins but spit-shined
Army boots. As he tried to make sense out of what was happening,
the chopper pilot barked out an order: "Fire!"

And the soldier behind the machine gun squeezed the weapon's trigger.

The blast was so loud that Jack barely heard Private Baldwin
when he shouted. "Hey Logue, you better get ready to feed me
those rounds!"

Jack stared at Baldwin, agape-mouthed, as the soldier swept
the machine gun from side to side. "Rounds?" Jack wondered what
the fuck the man was talking about.

When he got no response from Logue, Baldwin shouted louder.
"Come on, man, I'm runnin' out!"

He took his hand from the trigger just long enough to point.
"The ammo! In the crates! Hurry the fuck up!"

Captain Wallace and Private Baldwin did not observe the
change that had taken place. Jack King was now the co-pilot!

Panic swept over Jack as he looked at the wooden crates that
Baldwin pointed to. He had no idea what he was supposed to be
doing, but the lurching of the helicopter seemed so real that he
thought that he'd better play along with the nightmare. A burst of
bullets slamming into the side of the chopper sent Jack reeling into
the wooden crates. The compartment was filling with acrid black
smoke.

Jack was pulling at the lid of one of the ammo crates when
Captain Wallace screamed. "We're hit hard! We're going down!
When she hits the ground, run! The gooks will be on the wreckage
in no time!"

Jack wondered if this nightmare would end before the chopper
crashed. At the rate that they were plunging toward the earth, he
doubted if any of them would survive the impact. He braced himself against a wooden crate and waited for the dream to play itself

out. Choking in the thick black smoke, the pilot was wrestling with the helicopter's controls, and Baldwin was still gamely firing the machine gun, though God only knew what his target was. The Huey lurched sickeningly to the right as it's belly brushed the treetops. The metal propellers groaned then snapped off. Jack heard the shriek of metal on metal as the propeller slammed into the side of the chopper. He scrambled to the top of the crate and hung on for dear life as the Huey plummeted through the jungle, wincing at the screeching sound of snapping tree limbs scraping against the hull of the doomed aircraft. He closed his eyes and waited for the nightmare to end.

Chapter 39

August 28,1999

Chris awoke in the soft bed, the pillow under his head caressing his face like a cloud of cotton. He stretched luxuriously and wondered if it was time to get up and go to school. As the sleep-fog slowly lifted, he remembered that he had graduated a few months earlier. He sat bolt upright as he realized that he should be in a helicopter over a Vietnam jungle heading toward the Shau Valley, not a comfy bed.

"Where the hell am I?" He asked out loud as his eyes adjusted to the darkness. Now he could see dim shapes of the furniture in the room, and none of the shapes were familiar. Was he in a hospital bed? He took a quick inventory and found no wounds on his body.

Chris swung his feet over the side of the bed and carefully navigated around the walls of the room until he found a light switch. He closed his eyes against the harsh lamplight as he flipped the switch. When he opened them again, the first thing his eyes came to rest on was a poster of Adolph Hitler in full salute.

"Where the hell AM I?" He asked again, dumfounded.

The walls of the small room were plastered with Nazi memorabilia: swastikas and SS symbols. Chris wondered if he had come to in the bedroom of a Nazi soldier during the Second World War, then he spotted the boom box sitting on a scratched wooden dresser.

Definitely not World War Two, he thought, *kinda looks like World War Three.* The strange looking contraption was obviously some kind of radio, but Chris had never seen anything like it. He was tempted to turn it on, but it occurred to him that someone else might be in the house. The thought made his stomach clench with fear.

Chris opened the bedroom door a crack and peered out into the darkness. There was no sign of life in the hallway, no sound from the rest of the house. He sat on the bed and thought about what he should do next. For the first time, he looked down at his body and discovered that he wasn't wearing his green Army-issued shorts, but white Jockeys. He looked around and saw an untidy pile of clothes at the foot of the bed. He held up the wrinkled T-shirt and wondered what the hell the letters O.W.O. stood for.

"Doesn't matter," he mumbled. "I need to get the fuck out of here and figure out how to get home, or back to 'Nam, or whatever."

He was beginning to feel cold fingers of panic tickling his spine.

The first order of business was to figure out a way to sneak out of wherever the hell he was. Chris pulled the black T-shirt over his head and shuddered slightly as the damp fabric came to rest on his bare skin. He wriggled into the tight, clammy camouflage pants. These pants definitely weren't Army issue. There was a bulge in the back pocket. With no difficulty, Chris slid his hand into the pocket and extracted a worn leather wallet. His hands shook as he opened the billfold. He breathed a sigh of relief as he pulled out a few wrinkled dollar bills. The currency was American so he was probably in his homeland, at least. He began to count out the money; he might need it. If he wasn't in Devine, he would have to find his way home somehow.

The one-dollar bills looked completely normal, but he found a twenty that looked odd. The portrait of Andrew Jackson was larger than normal. Chris examined the bill closely, turning it over in his hand. Maybe it was some kind of joke money, like Monopoly money or something. He inhaled sharply when he saw the date on the bill,

1999. His legs shook, and he sat back down on the bed with a soft thump. *This can't be, this fuckin' can't be happening*, he thought. *Must be joke money*, he assured himself? He took a few deep breaths to steady his jangling nerves and stood again, stuffing the cash into the front pocket of the jeans.

Returning to his search of the wallet, Chris found a few business cards in a side compartment. The names on the cards didn't mean anything to him, but the addresses were in El Paso, he noted with some relief. He dropped the cards onto the bed and continued dissecting the billfold. The driver's license that he found had been issued by the state of Texas, Jack K. King, 42 Sunset Parkway, El Paso, Texas, D.O.B. 2/17/81 Issue date: 3/12/98 Expires on birthday 2002. Chris blinked and read the date again, 2002. His legs threatened to go out from under him, and he slumped down on the bed again. He stared at the picture on the plastic license. The face that stared back at him looked like it belonged on a mug-shot. The long thin face topped by a Mohawk. He looked slightly demented, but the icy blue eyes were what sent a new chill down Chris's spine. If this was some kind of a joke, it was not only an elaborate prank, but a creepy one to boot.

With a sudden feeling of revulsion, Chris flung the license on the bed where it joined the discarded business cards and scraps of paper. He wiped his palms on his thighs then raised them to his throbbing temples. As he kneaded the sides of his head, his rational mind slowly began to function again. If he really was in Texas in 1999, there must be an explanation. Though not necessarily a logical one. In times of stress, he had developed a habit of rubbing the smooth stone arrowhead that he had always worn on a leather thong around his neck. Now his hand automatically reached for the cool comfort of the stone and came up empty. Remembering that he had left the arrowhead with Brian in the Intensive Care Unit to bring him good luck. *Shoulda kept it*, he thought ruefully.

Thinking about the arrowhead jogged another memory, the face of Matachias flashed through Chris's mind. He had tried to forget about the spooky old Indian and his macabre ceremony, but now the memory played in his head like a bad movie. Chris had wished to skip the Vietnam War and the next 30 years.

The medicine man had told him that his wish would be granted. "No," Chris corrected himself. "The old man said that my wish had been granted. Oh, shit," he moaned, "I was only kidding!" Could that be the reason that he was in this crappy little bedroom wearing someone else's cold, wet clothes? Did that creepy old medicine man and his wolf jaw and smelly herbs send him to the future? If that was the case, maybe Jack King had taken his place in the Huey.

Chris knew the answer wasn't here in Jack's bedroom in El Paso. He would have to get himself back to Devine somehow, but how could he contact anyone that he knew? If 30 years really had passed, then he would have been given up for dead long ago.

The thought made him terribly sad. His parents must have suffered so much. How could he just pop in and say, "Hi, I'm back." The thought of how they would react to their son's sudden resurrection made him smile a little in spite of himself until he realized that they might not even be alive. If there was a way to go back to where he belonged, Chris would have to find the arrowhead. It occurred to him then that Brian might not have survived the accident. Maybe if Brian had died, Carolyn would have buried the necklace with him. The thought made him shiver. He suddenly wanted nothing more than anything to be back in the helicopter heading west toward the Shau Valley.

He hadn't wanted to be in Vietnam, but it was where he was supposed to be, no matter the outcome. As intriguing as it was to see what the world had become, Chris already felt isolated and alone. The relationships that he had in the '60's were over. If he couldn't get back to his own time, he would have to build a life from nothing.

Chris looked around the room one last time. He caught sight of his reflection in the mirror over the dresser and was relieved to see that he was still 18. The lighted dial of the clock on the dresser read 3:47. It would be getting light soon. Surely El Paso had a bus station. If he could find it, he could get to Devine in a few hours. His eyes came to rest on the assault rifle propped in the corner of the room. The Nazi posters and the icy blue eyes in the driver's license made the sight of the rifle all the more chilling. *King, you must be a real fuckin' prince*, Chris thought, shaking his head slowly. *If I do get back to 'Nam, I hope to hell you're not there.*

He slipped out of the bedroom and made his way quietly down the narrow hallway. As he tiptoed into the small living room of the trailer, he saw the shadow of a form slumped in a recliner that sat between him and the front door. Chris held his breath as moved closer to the chair. In the dim light from a street lamp that filtered through the tiny front window, he saw the unmistakable shape of a Jack Daniel bottle on the table near the recliner. "Well, at least that hasn't changed," he chuckled. The figure in the chair didn't stir as Chris eased the front door open. He hit the gravel running and didn't stop until he came to the gate of the Sunset Trailer Park. He had decided to go to the house that Carolyn, Matt and Brian had lived in when Chris had left for Vietnam. If it was possible to find his way back to the Huey, Brian's house was as good a place to start as any.

Chapter 40

Brian Boscorelli had just arrived home after dropping his mother off at her job at the nursing home. He parked the 1985 Honda Accord in the drive and hurried into the house. He darted for the ringing phone, hoping that it might be his bookie. He was hoping to get his bet in before the baseball game between Houston and San Diego started, and his bookie was harder than hell to get a hold of on Sunday mornings.

"Yeah, hello," he panted into the receiver.

There was a moment of silence before a soft voice asked hesitantly, "Brian?"

Brian thought that he heard the line click, but he answered anyway.

"Yeah, this is Brian."

The line went dead. He felt the tickle of fine hairs on his arms as he hung up the phone. Even though he had heard only the one word, the voice had been eerily familiar.

Brian grabbed a beer from the fridge and flopped on the couch with the sports section of the Sunday paper. He wanted to analyze the odds on the games that were going to be played that day. As he read the sports page, the soft voice on the phone nagged at the back of his mind. He wished that he could place it.

"Chris," his mind said. "It sounded like Chris." Brian shook his head and took a long swallow of beer. Chris was dead. The voice on the phone was someone else, someone that sounded like his dead friend, that was all.

The 30 years that had passed since Brian had seen his best friend had not been kind. A graying horseshoe of fuzz had replaced his crop of thick curly hair. A few stray wisps were scattered above his forehead. Four days worth of gray stubble on his chin and deep crow's feet at the corners of his eyes made him look ten years older than his true age. Alcohol was catching up to Brian, at 48 he looked withered and washed out.

The words on the sports page became blurred. Now that the memory of Chris had intruded on his Sunday, Brian couldn't shake it loose. He put the newspaper down and rested his head on the back of the couch. The knock on the front door startled Brian, he and Carolyn didn't get many visitors these days. *Probably some holy roller coming to save my soul,* he thought as he headed for the front door.

A man with shot-cropped dark hair stood with his back to Brian as he swung the front door open. He was staring at the Honda, he was gazing at the Honda in the driveway. The man was wearing a black T-shirt and camouflage pants. Brian thought that he must have the wrong address.

"Yeah, what can I do for you, buddy?" Brian asked curtly.

When the man on the doorstep turned to face him, Brian's legs failed, and he sat back on the carpet with a spine-jangling thump. His mouth agape, Brian tried to speak, but all that came out was a croak. The young man moved to help Brian, a look of alarm on his handsome face. Brian skittered backward on the carpet, looking for all the world like a deranged crab. Chris had to bite his lip to keep from laughing.

"Brian, it's okay, man, it's me," Chris said, holding his hand out to the man on the floor. Brian shook his head and scooted farther away.

"No, it can't be," he explained, his voice catching in his dry throat. "You're dead."

Chris smiled and held his hand out to Brian.

"No I'm not. I'm as alive as you are. I don't know how this happened, well maybe I do, kind of, but anyway, you're not seeing a ghost," he assured his stricken friend.

Brian allowed Chris to help him to his feet.

"Your parents told me that your helicopter was shot down, and you were killed the day you got to Vietnam," Brian argued. "And look at you! You're not a day over 18. What the fuck is goin' on here? Am I dreaming?" A look of alarm flitted across Brian's face.

"Hey wait, am I dead, too? Are you here to meet me?"

Chris started to laugh. "Would I come to take you to Heaven in this get-up?" he asked, pointing to the wrinkled T-shirt and pants. "I'll explain as much as I know, buddy. I really am alive and I need your help."

Brian still looked bewildered, and he reached out a forefinger and touched his friend's chest. "Well, you feel real enough," Brian said dubiously.

A smile creased his weathered face, and he enveloped Chris in a bear hug.

Both men had tears in their eyes when they broke from the embrace. After all the agonizing nights that Brian had passed in the last 30 years feeling guilty that he had not been able to go to Vietnam with Chris. All the booze in the world would not have made him forget that it was his fault that Chris had joined the Army. Now maybe he would have a chance to tell his best friend how sorry he was. He wiped his eyes with the sleeve of his sweatshirt.

"C'mon, sit down and tell me what the hell is happening," Brian motioned Chris to the couch. "Do you want a beer?" he asked. "I could use one, myself."

He grinned sheepishly and patted his expanding beer gut. "I guess you can tell."

Chris shrugged. He looked around the living room. Except for a new sofa and chair, the room looked the same as it had when he was 18. Chris tried not to stare at his old friend, but his eyes were drawn to the sallow face. Brian looked like hell. Chris wondered how many beers it had taken for him to age this badly.

"Yeah, sure, Why not?" he answered finally.

The two friends, the young man and the prematurely old one, sat and stared at each other in silence for a few moments, sipping their glasses of beer. Neither one could really believe that this was happening. Chris cleared his throat and told Brian the story of Matachias and Tory and the arrowhead. Brian listened quietly, astonished. He had always wondered what had happened to Chris the night that they had spent in Piedras Negras. Chris had not wanted to talk about it at the time, but Brian had known that something was wrong. His friend had seemed shaken; not his usual cool and calm self at all. Chris finished up his unbelievable tale by describing how he had passed out aboard the Huey and had come to in Jack King's bed.

Brian shook his head in wonderment. It sounded like a movie plot, but it must be real. The proof was sitting right in front of him. He got up to get another bottle of beer. Chris followed him into the kitchen.

"Man. I was really surprised when I found your mom's name in the phone book and at the same address. I swear I thought it was a miracle."

Brian handed a bottle of beer to Chris, then twisted the cap form his own bottle and tossed it in the trash can next to the stove. Chris watched him, puzzled, then looked down at the beer bottle in his hand.

"How did you do that without an opener?" He wondered.

With a grin, Brian grabbed the bottle from his friend and twisted the cap off effortlessly. "Believe me, a lot had changed," he told Chris.

"I looked my parents up in the phone book and couldn't find them," Chris said. "Did they move or something?"

Brian sat heavily in the nearest kitchen chair. Chris sat down across from him. Something in Brian's expression told him that wasn't going to like the answer. Brian was looking down at his hands.

"Where are they?" Chris asked softly.

"Your parents are dead, Chris. I'm sorry man."

He looked at Chris, then down at his hands again. "Your mom died of breast cancer in 1982 and dad..." His voice trailed off. This one was going to be even harder to say. "Your dad committed suicide two years later."

Brian heard Chris let out a muffled sob. He reached across the table and took his friend's hand.

"Your parents never got over your death," Brian explained.

He cleared his throat again. "As a matter of fact, I came out of my coma the day you were killed, or the day you were supposedly killed, I guess," he finished lamely.

"I had quite a lot of brain damage. It took over four months just for me to be able to walk right again," he continued. "I went over to your parent's house to visit once, but even though they were nice to me, I think I made them uncomfortable. I reminded them of you, I suppose." Brian's voice was barely a whisper now. "I guess maybe they blamed me for your death. If it wasn't for me, you would have gone off to college just like they always wanted."

Chris rested his forehead in his hands and shook his head. "It wasn't your fault, man. No one ever made me do anything that I didn't want to do."

They sat in silence for a few moments.

"I can't believe that my dad killed himself. How did it happen?" he asked in a low voice.

"My mom told me that when your mom got sick, she just gave up, didn't fight the cancer at all. Just didn't have the will to live, I guess," Brian said. "After she died, your dad became depressed and started drinking. He lost his job at the plant and became pretty much a recluse. I ran into your brother ,Jon, one time, and he told me that your dad never ate and hardly ever bathed. Jon tried to get him to see someone, made doctor's appointments for him, but he wouldn't go. One day Jon couldn't get a hold of your dad by phone, so he went over to his house to see if he was okay. He found your dad in the garage. Apparently, he had connected a hose to the exhaust pipe of his car and had run the hose in through a crack in the driver's side window. Jon said that he had been dead for a few days."

Chris couldn't fathom what he was hearing. His parents had been fine when he had flown off to Southeast Asia just a few days earlier, and now he was being told that they had been dead for years. Maybe if he could find a way back to 1969 things would turn out differently. Another thought popped into his head.

"What about Jon?" he asked, a little scared to hear the answer.

"He's still alive," Brian assured him. "At least he was last time I heard. He moved back to Pennsylvania after your dad died. I haven't heard from him since."

Chris knew that there was no use in agonizing over events that he had no control over, but he asked one more question. "How about your mom and Matt, how are they doing?" Brian sighed and shook his head.

"They split up a few years after you left. The medical bills from my accident pretty much broke them, I guess. I had permanent damage to my spine, and I still can't walk without limping. I started collecting disability checks not long after I came home from the hospital."

Brian hesitated before finishing. He sat looking at his hands, his face a mask of defeat.

"Matt got sick of me doin' nothing. I wish that I had been a little smarter back then. Maybe if I had found something to do with my life instead of drinking away my Social Security checks, they would have stayed together. My mom didn't care about anything but taking care of me, and Matt couldn't win."

Brian laughed bitterly. "Now she's still working at the nursing home, and I'm sitting here feeling sorry for myself 'cause I pissed my life away."

He looked up at Chris and smiled wanly. "Want another beer?"

Chris smiled and shook his head. It was time to change the subject. This was getting way too depressing.

"Listen, man", Chris said. "Do you still have the arrowhead necklace?"

To his relief, Brian nodded immediately.

"Sure", he answered. "It's sitting right on my dresser. I keep it in the old bowl that we put back together. I've kept those things as a sort of a shrine to your memory. I swear to you, Chris, I don't think that a day has gone by that I haven't thought of you." Brian's eyes were beginning to tear up again. Chris reached over and gave his friend a shot on the biceps, just like in the old days.

Brian brought the arrowhead from his bedroom and silently handed it to Chris. The smooth stone felt cool to the touch and utterly innocuous, but Chris felt the hair on the back of his neck stand up as though touched by a chill wind.

"If there's a way for me to get back to where I belong," he said, draping the necklace around his neck with a small shudder, "this is definitely the key. Maybe if I can go back to 'Nam, it will change the way things turn out, hopefully for the better."

Brian brightened visibly at the thought.

"Ya' know," Chris continued thoughtfully, "we gotta find out exactly what happened when the helicopter went down because that didn't happen when I was still on it." He cleared his throat. "Tell me, did they recover my body?"

Just asking the question reminded Chris how surreal the situation really was.

Brian thought for a moment before answering.

"No, they never recovered your body. From what I remember, you and the pilot were presumed dead. They said that your bodies were blown apart by the ammunition aboard the helicopter and incinerated in the fire." Brian swallowed hard before finishing his thought. "They never even found your dog tags. You were listed Killed In Action instead of missing, which really upset your family 'cause they thought that you might still be alive. After all of the

POWs were released, and you weren't with them, your folks finally gave up hope."

Chris tried not to think of the grief that his parents must have
suffered. Wallowing in it wouldn't help him out of this. He got up
and began pacing around the small kitchen, turning ideas over in
his head. His analytical mind was beginning to reassert itself again,
and he needed to have a plan. It made him feel at least a little
normal.

"You said that the pilot and I were listed as killed, but there
was another guy in the chopper. Was there a survivor?"

Brian wrinkled his brow in concentration. It was hard for him
to remember the details of his friend's death. He had killed a lot of
brain cells with booze in the last 30 years trying to forget.

"Yeah, I think there was a survivor, a gunner, if I'm not mistaken. I don't know his name," Brian finally remembered. "He was
thrown from the helicopter just before the crash. He was torn up
pretty badly, but he lived, as far as I know."

Chris pondered this for a time. "I must have been taken off of
the chopper just before it crashed because there was nothing wrong
with it when I was still aboard. The survivor must have been Phil
Baldwin. If we could only find him, maybe he would remember
when I disappeared." Chris laughed bitterly.

"Man, I can't believe how stupid this sounds." He sat down
heavily in the nearest chair and lay his head on his arms on the
table.

"This is fuckin' hopeless," Chris moaned. "Even if Baldwin is
still alive, we'll never find him. I only knew him for that one day.
I have no idea where he's from. He could be anywhere in the world
now." Chris was becoming truly scared. He felt certain that the
more time he spent in 1999 the harder it would be to get back.

Brian jumped up from his chair with a wide grin creasing his
face.

"C'mon, man, we'll look him up on the internet," he said, heading down the hallway toward his bedroom.

Chris followed him, looking genuinely puzzled. "The what?" he asked, flopping down on Brian's bed.

Brian ignored him, sitting down in front of what Chris thought was a television that sat on a small desk and started fiddling with the machine. Chris looked around the bedroom and was amazed to see that this room, like the living room, had hardly changed. It almost felt like Brian and Carolyn were living in some kind of time warp, unable to let go of the past or indifferent to the future.

"There' a bunch of different Vietnam veteran websites where vets can contact each other. Maybe we can find Phil Baldwin there."

Chris looked at Brian as though he war speaking Chinese.

"What the hell are you talking about?" he asked.

Brian turned the computer on and began to log on to the Internet.

"I guess you haven't heard about PC's, I mean personal home computers." he answered. "They came on the market about ten years ago. You can connect to a phone line and pick up all kinds of Internet services."

Chris stood looking over his friend's shoulder. The only computers he had ever heard of were on Star Trek and they were enormous with panels of blinking lights and reel-to-reel tapes. He still had no idea what Brian was talking about, but if it could help him find his way back to 1969 then he was all for it.

"So where do you keep your computer? In the garage?" he asked. Brian laughed and shook his head.

"No, it's not that big. I forgot, this is all ahead of your time," he answered, gulping the last of his beer. He pointed to the computer tower that sat on the floor by the desk.

"That thing down there is your hard drive where the discs go. That's where the computer stores information. It's also the modem so you can hook up to the phone line and get on the Internet." Brian explained. He smiled to himself as he continued to boot up the computer.

Being able to help Chris made Brian feel better than he had in a long time. Maybe he could undo some of the harm that he had

done to the people who loved him, and having Chris around almost made him feel young again.

Chris sat back down on the bed. "Except for the word 'phone'
I don't understand a word you just said," he sighed.

Brian searched for a website that might help them.

"Let's try 'Vietvet directory dot com," Brian mumbled. They
both watched anxiously as the WebPages popped on the screen.
Brian began clicking on icons as Chris wondered what the hell his
friend was doing now.

"Okay, what division were, are, you in?" Brian asked after he
had gotten where he wanted to be on the website. "First33 Air Cavalry Division, 163th3 Infantry, Platoon B," Chris answered.

Brian typed the information on the keyboard and hit the 'enter' button. "This site should bring up all of the names of the men
who served in that division, including yours," Brian explained.

Again they watched as the loading bar at the bottom of the
screen made it's way from left to right. Chris had no idea what to
expect, but Brian seemed to know what he was doing. As the names
began to roll down the screen in alphabetical order, Chris gaped.
He had never seen anything like this.

"Look," Brian pointed to the screen, "they list the name, rank,
and where they served, the months and years that hey served and
most recent address. We hit a gold mine, Chris," he said excitedly,
"let's just hope your friend Philip Baldwin's in here."

Brian rolled the screen with the computer mouse. Sure enough,
in the Bs they came to Baldwin, Philip, Private First Class, Served
in Hue from Jan. 1969 to Sept. 1969. Status, Wounded in Action,
received Purple Heart, Honorably Discharged.

"Sorry, Chris," he said, patting Chris on the shoulder. "I have a
lot to catch you up on. Anyway, you're not going to believe this,
his e-mail address is right here!" Chris looked bewildered again.

"That means that he has a computer, and I can send him a message right from my computer to his. It's instant mail as long as he's
on his computer," Brian spelled out patiently.

"Are you sure it's him?" Chris asked skeptically. "Maybe there was more than one Philip Baldwin over there. What if this is the wrong guy?" Brian had already started to address his e-mail, but he dutifully dropped the letter to the bottom of the screen and pulled up the list of names again. There were 34 Baldwins, starting with Aaron, but only one Philip who had served during that time period.

"Chris, that's got to be him. There's only one Philip Baldwin on here. Are you positive that Philip was his name?"

Chris snorted bitterly. "Oh, yeah, I'm sure. I just met him about 12 hours ago, remember?"

Brian nodded his head as he stared at the screen. "It's him, my friend," he assured Chris. "How about if I tell him to call here on the phone? I can tell him to call collect."

That sounded good to Chris although he thought it would be kind of weird to hear Baldwin's voice across the years. This all seemed to be going too smoothly.

"I'm sure he's gonna wonder who you are, though," he said doubtfully. "What will you tell him when he asks why you want to talk to him?" Brian pondered this for a moment. "Why don't we tell him that you're Jon, and you'd like to talk to him about your brother's death. You can say that you have some questions about the crash, and that you'd sure appreciate a few minutes of his time, blah, blah, blah."

He was typing busily as he spoke, not waiting for a response. The story sounded simple enough to be believable.

"Sounds like a winner," Chris agreed. "How long will it take for him to get the message?"

Brian shrugged. "Not long if he's got his computer turned on, just a few seconds." He had finished the message and had pushed the 'send' button.

"I'll have to turn the computer off, though. It's hooked up to the phone line and I can't get incoming calls when it's on." He was shutting the computer down when Chris reached out a hand to stop him.

"Wait," he said quietly. "Don't turn it off just yet. Find my name, Brian. I want to see what it says."

Brian didn't much like the idea of reading about his friend's death even under these bizarre circumstances, but he reluctantly did as Chris asked.

The screen rolled as fast as Brian could wield the computer mouse. He slowed the rolling down as he came to the names that began with L: Lofter, Loftowitz, Logan, Loggens, and then there it was. Logue, Christopher, Private First Class, served in Shau Valley, August 1969. Killed in Action, August 1969. That was all. Seeing his life reduced to the terse epitaph: Killed in Action chilled Chris to the bone. It made his current situation seem all too real, and all too impossible to bear.

"Brian," he said pleaded fervently, "whether Phil Baldwin calls or not, I have to go to Mexico. I'm sure Matachias is dead, but if I can find another Kickapoo medicine man, or Tory, maybe I can get some help. I'm positive that the arrowhead is the key to my getting back to '69." He didn't add, *and whatever is waiting for me there.*

Brian mulled over his desperate friend's request as he finished logging off of the computer. He swiveled his chair around to face Chris. What Chris had said made at least as much sense as anything else had that day. Brian tried to forget that having Chris around was the best thing that had happened to him in a long time. He decided that it was time that he thought of someone else for a change. *Who knows,* he thought ruefully, *maybe I'll like it.* Brian glanced over at the alarm clock that sat on his dresser.

"I've got my mom's car until I have to pick her up at work at 11:00. It's almost 5 now," Brian mused. "Let's say 2 hours drive down to Mexico, that's 7. That would only give us two hours before we'd have to start back. That's not much time."

Chris looked deflated for a moment, then he squared his shoulders. "If the old Indian's shack is still standing, I'll find it. It looked like a good wind would blow it over 30 years ago, but you never know. Tory told me that a lot of Kickapoo had settled around Piedras Negras, So I'm sure that we can find someone who can help me."

His voice regained its old resolve as he spoke, but when Brian met his eyes, they still seemed clouded with doubt and fear.

Brian shook his head. "If we manage to find any Kickapoo Indians, they'll think we're crazy," he snorted, then sighed. "On the other hand, what have we got to lose? My mom would have a hemorrhage if she got home tonight and found you here."

The thought made him grin.

Chris grinned back, his spirits lifting a little. "Yeah, I don't want to have to explain this to anyone else. Let's get going, or I'll be looking at your homely face for a long time, you old buzzard. If this doesn't work, maybe you can hide me in your attic and tell everyone that I'm your illegitimate grandson."

Both men bellowed out a hearty laugh, which came as a welcome tension buster. When the phone rang, Brian tried to regain his composure as he reached for the cordless. When he picked up the receiver, pressed the 'on' button, and said "hello", Chris gawked at him.

Brian wondered what was wrong with him, then realized that, of course, Chris had never seen a cordless telephone.

"Hey, mom, what's going on?" Brian asked.

While Brian talked to his mother, Chris picked up a software box from the desk and examined it closely. Suddenly, he found himself hoping fervently that he would be around in 1999 to use all of the new technology that he was seeing now. This was a fascinating preview, but Chris wanted to go back to back to 1969 and live his entire life. If he was going to live to see all these new toys, he wanted to watch as they evolved. More importantly, he needed to be there when his mom got sick, to help to take care of her, and he needed to be there to help his dad and his brother to cope with her death when the time came.

"Okay, that works for me," Brian was saying. "I've got something to do tonight anyway."

He paused for a moment.

"Oh, nothing much. I'm just going to spend some time help-ing out an old friend." He winked at Chris, who was busy stifling a laugh.

"Okay, see 'ya later, mom." Brian pressed the phones 'off' button and sat it upright on the desktop.

"Well, that came in handy. Mom's going out for pizza with some friends after work. They're going to drop her off after, so I've got the car all night." He gave Chris a friendly punch on the shoulder. "C'mon, Mr. Buzzcut, we'd better get going. By the way, I forgot to tell you how handsome you look with your radical hair-cut. And where did you get those clothes?"

Chris tossed the software box onto the bed and looked down at the black T-shirt with the O.W.O logo on emblazoned on the chest.

"I guess they're Jack King's. Great taste, huh? What the hell does O.W.O. mean?"

Brian shrugged. "Turn around," he commanded, "there's some-thing on the back, too."

Chris turned around so that Brian could read the back of the T-shirt.

"Our time is coming," he read the message out loud. "I won-der what that means? Maybe Jack's a pro wrestling fan or some-thing," Brian suggested.

"I'll bet it has something to do with all that Nazi shit he had in his room," Chris muttered. "Do you have a shirt I can borrow?" he asked. "I don't want to be seen in this shirt in case the O.W.O is some Nazi group."

Brian dug in a dresser drawer and pulled out a clean white T-shirt.

"Here," he said, tossing the shirt to Chris. "This ought to fit."

As Chris was pulling the shirt over his head, the phone rang again.

"That thing sounds more like a bird chirping than it does a phone," Chris observed dryly.

Brian chuckled as he reached for the telephone, "This might be Baldwin. If it is, I'll let you talk while I get some shit together for the road."

The caller was indeed Phil Baldwin. He asked to speak with Jon Logue. Brian handed the phone to Chris, then left the bedroom. He heard Chris telling his fabricated story as he headed toward the kitchen. He retrieved his wallet from the top of the refrigerator and counted out 83 dollars and change. That would get them a motel room for the night if they had to stay over, and he still had a hundred dollars or so on his credit card before he reached his limit. Brian figured that would be enough. He slid the wallet into the back pocket of his jeans and opened the fridge to get another beer. He was still shaken from his friend's visit, which was unexpected, to say the least. He looked at the beer in his hand for a moment, then reluctantly put it back in the refrigerator door. As much as Brian needed the beer, Chris needed him to be sober for this trip. It might well be the most important trip of his life.

Chapter 41

Brian still couldn't swear that the eighteen-year old Chris talking on the phone in his bedroom wasn't an hallucination or a ghost. *Ghost or no ghost*, Brian told himself, *I've been feeling guilty about his death for thirty years now. If there's a chance that I can help him now and improve my karma and maybe his, well, what the hell. I've got to go for it.* He was lost in thought, staring out of the window over the kitchen sink. He jumped a foot in the air when Chris bounded into the room.

"What's the matter?" Chris asked, laughing. "You look like you just saw the ghost of a friend who's been dead for 30 years."

The color slowly seeped back into Brian's cheeks. He grinned sheepishly.

"Yeah, I keep wondering when I'll wake up and find out that this is all a dream, " Brian admitted.

Chris nodded. "Me, too, " he agreed. "I don't think that's gonna happen though. And now here's the latest twist, Baldwin told me that before the helicopter crashed, the pilot told them to run like hell when they hit the ground. I think maybe I remember hearing that. Anyway, Baldwin was too badly hurt in the wreck to get far, so he hid in some bushes near the crash site. He was watching when the Viet cong pull the ammo crates and weapons from the chopper." He paused dramatically.

"Here's the best part, guess what else the V.C pulled from the wreckage, go ahead, guess."

Brian pondered the question, then shrugged. "I don't know," he replied," Amelia Earhart?"

Chris grinned wickedly. "No," he said, "they found me."

Brian, looking dumfounded, had no response for this.

"I know," Chris assured him. "I was kind of freaked out too. But Baldwin was sure that he saw the Viet cong lead me away with my hands on my head. The only thing that I can figure is that King was somehow switched with me when I passed out. That would explain why I woke up in his bed. If he was captured and then killed and buried, they would never find my dog tags."

Brian didn't know what to make of this. "Listen, we'd better get going. We'll start in Mexico where this whole mess began, and if that doesn't work we'll pay El Paso a visit and see if we can find out where ol' King fits into all of this."

Chris breathed a sigh of relief. He felt a lot less alone now that Brian had committed to helping him. "Thanks," he said softly.

Brian waved the thanks away. "That's what friends are for. You ready?"

Chris nodded his head.

Brian patted the front pocket of his jeans to make sure that his keys were still there as they headed for the front door. Chris held the screen door for Brian as he locked the inside door. On the way to the car, he filled Brian in on his conversation with Philip Baldwin. Baldwin wasn't sure if Captain Wallace had really been killed in the crash or captured by the enemy and declared dead. The helicopter had begun to burn shortly after the crash, and once the remaining ammo crates began to explode, the Viet cong had hightailed it in one direction and Baldwin in the other. He had a badly broken arm and some deep lacerations and bruises, but was otherwise in pretty good shape. Somehow, Baldwin had managed to find his way back to camp. At the time of the chopper crash, he had been near the end of his hitch in the Army. He had finished his tour of duty in a hospital in Honolulu.

While Chris talked, he looked around appraisingly at the car's interior.

"This is a Honda?" he asked. "It's so small. When did Honda start making cars?"

Brain laughed. "This is big compared to the first cars that Honda made."

He pulled the safety belt over his shoulder. "Put your seat belt on, man. You can get a ticket now for not wearing one. Besides, this car doesn't have air bags."

As Chris complied, he asked what an air bag was. Brian explained the safety device, and Chris shook his head for the hundredth time that day.

"Well, in this little bug I guess you need all the help you can get," he observed.

"Yeah," Brian admitted, "this isn't the greatest car in the world, but it sure beats walking to Mexico."

On the 2 hour drive south, Chris listened, fascinated, as Brian filled him in on some of the other changes that had taken place in the world over the past 30 years. He explained the latest toys: cable television and home satellite dishes, VCR's, camcorders and video games. As he warmed to his subject matter, Brain told a bewildered Chris all he knew about the newest in medical advances: heart, lung and liver transplants, laser surgery, in vitro fertilization and cloning. On the downside, there was AIDS and flesh-eating bacteria to report.

Chris was amazed to hear that the cold war was over, and the Berlin wall was only a memory. As they neared the Mexican border, Chris asked how the Vietnam War had ended. Brian had no easy answer for this question.

"I don't really remember," he admitted finally. "I guess it just sort of petered out, and the soldiers just came home."

Chris didn't find this answer satisfactory. "Well," he asked impatiently, "at least you can tell me who won."

Brian shook his head. "No one," he answered sadly. "No one."

Chapter 42

August twenty-eight 1969

Jack King followed his captors through the jungle, his hands growing numb from the ropes that bound his wrists behind his back. Fear pulsed through his body with every heartbeat. The fear kept him silent, but an inner voice screamed. *When is this nightmare ever going to end?* He would never have believed that anything could be worse than the dream about vomiting swarms of insects, *it had seemed so fucking real!* but this was worse, *and it seemed so fucking real!* The jungle that surrounded him teemed with the sounds of animal life. The moist, earthy smell of the dense foliage assaulted his nostrils and sweat coursed down his cheeks and back. The steamy air made Jack feel dizzy and weak. He couldn't remember ever having nightmares like this before.

A hard shove to his back from the small Asian man behind him sent Jack stumbling forward. He landed on one knee on the soft jungle floor before regaining his balance. As he righted himself, Jack's eyes met those of the man who had shoved him. The raw hatred in the dark eyes startled him and sent a chill down his spine. The two young men that led the party turned to see what the commotion was about. Their icy stares were as cold as that of the man who had shoved Jack. He wondered why these men hated him so much. He also knew that he had better keep up if he wanted to survive.

Jack had only suffered minor scrapes and bruises in the heli-copter crash. The Asian soldiers had dragged him, dazed and bleed-ing from the wreckage. When the chopper had exploded, the men had forced Jack into the jungle at gunpoint. They had thrust a shovel into his hands and had gestured for him to dig into the soft earth. When the hole was deep enough to suit them, they had buried the ammunition that they had scavenged from the twisted wreckage of the helicopter and covered the hole with leaves. At that point, they had tied Jack's wrists behind his back and had started to march into the wilderness.

As he walked, the mixture of dried blood and sweat that trick-led down his face was driving him insane. He would have given anything to have his hands tied in front of him so that he could just wipe his burning eyes. He tried to shake the moisture off of his face, but that made him even dizzier. He lowered his chin to his chest to let the blood and perspiration drain from his forehead. He saw the nameplate that was sewn above the pocket of his torn and bloody fatigue shirt. The name was clear and unmistakable: PFC CHRISTOPHER LOGUE. *Who the fuck is Logue?* he thought, desperate to make some sense of all this. *This is no dream, this is way too real, how did I get into this?* He looked again at the men who had captured him. They were clad in what looked like black pajamas, but they were clearly soldiers of some kind. They were all heavily armed. They each carried AK-47machine guns with banana clips. They moved with graceful precision, rarely needing to speak. The awful truth began to dawn on him, *I'm in Vietnam and these guys are Viet cong.*

Jack's fevered mind began to piece things together. The image of the badly beaten woman in the mountains swam before him. The eerie chant that had spewed from her bloody lips drummed in his head with every step. The Indian bitch really had put a curse on him! *Didn't she say that I'd be cursed by having my next wish come true?* he thought, trying to remember the injured woman's exact words. The combination of English and the woman's native tongue had mostly sounded like gibberish, but he had been able to pick out a few phrases. *When did I wish to be in Vietnam?* Jack recalled the warehouse party. He had drunk so much beer that by the time he got to the party, he had been pretty well shit-faced, but he could remember talking to the two teenage girls. He knew that he had been trying to impress them, but what had he said?

Suddenly, the memory came back to him with crystal clarity, he had said that he wished that he could have been in the Vietnam War! He had bragged about how many gooks he would have killed. That was when he had started hearing the weird animal noises! *Horned panthers*, he thought, *She said that the horned panthers of the underworld would be waiting for me.* Jack looked at the soldiers walking ahead of him. *I guess the horned panthers waited long enough*, he decided miserably.

As they moved silently through the jungle, Jack remained focused on the two young men in front of him. *I gotta get outta here or these guys are gonna kill me.* he decided. *With this fucker walking behind me, I can't do anything. I need some sorta diversion, something to distract them for a second, so I can make a run for it.* Jack knew that he would not have much of a chance to survive in the jungle, but he also knew that dying in the jungle was better than what the Viet cong had in mind for him. He was trying to think of a diversion the leaders began to yell into the thick jungle. Their cries were answered by feathery voices in the distance.

Another hard shove to his back sent Jack sprawling to the ground. He moaned as the thin ropes that bound him and bit into the raw flesh of his wrists. The noise that he emitted caught the attention of the men who led the way. Both began yelling at him, and though Jack didn't understand a word that they said, he knew that it wasn't anything good. He had managed to roll over and work himself up to a kneeling position before they could get to him. Jack screamed as the man behind him slid the barrel of his machine gun under the ropes around Jack's wrists, pulling him upright. The first blows from the gun butts landed on his ribs and abdomen. Jack screamed again, louder this time, as he felt ribs cracking. His body went limp, and as the man behind him let go of the rope he fell face first to the ground. The three Viet cong circled him, beating him with the butts their guns. Jack could do nothing to fend off his attackers. He buried his face in the rotting foliage of the jungle floor to protect it from the vicious blows.

Two of the soldiers concentrated on his upper back, each chose a kidney to batter, while the third man rammed his arms and shoulders. Jack no longer had even the strength that it would take to scream. His captors slowed their attack when the distant voices drew nearer. Someone was approaching quickly; Jack could hear them crashing toward them through the jungle. The beating stopped entirely when two men dressed in khaki uniforms came into view. These men were older and clearly outranked the black-clad men.

One of the older soldiers began screaming at the younger men, pointing at Jack as he shrieked. From the body language that the men displayed, Jack surmised that the men dressed in khaki were regular North Vietnamese Army while the pajama-clad men were Viet cong guerillas. It appeared to Jack that the older man wanted to keep Jack alive. He was sure that his saviors didn't have anything good in mind for his future. *They probably just need live prisoners*, he hoped.

The three young guerillas stood silent, their eyes downcast, while their superior continued to berate them. He finally seemed to grow tired of screaming and gestured toward Jack. The three younger men hoisted him to a standing position, not bothering to be the least bit gentle about it. The pain in his back was so excruciating that he was only able to let out a strangled grunt.

With one pajama-clad man on either arm, Jack stumbled along through the jungle. The going was even more difficult in the small clearing that they came to. The ground was nothing more than fetid swamp. Jack slipped to his knees in the slime from time to time, only to be pulled roughly back to his feet. He was afraid that his legs would give out completely. It was only a matter of time. When that happened, there was no way that these guys were going to bother carrying him. He was certain that he would die wherever he landed.

As the world began to grow black around him, Jack's arms were released. He fell to his face in the muck, pain shooting through his chest like a jolt of lightning. He lay face down in the slime, unable to lift his head out of the stinking ooze. He concentrated on gulping in small whiffs of air. When he tried to take in a deep breath, the broken ends of his ribs ground together like steel crushing glass, making him nauseous to his stomach from the pain. His captors spoke quietly to each other now. Jack was certain that they were parlaying with his life. When their conversation was over, the younger men yanked him upright by his arms and began to move forward again. Jack was no longer able to move his legs, so they dragged him this time. Head down, he watched dispassionately as the toes of his boots raked small valleys into the mud.

After they had traveled a short distance, Jack was dumped unceremoniously near the base of a tree that stood in the center of a small clearing. What little air he had managed to take into his lungs escaped with a small, pained 'whuff.' He fought to stay conscious through the aching misery. His wrists burned as the ropes that bound him were released. He groaned softly as his captors flipped him onto his back. He was yanked into a sitting position and dragged across the ground until his back was against the rough bark of the tree. One of the younger men pulled his arms behind the tree trunk. When the tips of his fingers met, his wrists were tied again. He moaned as the ropes chewed into his bloody flesh, bringing small smiles of satisfaction to his captor's lips. They had no pity for the American dog that was invading their homeland.

When they had finished with their prisoner, the soldiers joined their comrades at a makeshift camp nearby. Jack counted a dozen Vietnamese soldiers. They stared back at him, their faces cold and expressionless. Jack's captors joined their comrades in the small camp, talking and laughing and pointing at their hapless prisoner. To Jack's immense relief, they seemed to be finished with him for the moment. He stole a final glance at the soldiers. They were huddled around one of the men who had dragged Jack from the wrecked Huey. They watched with rapt attention as the young soldier drew in the dirt with a stick. He didn't care what they were doing as long as they left him alone.

He rested his head against the bark of the tree, finally able to take a few small, relatively painless breaths. He was growing mercifully numb to the pain. Jack had not been a good student and history was not his best subject. As far as he was concerned it wasn't his problem, so why care. His only interest in the war had been the bloody images that he had seen in movies.

Jack's head lolled on his chest. Suddenly his neck seemed too weak to support his skull. As his thoughts began to drift the battered face of the Indian woman in the mountains swam before him. This time, her bloody lips were smiling with grim satisfaction. Jack couldn't remember for the life of him why it had seemed like a good idea to beat her senseless. She had done nothing to him, he didn't even know her. *It's payback time.* The thought came to him with sudden clarity. *She went for a bike ride in the mountains and I kicked the shit out of her because I wanted to impress those asshole's in the Old World Order. Now I'm getting the shit kicked out of me. Maybe this is justice.* It occurred to Jack that maybe he had died and gone to hell. That would explain a lot. Maybe Ron Shanak had killed him after all.

Jack opened his eyes, the disembodied face of the Indian woman was still floating in front of him, her macabre grin wider than before.

"Go away," he mumbled thickly and closed his eyes again. Now she began to chant in a weird singsong voice.

"No more," Jack pled softly, "Please, no more." The woman's voice seemed to change. It was deeper now and sounded more oriental than the combination Indian- English that she had spoken in the mountains. Reluctantly, Jack opened his eyes just a slit.

The face of the Indian woman was gone. In its place was the face of an elderly Asian man. The man was dressed in nondescript loose gray clothes and had a straw coolie hat perched atop his white hair. Beside him stood a small boy, perhaps nine or ten years old and dressed in a similar fashion.

The old man was screaming at Jack, a gnarled finger shaking inches from the prisoner's face. Jack didn't need a translator to know that the man hated him. Jack turned his head away to avoid the spittle that flew from the old man's mouth. The men in the camp were going about their business, not paying any attention to what was happening to their prisoner. Jack wouldn't have expected them to help him anyway. The old man apparently thought that the American was ignoring him. He backhanded Jack across the cheek surprising force. Jack's teeth split the inside of his cheek, and he tasted salty blood as it dripped down his throat. He began choking on the blood, then coughed reflexively. The punch to his stomach caught him off guard, and his head lurched forward. The blow wasn't hard, but in his weakened condition Jack had to wrestle for control of his conscious mind. He was afraid that if he passed out, he would choke to death on the blood.

"Please," he begged, his voice a strangled whisper. "Please stop, I can't breathe, I'm fuckin' dying, I can't take anymore." Jack turned his head and looked at the young boy who had stood by watching silently. "Please tell him to stop. I'm begging you, please."

The boy didn't move, but Jack could read sadness and pity in the soft dark eyes. That was the last thought that he had before he tumbled into darkness.

Chapter 43

August 28, 1999

Chris and Brian got through customs and into Mexico without a hitch, much to Brian's relief. He didn't want to scare Chris, but he was a little worried about what would happen when he tried to get Chris back into the states. The clean-cut young man in the Honda's passenger seat didn't look at all like the picture of Jack King on the driver's license that he carried.

As they neared Piedras Negras, Chris spoke up. He had one last question for his friend.

"Whatever happened with that stolen car thing? Did the police ever prosecute you because you couldn't go into the Army?"

Brian scratched the gray stubble on his chin, then began to root around in the Honda's ashtray. He pulled a half-smoked joint from among the cigarette butts and ashes and handed it to Chris.

"Here," he said. "Fire that up and I'll tell you." Chris stared at the roach with distaste.

"While I was in the coma, they put me on probation," he continued. "No one knew if I would ever wake up, so it just wasn't worth spending a lot of time prosecuting me, I guess. By the time I finished rehab, I only had a year of probation left, so it was no big deal. Brian looked at Chris with surprise when he threw the joint back into the ashtray.

"I can't believe that you still smoke that shit at your age," Chris said. "It was kind of cool when we were teenagers, but now it seems kind of pathetic."

Brian didn't bother to point out that Chris still was a teenager. He pulled a cigarette from the pack on the dashboard and held it up.

"Is it okay if I smoke this, mom?" he asked.

Chris laughed and pushed in the cigarette lighter. He realized that it seemed kind of absurd for him to be lecturing Brian at this stage of his life.

Piedras Negras had grown quite a bit in 30 years. The barren fields surrounding the town had sprouted small tidy storefronts and office buildings. The new structures were modern, with blond brick facades and airy windows. American fast food restaurants were plentiful. Brian whistled softly as they drove down the main street.

"Boy, this town sure looks different. If I hadn't seen the 'Welcome to Piedras Negras' sign I wouldn't believe that it was the same place."

The sign on the Hacienda Motel had been replaced with that of a popular chain. The withered powder blue paint was gone. Now the building sported a sedate dusty beige coat with pale yellow trim around the windows.

"Hey, look," Brian exclaimed pointing to the neon sign in front of the motel. "They sold out to Comfort Quarters Motels. They're popping up all over San Antonio."

Chris didn't respond. He was busy trying to get his bearings, worried that he wouldn't be able to find the medicine man's shack after all. Things had changed so damn much. He closed his eyes and tried to remember where the tavern had been in relation to the motel.

"I think we walked three blocks south of the motel," he said softly. "The tavern was on the opposite side of the street."

Brian looked to his left as he drove slowly down the street. "I think it should be right about here," he said finally.

Chris opened his eyes and looked across the street. To his dismay, the tavern had been replaced with a four bay oil change and lube shop.

"Oh, shit," he moaned.

Brian pulled the Honda to the side of the street and stopped.

"Don't panic, man," he said reassuringly. "Try to remember where Tory was parked that night. You said that you took a major road out of town. It should still be there."

Chris took a deep breath to calm his wildly beating heart. He was too close to lose his cool now.

"Pull around to the back," he suggested. "The road was back there, I think."

Brian started the car's engine and waited for a few cars to go by before heading around to the back of the shop. When they had reached the parking lot, Chris pointed to an alley off to the left.

"That's it!" he yelled. "We went down that alley. The road goes off to the right at the end of the alley!"

Brian followed his friend's directions obediently. Sure enough, the road was exactly where Chris remembered.

"Hang a right," he instructed, and Brian obeyed.

"We drove for about 15 minutes on this road," Chris said, looking at his watch.

They drove in silence. To his relief, Chris recognized the silhouette of the mountain range to their left. The town had changed, but the mountains were everlasting. He felt a shiver of déjàvu as the sun began to change from bright yellow to the soft twilight orange that announced the coming sunset. *This is where I came in*, he thought.

Fifteen miles out of town, Chris began scanning the landscape to the right of the highway.

"Slow down," he ordered. "I think we're getting close."

Brian slowed the car to a crawl, which was safe enough on the two-lane highway. They had seen only a handful of cars in the past 15 minutes. Suddenly Chris let out a squawk and pointed to a few dots in the desert.

"There it is!" he cried.

Brian pulled the car to the side of the road and stared into the desert doubtfully. He didn't see any buildings, but then his eyesight wasn't what it used to be. As his eyes adjusted to the waning light, he saw what could be a few small structures set among the cactus.

"Are you sure?" he asked.

Chris nodded. "Pull ahead a little," he said, and Brian complied.

After they had gone a few hundred feet, Brian saw what looked to be the remains of a dirt road leading to the distant buildings. He turned down the rutted path, the Honda bouncing on the rocks. Chris reached out a hand and touched Brian's right arm.

"I think I'd better walk the rest of the way. You might break an axle on these ruts." he said softly.

Gratefully, Brian stopped the car and turned off the engine. Now that they had reached the medicine man's shack, he hated to let Chris go. This had been the best day he had in a long time. "Good luck," was all he could think of to say.

Chris smiled wanly. "Yeah, I think I'll need it. This is some scary shit. I hope to hell I can find something to help me here because I haven't come up with plan "B" yet."

Brian laughed. "I'll wait right here for you, man." He leaned over and opened the glove compartment. He handed Chris a small flashlight made of pink plastic. "Here," he said, "it'll be getting dark soon. You'll need this if you have to walk back here."

Chris took the flashlight and opened the car door. When he turned to face Brian, his eyes were moist.

"Thanks for everything, man," he said, his voice cracking a little.

Brian leaned over and embraced his friend. "No sweat, pal."

Chris got out of the car and closed the passenger door gently. He leaned over and gave Brian a little wave. Brian smiled and held up his right hand in a thumbs-up gesture. He pulled the joint out of the ashtray and lit it as he watched his friend grow smaller in the distance.

"Well," he said softly, blowing out a thin puff of fragrant smoke.

" I hope you find what you're looking for, but I gotta tell you, if you don't come back, I doubt that my sanity will either."

Chapter 44

"Are you hungry, hon?" Stacey asked. Jack looked over at her standing in framed in the kitchen doorway. Her silky blond hair seemed to fall over her shoulders in slow motion as she turned to walk back toward the stove. He was struck by how beautiful she looked today, almost like an angel. He could feel her love bathing him in a soft warm glow. Her movements were slow and graceful as she reached to open the cupboard over the stove.

"Can I get you something to eat?"

White teeth flashed in her sweet smile. Jack couldn't seem to answer her question: her beauty transfixed him. His vision seemed to grow dim and tighten into a wavering tunnel. Stacey's image grew smaller, then disappeared altogether.

A blue light flashed in front of him, and Jack found himself standing in front of his bathroom mirror. The eyes that stared back at him were different somehow. There was peace and forgiveness in these eyes. The person in the mirror no longer looked to be at war with himself. After being with Stacey, his soul was cleansed and free. There was something else different about the man who stared back at Jack. The hair on his head was full and feathered back softly. Jack had never worn his hair like this in his life. In his early teens he had spiked and bleached his hair or had worn it in a jagged Mohawk before finally settling on the O.W.O. shave. He slowly ran his fingers through the thick dark hair. He decided that he liked the way he looked in this new style. It softened the angles of his sharp features and made him look almost handsome.

His trance was broken by the sound of running water. His eyes darted around the small white bathroom. The steam that billowed out from behind the shower curtain blurred the edges of the room. Through the translucent curtain, Jack could see hot water streaming from the tiny openings in the showerhead. There was no one in the tub. He wondered if the shower was meant for him.

Jack glanced back at his image in the mirror and was dismayed to see his old familiar face reflected back at him. His Mohawk was back, and his hollow cheekbones were smudged with dirt and blood. Worst of all, the eyes that stared back at him had gone cold and dead and his thin lips were twisted into a sneer of pure hatred. The core of his soul was exposed, and the portrait was grotesque. Why hadn't he been able to see that before? He knew that the truth had always been there he just hadn't been paying attention. Now it was so obvious.

Jack turned back to the steaming shower. It was time to cleanse himself of the filth that he had carried for so long. The hot water would purify his soul. He stepped into the tub and pulled the curtain closed. He rubbed his body vigorously. The hot water that puddled around his bare feet turned reddish brown from the dried blood that caked his body. The faces of the people in whose veins the blood had once flowed floated in front of him, and he washed faster. Some were old, some young, some male, some female, but that didn't seem to be important now. All that mattered was the pain that he had made them endure. None of them had deserved it. He knew that he had taken something from each one of the people that he had hurt in his lifetime. He had stolen a piece of each one's spirit, and now those pieces flowed down the drain, and there was nothing he could do about it.

The rust-colored water that swirled down the drain had begun to clear. Jack's eyes widened in alarm as the water grew pink again, then deep vivid red. Fresh blood ran freely from his raw skin. The face of the Indian woman in the mountains appeared in the steam.

She was smiling, but her smile held pity now. Dark purple bruises mottled her cheeks, and one eye was swollen shut. The lips that smiled at her attacker were split and bloody. Jack fell to his knees, tears mixing with the blood and steamy water. How could he have done this to her. Wasn't she some child's mother or some mother's daughter?

"I'm sorry," he moaned, "I'm so sorry."

He was crying uncontrollably now, great choking sobs that made his sides ache. The crying brought with it a sense of release that was like nothing Jack had ever experienced. He felt as though a heavy weight was slowly being lifted from his spirit. When he was finally cried out, he sat back in the tub. With eyes closed, he let the pulsating water wash over his face. Without warning, he had a sensation of his body being jerked from the tub. The air was still steamy, but there was a cloying odor of rotting vegetation mixed in with the steam.

Pain wracked his body now. The muscles in his chest and back spasm suddenly, causing fresh waves of agony. The water running down Jack's face had taken on a putrid odor and was accompanied by the sound of raucous laughter. Jack opened his eyes against the stream of warm water. The salty stream burned his eyes, but before he closed them again he saw laughing faces above, looking down at him. As he tried to move away, his tightly bound wrists brought more pain.

Jack screamed out loud at the horror of what was happening to him. His Vietnamese captors continued to howl with laughter as they urinated on their prisoner. Jack bowed his head to avoid the foul liquid and waited for them to run out of ammunition. He began to gag on the foul taste, the searing pain in his ribs leaving him breathless.

When the soldiers had finished their business, they simply turned back toward their camp and walked away. Jack remembered when he had gone to YMCA camp one summer. All of the boys had gone to the edge of the woods and peed against the trees before bedding down for the night. He was the toilet tree on duty for

262 Find The River

the night. Jack laughed hoarsely at the absurdity of the memory. He yelled out at the black clad figures as they disappeared into the darkness.

"Thank you and please come again. Please put the seat down and flush next time."

He tried to wriggle closer to the tree to take some of the tug off of his burning wrists. The ground under his bare legs scratched at his bare skin, and he realized that he had been stripped of his clothes when he had lost consciousness. The night was turning cold, and Jack shivered, the motion bringing on a spasm of pain. He was beginning to grow lightheaded again. "No," he murmured, "can't pass out again. I might not wake up. Come on, Jack stay awake, gotta stay alive somehow, gotta stay alive..."

Chapter 45

The desert sunlight was dying in the western sky as Chris approached the ramshackle outbuildings that surrounded the decaying shack. His heart sank as he realized that the buildings had been deserted, probably long before. The weeds and brush that had been knee-high when he had been here 30 years earlier were chest high now. The shack was still standing; in fact, it didn't look much different than it had the last time he had seen it. The house had been dilapidated even before it had been abandoned.

Chris waded through the brush and rock that led to the front door until he found the stone path that led around to the screened-in back porch. The screen that had protected the porch had long since rotted away, leaving only the withered dry-rotted wood frame. The frame that held the back door to the shack had begun to rot, leaving the scarred wooden door hanging askew by its lower hinge. Chris swept a thick layer of dusty sand from the porch floor, then stood and tested the wood with his left foot. The wood creaked alarmingly, but didn't give. He took a deep breath and put his full weight on the floor. To his immense relief, it held his weight. He skirted around the edge of the porch, holding on to the wooden railing for support in case the floor gave way. His stomach curled into a tight knot as he neared the door.

Chris didn't know what he hoped to find inside the shack; clearly no one had lived here for a very long time. Maybe the old man had left some sort of clue that would lead him in the right direction. Maybe he would find some papers, and old piece of mail or something that would lead him to Tory. He peered cautiously through the opening at the top of the doorway, looking for any sign of movement in the shadows. Even though the shack wasn't habitable for humans anymore, the wildlife in the area would probably find it most hospitable.

As his eyes adjusted to the darkness, Chris called out, "Hello, is anybody home?"

He took a quick step sideways as he yelled, just in case something such as an animal needed an exit path through the doorway. He listened carefully, but didn't hear the sound of any movement from inside.

After a few minutes, he moved back to the doorway and poked his head through the opening. "Hello" he called into the darkness. No sound at all. He tugged on the door, trying to right it, but the lower hinge gave way. The dry rot had rendered the door as light as balsa wood. He propped it against the wall and stepped cautiously into the room. The wooden floorboards groaned under his weight but held fast. Motes of dust swirled in the thin rays of light that streamed into the small room through the doorway.

Moving farther into the room, Chris wondered how long ago the old man had died. Except for a thick layer of dust, the room looked pretty much the same as he remembered it. In the shadows of the far corner, he could see the crates that he had slammed into stacked neatly against the wall. Dusty bottles that held murky, substances of long forgotten origin still lined the wooden shelves on the back wall. Chris sighed and shook his head.

"This is a dead end," he said. "What the hell am I going to do now?" He didn't see any point in hanging around here any longer. Maybe if he asked around town he could find another medicine man. It would be dark soon, and even with the flashlight finding his way back to the road would be difficult. He hoped that Brian would have the headlights turned on so that he could see the car.

As Chris turned to leave the shack, the sound of wood creaking against wood came from the shadows behind him. He stopped dead in his tracks, every hair on his body standing straight up. The single creak turned into a rhythmic *scree, scree, scree*. Chris told himself that the noise was just a critter in the woodwork. His brain almost believed it, but his gut was unconvinced.

The sound grew louder, *Scree, scree, Scree, scree*. Chris turned slowly, pulling the flashlight from his pocket and flicking the button. His first impulse was to run like hell. He really didn't want to see what was behind him, but curiosity was getting the better of him.

He swept the light slowly from left to right, illuminating the far end of the room. There was no sign of movement; the dust on the shelves lay undisturbed. As he played the light across the shelves, he saw that they ended a few feet from the corner. He hadn't noticed that before. Moving closer, he saw a small door tucked into the shadows of the corner. It was no bigger than five feet high and two feet wide. There was a small hole in the unpainted wood where a doorknob must have been. A small rectangular block of wood nailed to the wall served as a makeshift latch. The creaking grew louder as he neared the door.

There must be another room, he thought, *and whatever, whoever is making that noise is on the other side of that door.* The beam from the flashlight was growing dim. Chris shook the little pink plastic torch. *Just like Brian to give me a crappy little flashlight with dying batteries*, Chris thought with a trace of irritation.

"Well, it's now or never," he whispered out loud, his voice sounding shaky in the deepening darkness. His hand shook as he reached for the latch.

Chapter 46

Jack shivered as the cool night air wafted over his naked body. Mosquitoes had come with the darkness. The insects landed on his bare skin, tickling raw nerve endings and making him shiver. He tried to blow them away from his face, but the respite was only temporary. The pain in his torso and wrists overshadowed the tiny probes that drilled into his skin seeking nourishment. Soon a few insects became a swarm and Jack was engulfed in a small cloud of wings and stingers. The red welts that they raised as they stung began to itch, adding more agony to the mix. He closed his eyes and searched his mind for a peaceful place to go. He knew that he wouldn't survive the night, and he wanted to die with his mind free of pain.

He thought of Stacey was peaceful, the image of her sweet face bringing him some small measure of comfort. He imagined her as he had seen her in his fevered dream: cooking him dinner, sitting on the sofa watching television with him. He could almost smell her perfume as she rested her head on his shoulder. *"How the hell could I have ever let her go?"* he wondered.

His mind wandered, and he pictured his grandmother asleep in her old blue chair, the television droning in the corner. To his surprise, he missed her. He remembered when he had first moved in with her. She had tried to love him, but he had been so angry that he had pushed her away. After a time, she had just given up. For the second time that night, Jack began to cry. "I'm so sorry, " he moaned softly.

"If I ever get a chance, I promise that I'll do things differently." The tears brought relief, and Jack fell into a fitful doze.

The tugging on the ropes binding his wrists woke Jack instantly. "Oh, God, what now?" he said. The ropes loosened, then slipped away from his raw flesh. He brought his arms to the front of his chest, relaxing the tightness he felt in it. He leaned forward, hugging himself and trying to rub the feeling back into his numbed hands.

"Run," a small voice in his head commanded, but his body wasn't able to obey.

He wouldn't get ten feet without being shot. He rocked on the ground, waiting helpless for the soldier who had freed him to commence the next round of torture.

To Jack's astonishment, the face that came around the tree was that of the boy who had watched as the old man had peed on the American prisoner. Jack opened his mouth to speak, but the boy placed his finger over his lips to silence him. Wordlessly, he pointed to the jungle and gestured for Jack to follow him.

Chapter 47

Chris balled his right hand into a fist to stop the shaking. He turned and took a last look toward the open doorway. Even in the gray twilight the desert seemed mighty inviting, but the way back to his own time didn't lie out there. The rhythmic, hypnotic creaking from the other side of the door was calling to him.

He reached out to open the latch, and this time his hand was as steady as a rock. The small door swung open with surprising ease. The only illumination in the small dark room came from the cracks of a boarded up window. Thin rays of light streamed through the board, speckling the floor below, but not casting much light. The flashlight was nearly dead, but Chris swept the meager beam across the shadows as his eyes adjusted to the darkness. The only furniture in the room was an old metal bedframe sitting on the rotting boards. Chris wondered how many nights the old man had slept there.

The creaking had stopped when Chris had opened the door. *Maybe it was an animal and I scared it off*, he thought. Disappointment flooded over him. This room didn't hold anything more helpful than the other one had. The flashlight finally gave up, and Chris absently placed it on the shelf next to the doorway. *What the hell do I do now?* he thought.

Cold fingers of panic knotted his stomach as he tried desperately to come up with a workable plan "B." Without a light, he would never be able to find his way back through the desert to

Brian. The only alternative was to stay here until the sun came up, but the thought of spending the night in the old medicine man's rotting shack was about as appealing as sleeping in an open grave. His right hand toyed with the arrowhead necklace. The stone felt warm and strangely reassuring against his skin. He closed his eyes and visualized the Kickapoo Indian men sitting by the deep blue lake, the huge gray wolf lying by the fire warming his belly like a contented old dog. He remembered the hundreds of dreams of different times and places that the arrowhead had brought to him. He was convinced that the arrowhead had been the gateway to another life. The stone had passed from generation to generation in the Kickapoo and carried with it a little of the spirit of all who had touched it. He was not born into the Kickapoo tribe, but when he had found the arrowhead, he had been somehow adopted into their family. He knew it every time he held the stone. Surely it held the key to returning to his own time.

Chris held the arrowhead tightly, trying to extract the secret from the veined flint. A voice from the darkness sent a chill through his entire body.

"It is time for you to return, Chris."

Chris looked around the small bedroom for the source of the voice. A pale blue light illuminated the back of the old man's rocking chair. The corner had been in total darkness when Chris had first ventured into the room. The soft shimmering light reminded Chris of the halo from a full moon at midnight. The surreal glow surrounded the figure of a man sitting in the ancient rocker. The floorboards issued a now familiar creak as the man stood and turned to face Chris.

Chris took a step backward, stumbling against one of the wooden crates.

"Who are you?" he asked, his voice a pleading whisper.

He felt a rush of calm wash over him as the ghostly figure moved closer. Chris now recognized the man he had seen at Eagle Pass Park when he had found the arrowhead. The kindly weathered features also belonged to the man who had taken Chris's arm and pulled him and his injured friend from the raging river.

The man spoke again. "I am Hupa."

His smile held a trace of sadness. "You must return to where you belong now," he said softly. "You have learned that the future holds nothing for you unless you use the hours of the day to course it. The gift that the Great Spirit has given to you is the knowledge to change the course of your life and the lives of those that you love."

Chris stood speechless, his eyes fixed on those of his guardian angel. He no longer felt any fear at all. That he was having a conversation with a ghost didn't seem to be the least bit odd. He felt as if his thoughts were intertwining with those of the Indian's spirit. Memories and emotions flooded together, holding him transfixed.

Hupa held out a ghostly hand to Chris. "Come with me," he said. "I will take you to the places that you have only been able to visit in your dreams. There are people who are waiting to meet you. They are your friends and have watched you grow into a man." He moved closer to Chris. "Come, take my hand."

The shimmering blue light that emanated from Hupa expanded to fill the small room. The spirit's hand felt warm and comforting. A heady feeling of a weightlessness shot through Chris as the room began to fade from view.

Chapter 48

Brian woke up in the Honda's front seat as the first thin rays of sunlight began to streak the eastern sky. He looked around groggily, trying to figure out where the hell he was. The memory of the night before came back to him slowly. His patience had worn thin after Chris had been gone for an hour. He had listened to the car's cassette player for a while then had turned it off, so he wouldn't wear out the Honda's battery. Luckily, he had found Carolyn's emergency stash of Twinkies and a warm can of Pepsi, so at least he had a little dinner. Afterwards, he sat and smoked the better part of a pack of cigarettes as the sun disappeared behind the mountains. As the sky turned from deep blue to pitch black, Brian had cursed under his breath and slammed the palm of his hand on the steering wheel. Going after Chris was out of the question now. He wasn't about to go wandering around the desert in the dark. Not knowing what else to do, he had lowered the back of the driver's seat back as far as it would go and had settled in for a nap.

Now he crawled stiffly from the car massaging his aching back and yawned as he emptied his bladder against a nearby rock. *Where the fuck is Chris?* he wondered. *Where indeed,* he answered.

"Excellent question, Brian my man," he said out loud. *If Chris had been successful, he was back aboard a doomed helicopter over the Vietnamese jungle.* The thought made Brian unspeakably sad. He wanted what was best for Chris, but it had been so damn good to have him around again.

He looked at the small collection of buildings in the distance, then back at the car. Maybe Chris had been afraid to try to find the car after dark and had fallen asleep in the old man's shack. "Aw, screw it," Brian said finally. He started down what was left of the dirt road toward the shack. He didn't want to know, but he had to know, what had become of his friend.

What was left of the dirt road that led to the ramshackle collection of buildings faded in the distance as Brian got closer. Tall weeds surrounded the shack and its decrepit outbuildings. Brian guessed the old man had once planted grass and maybe a garden. He didn't much like the idea of wading into the chest-high growth. It looked like it would be a haven for snakes and desert tarantulas, but there was no other way to get to the shack. The decaying buildings didn't look all that appealing either. The air of rotting mildewed wood reminded Brian of an old western ghost town. "*Just turn around and go back to the car and get the hell out of here*," a small voice within him advised. "*Forget about this nightmare. Chris died in Vietnam 30 years ago, and all of the rest is pure bullshit.*"

While Brian thought that the small voice had a very good point, he reluctantly rejected the idea of turning back. He had come too far, and he knew that if he walked away now he would always wonder what had happened to his friend.

"Hey, Chris, you in there?" he called hopefully. The only sound that he heard was the rustling of the tall grass in the desert wind.

He waded into the chest-high grass, tiptoeing like a swimmer testing the temperature of the water. Fear of what might be in there with him propelled Brian along very fast indeed. He breathed a sigh of relief when he reached the clearing around the shack. The single window on the side of the cabin that faced the road had been boarded up. Chris couldn't have gotten into the shack that way. Flat stones had been laid out to form a walkway around the side of the shack. Brian followed the path that led to the screened- in porch.

The wind had not quite obliterated the fresh footprints in the sand and dust on the porch. The footprints reassured him that it was all too real. Chris had come this way. Brian had begun to wonder if he had been having some sort of mental breakdown and had imagined the whole thing. *He's probably asleep in the shack*, Brian thought, gingerly stepping onto the sagging porch. "Chris?" he called out as he approached the door. There was no response. Brian looked into the small room through the open doorway. Tingles of fresh anxiety breathed heavily across his skin as he realized that the footprints stopped at the threshold. A thick layer of dust on the floor of the shack lay seemingly undisturbed. *"Oh, crap,"* Brian thought. He ventured a foot into the small room. There was no trace of anyone having been there for a very long time. He was about to turn toward the open doorway when a small finger of light coming from the far corner caught his eye. The wooden door to the other room was ajar.

"Chris? You in there?" Brian called softly, his breath raising a small whirlwind of dust. He didn't really expect a reply and heard none.

"This is too fucking weird," he said as he crept toward the far corner, careful to go slowly on the creaking floorboards.

The door whined softly as he opened it wide. The room was empty except for a rusty iron bedstead and an old rocking chair lying on its side in the dust.

"This is hopeless," he sighed. "No one has been in here in, like a century." Brian turned to leave the shack, banging his elbow on a wooden shelf as he turned.

Something on the dusty wooden shelf caught his eye. His mind refusing to believe what his eyes saw, he reached out with a shaking finger and touched the dust that covered the pink plastic flashlight.

Chapter 49

Jack stumbled to the line of trees that edged the jungle, struggling to keep up with the boy. He was only 20 yards from the camp, and already the pain and fatigue were wearing him down. He was unable to stand upright without bringing on agonizing spasms of pain, so he ran in a weird, crablike skitter. Low branches left deep scratches on his naked flesh as he pushed through the dense foliage. He resisted the urge to call to the boy to wait. The sound of his voice would surely alert the soldiers to his escape. Jack silently commanded his legs to move forward.

Jack didn't know about the pan mines that had been sown sporadically around the perimeter of the camp. Miraculously, his feet didn't find any of the deadly mines. Instead, he hooked one of the thin brass trip wires that released a small stick that supported the firing mechanism of a phosphorus flare. As his foot hooked what he thought was a vine, Jack stumbled but managed to right himself. His head swivelled as he heard the sharp click of the firing mechanism. The fireball hissed into the air and exploded 15 feet over his head. In an instant, the blinding white light of the flare lit up the jungle around him.

Like a deer caught in the headlights of an oncoming car, Jack watched in mute horror as the burning flare fell to earth. The sound of angry voices coming from the direction of the Vietnamese camp mobilized him, and he headed deeper into the jungle. The little boy was no longer in sight. Guns cracked in the distance. His pain forgotten, Jack pumped his legs as hard as the undergrowth would allow. A few slugs whizzed past him, forcing him to dodge left, then right. The gunfire slowed, then stopped at about the same time that Jack's injuries caused him to drop to the jungle floor, gasping in a few agonizing breaths. He knew that he didn't have long to rest. The soldiers would be able to track him easily now that the flare had shown them his position. The sounds of voices and breaking branches got him moving again, zigzagging through the dense brush. The voices were getting closer all the time. Jack knew that they would be on him in a matter of seconds.

The dream that had begun this strange nightmare flashed vividly through his mind. He saw himself running through the jungle naked, just as he was now. In the dream, he had hidden on the ground, covered with leaves torn from the thick tangle of bushes that surrounded him. Sticks tore at his naked flesh as he threw himself on the ground and crawled under a low-hanging bush, tearing branches from the lower limbs of trees and yanking plants out by their roots as he went. Covering himself as best he could, he lay motionless, listening to the voices draw nearer. He held his breath and listened to the pounding of his heart as two soldiers passed by, their footfalls so close that Jack was sure that they would step on him.

The shadowy figures disappeared into the blackness, their whispers fading in the dark as Jack lay frozen with fear, still not daring to breathe. No new footfalls broke the stillness of his hiding place, and he was finally forced to breathe again. He would not stir from his cover until he was absolutely sure that it was safe to do so. The pain from his injuries had abated somewhat. He closed his eyes to rest them for a moment. He fell into a light doze, the crackle of brush trampled by booted feet brought him awake in a heartbeat, threatening to drown him in storms of fear.

Oh, Christ, they're coming back, he thought. *Why didn't I run when I had the chance?* He could make out the dark silhouette of someone standing next to his hiding place.

Chapter 50

Enveloped in the cool blue cloud, Chris felt a peculiar floating sensation. The cloud began to disperse slowly and he found himself standing by the side of *Lake Kahooga*, a place that he had seen so many times in his dreams. The cloud had receded into a pale, eerie mist that settled above the still surface of the water. Hupa sat, as he had in Chris's vision, by a smoldering fire alongside a handsome young Indian man. The gray wolf lounged by the warmth of the fire. He raised his massive head and regarded Chris calmly. Chris recoiled in fear, but the wolf made no move toward him, resting his head on his paws, he appeared to be content lying on his soft pine needle bed. Hupa rose and smiled broadly, holding a hand out to Chris in a welcoming gesture.

"My young friend," he said warmly. "Come and meet Seeing Eye."

Chris didn't know what to say, so he settled for an awkward. "Pleased to meet you."

Seeing Eye stood and embraced the startled young man, then stood back and held Chris at arms length.

"You have had quite a journey," he said. "Now you have come full circle, and your journey is nearly at an end."

"I don't understand any of this," Chris replied, bewildered. "Why has this happened to me?"

Seeing Eye shrugged as if this was a stupid question. "Because the arrowhead chose you," he replied. "You have made a great sacrifice for the Kickapoo people, and we are grateful. Now you must return to your own time. You have much to do." Chris was beginning to grow tired of the riddles. "I don't understand, what sacrifice?" He asked impatiently. "Through the magic of the arrowhead, you allowed me to steal your life for a time." The deep voice came from the trees behind Chris. He wheeled around and came face to face with Matachias. The medicine man's hair was still gray and his skin weathered, but he stood straight and tall now. A beautiful young Indian woman stood at his side, her arm hooked in his.

"There is a confused and angry young man who planned to do great harm to our people," he continued. "To release his anger this young man, known as Jack King, planned to bring powerful weapons to a tribal celebration and kill as many Kickapoo tribesmen as possible. Our tribe would have been destroyed. The wish that you made in my cabin allowed me to send him to war in your place. The only way to change Jack King was to let him see firsthand the cost of hatred and prejudice. Now he has had the time to reflect. You must return to your own life and Jack to his, come what may."

The fog that had hovered over Lake Kahooga began to float toward Chris, forming undulating fingers of pale blue. He shivered as the mist snaked around his ankles. Chris knew that he had better hurry if he was going to get the answers to his questions.

"You said that I still have much to do. What does that mean?" he asked.

"There is much that a man with a heart as true as yours can accomplish in a lifetime," Matachias replied enigmatically. "I thank you for returning my father, Hupa, to the spirit world to join my mother and me."

Chris saw that Hupa and Seeing Eye now stood with Matachias and his mother, though he had not seen them move. Their figures had taken on an unearthly glow, and Chris could see the outlines of the trees through their rapidly fading bodies.

"You'll return me to Vietnam, then?"

This time Hupa answered the question. He looked at Chris sadly as he shook his now- translucent head.

"I must send you back to where I found you. I belong fully to the spirit world now and will not be there to help you this time. May the Great Spirit send you home safely." Hupa's words trailed off. All Chris could see now was the forest.

The mist swirled around his chest, chilling him to the bone. As it rose to cover his face, Chris began to feel the strange floating sensation once again. *"What a hell of a day this has been, "* he thought as the darkness claimed him.

Chapter 51

Jack waited in his cocoon of leaves and twigs, eyes shut tight, for the bullet to the head that he was sure was coming. He didn't feel any fear, he would rather die quickly than be recaptured and tortured. He was startled to hear a deep voice speaking to him in English.

"The Great Spirit has sent me to release your soul from the Horned Panthers. They would guide your enemies back to watch you suffer before they finally put you to death."

Jack's eyes flew open in surprise. Was he dreaming again? Still? In the darkness, he could only see the outline of the tall man who stood beside him. The man knelt next to Jack and touched his arm lightly. The hand felt warm and soothing.

"We must go now, your enemies will be here soon."

Jack struggled to sit upright. He could see the tall man now. His skin was dark and smooth. His handsome face was surrounded by long black hair topped by a floppy suede hat with a single feather in the brim. He wore only a tanned suede vest and leggings. Several small leather bags hung from a thong around his waist.

"Who are you?" Jack whispered. "What is happening to me?"

"I am Hupa," the man replied. "The Horned Panthers have cursed your spirit because you have washed others with the pain that fills your heart. The marks of hatred that are inked on your arms scar your entire life with evil. You must now rid yourself of both if you are ever to find peace."

Jack looked down at the swastikas tattooed on his biceps. The symbols that he had taken such pride in now looked ugly and alien to him. He was ashamed to have the emblems of hatred branded into his flesh. He heard voices in the distance and recoiled in fear. There were tears in his eyes as he looked up at the handsome dark face of Hupa.

"Am I going to die?" he asked in a hoarse whisper.

Hupa didn't reply. He stared deep into Jack's eyes and lifted a hand to gently touch Jack's tear stained cheek.

Jack felt a sense of calm that was foreign to him even though the voices of the Vietnamese soldiers were growing louder. Hupa's face had taken on a faint bluish glow that spread to obscure everything around him. As the blue mist engulfed him, Jack felt the pain in his ribs and back begin to ease, then vanish altogether. Hupa's voice sounded hollow as he answered Jack's question.

"No, Jack. You have suffered enough. It is time that you have the chance to change the things that you can. To begin with you must stop the chain of events that you set in motion up in the mountains. Mary's life, as well as your own, will be in your hands now. Let your wounds heal, Jack. I warn you that if you tear them open again they will bleed forever."

Chapter 52

A foul stream of muddy water running into his open mouth brought Chris back to consciousness. He choked and gagged on the filthy liquid, spitting out as much as he could. He felt a rush of nausea and wondered how much of the river he had swallowed while he was passed out. His thoughts swirling in his head seemed to be moving faster than the turbulent water around him. Nightmare images crowded his brain: crashing helicopters and Indians and swastikas all fought their way forward.

The pain in his arms forced Chris to concentrate on surviving. He pushed the other thoughts aside. His left arm was hooked around a branch of a tree that had fallen into the rain-swollen river. His right arm held his wounded friend in a death grip. Chris looked at the top of Brian's head and was momentarily surprised to see that the wet, bloody hair that was plastered to his scalp was thick and dark. Chris had half expected to see thinning gray curls surrounding a bald spot. As Chris tightened his grip on his friend, Brian moaned softly.

"*I'm back*," he thought happily. "*Hupa sent me back.*"

His relief was short-lived as he remembered the medicine man's last words.

"I will not be there to help you this time."

Chris craned his head, scanning the riverbank, hoping that Hupa could find a way to help him after all. As promised, the Shaman was nowhere to be seen. *Shit*, Chris thought. *I'm really on my own this time.*

This realization was cut short by a loud creaking noise coming from the roots of the tree that Chris clung to. The rushing water was slowly loosening the roots from the soft mud of the riverbank. The tree shifted as the roots began to pull free. Chris attempted to tighten his grip on the branch, but his arm was rapidly growing too numb to function. He tried to quell the panic that was threatening to tie his gut into knots. The tree would be swept down river soon. Chris knew that now it was only a question of which would give out first, the tree roots or his arm. If he couldn't find a way to shore, he and Brian were goners.

Chris wondered what it would be like to drown. He remembered that he had once read that it was a relatively painless way to die, but that was small comfort now. He had watched in horror as Brian had been dragged under the water by a branch. It had looked pretty damn painful to Chris. *Maybe it would be better if I just give up and let go*, he thought miserably. *Fighting is just prolonging the pain.* The tree jerked in the water as another root pulled free.

Chris was losing strength rapidly. His lungs gurgled when he breathed from the water that he had inhaled. He thought about Hupa and Matachias. They had seemed so happy in the spirit world. Chris hoped that he would join them if the river claimed his life. He was having trouble keeping his eyes open and was beginning to shiver from the cold. His ears rang unpleasantly as he began to fade in and out of consciousness. *Maybe my only purpose in life was to stop Jack King from going on a rampage against the Indians,"* he thought.

It was to be his last thought. With a final sickening swosh, the mud of the riverbank gave up its grip and released the tree. Unable to free his useless right arm, Chris was swept away by the rushing torrent, taking Brian with him toward the Rio Grande.

Chapter 53

Jack woke up screaming, flailing his arms and legs to free himself from the twisted knot of sweat-soaked sheets. When he had finally thrown the covers to the floor, he sat up and stared wildly around the small bedroom.

"It was all a nightmare," he breathed as his surroundings registered on his fevered brain.

As the pounding in his chest slowed, he swung his feet over the side of the bed, padded to the bathroom and flipped on the light. As he emptied his aching bladder, Jack caught sight of his reflection in the clouded mirror that hung over the sink.

His thin face was caked with blood from the wound on his forehead. His naked body was covered with insect bites and bruises. The stubble on Jack's neck stood straight and stiff on his scalp as he looked down at his mud-caked, bloody feet. Jack turned slowly, looking over his shoulder at the bruises on his back. The bruises matched the beating that he had taken in his dream, but there was no pain.

Jack's mind reeled at the possibility that he really had been captured and beaten by Viet cong guerillas in the year 1969. "Oh, screw it," he said out loud. "I'll never figure it out and I'm just wasting time."

Whatever the hell had happened the night before, dawn was breaking, and he had a lot to undo. If by some miracle the Indian woman had survived the night, he had to hurry and get her to a hospital.

Jack ran back to his bedroom and grabbed the O.W.O. shirt from the crumpled heap of clothes that lay on the floor by the bed. The emblem seemed alien to him now. He turned the shirt inside out and slid it over his head. He would throw it out later. He pulled on his rumpled jeans and damp boots and headed down the narrow hallway toward the living room.

His grandmother was still sleeping in her recliner in front of the television. Jack stopped for a moment by her chair and looked down at the old woman. The rush of love and compassion that he felt for her surprised him.

Bending to kiss her wrinkled cheek, Jack whispered. "I'm sorry, grandma. I've been a real shit and I'll try to make it up to you."

The old woman stirred in her sleep and mumbled, but did not wake up. Jack moved quietly to the front door and jumped over the three steps and down to the gravel below.

Butterflies the size of B-52's formed in his stomach as he headed to Stacey's trailer. He had no idea how he would explain to her that he needed her to help him rescue an injured Indian in the mountains. The small voice that he was beginning to recognize as the voice of reason spoke inside his head. "*Just keep it simple*," the voice advised. "*Tell her the truth*." Jack took a breath and calmed down. The butterflies subsided.

"Where have you been all my life?" he asked the voice wryly.

Stacey's trailer was dark. After Jack had pounded on the door for a few minutes, a light came on in a back room. Stacey peeked around the lace curtain that covered the window in the front door and asked in a sleepy voice.

"Who is it?"

Jack wiped his sweaty palms on his thighs before answering.

"It's Jack. Please, I really need to talk to you, I really need you right now, please," he said in a desperate tone.

Stacey answered her door with a cool. "What do you want?"

"I injured a women, she's up in the mountains, I have to go get her to a hospital. Please, I need your help. Jack could barley get to of the words out before the tears came steaming down his face.

"What are you talking about ,Jack"

"I promise I will explain everything to you but I have to get up there right now before it's to late. Will you help me?"

She reached for her car keys without hesitation. "I'll go get Kevin."

Jack marveled at how quickly she agreed to help, but he wasn't really surprised. That was just her nature.

Stacey handed the car keys to Jack and strapped Kevin into his car seat.

"You know the way, so you'd better drive," she instructed.

As she climbed into the passenger seat, Stacey dug in her purse and pulled out a cellular phone.

"I'll call 911 and then you can give directions to the ambulance dispatcher," she said.

Jack hadn't thought about calling for help. He had been alienated from society for so long that calling for help had never occurred to him.

What did I think I was going to do? He wondered silently. *Just load the poor woman into the back seat of Stacey's Toyota and drop he off at the nearest Emergency Room?* He shook his head as Stacey handed him the cell phone.

As Jack gave directions to the dispatcher, Stacey studied him out of the corner of her eye. He looked like warmed-over death in wrinkled jeans and his tee shirt on inside out. Dried blood was crusted on his pale face and he looked like he had been stung by every mosquito in west Texas. Something was different about him though. His edginess was gone and he seemed to be more comfortable in his skin than she had ever seen him. The fact that he was going out on a limb to rescue her was definitely a good sign.

They rode in silence. Jack wanted to tell Stacey about all that had happened the night before, but he didn't know where to start. He decided that she had enough to think about already. For her part, Stacey was dying to ask what the hell all of this was about, but she knew that she wouldn't like the answer so in the end she kept quiet.

Jack slowed the car as they headed up the mountain road. He pulled over to the side and turned the car's engine off about half-way up the mountain.

"Stay here," he instructed as he got out of the car.

Stacey ignored him, of course. She checked to make sure that Kevin was still asleep in his car seat. When she was satisfied that he was safe, she got out of the car and followed Jack.

The Paramedics would see the car.

Jack had climbed over the guardrail and was searching for the broken tree when he heard a low moan. He hurried in the direction of the sound and found the women lying where he had left her. She was barely breathing, but her eyes widened in terror when she saw Jack heading toward her.

Her whisper, "No," was barely audible.

Jack knelt by her side. "Don't be afraid," he begged her in a hoarse whisper. "Help is on the way."

He began to cry again, his face contorting as the tears ran down his cheeks. Her injuries looked horrendous in the clear morning light. The silence was broken by the sound of approaching sirens.

"We called for help," Jack explained. "They'll be here in a minute."

She looked past Jack at the small blonde woman who stood behind him, her face a mask of compassion, and felt a ray of hope. Jack had regained control of himself a little. He pulled his tee shirt off and folded it into a pillow, gently placing it under her battered head.

"I'm so sorry," he said softly. "I know that it doesn't help, but I truly am sorry."

Her only response was a pitiful shiver. Jack realized how cold it was and turned to yell for Stacey to bring her jacket to cover up the women.

Stacey backed toward the car as Jack apologized. She didn't know how to react. How could anyone do this to another human being? Jack saw her retreating to the car and asked Stacey to bring something to keep the injured woman warm. Stacey retrieved a blanket from the back seat of the Toyota and handed it to Jack without a word.

The ambulance driver parked behind the Toyota, and the Sheriff's deputy who had escorted the ambulance parked in front, blocking Stacey's car in.

Stacey called out. "Over here!"

Two paramedics jumped from the van and hoisted a collapsible Gurney from the cargo bay. They headed toward the sound of Stacey's voice with the deputy right behind them, unsnapping his holster as he ran.

The paramedics pushed past Jack and knelt on the ground by the women's side. "Can you tell me what you name is sweetheart?"

"Mary Roundtree,"she said in a soft whisper.

They examined her quickly and efficiently, speaking to each other in clipped phrases.

"Compound fractures, probable concussion, hypothermia, airway patent," and other medical terms that were Greek to Jack.

"Let's get her back to the truck and get an I.V. started," was the first sentence that he understood.

Mary groaned as they lifted her gently onto the Gurney and covered her with a blanket. Jack, Stacey and the deputy watched in silence as the paramedics wheeled the Gurney to the ambulance. The deputy broke the silence.

"What happened here?" he asked. "Who did this to her?"

Stacey watched Jack's face intently as he decided on an answer. He finally took a deep breath and said "I did."

The look of pain and revulsion on Stacey's face hurt Jack more than anything else that had happened to him that night.

The deputy lit a cigarette and blew out a plume of smoke.

"You know I'm gonna have to arrest you, son," he drawled, not unkindly.

Jack nodded and held his hands out to receive the handcuffs. For a moment, he had been sorry that he had decided to help his victim, but that changed when he looked down at his wrists. The red welts, ugly but painless, circled his wrists, standing out in stark contrast to his pale skin. Jack had no doubt that the nightmare had been real, and that for once in his miserable life, he had made the right choice.

Part 6
Chapter 54

Friday, May 16, 2002 5:35 P.M. Brunswick, Ohio

Gravel crunched noisily as the white Chevy van swung into the driveway in front of the little blue ranch house. Bold painted lettering on the side of the van read: NORTH COAST ELECTRICAL, RESIDENTIAL AND COMMERCIAL, FREE ESTIMATES, followed by a local phone number.

Jack King sat in the driver's seat, staring at the house as he had every night for the past month. The house had been painted five years earlier by the previous owner, but the blue siding and white trim were holding up pretty well. Jack sat for a while, admiring the Homburg gray shutters that he and Stacey had put up, and the flowers that they had planted in April. They had bought the tidy little house in March, and Jack still couldn't believe that it belonged to him.

Good luck had finally come Jack's way after he had been arrested. Rich Shanack and a few of his Old World Order lackeys had pulled the robbery of the drug dealer the night of the warehouse party. Unfortunately for them, they picked the night that the D.E.A. also picked to bust the dealer. Jack testified against the Shanack brothers and they had gotten some heavy prison time. The O.W.O. had fallen apart before the Shanack brothers were even sentenced.

Jack had worked hard for the past four years and was proud of all that he had accomplished. While he had been on probation for the assault on Mary Roundtree, Jack had studied for his high school diploma and worked two minimum wage jobs to boot. After obtaining his diploma through a G.E.D. program, he had gone on to trade school and had become a certified electrician. After completing an apprenticeship, he had worked for an electrical contractor until he and Stacey had saved enough money to start his own company. North Coast Electrical was out of the red now, and Stacey had been able to go to part-time at her secretarial job.

Marrying Stacey was the accomplishment that Jack was the proudest of. He considered it a miracle that she had stuck by him through it all. Somehow she had sensed that the change in him was genuine, and her trust had been what kept him going. Becoming father to a great little guy like Kevin had really been the icing on the cake. Jack had adopted Kevin after he and Stacey had married. He was the only father that Kevin had ever known.

"So what's missing?" Jack said out loud. Sometimes late at night, lying in bed waiting for sleep to come, or when he worked alone like he had that day, Jack had the nagging feeling that he had some kind of unfinished business to complete. He tried to convince himself that it had to do with the responsibility of running a business or paying household bills, but he knew that it ran deeper than that. Jack had dreamed about his night in Vietnam many times, but the dreams were becoming more frequent and vivid lately. Jack felt that Hupa had something for him to do, but he had no idea what it was.

The light in the kitchen went on and Jack smiled. He knew that Stacey would be starting dinner and that the house would be warm and warm and cozy when he stepped inside.

"Hi, hon, how's it going?" he asked as he shut the screen door behind him.

Stacy came out of the kitchen and flopped down next to him on the sofa, planting a kiss on his near cheek. Her smile, always infectious, lit up her face.

"Hi, babe. Besides the fact that I'm a big fat cow, I guess I'm doing okay. How was your day?"

Jack placed a hand gently on his wife's beach ball sized belly. Stacey was due to deliver in three weeks and was having a hard time getting around now, but she looked better than ever to Jack.

"My day wasn't bad," he replied. "I finished off that punch list at the Shee's house, so we should be getting the check pretty soon. How's Jack junior doing today?" he asked, rubbing Stacy's tummy.

"You mean Kaleigh or Sydney," she corrected with a laugh, "She's doing fine. Let's just say that she's very active today. She must think that she's in a swimming pool and she's doing the backstroke."

They were both laughing now.

Stacey rocked her unwieldy body forward twice and on the third attempt she managed to get to her feet. Jack watched in amusement as she maneuvered around the coffee table and into the adjoining kitchen.

Jack picked up the remote and turned the television on, leaning back on the sofa with a contented sigh.

"Are you hungry?"

Stacey's voice from the kitchen sent an unexpected shiver up Jack's spine. His eyes locked on her as she reached into the cupboard above the stove. She turned and smiled at Jack over her shoulder.

"Would you like something to eat?"

Now he remembered: this exact scene had been played before in a feverish dream while he had been tied to a tree in the Vietnam jungle. Why had he been given a glimpse into his future? He wiped the cold sweat from his forehead and ran a trembling hand through his thick mop of hair.

"I guess your mom and grandma and I are going shopping tomorrow for some stuff for the baby's room. They're going to pick me up around noon. Is there anything you need at the mall?" Stacy asked from the kitchen.

Jack was lost in thought and didn't hear her. The sudden intrusion of images from the past had left him dazed.

"Jack, did you hear me or is the TV more interesting?" Her voice finally broke through his trance.

"I'm sorry, yeah, I heard you. I can't think of anything I need. Maybe I'll take Kevin to North Park and we'll do some fishing." He hoped that she didn't notice how shaky his voice sounded.

Stacey returned to her cooking, and Jack picked up the remote and began to channel surf. There was no point in dwelling on the past. *If Hupa has something that he wants me to do, then he ought to just spit it out and let me get on with my life,* he thought bitterly.

After going around the dial a few times, Jack settled on the 6:00 news. An attractive blonde talking head was leading into a new story.

"We now take you live to correspondent Tom McCreary in Clarion, Pennsylvania, just outside of Pittsburgh where environmental activists have been demonstrating for the past two days."

The television picture switched to a blandly handsome young reporter standing a safe distance from a group of demonstrators waving hand-lettered signs.

"Thank you, Stephanie," the reporter intoned. "This rural area outside of Clarion has been proposed as a possible site for a nuclear power plant. These protestors are concerned about the loss of wildlife that would be inevitable if a nuclear plant is built in this heavily forested area."

The camera panned to a man speaking to he crowd through a bullhorn. The speaker was a lean, handsome man somewhere in his forties. He appeared to be clean cut and conservative until the camera moved behind him showing the dark brown ponytail streaked with gray cascading down his back. The crowd responded to his speech with cheers and more sign waving.

Jack leaned forward on the sofa, watching in fascination. The reporter was rattling on, and Jack paid no attention to him until he said the name.

"Christopher Logue."

The name hit Jack like a bucket of cold water. He had seen that name stitched above the pocket of the fatigue jacket that he had been wearing that long, horrible night in Vietnam.

Jack leaped across the coffee table and landed on one knee in front of the console television. The reporter was leading into a conversation that had been taped earlier that day.

"The group of 50,000 protesters here today is by far the largest turnout for this issue in many years," the reporter said, thrusting a microphone toward the handsome man with the ponytail. "This is Christopher Logue, the head of the Wildlife Conservation Corps. Chris, what do you think is going to be the outcome of this demonstration?"

Chris smiled at the question. "The people of Clarion, and the surrounding areas have been fighting this proposal for 10 years, and we're going to keep coming back until the politicians wipe this proposal off of the slate."

Chris was the picture of charm as he smiled at the camera. He was clearly at ease in front of the lens. Also obvious was his sincerity and belief in his cause. There was no doubt in Jack's mind that this was the Christopher Logue who owned the fatigue jacket.

"I grew up in Clarion, and most of the people here have lived here all of their lives and have voted to keep this county free of the pollutants that would eventually destroy the rivers, streams and forests," Chris continued. "The loss of another wetland would be tragic. One accident would destroy it all. The people here today know what's at stake, and they're committed to keeping the plant from being built here, or anywhere else for that matter. It's high time that the politicians start spending our tax dollars to seriously explore the use of alternative sources that are safer and cheaper in the long run and could be available if enough people care about our environment." Now he was looking directly into the camera. "For more information, we have a toll-free number."

At that point, an 800 number appeared at the bottom of the screen.

Jack sprinted to the kitchen, silently repeating the phone number. He frantically pulled open the junk drawer and began to rummage through it, looking for something to write with.

"Jack, what's wrong? What are you looking for?"

Ignoring Stacey's question, Jack caught sight of a broken green crayon lying in the bottom of the drawer debris. He snatched it up in triumph and scribbled the number on the counter top.

"What in the world are you doing?" Stacey's face was a mask of concern. "My God, you look like you've seen a ghost."

His mission accomplished, Jack slid into one of the kitchen chairs. He took a deep breath to slow his racing heart and looked up into Stacey's beautiful eyes. Christopher Logue was the piece that had been missing from Jack's life, but Jack didn't know how to explain that to his wife.

After his arrest, he had said that he had attacked Mary Roundtree on the orders of his superiors in the O.W.O., which was true enough. Explaining why he had returned in the early morning to rescue her, knowing that it would mean turning himself in, had been a little more difficult. In the end, he had simply said that he had a change of heart. Stacey had been skeptical; she had seen such a profound change in Jack that she believed there was something bigger behind it, but she had kept her doubts to herself.

Now, in typical Stacey fashion, she waited silently for Jack to speak. She handed him a glass of cold water. He took it with a wan half-smile and gratefully drained the glass in one gulp.

"Honey, sit down," he said, pointing to the chair next to his.

He had not spoken of that long-ago night in the Texas mountains in ages. He didn't know if Stacey would believe his story, but she had believed in him all of these years, so she had to be the most trusting soul on the planet. He would just have to tell her and hope for the best. Now that he knew that Christopher Logue was just a phone call away, Jack would never rest until they met.

Chapter 55

May 30, 2002 Clarion, Pennsylvania

Chris Logue sat behind his battered oak desk staring absently out of the small window. His mind wandered as it had frequently over the past two days, making it impossible to concentrate on his work. He had been thrown for a loop when Jack King had called. Hupa had told Chris years before, in a particularly vivid dream, that Jack would one day form a partnership with him and would one day become his successor. Chris had expressed doubt at this prediction. His limited contact with Jack's world had left Chris unimpressed with Jack's character, to say the very least. He remembered the Nazi posters that decorated the walls of Jack's cramped bedroom. His Indian guardian had assured Chris that Jack King was a changed man and a true believer in the magic of that change.

In the years after this dream, Chris had put the question of Jack King's transformation on the back burner. College, then law school, then a wife and children and work as an environmental lawyer had left little time for Chris to reflect on the past. At night, though, in dreams, the past was as real as the present. Over the years, Chris had become adept at shaking his dreams off when the alarm clock buzzed. He had too much to do to worry about Hupa's prophecies. Now one of those predictions appeared to be coming true.

Chris sighed and swivelled his desk chair around to face the wall of photos that hung over a worn leather sofa that was the only uncluttered surface in the tiny office. There wasn't a chance in hell that he was going to get any more work done today, so he might as well let his thoughts wander free for a while. He gazed at the photos that told the story of his life. A lump formed in his throat when his eyes landed on the grainy black and white picture of Brian leaning against the side of Matt's old Bonneville.

Chris still missed his childhood friend. At 18, Chris had not had to deal with the loss of a loved one and Brian's death had the added whammy of guilt heaped on the loss. Chris wiped moisture from his eyes as he remembered the last time he had seen Brian in the river at Eagle Pass Park. Right 'til the end, he had hoped that somehow Hupa would be able to rescue them after all, but it was not to be. Chris had been unable to hold on to his friend when the tree had been pulled loose from the soil. The boys had been swept away toward the center of the swirling river. Cold and exhausted, Chris had tried to keep his death grip on his friend's neck, but the rushing water had won the battle for Brian's life.

The last time Chris had seen him, the current was dragging him under for the last time.

Unable to fight any more, Chris had let the water carry him away. He had been barely conscious when two campers who had seen his head bobbing above the water's surface fished him out of the water a mile down river. Chris had sucked in what seemed like half of the river, and he was battered and bruised, but the Emergency room Doc had pronounced him fit enough to join Uncle Sam as scheduled after a few days rest. Chris and his parents had waited with Brian's stunned family while search parties dragged the rain-swollen river for Brian's body. Chris had still been numb when he had climbed aboard the bus for boot camp.

Brian's lifeless body had surface while Chris was still in boot camp. Ryan and Laurie had decided to wait until he came home on leave to tell him about his friend's death. Carolyn had comforted

Chris when he had broken down at the cemetery. Amazingly, she hadn't blamed Chris for her son's death. "It was an accident, pure and simple," she had assured him as she stroked his back while he cried. "You have to let it go."

Letting it go had been easier said than done, but Chris had finally managed to forgive himself. He figured if Brian's mother didn't blame him for her only son's death then maybe he should give himself a break.

Still, he couldn't help wondering what Brian would be like as a middle-aged man. The waste case he had met on the night of his switch with Jack King would probably be different if he had survived the river. Chris would have been a part of his friend's life, and he thought that he could have made a difference.

"Oh, well," he sighed. "If I had wheels, I would have been a bicycle." That had been one of Laurie's favorite sayings.

Chris looked at the photo of Matt and Carolyn sitting on his patio, smiling into the camera. He had taken it the summer before when they came to visit his family in Clarion. After they had retired, Matt had bought a used recreational vehicle, and they now spent their summers in the north, away from the heat of the Texas summers at last. They would always grieve the loss of their son, but Matt's nieces and nephews had helped to fill the void, and life had gone on.

The next photo that caught his eye was one of Ryan and Laurie, taken shortly before her death. His mother had been going through one last bout of chemotherapy to try to halt the progress of her breast cancer. She looked pale and thin, her alabaster skin a sharp contrast to the brightly colored scarf wrapped in a turban around her head, but her smile was bright. With the emotional support of her husband and sons, she had fought bravely, but in vain. Ryan had been devastated by her death. Chris had transferred his college credits to a school closer to home when Laurie had become ill, and he stayed on with Ryan for two years after his mother died. He and Pam Case had tried to renew their relationship when he returned to Texas, but they had never really been able to connect. Chris had met Sara in law school, and they had married a year later. When Chris had moved Sara and their three daughters back to Clarion, Ryan, now retired, had bought a condominium a few miles away from his son. He kept himself busy by doing some consulting work and playing golf with Chris and Jonathan when the Pennsylvania weather allowed.

"Enough with the memories, already," Chris said out loud. "Time to go home."

As he stood up and turned toward the window, Chris was surprised to see that it was dark outside. Sara would be wondering where the hell he was. She was used to his long working hours by now, and he was sure that she would take one more late evening in stride. His bad hip creaked as he pulled his jacket from the hook by the office door, and Chris stopped to rub his cramped muscles. The injury that he had received in the helicopter crash in Vietnam had earned him a Purple Heart and a medical discharge from the Army. His wish to Matachias had been granted after all. Chris had never had the chance to fight in the war. He still limped a little now and then when his hip stiffened up, but he was used to it by now. The ache always reminded Chris of Phil Baldwin. They had become good friends during their stay in the military hospital in Honolulu and still compared war wounds whenever they talked on the phone.

As Chris drove to his log home on the edge of Cook's Forest, he thought about his meeting with Jack King that had been scheduled for the next day. Their phone conversation had been brief, but Jack had sounded enthusiastic about meeting him. He wondered if Jack knew that Chris had lived his life for one very long day.

Chapter 56

It was a few minutes before 11:00 a.m. the next morning when Stacey's maroon mini-van pulled into the parking lot of the Krazy Kone ice cream stand across from Chris Logue's office. The ice cream stand was about to open for business, and a line was starting to form in front of the serving window. The mini-van pulled into one of the spaces in front of the window. Chris had been looking out of his office window for the better part of an hour, anxious for Jack King to arrive. A young man and woman were visible in the front seats of the van, and Chris could see someone moving in the back seat. He watched as the young man got out of the driver's seat and walked around to the passenger door to help an obviously pregnant blond woman out of the front seat and over to the sidewalk. He returned to the van and opened the side panel and waited until a little boy got out and joined his mother on the sidewalk. Chris knew from the Ohio license plate on the van's bumper that Jack and his family had arrived.

Chris had the unexpected sensation that an unknown son he had never met had finally returned home. They were bound together by a tie that the Kickapoo had knotted in another time and place. He found that he was looking forward to swapping stories with the person who had shared the brief body-switching experience with him. He had no idea what Jack had experienced during his night in Vietnam, but it must have been quite a night to have changed him so much. He leaned back in his chair and closed his eyes, waiting for Jack to knock on his office door.

"Jack, honey, why don't you go in by yourself. I feel kinda strange about this. I'll get Kevin an ice cream cone while we wait for you. Besides, you guys need a chance to talk in private."

Jack smiled and kissed her pale cheek. He could understand her mixed emotions. He was feeling a little weird about this himself.

"Yeah, sure, that works for me," he answered. "Could you get me a chocolate malt while you're at it?"

Stacey nodded and returned her husband's kiss. "Good luck in there. I hope this is what you're looking for, Jack. You know that I trust you with my life," she said, hugging him awkwardly. "For the past four years you've never given me a reason not to believe in you. I'll always trust in your decisions because you've brought me the most happiness that I've ever had in my life."

Jack smiled down at her. "Right back at you, hon," he whispered. He reached down and ruffled Kevin's blonde hair.

"Kevin, take good care of your mother. I'll be back in a little while."

Kevin's mind was occupied with the ice cream selection. "Dad, can I get a banana split instead of a cone? I had one at my friend Kyle's house once and it was really good."

"Sure, buddy," Jack replied over his shoulder as he started across the street. "Just don't get it all over your shirt."

Chris stood when he saw Jack double-checking the address over the office door. He opened the door as Jack reached for the knob. The two men smiled as they locked eyes. Chris was the first to break the silence.

"Hello, Jack, how was the drive down?" he asked, holding his right hand.

The question sounded a little lame to Chris as he said it, but Jack seemed to relax as he took the older man's hand in a firm grip. A little small talk gave him time to get his bearings.

"Not bad at all," Jack answered as Chris steered him to the leather love seat. "We made it in three hours. Once we got on the turnpike, it was smooth sailing."

Jack sat down while Chris poured a cup of coffee from the old-fashioned percolator that sat on a small sink top in the corner of the office. Jack shook his head at the offer of a cup.

"I like your small town," Jack said. " It seems real cozy. I'll bet everyone knows everyone else, huh?"

Chris chuckled as he sat on the love seat next to Jack. "Yeah, I'll say. It's like one big happy family, warts and all. We do watch out for each other though. That's the upside to small town life."

He pointed in the direction of the front window. " Looks like you have a nice family," he said, smiling. "I see that your son found the Krazy Kone."

Jack grinned proudly. "Thanks. Stacey and I thought that we needed some time to talk alone, and Kevin was glad to oblige. I told her everything before I called you. She doesn't know what to make of my adventures in Vietnam, and to tell you the truth, neither do I I'm hoping that you can tell me what really happened to me and why."

Jack was relieved that Chris didn't seem to be the least bit surprised by the question.

"I'll tell you my story if you'll tell me yours," the older man offered with a lopsided grin. "That should fill in some of the blanks for both of us."

Chris rearranged some of the papers that littered the coffee table and leaned back into the soft leather, plopping his feet onto the table and gesturing for Jack to do the same.

"Might as well get comfortable," he advised.

Chris listened intently as Jack told his story for the second time that week then he filled Jack in on his short stay in Jack's life. After Chris had finished telling Jack about how his life had changed after he had found the arrowhead, the two men sat for a while in companionable silence.

"Well, now we know what happened," Jack said finally.

"Now, I'd like to know why, if you can tell me."

Chris sipped his cold coffee as he searched for the right words. He leaned toward Jack and spoke softly.

"You were going to hell in a basket, son, and you were planning to take a whole lot of people with you," he said, not unkindly. "The Great Spirit sent Hupa to stop you, with the power of the arrowhead, of course."

Jack flushed red, embarrassed that Chris knew the truth about his teenage years. He couldn't argue with any of it though.

"Well, what now?" Brian asked.

Chris smiled and gave Jack a friendly slap on the shoulder. "You've come a long way already, my friend. Now it's time that you learn what Hupa has taught me, that the smallest things that we do can make a difference.

Jack looked confused and a little disappointed. "That's it?" He asked doubtfully.

Chris thought for a moment and then explained. "Look, the smallest pebble thrown into a pond can create a lot of ripples. If one thing had not changed, if you had been allowed to take a rifle to the Indian Jamboree, so many lives would have been ruined in a single day. Not just the lives that you would have taken, but the lives of their loved ones and the children who would never have been born, it goes on and on. One single, thoughtless act of anger and hatred would have gone on forever." Chris spoke passionately now, clearly warming to his subject.

"If you could cause that much damage in a single day, Jack, just imagine how much good you could do in an entire lifetime!"

Jack mulled this over for a while, then sighed. "I wouldn't know where to start. I'm an electrician, not a lawyer or a doctor. "

Chris laughed. "The demonstrators that you saw on television the other day come from every walk of life, and each one makes a difference. All they have going for them is their belief in a cause, and the willingness to do something about it."

He waved his hand in the direction of his cluttered desk. "This is my thing, Jack. It may not be yours. Hupa and his ancestors died trying to save the wilderness for their tribe. Their sacrifice convinced me that I wanted to help save the wilderness for everyone. Maybe that isn't your task though."

Chris reached under his shirt and pulled a worn leather thong over his head and held it out to Jack. The arrowhead suspended from the thin strand of leather gleamed dully in a ray of sunlight that shone in through the office window. For a second, Jack thought that he saw the thin veins of gold and silver writhe like tiny snakes captured within the polished stone. He shook his head a little to clear his eyes. *Must be a trick of the light*, he thought. He reached out tentatively and took the arrowhead from Chris with a trembling hand. The stone felt warm, like a living thing.

Chris suppressed a grin at the look of startled revulsion that flashed across Jack's face. It had been a long time since he had first held the arrowhead, but he remembered the feeling well. Jack gave Chris a questioning look.

"That's the key to your dreams, son," Chris said, a trace of irony in his voice. "Just put it on and Hupa will take it from there."